D0016052

Herons
Landing

JoAnn Ross

Herons Landing

ISBN-13: 978-1-335-54191-8

33614080647299

Recycling programs
or this product may
ot exist in your area.

Herons Landing

This edition published by arrangement with Harlequin Books S.A.

For questions and comments about the quality of this book, please contact us at CustomerService@Harlequin.com.

® and TM are trademarks of Harlequin Enterprises Limited or its corporate affiliates. Trademarks indicated with ® are registered in the United States Patent and Trademark Office, the Canadian Intellectual Property Office and in other countries.

www.HQNBooks.com

Printed in U.S.A.

Again, to Jay, for all the years.

CHAPTER ONE

Seth Harper was spending a Sunday spring afternoon detailing his wife's Rallye Red Honda Civic when he learned that she'd been killed by a suicide bomber in Afghanistan.

Despite the Pacific Northwest's reputation for unrelenting rain, the sun was shining so brightly that the Army notification officers—a man and a woman in dark blue uniforms and black shoes spit-shined to a mirror gloss—had been wearing shades. Or maybe, Seth considered, as they'd approached the driveway in what appeared to be slow motion, they would've worn them anyway. Like armor, providing emotional distance from the poor bastard whose life they were about to blow to smithereens.

At the one survivor grief meeting he'd later attended (only to get his fretting mother off his back), he'd heard stories from other spouses who'd experienced a sudden, painful jolt of loss before their official notice. Seth hadn't received any advance warning. Which was why, at first, the officers' words had been an incomprehensible buzz in his ears. Like distant radio static.

Zoe couldn't be dead. His wife wasn't a combat soldier. She was an Army surgical nurse, working in a heavily protected military base hospital, who'd be returning to civilian life in two weeks. Seth still had a bunch of stuff on his homecoming punch list to do. After buffing the wax off the Civic's hood and shining up the chrome wheels, his next project was to paint the walls white in the nursery he'd added on to their Folk Victorian cottage for the baby they'd be making.

She'd begun talking a lot about baby stuff early in her deployment. Although Seth was as clueless as the average guy about a woman's mind, it didn't take Dr. Phil to realize that she was using the plan to start a family as a touchstone. Something to hang on to during their separation.

In hours of Skype calls between Honeymoon Harbor and Kabul, they'd discussed the pros and cons of the various names on a list that had grown longer each time they'd talked. While the names remained up in the air, she *had* decided that whatever their baby's gender, the nursery should be a bright white to counter the Olympic Peninsula's gray skies.

She'd also sent him links that he'd dutifully followed to Pinterest pages showing bright crib bedding, mobiles and wooden name letters in primary crayon shades of blue, green, yellow and red. Even as Seth had lobbied for Seattle Seahawk navy and action green, he'd known that he'd end up giving his wife whatever she wanted.

The same as he'd been doing since the day he fell head over heels in love with her back in middle school.

Meanwhile, planning to get started on that baby making as soon as she got back to Honeymoon Harbor, he'd built the nursery as a welcome-home surprise.

Then Zoe had arrived at Sea-Tac airport in a flag-draped casket.

And two years after the worst day of his life, the room remained unpainted behind a closed door Seth had never opened since.

Mannion's Pub & Brewery was located on the street floor of

a faded redbrick building next to Honeymoon Harbor's ferry landing. The former salmon cannery had been one of many buildings constructed after the devastating 1893 fire that had swept along the waterfront, burning down the original wood buildings. One of Seth's ancestors, Jacob Harper, had built the replacement in 1894 for the town's mayor and pub owner, Finn Mannion. Despite the inability of Washington authorities to keep Canadian alcohol from flooding into the state, the pub had been shuttered during Prohibition in the 1930s, effectively putting the Mannions out of the pub business until Quinn Mannion had returned home from Seattle and hired Harper Construction to reclaim the abandoned space.

Although the old Victorian seaport town wouldn't swing into full tourist mode until Memorial Day, nearly every table was filled when Seth dropped in at the end of the day. He'd no sooner slid onto a stool at the end of the long wooden bar when Quinn, who'd been washing glasses in a sink, stuck a bottle of Shipwreck CDA in front of him.

"Double cheddar bacon or stuffed blue cheese?" he asked.

"Double cheddar bacon." As he answered the question, it crossed Seth's mind that his life—what little he had outside his work of restoring the town's Victorian buildings constructed by an earlier generation of Harpers—had possibly slid downhill beyond routine to boringly predictable. "And don't bother boxing it up. I'll be eating it here," he added.

Quinn lifted a dark brow. "I didn't see that coming."

Meaning that, by having dinner here at the pub six nights a week, the seventh being with Zoe's parents—where they'd recount old memories, and look through scrapbooks of photos that continued to cause an ache deep in his heart—he'd undoubtedly landed in the predictable zone. So, what was wrong with that? Predictability was an underrated concept. By definition, it meant a lack of out-of-the-blue surprises that might destroy life as you knew it. Some people might like change. Seth was not one of them. Which was why he always ordered takeout with his first beer of the night.

The second beer he drank at home with his burger and fries. While other guys in his position might have escaped reality by hitting the bottle, Seth always stuck to a limit of two bottles, beginning with that long, lonely dark night after burying his wife. Because, although he'd never had a problem with alcohol, he harbored a secret fear that if he gave in to the temptation to begin seriously drinking, he might never stop.

The same way if he ever gave in to the anger, the unfairness of what the hell had happened, he'd have to patch a lot more walls in his house than he had those first few months after the notification officers' arrival.

There'd been times when he'd decided that someone in the Army had made a mistake. That Zoe hadn't died at all. Maybe she'd been captured during a melee and no one knew enough to go out searching for her. Or perhaps she was lying in some other hospital bed, her face all bandaged, maybe with amnesia, or even in a coma, and some lab tech had mixed up blood samples with another soldier who'd died. That could happen, right?

But as days slid into weeks, then weeks into months, he'd come to accept that his wife really was gone. Most of the time. Except when he'd see her, from behind, strolling down the street, window-shopping or walking onto the ferry, her dark curls blowing into a frothy tangle. He'd embarrassed himself a couple times by calling out her name. Now he never saw her at all. And worse yet, less and less in his memory. Zoe was fading away. Like that ghost who reputedly haunted Herons Landing, the old Victorian mansion up on the bluff overlooking the harbor.

"I'm having dinner with Mom tonight." And had been dreading it all the damn day. Fortunately, his dad hadn't heard about it yet. But since news traveled at the speed of sound in Honeymoon Harbor, he undoubtedly soon would.

"You sure you don't want to wait to order until she gets here?"

"She's not eating here. It's a command-performance dinner," he said. "To have dinner with her and the guy who may be her new boyfriend. Instead of eating at her new apartment, she decided that it'd be better to meet on neutral ground."

"Meaning somewhere other than a brewpub owned and operated by a Mannion," Quinn said. "Especially given the rumors that said new boyfriend just happens to be my uncle Mike."

"That does make the situation stickier." Seth took a long pull on the Cascadian Dark Ale and wished it was something stronger.

The feud between the Harpers and Mannions dated back to the early 1900s. After having experienced a boom during the end of the end of the nineteenth century, the once-bustling seaport town had fallen on hard times during a national financial depression.

Although the population declined drastically, those dreamers who'd remained were handed a stroke of luck in 1910 when the newlywed king and queen of Montacroix added the town to their honeymoon tour of America. The couple had learned of this lush green region from the king's friend Theodore Roosevelt, who'd set aside national land for the Mount Olympus Monument.

As a way of honoring the royals, and hoping that the national and European press following them across the country might bring more attention to the town, residents had voted nearly unanimously to change the name to Honeymoon Harbor. Seth's ancestor Nathaniel Harper had been the lone holdout, creating acrimony on both sides that continued to linger among some but not all of the citizens. Quinn's father, after all, was a Mannion, his mother a Harper. But Ben Harper, Seth's father, tended to nurse his grudges. Even century-old ones that had nothing to do with him. Or at least hadn't. Until lately.

"And it gets worse," he said.

"Okay."

One of the things that made Quinn such a good bartender was that he listened a lot more than he talked. Which made Seth wonder how he'd managed to spend all those years as a big-bucks corporate lawyer in Seattle before returning home to open this pub and microbrewery.

"The neutral location she chose is Leaf."

Quinn's quick laugh caused two women who were drinking wine at a table looking out over the water to glance up with interest. Which wasn't surprising. Quinn's brother Wall Street wizard Gabe Mannion might be richer, New York City pro quarterback Burke Mannion flashier, and, last time he'd seen him, which had admittedly been a while, Marine-turned-LA-cop Aiden Mannion had still carried that bad-boy vibe that had gotten him in trouble a lot while they'd been growing up together. But Quinn's superpower had always been the ability to draw the attention of females—from bald babies in strollers to blue-haired elderly women in walkers—without seeming to do a thing.

After turning in the burger order, and helping out his waitress by delivering meals to two of the tables, Quinn returned to the bar and began hanging up the glasses.

"Let me guess," he said. "You ordered the burger as an appetizer before you go off to a vegetarian restaurant to dine on alfalfa sprouts and pretty flowers."

"It's a matter of survival. I spent the entire day until I walked in here taking down a wall, adding a new reinforcing beam and framing out a bathroom. A guy needs sustenance. Not a plate of arugula and pansies."

"Since I run a place that specializes in pub grub, you're not going to get any argument from me on that plan. Do you still want the burger to go for the mutt?"

Bandit, a black Lab/boxer mix so named for his penchant for stealing food from Seth's construction sites back in his stray days—including once gnawing through a canvas ice chest—usually waited patiently in the truck for his burger. Tonight Seth had dropped him off at the house on his way over here, meaning the dog would have to wait a little longer for his dinner. Not that he hadn't mooched enough from the framers already today. If the vet hadn't explained strays' tendencies for overeating because they didn't know where their next meal might be coming from, Seth might have suspected the street-scarred dog he'd rescued of having a tapeworm.

They shot the breeze while Quinn served up drinks, which in this place ran more to the craft beer he brewed in the building next door. A few minutes later, the swinging door to the kitchen opened and out came two layers of prime beef topped with melted local cheddar cheese, bacon and caramelized grilled onions, with a slice of tomato and iceberg-lettuce leaf tossed in as an apparent nod to the food pyramid, all piled between the halves of an oversize toasted kaiser bun. Taking up the rest of the heated metal platter was a mountain of spicy french fries.

Next to the platter was a take-out box of plain burger. It wouldn't stay warm, but having first seen the dog scrounging from a garbage can on the waterfront, Seth figured Bandit didn't care about the temperature of his dinner.

"So, you're eating in tonight," a bearded giant wearing a T-shirt with Embrace the Lard on the front said in a deep foghorn voice. "I didn't see that coming."

"Everyone's a damn joker," Seth muttered, even as the aroma of grilled beef and melted cheese drew him in. He took a bite and nearly moaned. The Norwegian, who'd given up cooking on fishing boats when he'd gotten tired of freezing his ass off during winter crabbing season, might be a sarcastic smart-ass, but the guy sure as hell could cook.

"He's got a dinner date tonight at Leaf." Quinn, for some damn reason, chose this moment to decide to get chatty. "This is an appetizer."

Jarle Bjornstad snorted. "I tried going vegan," he said. "I'd hooked up with a woman in Anchorage who wouldn't even wear leather. It didn't work out."

"Mine's not that kind of date." Seth wondered how much arugula, kale and flowers it would take to fill up the man with shoulders as wide as a redwood trunk and arms like huge steel bands. His full-sleeve tattoo boasted a butcher's chart of a cow. Which might explain his ability to turn a beef patty into something close to nirvana. "And there probably aren't enough vegetables on the planet to sustain you."

During the remodeling, Seth had taken out four rows of bricks in the wall leading to the kitchen to allow the six-foot-seven-inch-tall cook to go back and forth without having to duck his head to keep from hitting the doorjamb every trip.

"On our first date, she cited all this damn research claiming vegans lived nine years longer than meat eaters." Jarle's teeth flashed in a grin in his flaming red beard. "After a week of grazing, I decided that her statistics might be true, but that extra time would be nine horrible baconless years."

That said, he turned and stomped back into the kitchen.

"He's got a point," Quinn said.

"Amen to that." Having learned firsthand how treacherous and unpredictable death could be, with his current family situation on the verge of possibly exploding, Seth decided to worry about his arteries later and took another huge bite of beef-and-cheese heaven.

CHAPTER TWO

The bride was beautiful, as all brides are. It was, of course, easier when you had unlimited funds at your disposal. The white couture gown, flown in especially for the event from Paris, was a cloud of diamond-white tulle, embroidered with seed pearls and Swarovski crystals. The Belgian lace veil was attached to a diamond tiara that was a duplicate of the one worn by Audrey Hepburn in *Breakfast at Tiffany's*.

As chief concierge of the butler floor at the Las Vegas Midas Resort Hotel and Casino, Brianna Mannion had arranged for a stylist to ensure perfect hair and nails for the bride and her seven attendants, all in poufy pastel taffeta gowns that would never be worn again.

The groom, while not as flamboyantly attired, nevertheless was handsome in a black tux. His concession to glitz was the crystal-studded bow tie designed to coordinate with the bride's gown. There'd originally been plans for him to wear a top hat, but when he'd steadfastly objected, the bride's harried mother had thrown up her hands in defeat.

"Well, I did want our princess to marry an alpha male," she'd said to the bride's father. Who, Brianna noted with a

bit of trepidation, was pouring his third Scotch since arriving at the wedding preparation suite. Typically the suite was
a women-only zone, but this was far from a typical wedding
and since the bride's mother (who had a strong alpha streak
herself) had insisted her husband be there for the preparations,
he'd apparently caved rather than risk a scene.

Because the Midas prided itself on the extreme level of privacy afforded to its guests, this particular suite had its own
high-speed elevator that opened onto the ballroom booked
for the event. Although it took four trips, Brianna managed
to herd the party down the sixty-five floors to the ballroom,
which took some logistics when a trio of bridesmaids, having
lost patience during their styling, had begun nipping at each
other. Fortunately, she was able to calm things down before
the pink, yellow and aqua taffeta started getting ripped apart.

The ceremony, presided over by the top Elvis impersonator
in the country—no mere local Elvises (Elvi?) need apply—
amazingly went off without a hitch. And although the reception might have gotten a little rowdy, both the wedding party
and the guests invited to this special occasion all seemed to
enjoy the tiered white wonder of a wedding cake created by
the Cordon Bleu–trained top chef. But it was the gilt doggie
bags filled with a variety of gourmet dog biscuits dusted with
edible twenty-four-karat gold that proved the hit of the party.

After escorting the happy couple up to their honeymoon
penthouse suite that adjoined that of the bride's parents, Brianna finally blew out a long breath of relief.

The good news was that the wedding of the tech mogul
and his wife's award-winning King Charles spaniel to a male
belonging to a distant member of the British royal family (the
first high-end dog ceremony Brianna had arranged) had gone
off without a hitch. The bad news was that if word got out
of its success, it might not be her last.

She'd just returned to her desk, which, like everything

else in Midas, was heavily gilded, when a guest she recalled from yesterday came marching toward her. Unfortunately, the man's lobster-red complexion, furious scowl and steam she could practically envision coming from his ears were not encouraging signs.

"I have a complaint," he bellowed as he approached the desk. Like she couldn't hear him from three feet away?

"I'm so sorry to hear that." Brianna pasted on her most conciliatory, caring smile. "What can I help you with?"

"The concierge from yesterday was terrible. I want her fired."

"May I ask why?"

"Because she's obviously not working up to the standards of this hotel."

"Sir, I'm the concierge you spoke with yesterday. And again, I'm sorry that you had a less than satisfactory experience. What's the problem?"

He gave her a long, hard look. Leaned over the desk, and squinted at her gold-plated name tag. Then straightened, and squared his shoulders like a man about to go into battle. "It's about that restaurant you sent us to last night."

"Bombay Spice."

"Yeah. That one."

"You didn't care for your meal?" Bombay Spice, located a block off the strip near the Taj Mahal, was one of Brianna's personal favorites, serving deliciously prepared authentic Indian cuisine.

"It was fucking vegetarian!" His tone rose again with indignation.

Having grown up working on the Mannion family Christmas tree farm, Brianna had learned at an early age how to deal with difficult customers. She'd also discovered, while working her way up the chain of the hotel hospitality business, that in some cases, the higher the income, the more escalated the sense of privilege. Apparently this was going to be one of those cases.

"I believe I mentioned that when you asked about it," she said with measured calm.

"Well, dammit to hell, I expected them to serve *some* meat dishes. None of the five-star reviews my wife read online said anything about them not at least having a damn rib eye steak." His color rose to a hue that had her prepared to call 911 in case he keeled over from a blood pressure spike.

"I suspect the reviews didn't mention the lack of meat because online diners were reviewing the restaurant's vegetarian dishes."

Brianna wished she had a dollar for every time a guest came up to her with a list of restaurants in hand, asking her to recommend one. The problem with online review sites was that they reflected only the experience of the person writing the reviews. She'd spent her first six months in Las Vegas eating at as many restaurants as she could, meeting the owners and managers, in order to get firsthand knowledge. Some guests might like a noisy, busy brasserie, while others might prefer a quiet, romantic dining experience. Some might like bright lights. Others might go for candles on the table. Her job was to ask questions to determine what restaurant might work for that particular guest. Which she'd tried to do with this agitated man yesterday.

"You shouldn't send people there."

"I *did* recommend two steak houses," she reminded him, practically having to bite her tongue at this point.

"But Bombay Spice had great reviews," he insisted. "Which is why my wife wanted to go there. She was determined to try the gobhi mattar masala with truffle rice because it had all five stars. But if a restaurant doesn't have meat, you should warn people! You ruined our anniversary dinner!"

"I'm sorry you had a less than satisfactory experience." The cauliflower/green peas/cumin/ginger/cashews dish was one of Brianna's personal favorites. But she did find the truffle rice a bit rich for her taste.

"Less than satisfactory? It sucked! Of course we left the place, but by then it was impossible to get a table anywhere decent, so we just came back to the hotel."

"We have several fine restaurants in the hotel," she pointed out in her most cordial, professional voice. "All which have received excellent reviews by both critics and diners alike. I, or the night concierge, would have been more than happy to arrange for you to have dinner on us if you'd only let us know you were dissatisfied."

"My wife had lost her appetite by the time we got back here and just wanted to go to bed." He ripped off his black-framed glasses. If fiery glares could kill, Brianna would have burst into flames on the spot. "Which is why you owe me fifty fucking thousand dollars."

That got Brianna's full attention. "Excuse me?"

"My wife went to bed. *Alone*," he stressed in the event Brianna hadn't gotten his meaning. "Since our anniversary night was toast, I decided, what the hell, I might as well go down to the tables."

Where he'd lost fifty thousand dollars. Brianna restrained herself from suggesting he Google the meaning of *gambling*.

"I'm thinking of reporting this place to the state gambling commission for rigging the games."

"That's certainly your right. But I can assure you that nothing at the Midas is rigged."

Her roots may be Irish, from a many-times-great-grandfather who'd arrived in the Pacific Northwest where he'd gotten the dangerous job of driving the dynamite wagon for the construction of the railroad, but somehow Brianna must have been busy meeting and greeting people when God had handed out tempers, because she hadn't inherited the trait. Still, this man was beginning to test her limits.

"I've never lost that much in any casino in two fucking hours."

Wow. He'd really been tossing down the high dollar chips. And, from the red veins crisscrossing his eyes like lines on a Nevada roadmap, he hadn't turned down any of the free drinks handed out to high rollers.

"I'm sorry for your bad luck." Having never dropped as much as a dollar in a slot machine, Brianna didn't comprehend why anyone would want to risk hard-earned money when everyone knew that in the end, the house always eventually won, but enough people seemed to feel different to allow her to be paid a very lucrative salary with benefits and generous tips from happy guests. Especially those who'd walked away after a winning streak. "But it certainly wasn't due to any rigging."

He shoved the glasses back on his face. "I'm going to report you to the manager."

"Again, that's your right."

Having received not only high marks, but a bonus at her annual review, Brianna wasn't concerned about her job being in jeopardy. Usually before a guest arrived on the butler's floor, she'd wade through her files of past likes and dislikes to ensure a stay tailored to that particular party. But because this man and his wife were first-timers, there was no previous record. And unfortunately, he'd added nothing to the comments section in the online reservation form. Such as his intense dislike of vegetarian meals.

"And after I report you, I'm going to write the worst goddamn review ever published on Yelp." He spun on a heel and stomped off toward the gold-embossed elevator.

"I hope you have a safe and uneventful trip back home,

sir," she called after him. It was the same thing she told all the guests as they'd leave.

"I intend to, since you won't be the one doing the planning. And quit calling me *sir*, bitch," he roared back over his shoulder. "I'm an orthopedic surgeon, dammit!"

"Doctor Dick," Brianna murmured under her breath, reminding herself that although this might not be her most fulfilling day, she was exactly where she'd always dreamed of being.

Working at the family tree farm had taught her she enjoyed working with people, helping each family find the perfect tree just for them. Watching *Gilmore Girls*, she'd always identified with Lorelai's dream of creating a warm and caring environment in her very own inn, rather than working for someone else. And she'd even had a specific house in mind.

Then, while earning her degree in hospitality and hotel management, classmates and professors had tried to convince her that she'd be wasting her talents on a small town of seven thousand plus, stuck out on the Washington peninsula, where guests would have to travel by ferry or a long car ride over twisting mountain roads to visit. No, she'd been born for more important things, she'd been told. All she needed to do was give up those childish dreams of creating a life in the Pacific Northwest's version of Star Hollow, and dream bigger. Bolder. Brighter.

It was during summer break between her sophomore and junior years, with more time to watch TV, that she'd become hooked on the Travel Channel, drinking in the splendor of the world's grand hotels. By the time she returned to UW, she'd changed her focus, and after graduation and playing maid of honor at her best friend Zoe's wedding to Seth Harper, she'd begun her gypsy life of traveling the country, working her way up to this gilded desk.

Dealing with demanding high rollers who expected their

needs dealt with immediately, if not before they even realized they were going to want something, she'd honed her skills at making the impossible possible.

But while she might be near the pinnacle of her specialized hospitality world, there were times Brianna found herself missing those early days when she worked in less luxurious surroundings, dealing with more cordial families. Parents who'd appreciate a bowl of chicken noodle soup sent up to the room for a sick child, or honeymooners excited about something as simple as a bottle of house-labeled champagne and chocolate-dipped strawberries in their room. And later showing her that they'd put a photo on their wedding Facebook and Instagram pages.

Be careful what you wish for, she thought as she cleared the desk of her planner and files to make room for the night-shift concierge to take her place.

Although she'd been offered housing in a wing of the sprawling resort away from the casino, Brianna had opted to rent a studio apartment away from the noise and bustle of the strip. Along with the rise in income, each step up the hospitality ladder had brought additional responsibility and increased stress, but whenever she drove into the quiet, green environs of The Sanctuary with its sparkling blue pools and xeriscape, drought-resistant gardens that appealed to her inner environmentalist, the stress of her workday began to flow away.

But not tonight. She'd always been a positive person. Anyone who had a flash fire temper, or was even easily annoyed, would never succeed in her career. But as she reran the conversation with the doctor who wore his privilege the same way he undoubtedly wore his white hospital coat, a low, simmering irritation flowed through her. And had her thinking, yet again, of those happier early days. She considered going to the resort's exercise room and working it off on the treadmill and elliptical, but opted instead for take-out pizza, a glass of wine and streaming a movie.

Another reason she'd chosen this apartment was that its white walls offered a blank canvas. As did the white furniture and white kitchen. A person could do anything they wanted to make it their own. But, she realized now, though it was a respite from the overexcessive gilt of Midas, it didn't offer a single clue to the person who lived here. She hadn't bought any posters, or paintings, or even colorful throw pillows. And although she'd practically grown up in her mother's farm kitchen, she owned one frying pan, two pots, a teakettle, a coffee maker and a set of four white dishes and bowls she'd bought online. A nun's room at a convent would undoubtedly have more personality.

Then again, she reminded herself as she kicked off her sensible black pumps, changed into yoga pants and an oversize Gotham Knights football jersey her brother Burke had sent her, she didn't exactly live here. She ate takeout and slept. Her life was at Midas. Same as it had been at every other hotel she'd worked at over the years. Which was fine with her. Dedication to her career had paid off in escalating achievements and money. And although she experienced a sense of satisfaction when she waved her magic concierge wand and provided a magical happy outcome for guests, when was the last time she'd felt happy?

"You're just in the dumps because of Doctor Dick," she assured herself as she poured a glass of chardonnay. After calling in her take-out order, she sat down on the hard, snowy white couch, turned on her iPad and logged into the Honeymoon Harbor website, which she'd been doing more and more often since moving to the desert two years ago.

Clicking on the link to the town's newspaper, the *Honeymoon Harbor Herald*, she scrolled through announcements of births, weddings, anniversaries and deaths, recognizing the names of people she'd known all of her life. People she'd grown up with. Harper Construction had renovated the old library, which had earned a national award for innovative green historical renovation. Seeing the photo of Seth Harper, appearing uncomfortable in a suit and tie, caused a twinge in Brianna's heart.

She'd had a crush on him going back to first grade, when he'd shared his lunch box Ding Dong with her. Her mother was a farm-to-table cook who hadn't allowed processed food in their home. Even now, looking back, Brianna wasn't sure whether it was Seth's dark-chocolate-brown eyes with their ridiculously long lashes or the sudden burst of sugar on her tongue that had caused her to fall.

Despite being a Harper, he'd been friends with her brothers, which had him around the farm a lot. During her elementary school years, whenever she'd play with her Barbies, she'd be bridal Barbie, and groom Ken had been renamed Seth. Unfortunately, he'd always viewed her as either his friend's sister who'd insist on tagging along with them, or worse, one of the guys. By middle school, she still hadn't caught his attention, but Brianna knew, with every fiber of her young, not-yet-budding body, that once they got to high school and her breasts grew larger than the puny little bumps sticking out from her chest and she got curves in other places—like maybe some hips that didn't look like a boy's?—Seth Harper would finally look up and notice that the girl of his dreams had been in front of him all along.

Maybe she'd even get a locker next to his. Those things could happen, right? After all, all those book writers and movie makers had to get the "meet cute" idea from somewhere. And one day, while he was taking out his book for their shared first-period English class, their eyes would meet, bells would chime, Disney bluebirds would sing and, forever and ever afterward, they'd be known to one and all as "Sethanna."

Unfortunately, when they'd returned to school after the Christmas break their last year of middle school, he'd looked up, all right. But instead of being blinded by her not-yet-achieved perfection, instead he'd noticed Zoe Robinson, a new girl from Astoria, Oregon, whose father had brought the family across the Columbia River back to his home-town. From the moment Zoe had walked into that first-pe-riod homeroom, Seth's swoony brown eyes had locked on to her. And Zoe had tumbled just as fast.

Brianna could have hated her. At first, she'd wanted to hate her. But the petite girl with the long dark curls turned out to be as friendly as she was pretty. With Seth seeming destined to forever stay in brother mode, and unable to ignore the little sparkly hearts that appeared to follow the couple around like fairy dust, by the summer of their sophomore year of high school, Brianna had resigned herself to the fact that the two were, in fact, the perfect couple. And over that time, Zoe had become like the sister Brianna had always dreamed of.

Not that any of that had stopped her from dreaming of Seth. Mature Audience Only dreams (she hadn't had the ex-perience to imagine the R-rated yet) that had her feeling guilty when she woke up, and making it hard to face either one of them the next day.

After graduation, Zoe had joined the Army, something she'd been talking about all through school, but Brianna hadn't really believed she'd go through with. And, from what she could tell, her visit to the Port Angeles recruiting center had surprised even Seth. She'd always wanted to be a nurse, but loggers didn't make that much money, and even with her part-time job waiting tables at the diner, her family hadn't had the money for nursing school. Beginning with a descendant who'd first arrived on the peninsula from Seattle to serve at

Port Townsend's Fort Worden in the early 1900s—theoretically to thwart any invasion from the sea—every succeeding generation of Robinsons had had at least one military family member. Which was why Zoe, an only child without any brothers to carry on the tradition, had decided that letting the Army pay for college only made sense.

She and Seth had continued to date while she'd gone to school at UW, returning home on the weekends and for holidays. Although everyone in Honeymoon Harbor knew they were destined to spend their lives together, Seth had officially proposed on New Year's Eve of Zoe's final year, and after her graduation, once she'd been commissioned as a second lieutenant, they'd married in a simple ceremony held in the Moments in Time meadow at Lake Crescent Lodge in Olympic National Park.

Because Seth was a civilian, rather than wear her dress uniform, Zoe had chosen to be married in a simple white silk shantung sheath, while Brianna, who'd returned home from her job at the Winfield Palace Hotel in Atlanta to serve as one of Zoe's two attendants, had worn a sleeveless dress with a flared skirt in a soft, dusty pink that mirrored the mountains' icy glaciers at sunrise. The other bridesmaid, Kylee Campbell, had gone with a matching style in a kelly green that echoed the bright new needles on the fir trees surrounding the town.

After a weekend honeymoon at the lodge where President Franklin Roosevelt had once slept, Seth had stayed behind on the peninsula while Zoe headed off to San Antonio for more training. Afterward she'd gotten her choice assignment to serve at Joint Base Lewis-McChord's Madigan Army Medical Center north of Olympia. So they'd moved into a rental near the base and considered themselves even more fortunate when she'd gotten to stay there for all four years of her active duty.

Although Brianna was busy moving from town to town, hotel to hotel, Zoe had kept her up to date with phone calls and texts. After finishing her active duty, the couple had re-turned to Honeymoon Harbor, where they moved into a house Seth got busy renovating. Zoe had been so excited about the house, texting pictures of the progress and links to Pinterest pages of ideas she had for making the small cot-tage perfect. She still owed the Army four years of Individ-ual Ready Reserves, which apparently hadn't seemed any big deal because it only involved mustering once a year, which she could even do online.

Tragically, just as her IRR time was coming to an end, she'd been deployed to Afghanistan, only to be killed in a suicide bombing at the hospital while on duty.

In the midst of transitioning from the Ritz-Carlton, Ka-palua on Maui to the soon-to-be opened Midas, Brianna had flown home across the Pacific for her BFF's burial in the vet-erans' section of the Harborview Cemetery, where generations of Robinsons were buried. At the time, Seth had appeared numb. Now, looking more closely at his face on her iPad's screen, his face appeared haggard, his dark eyes haunted.

Brianna sighed at the painful memory, swiped at a tear, checked her watch and saw that she still had another ten minutes before the pizza delivery. While Vegas might be a 24/7 city, when it came to takeout, weekend nights were es-pecially heavy. So rather than have to interrupt her movie when the delivery guy finally arrived, she took another sip of wine and impulsively clicked on the link to the town's real estate listings.

When she saw the Victorian on the bluff overlooking the harbor at the top of the For Sale column, Brianna's heart, which had been hurting for her lifelong friend and former crush, took a leap.

Despite the unfortunate color choice someone had chosen for the exterior, it was *her* house! Growing up Catholic, with a high school principal for a mother, Brianna had tended to be a rule follower. One exception had been all those times she'd sneak into the abandoned three-story house with her brothers and Seth. Her brothers had claimed the house was haunted. Brianna hadn't believed in ghosts, but even if it did have a resident wandering spirit or two, she wouldn't have cared. The creaky old Victorian spoke to her in some elemental way. Much as that first amazing taste of a Ding Dong had done.

Even in those days, as she'd wandered through the dusty, cobweb-strewn rooms, she'd pictured it as it must have once been. And could be again. All it had needed, she'd believed, was some love and tender care. The house, named Herons Landing by its original timber baron owner for the many great blue herons that would roost in nests in the property's towering Douglas fir trees, was, quite literally, Brianna's dream home. But, like her youthful dreams of Seth Harper, it would remain someone else's reality.

The doorbell rang, signaling the arrival of her spicy buffalo chicken pizza with Greek yogurt dressing. She logged out of the computer, paid for the meal and settled down to watch the opening of the Dragonfly Inn *Gilmore Girls* episode, which had inspired her to get into the hotel business. By the time all the first guests had arrived, Brianna had managed to put her encounter with the rude, gambling doctor behind her.

Spoiler alert: it wasn't going to prove that easy.

CHAPTER THREE

The Leaf restaurant was located on Rainshadow Road in a bungalow in the center of town across from Discovery Square.

In contrast to the Victorian gingerbread exterior—which the town's historical planning commission had refused to allow to be modernized—the owner of the restaurant, a transplanted chef from the San Francisco Bay area, had opted for a clean and simple Scandinavian look. Posters of vegetables, framed in light wood, brightened the glacier-white walls. Harper Construction had done the work, and although the furniture chosen by the Portland designer made Seth feel as if he were having dinner in an IKEA store, he was, nevertheless, pleased with how it had turned out.

He spotted the couple as soon as he came in. They were seated at a white table by the window overlooking a garden from which the chef sourced much of the restaurant's herbs and vegetables. When Mike Mannion leaned across the table to take hold of his mom's hand, Seth felt a very familiar twinge of loss.

There were too many reasons he'd missed Zoe two years after her death to catalog, but one of the worst was those random, impulsive moments when the two of them would get lost together in their own private world. He missed touching her. Tasting her...

No. Don't go there. Remembering making love to his wife while having dinner with his mother and her maybe boyfriend, who she might even be having sex with (and didn't that idea make him want to wash his mind out with bleach?), made this already awkward situation even weirder.

He cleared his throat as he approached the table. They moved apart, but easily. Naturally. Not at all as if they'd been caught in any inappropriate display of affection. Yet another possible indication that they'd moved beyond dinner dates that ended with a chaste good-night kiss at the door.

"There's my handsome boy now!" Looking like a wood nymph in a long green suede dress and some sort of colorful stone hanging on a black velvet cord around her neck, his mother rose with a warm and welcoming smile. It had been a long time since he'd seen that smile. Having been wallowing in his own dark pit of grief for two years, Seth hadn't paid all that much attention to gradual changes in his mother.

Seeing her now, so vibrant and joyful, as she'd been while he'd been growing up, he realized that her vibrancy had been fading away the last few years.

"I'm so glad you could join us!" Despite having lived nearly four decades in the Pacific Northwest, Caroline Harper's Southern roots occasionally still slipped into her voice, bringing to mind mint juleps on a wide wraparound porch while a paddle-bladed fan spun lazily overhead.

Seth had visited his mother's childhood home a few times as a kid, but hadn't been back to the South since his grandparents had died. Both on the same day, he remembered now. His grandmother had died of a sudden heart attack while deadheading roses in her garden. Her husband of sixty years had literally died of a broken heart that same evening.

Maybe, he considered now, deep, debilitating grief ran in his family's DNA. If so, his grandfather Lockwood had been more fortunate than he. At least the old man he remembered always smelling of cherry tobacco from his pipe hadn't had to linger for years and years, suffering the loss of his soul mate.

Unlike so many in the Pacific Northwest, whose wardrobes tended toward hoodies, flannel, T-shirts and jeans, his mother had started dressing all New Agey, which could have looked ridiculous, but suited her perfectly.

Going up on her toes, she kissed his cheek. Then leaned back and sniffed what he realized was undoubtedly the aroma of grilled beef he'd brought with him from the pub. Laughter danced in her green eyes. "Seems this is your second meal of the night."

"Consider yourself busted," Mannion said on a laugh as he stood up and held out a hand. "I stopped in Port Angeles on the way back from the coast last week for some ribs and brisket and I'd no sooner walked in the door of your mother's place when she asked me if I had a death wish."

"You smelled of pit smoke," she scolded him. "And that barbecue platter is a heart attack waiting to happen. At our age, we have to start taking care of ourselves. I don't want you keeling over on me."

"Not going to happen," the older man countered. "You're not going to get rid of me that easily."

His mother's obvious concern, along with that casual mention of him spending personal time at the apartment she'd moved into, as if they might already be a couple, was yet more indication that she'd moved on. While meanwhile her husband continued to insist that his wife had merely gone menopause crazy and would return home any day.

"What do you mean, at your age?" Seth asked, determined to stay out of his parents' personal lives as much as possible.

"You look as terrific as you did back when I graduated high school."

"And isn't that exactly what a dutiful son is supposed to say," she said, dimpling prettily. He'd heard it said, down at Oley Nilsson's barbershop, that when Caroline Lockwood had hit town, there'd been a stampede of single men vying to pass time with the pretty Georgia peach. But for some reason he'd never figure out, his gruff, uncommunicative contractor father had won not just Caroline Lockwood's hand, but apparently her heart, as well.

Until recently.

As he slipped into the booth next to Mannion, she turned toward him, her smiling eyes turning as serious as a heart attack as they moved over his face. "How are you?"

"Fine." Another thing that might be in his Harper DNA was that the men in their family would rather have their fingernails pulled out with a pair of needle-nose pliers than ever talk about their feelings.

He'd never cried over Zoe. Not even when he'd insisted on seeing inside the polished wooden casket that didn't carry her body, because it had been blown to pieces, but merely an empty starched green uniform carefully pinned to the sheet and blanket inside which, he knew from reading up on the topic online, carried a plastic bag with what little searchers were able to find of his wife after the explosion. Some caring soldier—who had to have one of the toughest, most unappreciated assignments in the military—had shined the buttons to a bright glossy sheen, never knowing if anyone would see them. It was, Seth had recognized, even through the cloud of pain, a matter of respect.

He hadn't cried when he'd placed her wedding band, which had been recovered and delivered to him in person, along with some rescued uniform patches, into the casket. Although the heat of the blast had turned her ring into a metal lump, since she'd never taken it off from the moment he'd slid it on her finger during their Crescent Lake ceremony, he'd felt it belonged with her. And truth be told, he wasn't about to let her parents see it. They probably had the same horrific images in their mind as he did in his and the least he'd felt he could and should do was spare them this one piece of pain. He did, however, save out the Purple Heart and Bronze Star he'd received, knowing the Robinsons would want them. As far as he was concerned, they were of no comfort and he wouldn't mind never seeing them again.

He hadn't so much as misted up when the uniformed officer had handed him the flag that had seemed to take freaking forever to fold. Nor during the ceremonial volley performed by a team of eight volunteer soldiers who'd shown up from Fort Lewis–McChord to honor one of their own.

All around him, people, even men, had been sniffling. Others, like his mother, had openly wept, while Helen Robinson, Zoe's mother, keened in a way that had him afraid she'd throw, prostrate, herself over her daughter's casket. Brianna Mannion, Zoe's best friend, who'd flown in from Hawaii, had had silent tears streaming down her cheeks.

Burke, Brianna's older brother, who'd gone on from being a high school quarterback to play in the NFL, had flown in from a spring skiing vacation in the Swiss Alps, arriving in town minutes before the funeral due to flight delays. Even he'd been uncharacteristically somber and had bitten his bottom lip during the gravesite military ceremony.

But not Seth. He'd felt as if he'd turned as dry as dust. As dry as that damn violent, fucked-up country that had killed her. His only emotion was a low, seething anger that Zoe hadn't just taken out a student loan like any normal person.

It wasn't like he didn't have a good job, he'd told her during their many heated arguments over her decision. With his income from the construction company, and her earning a civilian nursing salary, they could have paid off the damn loans. Sure, it would've taken time. But they could have done it. Together. Unfortunately, that same tenacity he'd always admired had a flip side. She was, hands down, the most stubborn person he'd ever met. And once Zoe Robinson decided on something, heaven and earth couldn't have budged her.

Now, as a line furrowed his mother's forehead, he dragged his thoughts back to their conversation and ratcheted up his blatantly fake response. "Seriously, things are going great. We've got a lot of work lined up, which is always good. Seems everyone wants to be ready for summer." And punching holes in other people's walls kept him from abusing the ones in his and Zoe's house.

Another furrow etched its way between her eyes. "You work too hard."

"When you love what you do, it's not work." Terrific. Now he was talking like that motivational desk calendar his insurance agent had sent him at Christmas.

"Yet it's necessary to have downtime," she scolded him gently. "Silence is important. We need it to connect with our inner selves. Which then allows us to make sense of the disturbances surrounding us."

Seth had many words he could use to describe Zoe's murder. *Disturbance* didn't come close.

"You used to like to sail. And hike. Fish. Go over to the coast. Or the park."

He used to like to do a lot of things. Some of those with the Mannion brothers. Others with Zoe. The first time he'd touched her bare breasts had been one sunny summer afternoon he'd dropped his boat's anchor in a hidden cove rumored to have once been a pirate hangout. Two years later, they'd returned to that same cove and lost their virginity beneath a huge white moon.

But that was then and this was now and rebuilding other

people's houses was what was left of what had once been his life. Which was working for him just fine.

"I still make it up to the park." Which he did every weekend, but she didn't need to know why.

"Good." She patted his cheek. "Because I worry."

"You don't have to."

"Which shows how much you know. Mothers are genetically programmed to worry."

Seemingly unaware she'd sent a dagger straight to her heart as he thought about that nursery Zoe had designed waiting behind the closed door for a baby that would never come, she reached down and retrieved a gift-wrapped package. "I brought you a present."

"It's not my birthday."

"Well, of course not. I'm not so old and senile that I'd ever forget that day I took part in a miracle. This is a 'just because' gift." Her smile wavered, giving him the feeling that she might be concerned about how he felt about whatever it was.

He untied the cord, sliced the tape and gingerly pulled back the brown kraft paper. "Wow. This is nice." A huge whoosh of cooling relief came over him as he looked down at a misty painting of the Olympic rainforest that suggested at any moment fairies would come out from behind the moss-draped trees and begin dancing in a magic circle. It was, to his admittedly untrained eye, really, really good.

"It's my first watercolor," she said. "I've been taking Michael's classes."

Along with his real estate investments, and his own painting, Mike Mannion taught various art classes, charging only for the supplies. Seth's father, unsurprisingly, claimed it was a ruse to meet women. Given that the artist had inherited the Mannion men's black Irish looks, Seth was pretty sure he wouldn't need to go to that much trouble to attract a woman. But why did the woman in question have to be his mom?

"Your mother's got a natural talent," Mike said.

"I don't know about that," she said, patting her newly streaked blond hair in a way that was as close as Seth had ever seen her come to preening. It also called his unwilling attention to the gold wedding band on her left hand. At least she hadn't taken it off. Yet. That was something, right? "It's more that Mike is a marvelously patient teacher. And so inspirational."

"I keep telling Caroline that she needs to overcome all that Southern belle breeding to work on her artistic arrogance," Mike said on a hearty laugh. "She is, hands down, the best student I've ever taught. I'm trying to talk her into exhibiting at the annual boat festival for Harbor Days."

"I'm certainly not at that level," she protested.

"There she goes again. Underestimating herself." The artist/entrepreneur shook his head. "That's something we're going to have to work on."

As they smiled across the table at each other, getting lost in each other's eyes—oh, hell—they could have been two teenagers in the throes of first love. Seth had no problem remembering that morning Zoe had walked into middle school class, their eyes had met and, at thirteen, he'd fallen like a stone rolling down Mount Olympus.

"Well, not that you asked me, but if Mike thinks you'll be ready to take part in the exhibition, I think you should go for it," Seth said. "As for your natural talent, you did, after all, attend the South Carolina School of Art and Design."

"Only for two years. And I was studying fabric design, not painting, before I dropped out."

To marry his father. No way was Seth going to go there. "Their loss. And you've always drawn the architectural renderings of the company's projects." Not just to promote the company on its website, but to give clients an idea of how their buildings would turn out.

"Those are only illustrations."

"Only snobs draw a strict line between fine art and illustration," Mike said. "Both forms need the same elements: successful lighting, color and composition. And while the argument will probably rage forever, because everyone's definition of art is a personal one, if art is about communicating a message, then illustration is definitely fine art."

They were getting over his head, but there was one thing Seth did know. "Blueprints don't tell anyone who can't envision them in three dimensions anything. But when clients see your illustrations, with the interiors, exteriors, even landscaping, they can imagine themselves living there. They see themselves on that porch swing, or playing with their children in the backyard. Or having summer dinners on the deck or patio. You bring the blueprints alive and allow them to keep the faith during all the hectic months of construction, which can be depressing for even the most optimistic buyer."

All the years he'd been growing up, she'd carried around a sketchbook in her oversize purse so she could draw scenic sites around the peninsula. When had she stopped doing that?

"Your son," Mike said, "just made my point. You're definitely an artist."

"My son is prejudiced."

"Probably so. But that doesn't mean he also isn't right."

"And hey," Seth said, "when you're a famous watercolor artist, I'll be able to boast that your very first painting is hanging on my wall."

Caroline laughed, then opened her menu—which, natch, boldly proclaimed to be printed on recycled paper—and began pointing out items that he'd enjoy. She'd always been a warm and caring person. But this laughing, *happy* New Age druid earth mother sitting across the wooden table reminded him of a bright butterfly newly emerged from a chrysalis.

Michael Mannion was a long way from a starving artist. Although Seth wasn't into Honeymoon Harbor's art scene, he knew Michael's work must sell well enough to allow him to spend years traveling the world. And now he'd returned home to buy another of the abandoned warehouses rebuilt by one of Seth's ancestors after the fire. Unlike the pub's bricks, it had been built with rocks that had originally served as ship ballast.

A gallery, featuring not just Mike's but other local artists' and artisans' work, took up the street level floor; his loft and studio took up the entire third floor. At the moment the second floor was vacant, but plans were for Harper Construction to turn it into a communal work space for Olympic Peninsula craftspeople.

The conversation, which Seth had admittedly not been looking forward to, flowed easily, covering the weather, always a topic in the wait-a-minute-and-it'll-change Pacific Northwest; the pod of orcas they'd seen this morning, three calves breaching playfully; and the news that an award-winning woodcrafter from Seattle, who'd created artisan furniture for some of Seth's wealthier clients, was close to becoming the first tenant to take space on the second floor of Mike's building.

Since he'd been hired for the initial work, Seth had come to know both the building and the painter well. Remodeling, especially a building dating back to the late 1800s, was not for the fainthearted. Having been forced to be the bearer of bad construction news on more than one occasion, Seth knew Mike Mannion to be a patient and good man. One who'd treat his mom well.

Still, as he dug into his surprisingly not bad cremini mushroom meatloaf topped with cornbread made with organic cornmeal from Blue House Farm outside town, Seth realized that wherever this budding romance was headed, Caroline Harper might not be returning home. Which, as happy as he was to see his mother enjoying her life, meant that his already strained situation with his dad was about to get a whole lot worse.

CHAPTER FOUR

One of the things Brianna loved best about her profession was that, on any given day, she never knew what was going to happen at work. Which typically was nonstop. She needed to be ready for any question, any request, because, as she'd discovered, any guest could ask her anything. This morning, as she arrived at her office, her assistant, Brad, was waiting with her coffee. Something she'd never requested, but since he'd started the habit his first day and was inordinately proud of his French press, she certainly wasn't going to turn him down.

"The man called," Brad said before she'd even sat down at the cluttered work desk guests never saw. Which, because she'd insisted she couldn't work on something that looked as if Marie Antoinette might have chosen it, was simply painted a fresh, clean white. The Cape Cod style reminded her of her Honeymoon Harbor roots and helped keep things in perspective when she spent sixty hours a week in a gilded palace. "He asked to see you as soon as you got in."

That, in itself, wouldn't have triggered any concern. Hyatt Huntington, general manager of both the resort hotel and the casino, was even more of a workaholic than Brianna, often boasting that he had no trouble getting by on three hours of sleep a night. There were many days when she'd arrived early to find a stack of messages already waiting. She had, after several weeks of sleepless nights, convinced him that she didn't have his superpowers and could do her job much better if he stopped texting her all night.

Still, she couldn't miss the seeds of worry in Brad's normally smiling blue eyes. "Sure. Would you let him know I'm on my way?"

"Of course."

With his romance cover model looks, Brad could have made a bundle in tips if he'd chosen to work on the casino floor. But, as she'd once done, he'd opted to work his way up the ladder, learning the ropes at previous hotels before this one, that would hopefully someday earn him entry into the prestigious Les Clefs d'Or. It had been Brianna's membership in the international organization of concierges at the pinnacle of the profession, along with stellar recommendations from previous employers, that had won her this job, which had been the most sought-after position in the city.

Grateful for the burst of caffeine before meeting with the high-energy hotel manager, she took a sip of the perfectly brewed coffee. Oh, yes, with his ability to anticipate every need, Brad had a successful career ahead of him.

"Did he mention what it's about?" The general manager usually sent her a blizzard of messages every day. Ones that Brad, who had to triage them by importance, had taken to calling Huntington's snowflakes.

"No. But he didn't sound very happy."

"Then it's situation normal." Brianna never got called to her boss's inner sanctum to be rewarded for a job well done. She was expected to provide guests with perfection. Anything less was unacceptable. Wondering if her furious physician had followed through on his threat to report her, she paused before leaving the office.

"Would you please check the latest Yelp reviews?" she asked Brad. "And text me if we've got a new negative one?"

"Sure. Let me do it now. It'll just take a sec." Without missing a beat, not bothering to inquire why, he began tapping on his computer.

Hopefully he wouldn't find anything. But it was always good to be prepared.

Unfortunately, the review was already there. As soon as she got back from her meeting, she was going to have to take several deep breaths, switch from coffee to more calming tea, and respond. Bad reviews were never a good thing. But letting them go unacknowledged suggested the hotel didn't care about its guests, which was even worse.

Brianna buttoned her jacket over her ivory silk blouse, smoothed out nonexistent wrinkles in her black pencil skirt, and ran a hand over her hair, which she'd coiled into its usual tidy chignon. Then, after changing from the flats she'd worn for driving into her official work pumps, she squared her shoulders and headed toward the express elevator leading directly to the executive floor.

Her boss's secretary waved her right into his private office. The sympathy in the woman's eyes was not encouraging.

The office, which was spacious enough to hold Brianna's entire apartment, was situated at the very top of the Vegas strip high-rise, which not only offered real-time viewing of all the hotel's public places on the multiscreen TVs that were duplicates of the ones in the security offices, but also a stunning view of the entire valley out the glazed window wall.

"Brianna." Hyatt Huntington didn't get up from behind his huge, imposing desk. Having seen the invoice when the Louis Quatorze polished black desk covered in ornate gilded friezes of lions' heads and acanthus leaves had arrived, Brianna knew that the cost had topped twenty thousand dollars. Paid for by gamblers like the angry, Yelp-reviewing physician. Not only had Hyatt not stood up, as he usually did, he hadn't wished her a good morning.

"Mr. Huntington." Her three-inch heels clicked on the miles of marble as she approached the desk. Then, unsure whether or not she should sit down, Brianna stayed standing in front of him.

"It's Hyatt," he said on an exasperated breath. "I told you when this place opened two years ago that you needn't be so formal when we're in here alone together." His brows dove toward his blade of nose. "And would you please sit down and stop looking as if you're on the way to the guillotine?"

Resisting mentioning that the furnishings brought to mind all those executions after the French Revolution, Brianna sat down in the neoclassic reproduction chair on the visitor's side of the desk. His own high-backed baroque chair with its red velvet upholstery could have belonged to the Sun King himself.

He might not be about to chop off her head, but the fact that he hadn't offered her coffee and his hands were folded tightly atop the gilt leather desktop told Brianna what was coming. But rather than volunteer and risk telling him something he might not yet know—like that damn Yelp review—she folded her own hands and waited.

"I received a call first thing this morning," he said.

Still she waited.

"From a guest. Does the name Dr. Aaron Michaelson ring a bell?"

"Yes. He was unhappy about a less than satisfactory experience he had at Bombay Spice."

"Which he says you highly recommended."

"No." Brianna was not going to back down on this point. "He came to me with a printed-out page of reviews. As you undoubtedly realize, online reviews only reflect that one diner's experience. I told him that Bombay Spice was one of the better Indian restaurants in the city. Then, after asking him what his favorite restaurants back home were, in order to get more information on his personal tastes, which turned out to be all steak houses, I recommended a few of those, as well. Including our own Chops, but I could tell that his mind was already made up when he arrived."

"He was angry because there wasn't any meat on the menu."

"It states quite clearly on the restaurant's website and the menu that it's vegetarian. Perhaps he's never heard of the concept of sacred cows?"

Realizing she'd come off snarky, Brianna held up her hand and took a deep breath. "Sorry. Did he happen to mention that I offered him a free meal here?"

"On a day he was checking out."

"If he'd first complained when he'd returned from Bombay Spice, Greg, the night concierge, would have done the same thing." He'd even have had his overpriced dry-aged prime steak delivered to the doctor's damn room, which could have prevented him losing a bundle on the tables out of pique.

"I get your point. But he's insisting you owe him fifty thousand dollars."

"To which you told him, 'No way,' right?"

"Of course. The idea is ridiculous. You didn't drag him down to the casino and force him to keep throwing his chips around the roulette table."

She breathed a sigh of relief. Not that she'd expected Hyatt to take that complaint seriously, but it was encouraging that he found the idea as ludicrous as she had.

Her relief was short-lived.

"We came to a compromise."

Her knuckles whitened from the pressure of her hands being squeezed together so tightly. "Oh?"

"I offered him the Golden Treasure suite, on the house, the next time he's in town."

"I assume he accepted." King Midas himself might have found the suite blindingly overgilded. Which undoubtedly would suit the status-conscious doctor and his apparently privileged wife to a T.

"He did. After I assured him that you'd write him a note of apology."

"What?" Brianna crossed her arms. "No. Period. Way."

He arched a blond brow. It was not often that they were at cross-purposes. And never, in her two years of working together, had she ever refused a directive.

"He called me a bitch."

"That's unfortunate. But it was obviously in the heat of the moment. He was a guest. And the single most important tenet of any business, but especially hospitality, is that guests are always right."

"No, not always." This one had been rude, sexist and wrong.

"Give me a break, Brianna. The guy might be an asshole, but he also just happens to be one of the biggest whales in this town."

That she hadn't known. Not that it made a difference in the treatment she would have provided. Still, while all the elderly men and women who came on the chartered buses to add some excitement to their retirement brought in a nice bit of change, it was the high-stakes gamblers, aka the *whales*— who couldn't stay away, who'd keep betting, even when they were losing—that kept all those chandeliers lit and indoor fountains flowing. Not to mention paying her salary.

"Why didn't I know him?"

She was familiar with all their regulars. She created files for every one with all their likes and dislikes. She never missed sending birthday or anniversary cards (not always easy to keep up with, considering the number of divorces many went through), enclosing vouchers for chips. Some took advantage of their status to the point her dentist had warned her that if she didn't stop grinding her teeth, she'd end up eating baby food.

Others, more reasonable, nice ones, Brianna had become close with. Enough that she'd spent part of her Christmas holiday in Florence, shopping with a bond fund manager's wife and taking care of their children while they'd gone on a Tuscany wine tasting tour. All expenses paid, of course, along with a nice check and a gold mesh bracelet the wife had insisted on buying her at one of the shops on Florence's Gold Bridge.

"You don't have him in your book because he's from Des Moines and usually stays at Wynn Tower Suites or the Mansion at MGM Grand. Which, given his tendency to jump back and forth, suggested that he might be induced to make us his home base when in town."

"He's a doctor. Granted, it's a good profession, but he's not exactly the type of gambler either one of those places or we would be vying for."

"Ah, but he's a doctor who happens to have established a national chain of for-profit medical clinics and is part owner in three more hospitals in Miami, Phoenix and Honolulu. The guy's rolling in dough. Which, as last night proved, he's more than willing to throw around. We want him throwing it around at our tables."

It made sense. And surely Doctor Dick hadn't been the first rude or even obscene guest she'd dealt with over the years. But, as she sat across from this man she knew to be the son of two high school teachers in Mesa, Arizona, Brianna realized the incident yesterday was close to becoming her last straw.

"What happens if I refuse to write the letter?"

"Of course I can't force you." She could tell that Hyatt

wasn't enjoying this any more than she was. One difference was that she was single, responsible only for herself. While, with two kids in college, one of whom was currently in Italy, studying for her PhD in art history, her boss had a great deal more to lose if the gambling doctor went over his head to Midas's owner, a billionaire who always ranked in the top fifty on the annual Forbes richest list.

"Not that you'd ever try," she allowed. Hyatt was a good guy who, through no fault of his own, had landed in an un-tenable situation. Which was only one of the reasons she de-cided to help him out. "But you *would* accept my resignation."

He stared at her for what seemed a full minute. Then dragged his hand down his face. "Oh, hell. You don't want to do that."

The idea hadn't occurred to her as she'd taken the eleva-tor up to this floor. Neither had it crossed her mind as she'd made the long trek across the ocean of pink marble and sat down in the fake antique chair. But as soon as she'd heard the words leaving her mouth, Brianna knew it was exactly what she wanted to do. And fortunately, thanks to a recent surprise inheritance from another favorite guest whose family she'd become personal friends with, she could afford to walk away.

"Yes," she said, "I do. I assume you'll want me to leave im-mediately, so you can assure Dr. Michaelson that I no longer work here. Hell, tell him you fired me. That should gain you points over the MGM Grand and Wynn."

"Does it matter that I don't want you to leave?"

"Yes." He did not, she noted, insist that he wouldn't play the fired card. She watched the tension in his shoulders, clad in a suit that she guessed cost as much as either of his par-ents' annual salaries, loosen slightly. "It matters a great deal and I appreciate it. But it doesn't make any difference, Hyatt. It's not the first time I've felt that I'm not the best fit here at Midas. So I think it's for the best."

He blew out a breath. Then finally stood up, went around the desk and, instead of shaking her hand, surprised her with a hug. Not a creepy boss-copping-a-feel hug, but the kind two close friends would share. "I'll miss you," he said.

"Back at you," she said, meaning it. He'd been not just a mentor, but a friend. Perhaps, she'd often considered, because they'd both come from similar middle-class backgrounds.

Her second thought, coming right on top of the first, was that although she was friendly with many people, she no longer had anyone she could consider a true friend. At least not the kind she could share secrets with, or who'd play designated driver while you got drunk because you'd been dumped by some guy your always loyal friend would assure you was a tool who'd never been, and would never be, good enough for you.

Zoe had been that type of friend. But now, although she'd have been the first person Brianna would have called, she was gone. Forever. And although Brianna had exchanged emails back and forth with Seth for the first few months after the funeral, their correspondence had drifted off when he'd stopped responding, suggesting he'd moved on with his life.

"You'll be impossible to replace," Hyatt said, breaking into her thoughts.

She laughed at that and felt the tension inside her melt away, like one of the glaciers on Mount Olympus back home at spring thaw. "You know that's not true. No one's irreplaceable." Except possibly George Clooney. "You might take a look at Brad," she suggested.

"Are you sure he's ready?"

"He's young," Brianna allowed. "But he's been in the business since he was eighteen and has worked hard to learn the job along the way. He's also eager to please and is a natural at this business." She knew he had three younger sisters and had often thought that when they'd played tea party, he'd have been the one setting up the table and pouring the pretend tea. "If you move Greg to days, Brad should be able to handle nights. Especially with Greg to act as a mentor."

"I'll give it a thought. Thanks for the recommendation."

He'd already mentally moved on. As he should.

"You're welcome." She patted his arm. "Take care. I'm off to write a polite, gracious response to the not-the-least-bit-truthful Yelp rant, pack up my desk and be on my way."

"I'll write a glowing referral. Just let me know where to send it."

"It's not necessary."

Again an arch of the brow. "You already have a new place in mind?"

"I do." The answer was so obvious she was surprised it wasn't flashing in neon bright lights over her head. "I'm going home."

CHAPTER FIVE

It was morning in Kabul, Afghanistan. Traffic was streaming through the Bagram Airfield gates: suppliers, contractors, civilian workers, local residents who were members of the ANA, the Afghan National Army. The sun was rising, the base buzzing as the day medical staff at the state-of-the-art Craig Joint Theater Hospital caught up with patients who'd transferred in or out during the night. Widely recognized as one of the most advanced hospitals in the US Central Command, as well as the premier medical facility in Afghanistan, CJTH had the admirable record of a 95 percent survival rate. Thanks to dedicated medical personnel like Army Captain Zoe Harper, who was currently assigned to the intensive care department.

She was busy mentoring a local nurse, teaching her to tend to one of the unit's favorite patients, a nine-year-old boy who'd been burned when the family's propane tank blew up, when shouts started ringing out through the wing. Then automatic gunfire.

Instructing the nurse to bar the heavy metal door, she threw herself over her patient just as the world blew up.

When his phone alarm crashed into the all-too-familiar nightmare, Seth, drenched in sweat, dragged himself out of the inferno and threw the damn phone across the room. He resisted, just barely, taking a hammer to it.

The events that invaded his sleep weren't real. Or maybe they were. He had no way of knowing because the only facts the Army would share with him were that his wife had been working in the IC ward when security had been breached, allowing suicide terrorists dressed in medical uniforms to attack the hospital.

She'd told him about her patients. Both military and civilian, but he could tell that the little boy, whom she'd been treating for six months, had been a favorite. She'd even asked Seth to send a box of birthday party paraphernalia and Star Trek and Star Wars figures. Which he'd done. She'd emailed pictures of the birthday party two days before her death. The boy had been grinning up at Zoe, who was wearing a silly, definitely not standard issue Princess Leia wig with her military scrubs. It was obvious the kid had fallen in love with her. As everyone always did.

Her stories had created endless possible scenarios of her death. All were violent and horrific, and too often, followed Seth throughout the day. Which, in its own way, was even worse than the nights.

And not just because morning meant going out into the world where he might be forced to interact with people, but mostly because the one person he would not be able to avoid was his dad. Who, if Seth arrived at the job site a nanosecond past the seven o'clock start time, would spend all damn day complaining about the supposed lack of the younger generation's work ethics.

Stumbling out of his side of the bed (he couldn't make himself breach his wife's cold, empty side), he let Bandit out to do his business, then opened a can of dog beef stew that had more vegetables than Seth ate in an average day. He figured he'd banked about a month's worth at last night's dinner.

Drawn by the sound of the electric can opener, the mutt came racing back in, skidded across the wood floor, dove his head into the bowl and dispensed with breakfast in three huge gulps.

He followed Seth into the bathroom and would have continued right into the shower if not barred by the ceiling-high glass door. The vet had explained that along with eating issues, separation anxiety wasn't uncommon in rescues. Especially one who'd been all mangy skin and bones when he'd started showing up at the job site.

Having learned to ignore the unwavering eyes watching his every move, Seth braced his hands against the tile walls of the shower, lowered his head and let the cold water pouring out of the rain shower slam down the hard-on that continued to taunt him every damn morning. Closing his eyes, he kept his hands flat on the walls because even getting himself off would feel like he was committing adultery.

But not taking care of the ache wasn't easy as he fought against envisioning what he'd be doing if Zoe was in this multihead shower he'd built solely with her in mind. She'd seen one on an HGTV makeover show, and sexted him with ideas of how much fun it would be to work on their baby making in one. Graphic, hot ideas that had had him immediately driving to the plumbing supply store.

There were days, and this was one of them, when he thought he ought to just sell the damn house. But then he'd wander through the rooms and see things like the rooster wall clock in the kitchen and the trio of small, seemingly useless little porcelain boxes she'd bought for the bedroom side table, or photos of her planting the living Christmas tree they'd bought from the Mannion farm so their future children could grow with it, and he knew that there was no way he was ever going to be able to abandon this house that he'd remodeled, but she'd turned into a home.

After he'd toweled off, dressed in boxer briefs and jeans, lay-
ered a flannel shirt over a black Harper Construction T-shirt
and pulled on his socks and work boots, Seth took off his wedding band and put it into the box in the bedside table drawer.

One of the few things he and his father agreed on was that
wearing rings when doing construction could be dangerous.
Seth himself had seen guys seriously bruised, had one guy on
his sheet metal crew whose finger had been amputated when
the ring caught in a piece of machinery, and his electrical
contractor's finger was burned to the bone from an electrical
arc during his apprentice days.

So, every work morning since returning home from his
weekend honeymoon, he'd put the ring away in its black box
in the drawer of the table that still held a framed photo of
Zoe and him on their wedding day. And every evening, as
soon as he walked in the door, he'd put it back on. Although
his main reason was that wearing that simple gold band was
a way of keeping his wife close, of not forgetting her and all
they'd shared together, the simple truth was that after all these
years it had become a habit.

Not a habit, he decided as he walked, with Bandit following
right on his heels, out to the garage. Habits, both good and
bad, became mere routines, something done without thinking. Taking off and putting on his wedding ring was more
like a ritual. Which was a good thing, right?

Rituals were important. They were what bound societies
together. Without them, the world would spiral into disor-
der. The type of chaos that could blow up a beautiful young
woman, who'd never done anything to hurt anyone, in the
bloom of her life.

Two years after its detail job, Zoe's Civic still sat in the
second car stall. It was concealed by the cover he'd bought
after seeing her off on her deployment, but he could still envision it in all its Rallye Red glory. Many people in town,

including Quinn, who'd actually shared a personal opinion for once, had suggested he sell it. Easy for them to say. Seth would rather cut off a limb with a rusty chain saw.

He wondered what all those well-meaning folks would say if they knew that once a week he'd drive it to Olympic National Park, up to Hurricane Ridge and back (except in the winter when snow closed the road), to keep the battery charged and gunk from building up inside the various internal parts, none of which he knew all that much about, but it's what the guys on the car radio shows when he was growing up were always saying. The ranger at the Heart O' the Hills entrance station, whose kitchen he'd remodeled, had quit asking for his park pass and merely waved him through. She'd also never, not once, asked him the reason for such regular visits.

It wasn't easy keeping a secret in Honeymoon Harbor, but the fact that his mother hadn't known about his weekly trips to the ridge suggested he owed that ranger a debt of gratitude.

Over the past years, Seth had learned a funny thing about death. The funeral, held in St. Peter's because Honeymoon Harbor wasn't a big enough town to have a Greek Orthodox congregation, had been packed, with every pew filled and standing room only in the side aisles and at the back. The townspeople, along with soldiers from Fort Lewis–McChord who'd come to honor one of their own, had even spilled out into the church parking lot.

Even more people from the peninsula lined the sidewalks on the way to the cemetery, holding their hands over their hearts, their kids waving miniature flags. Although much of that time was a blur, Seth remembered the members of the fire department, dressed in full uniform, standing at attention in front of their gleaming red trucks, having to stop for a freight train carrying a load of logs, and how the engineer had respectfully left his finger off the whistle at the crossing. He also recalled how, as the cortege wound its way along the waterfront, one old man, wearing fisherman's rubber overalls and black boots, stood on the dock beside his trawler, shoulders squared, back straight as a ramrod, briskly saluting as the hearse drove past.

They were forced to hold the lunch after the internment in the parish community hall because neither his and Zoe's home nor her parents' house had enough room for everyone who'd wanted to attend. Tables groaned with casseroles, salads and cakes, and although he'd protested, the women who'd planned the occasion with the precision that Eisenhower had probably used for the D-Day invasion had sent him home with Tupperware and foil-wrapped packages labeled with the contents and name and mailing addresses of who'd made them so he could send thank-you notes. Yeah. Like that was going to happen.

Unwilling to allow people to believe their efforts weren't appreciated, his mother had handwritten notes on cards she'd made herself. Later, he'd learned from Ethel Young, who ran Harper Construction's office, that she'd taken time to write a different, personal message on each card.

The first few weeks after the funeral, everywhere he went, people would stop to tell him how sorry they were for his loss, and ask—with great concern in their eyes and sadly sympathetic expressions—how he was doing.

To which he always lied and said something along the lines of, "Well, you know, it's not easy, but I'm doing okay." To which all those who'd told him that if he ever needed something, *anything*, to give them a call, looked openly relieved that they wouldn't be roped into dealing with Honeymoon Harbor's youngest widower.

Widower. Seth hated that word, which sounded like something from one of Zoe's downloaded Jane Austen movies that he couldn't bring himself to delete from their DVR menu.

But time moved on and apparently everyone had expected

him to, as well. Because, except on Memorial Day, when Boy and Girl Scouts put flags on all the veterans' graves and the VFW held a remembrance ceremony at the Harborview Cemetery, it was as almost as if his wife had never existed. As if she'd never twirled across the stage in a tutu playing the Sugar Plum Fairy in the eighth grade production of *The Nutcracker*, never waved her blue-and-white pom-poms while he was racing down the high school football field to catch Burke Mannion's passes, never marched in perfect military formation in her JROTC cadet uniform. As if she'd never exchanged wedding vows with stars in her eyes, dreamed about babies who would never be born, never gone to war to save lives, only to lose her own.

"Fuck." Although it never got easy, some days were tougher than others. Realizing that this was going to be one of the tough ones, he yanked open the door for the dog, who jumped into the passenger seat. Then he climbed into the truck, punched the button for the garage door opener and headed to work.

As imagined images of the aftermath of the hospital bombing that had seemed to run 24/7 for days on cable TV and were probably burned forever on the inside of his eyes, Seth pulled up in front of Cops and Coffee, conveniently located next to the police station and across the ferry dock from the pub. The coffee shop was operated by three retired Seattle detectives, thus the name and the flashing red, white and blue police light. They'd wanted to put the sign above the door, which the town's strict historical design committee had quickly nixed, but Seth, who'd done the remodel, had managed to get them to give him a permit to place it in the front window, where visitors coming in or leaving on the gleaming white ferry couldn't miss it.

Bandit's ears perked up as soon as he cut the engine. His tail began to thump enthusiastically. And just in case Seth might forget the doggie bag, he reminded him with a loud woof.

"Got it," Seth reassured him. One thing about having a

dog…it was hard to feel sorry for yourself when you lived with an animal that, despite an obviously rough background, could remain optimistic. It occurred to him, not for the first time, that Bandit would've been a good dog for his and Zoe's kids. Which sent his momentarily uplifted mood diving again.

The decor, if it could be called that, was a hodgepodge of '50s blue vinyl booths and red Formica-topped tables, a counter with the same blue vinyl on the swivel stools and a separate room in the back where tourists could buy souvenirs. What elevated the joint from your average doughnut shop was the enormous stainless steel espresso machine with as many switches and dials as a fighter jet. Because, after all, this was Washington State, where coffee was the nearest thing to a religion and Folgers in a carafe just wouldn't cut it.

"You look like you're on the way to the chair," Dave, a former homicide detective sporting a Tom Selleck broom brush mustache, greeted him. The uniform of the day was a cop-blue shirt with a badge that read Doughnut Patrol. The badge, natch, was available for sale in the gift shop alongside the T-shirts and travel mugs reading Don't Dunk and Drive.

"Just the job site," Seth answered, handing over his oversize travel mug to Dave, who brewed him coffee just the way Seth liked it. Pitch-black and strong enough to stand a spoon up in.

"Meaning the job you're doing with your dad." The machine began pouring out the coffee. "The morning after you had dinner with your mom's new boyfriend."

"Well, that didn't take long." One of the good things about Seth's hometown was that it was, in many ways, like small towns anywhere. The type of close-knit community where everyone would band together in a heartbeat to support and protect their own. The downside was that same closeness had everyone privy to everyone else's business. "What, did someone put it on the damn Facebook page?"

"Not yet. But Emma Mae Graham, who came in for a

mocha latte and a chocolate glaze to take on the ferry for a day in the city told me she saw you with your mom and Mike Mannion at Leaf. Which makes it the first time they've gone public after the past two months, right?"

"Yet you already knew."

"Hey, I was a street detective before I got into this business." He tapped his temple. "And detecting in this town is a lot easier than back in the day. Hell, if I knew that everyone who comes in for a cup of joe feels the need to tell a story, I would've suggested we open up a Starbucks in the cop shop back in Seattle. It would've saved us a lot of interrogation time."

Fortunately, Seth's dad was even more of a hermit than Seth, so there was a chance that it might take him longer to find out that his wife, who'd filed separation papers three months ago, had found herself a new man. He skimmed a glance over the doughnuts in the glass-fronted case. "I'll take a box of six glazed crullers and six apple fritters to go."

"Breakfast of champions," Dave agreed as he began putting them into a dark blue box with the Doughnut Patrol shield printed in gold on the top.

"The fritters have apples in them," Seth said. "Which is a government-recommended fruit part of the food pyramid, right?" That was his story and he was sticking to it.

"Works for me," the former detective agreed. "Like carrot cake is a vegetable."

"There you go."

After boxing up the fritters and crullers, along with three doughnut holes in a small waxed bag for Bandit, Dave handed the complimentary baker's dozen thirteen deep-fried doughnuts to Seth, who bit into a cruller and enjoyed the rush of fat and sugar.

He drove along the water, turning up the hill to a gut-job he'd been working on for a month. Great. His dad's truck was already in front of the house. Seth didn't know how the old man did it, but he'd often thought he could arrive at two in the morning and Ben Harper would already be there.

He paused for a moment, studying the house, which was one of his favorites. Like the arts and crafts bungalows, Folk Victorians were one of the most often found styles of historical houses in the country, and what home buyers usually thought of when they went looking for "charm."

The homes had ruled the day from 1870 to 1910. Unlike the better-known high-style Queen Anne, a Folk Victorian was nothing more than a dressed up ordinary "folk house," so named because it had been built to provide basic shelter for the masses with little regard for changing fashions.

As growing railroads brought machinery into towns where workmen could produce inexpensive Victorian detail to be grafted onto existing homes, the decorated houses began to spread like wildfire.

What set the Folk Victorians apart from the earlier ordinary houses was the decorative detailing on the porches and cornice line. Porch supports were usually turned spindles or square beams with beveled corners. Other porch details were lacy or unique jigsaw-cut balustrades. The possibilities were as endless as the craftsmen's imaginations and reflected their own particular region. In this part of the country, silhouettes of trees, mountains, animals, whales and fish along with stylized Pacific Northwest Native American symbols predominated.

Their uniqueness, combined with a simple floor plan, made Folk Victorians as desirable today as they were when that first trainload of architectural trim had arrived in the 1800s. This particular house had been bought by a local photographer, Kylee Campbell—an old friend of Zoe's—and her photographer fiancée she'd met while traveling across Europe. While Kylee tended to focus more on portraits and the lucrative wedding business, Mai, her fiancée, was more into scenic shots she sold to magazines around the world. Some, taken in the national park and around town, were currently displayed in Mike Mannion's gallery.

While Bandit snuffled around the exterior, searching out any squirrels or raccoons that might have invaded during the night, Seth found his father inside what had once been a back kitchen and was in the process of becoming a darkroom. Although Kylee and Mai were both photographers, their methods were very different. Kylee preferred shooting digital so her clients could see the photo immediately, but Mai occasionally preferred working with black-and-white film, which she'd develop herself. While going over the plans for the darkroom, she'd jokingly told him part of the reason she preferred film over digital was that the Caffenol, which apparently had replaced the funky old developer, smelled so damn good. Especially early in the morning, when she claimed it was like breathing in hot coffee steam while meditating. He'd decided to take her word on that.

While working on this house, he'd thought how often marriages were a study in contrasts. Along with being a born nurturer, which had made her such a beloved nurse, Zoe had definitely been the more outgoing and talkative of the two of them. Even as she could be briskly efficient, she also wore her heart along with her combat patch on her uniform sleeve. One of his few positive takeaways from her deployment was how she would have made a bad situation better for any soldier who'd ended up in her care.

Similarly, in contrast to Mai's serenity, Kylee was an extrovert, as bright as her red hair, perfect for keeping stressed-out brides and grooms from freaking out before the ceremony, while at the same time being empathetic enough to catch those special moments that showed, far better than any posed photos, expressions of love.

Like the photos she'd taken for his and Zoe's wedding, which included one of Zoe's mother zipping up her wedding dress, another of his bride-to-be calling him one last time on her cell minutes before the ceremony to tell him how much she loved him. And one he hadn't realized Kylee had caught, of him pinning the rose boutonniere on the lapel of his father's seldom-worn, outdated suit. His father's expression had revealed a warmth of emotion Seth couldn't remember ever seeing before or since. Whenever he looked at that particular photo, Seth wondered if, just possibly, Ben Harper had been remembering his own wedding day to a woman as warm and open as he was distant.

Zoe had always been the outgoing one of the two of them. Middle school was hard enough to figure out your way through, even when you'd known everyone in your class forever. Coming in as the new girl midyear couldn't have been easy. But seemingly without any effort at all, she quickly began weaving herself into the fabric of the school, and by the time summer vacation rolled around, it was as if she'd been there all her life. All of his life.

After steaming off over a century's layers of wallpaper, Seth's dad was now down to getting rid of the paint before repairing the walls with a mixture of lime putty, fine sand and goat hair. Watching him, thinking back to that photo, Seth wondered, for the very first time, if, as much as he'd loved Zoe, because he shared the same difficulty in articulating his feelings as his father, they might have ended up like his parents. At a point when their love might not have been strong enough to overcome years of what Zoe might someday come to view as indifference.

Hell. And wasn't that a fun thought? Not that he'd ever get a chance to know. Or to try to fix things if they had gone off course. Because Zoe was gone. And he was still here. With a job to get done. On budget and on schedule.

Ben Harper might not be the easiest of men to live with, but no one could fault his attention to detail. The man was

one of the last of a dying breed of craftsmen whose knowledge of building had been passed down through the generations. Although many of the kids Seth had grown up with
couldn't wait to get out of their small, isolated hometown,
Seth's roots had always been deeply set in the area's glacial,
loamy soil. And he especially appreciated being part of a con-
tinual line of Harper males who'd built Honeymoon Harbor.

"'Bout time you showed up," his father, thankfully unaware
of Seth's earlier thoughts, muttered without turning around.
"Late night?"

"I stopped for fritters." He didn't bother to share that he'd
spent most of the night locked in the frequent nightmare of
the suicide bomb blowing Zoe's hospital ward to smithereens.

He put the box on top of a sheet of plywood being held
up by two sawhorses and could tell that he'd diverted his
old man's interest in this morning's delay when the steamer
paused. Fritters were Ben Harper's favorite. But apparently
this morning they weren't enough to stop him from his work.
"Humph." The steamer began moving again. "Didn't realize
Cops and Coffee had gone organic. Given that's what you
seem to be into these days."

"They haven't." Since he'd only begun to make inroads
in the oversize travel mug of coffee, it took a moment for his
dad's meaning to click in. Obviously he was talking about
the newest organic place in town. *Busted.*

"Word gets around," Seth said casually. Not that there was
anything casual about your parents' breakup. Whatever your
age, he was discovering.

"I was driving by and saw you going into Leaf after work."

"I remodeled the place. Makes sense I'd eat there from time
to time. The mushroom meatloaf's pretty good." Yet for the
life of him, he couldn't figure out why so many things on
the menu had appeared to be pretending to be meat. It wasn't

like you'd ever go into the pub and find Jarle's beer-battered fried cod and chips pretending to be a salad.

The older man grunted, then muttered something beneath his breath. "Like it makes sense for a son to turn traitor on his own flesh and blood?"

"Okay. I had dinner with Mom. So what?"

"You weren't eating with just your mother. You going to tell me you didn't know that she would be there with her new boyfriend? Wearing a dress she sure as hell never wore out to dinner with me?"

Seth was about to point out that he couldn't remember the last time his father had taken his mother out for so much as a burger at Dinah's Diner when the comment hit home.

"Nobody told you she was at Leaf." Gossip might always be swirling in Honeymoon Harbor's salty air, but he doubted anyone talking to his dad would bother to mention what his mom was wearing. "You *saw* her with Mannion."

"Like I said, I happened to be driving by."

"You said you saw *me* while driving by." Seth jabbed a finger at him. "I was ten minutes late because I stopped by the pub first." Unless his dad had been driving up and down the street, the odds of him seeing both his wife and son arrive was not only unlikely, it was flat-out impossible.

Ben backed down the ladder, switched off the steamer and put it onto the plywood next to the blue box. "I'll bet dollars to those doughnuts you brought with you that you stopped at the pub to have yourself a real dinner before eating the damn rabbit food they serve at Leaf."

Seth was going to neither confirm nor deny that guess. "I told you, the meatloaf was good. And the corn bread nearly as good as Mom makes. And trying to change the subject to a debate about vegetarian versus burgers isn't going to work. You were stalking Mom."

"Not stalking." His face settling into hard lines, his father reached into the box, took out a fritter and bit into it with enough force to send powdered sugar flying around like snow in a blizzard. "I was just watching out for her. She's not used to being on her own."

Even as he was annoyed by the stalking aspect, Seth knew that his father wasn't entirely lying. He'd always known Ben Harper loved his wife. In his way. Which, unfortunately, hadn't ever been the least bit demonstrative. Which caused a twinge of pain as he remembered the way Zoe would touch his arm, smooth a hand over his hair, nuzzle his neck while they were sitting and watching TV on the secondhand couch she'd unearthed at Treasures antiques shop.

"I suspect she's felt as if she's been on her own for a long time," he said, feeling his way across what was turning out to be a conversational minefield. "Given that you're not one for going out."

"A man puts in a hard day's work, he doesn't feel like getting all gussied up to stay out until all hours of the morning dancing," his father said around a second mouthful of fritter.

"Last I checked, movies only take a couple hours. And don't require either dressing up or dancing."

"Cheaper to stay at home and watch a show on the TV."

"Maybe. But did you ever think that attitude is what's got you living alone?"

"Your mother will be back."

Seth knew he'd hit a sore spot when his father grabbed the steamer, went back up the ladder and switched it on.

"It's been three months," he said to Ben's back.

"Took nearly that long to talk her into marrying me and staying here instead of going back east to that foo-foo art school." He began methodically moving the steamer over the wall. "I can wait her out."

"I'm no expert on women, but I'm not sure that's the best option."

The steamer paused as his father stiffened. Shoulders, arms, legs. "You saying she's serious about some pansy artist?"

Seth resisted rolling his eyes. "Did you ever think that mom might prefer you not to talk like Archie Bunker?"

"I liked Archie," Ben shot back. "It was good to see a regular guy on TV. So? Is she involved with Mannion?"

"I don't have any idea. All I know for sure is that she's taking classes from him in art." And how weird did it feel playing this stupid high school game of "does she like me or him best" with his dad? "Which, by the way, she's really good at."

"He's probably just leading her on by telling her that."

"She gave me a watercolor. Believe me, she's good."

"If she'd wanted to paint, I wouldn't have stopped her. Hell, she could've helped out on the houses instead of just doing the business's books. And those drawings of the houses."

Seth opted against mentioning that creating an actual piece of art wasn't anywhere the same as painting a wall. But then wondered if, just possibly, she'd like to try a mural. With Kylee and Mai both being visual types, a mural of the harbor, or snowcapped mountains, might make a nice feature wall.

"That wasn't my point. Whatever their relationship, Mike Mannion's not the only guy in town. Did you ever think that the longer she stays away, the more comfortable she might be with the new normal of single life?"

Ben shot a look over his shoulder. "She's my wife."

"For the moment, though I feel the need to point out that you *are* legally separated." Seth had been surprised when she'd gone all legal-ass on his dad, having those separation papers served on him. "But, just in case you missed the memo, the days of women being chattel are long gone. You don't own her."

Great. Now not only was he eating veggie meatloaf, he was paraphrasing Beyoncé.

"Never said I thought I did." Ben's scowl deepened. "Your

mother's always had a mind of her own. I used to call her my steel magnolia."

There was just a tinge of something that sounded like pride in Ben's tone. Which made sense because only a strong woman would've stuck around past the first anniversary. It wasn't that his father was a bad guy. But he was from another era, a hardworking, blue-collar guy who wasn't all that happy about a world that seemed to be moving too fast to keep up. And whereas some people might see the glass half-filled, Ben Harper always seemed afraid someone was going to steal his.

"*Used to* being the definitive phrase," Seth pointed out, wondering yet again how he got into this damn situation. "Do you want her back?"

That question had his father spinning around so fast Seth feared he might fall off the ladder and break his stiff neck. "What the hell do you think?"

"I've no idea. You damn well should," he said. "Not only is she smart, kind, loving and an all-around great woman, the one thing you and I have in common, along with the love of fixing up old homes, is that we both married above ourselves. Besides, living alone is the frigging pits."

Not that the way he spent his days was fully living. The truth was he was fucking tired of being lonely. If he hadn't been able to lose himself in his work, he probably would've just taken his boat out the strait into the Pacific and jumped into the icy ocean where Coast Guard PSAs were always reminding boaters to wear their life jackets because a fit person could swim only fifty yards in fifty-degree water, which just happened to be the summer temperature.

Another grunt. "You should know, given that you've turned into a hermit monk," his father said. "Hell, even I've played poker once a week for the last twenty or so years."

Which had always taken place at the Harper house, and which, Seth could have argued, wasn't exactly getting out.

"It's not the same thing," he insisted. "My wife died."

Zoe had been more than Seth's wife. She'd been his soul mate for over half his life. He'd lived for her weekend visits home while she'd been away at college, and it never would've occurred to him to so much as look at another woman while she'd been deployed, assuring him that she was in a well-guarded hospital and would be returning home to make a lot of babies, so he'd better be prepared to man up and do his part. Which had totally worked for him.

"That was two years ago," Ben said.

Two years, one month, two weeks and three days. But hell, who was counting?

He was.

"We were talking about you and Mom." Seth felt the damn plaster walls closing in on him. Inside his head, bombs were exploding. "And what you're going to do to win her back."

"She'll be back. Once she gets over this crazy hippy streak." He went back to working on the wall. "Town used to be made up of regular folks. Loggers, fishermen, boat builders. People who made this place. Now it's being overrun with all sorts of writers, musicians, artists and such. Who wouldn't even know how to bait a hook, fell a tree or hammer a nail into a wall."

Like most Harpers, Ben had a strong streak of mule in him. While his mother, despite what Mike had referred to as her Southern belle breeding, was, indeed, the steel magnolia his dad claimed she was to the core. Once the former Caroline Lockwood Harper made her mind up about something, she wasn't one to back down.

Reminding himself that his parents were adults who didn't need their only son to play marriage counselor, Seth went down the hall into what was going to be the en suite for a new master bedroom. Where he vented his frustration with a crowbar, attacking the crappy '70s lime-green and yellow-daisy ceramic tile in the shower.

CHAPTER SIX

One week after quitting her job, Brianna was standing at the railing of a Washington State ferry slowly chugging its way across Puget Sound. Although spring in the Pacific Northwest could be chilly, and she'd be warmer indoors, she enjoyed the briskness of the salt-tinged breeze ruffling her hair, which was no longer pulled back into its tight, tidy, professional chignon that had always given her a headache.

She'd lived life on a wildly spinning hamster wheel for so many years since leaving home, it took her a while to recognize the heady feeling that rushed through her as she drank in the sight of the shaggy Douglas firs spearing into the sky, the rugged white peaks of the Olympic mountains in the distance and seagulls noisily diving for fish in the water churned up by the gleaming white boat.

As she sipped from a cardboard cup of coffee, the drink that famously kept the Pacific Northwest humming, a brown pelican flew by, the ungainly, awkward-looking bird surprisingly graceful in flight. More pelicans perched on wooden pilings.

Freedom. For the first time since she'd left her family Christmas tree farm to go off to college, she had no demands from any calendars, clocks, hotel guests, and no one to answer to but herself.

The idea was both thrilling and a little daunting at the same time. After all, ever since graduating from college, she'd always moved on from town to city, hotel to hotel, place to place, never looking back. Her life had been like that old country video where the heroine had ripped the rearview mirror off the side of her car and headed, hell-bent for leather, out of Dodge.

And now here she was, on a ferry getting closer and closer to land, drinking in the familiar sounds, the smells and pretty sights, and hoping that Thomas Wolfe had been wrong about never being able to go home again. This was a new chapter in her life. A new beginning, and despite the butterflies that had begun fluttering their wings in her stomach, she would make it work.

Reminding herself that she'd always been a self-starter with strong organizational and people skills, instead of worrying about any possible pitfalls in her plan, she concentrated on the vision of what she'd always thought of as *her* house turned into a warm and inviting bed-and-breakfast. The type of place she herself would want to stay in.

Over the years, as she'd worked her way up the hospitality chain to the Midas, her surroundings had become more and more luxurious. And while each hotel offered additional amenities and increased pampering, they'd never been the type of place she would have preferred to stay herself. She wouldn't have chosen glitz and glamor, or bustling staff in crisp uniforms with shiny brass buttons and fringed epaulets that would make a banana republic general proud.

Rather than a crowded dining room abuzz with conversation drowning out the pianist playing Gershwin on a shiny black baby grand, she'd rather spend an evening enveloped in an overstuffed chair in a room with well-read books lining the walls, and a fire crackling away in an old stone fireplace.

Instead of shopping at designer boutiques with a platinum credit card, she'd rather stroll down tree-lined streets, dropping into small, quaint, locally owned shops that carried homemade fudge and desserts and whimsical, one-of-a-kind handmade pieces created by local artisans. And rather than being suffocated by ridiculously overpriced designer scents, she'd rather breathe in the tang of fir trees and salt air.

The sky turned a tarnished silver hue, hinting at rain as Honeymoon Harbor came into view, the stone Victorian buildings climbing up the steep hill, the now-automated white lighthouse at Pelican Point, and there, overlooking the harbor, was Herons Landing, unfortunately painted a Pepto-Bismol pink with purple trim and chartreuse shutters. Fishing and whale-watching boats bobbing in the water beside the sailboats and beautiful wooden boats the town was known for and what appeared to be a father and son stood on the pier, fishing lines dangling over the railing into the water, reminding her of childhood days when she'd done the same thing. Not that she'd been all that wild about fishing or crabbing, but if Seth was going to be out there with her brothers, she wasn't going to miss an opportunity to show him what a perfect girlfriend she'd be. The fact that he'd never experienced that hoped-for epiphany hadn't been for her lack of trying.

The announcement to return to her car came over the speaker and five minutes later, as she drove off the ferry onto the cobblestone street created from the same stones as many of the town's buildings, she felt an internal click that told her she'd made the absolutely right decision.

Pages from Captain George Vancouver's ship logs, housed under glass in the town historical museum, revealed his awe at the towering, snowcapped mountains, deep green rain forests that come nearly to the water's edge, crystal rivers, tumbling waterfalls, beaches and sapphire water studded with emerald islands.

By the late 1800s the town had become a bustling seaport, banking on a rich future. A building boom gifted it with an abundance of ornate Victorian homes perched atop the green bluff overlooking the bay. A town built and populated by dreamers, its port frequented by vessels from faraway places, the early economy had been built and supported by timber and shipping.

Unfortunately, too much of what was now Honeymoon Harbor had been constructed on the shifting sands of speculation that it was primed to become the capital of Washington State. Dreams were dashed when the boom collapsed and the population had declined drastically.

Although it never became the major shipping harbor people had hoped for, the royal trip that had resulted in the town's name change, along with the magnificent monument Franklin Roosevelt later designated as a national park, had created a renaissance that resulted in an influx of visitors who continued to arrive at the harbor's dock on gleaming white ferries like the one that had brought Brianna home.

The town had been divided between residential and business. Most of the buildings along the water were commercial, designed to serve arriving and departing ships. Originally built of wood from the bustling timber trade, they'd been reduced to ashes during a devastating fire that had swept through the waterfront. Meanwhile, the homes, including the Victorians the town had become known for, had been built on the bluff overlooking the harbor, which had allowed them to escape the firestorm.

Tempted as she was to drive out to the house, she reluctantly decided it made sense to go home, see her family and get a good night's sleep before contacting the Realtor in the morning. As much as Honeymoon Harbor looked much the same as it had when she'd been growing up here, there had been changes. An old warehouse had been turned into condos, the real estate sign out in front offering spacious, remodeled lofts. She dropped into a coffee shop by the ferry terminal that hadn't existed when she'd returned for Zoe's funeral two years ago, and stood in line to buy a salted skinny caramel mocha latte from one of the owners, whom, she learned from their brief conversation while he prepared her drink, was a former undercover Seattle vice detective. Which, she supposed, explained the earring and the dreadlocks.

There were other new businesses, as well, including her uncle Mike's art gallery, which would prove handy when it came to decorating her inn. Honeymoon Harborites preferred to buy local whenever possible, and in her case, it was even better when one of the businesses was owned by family.

She came up to the wide, grassy green square that had always been the centerpiece of the town. A lacy white Victorian gazebo—built by a Harper for the royal visit, where the Mannion mayor had handed the Montacroix king and queen the key to the city—had immediately proven popular with the honeymoon trade. Even today Brianna's attention was drawn to a tall, familiar redhead snapping wedding photos of a smiling bride and groom.

Growing up, Kylee Campbell and Zoe Robinson had been Brianna's best friends. They'd been inseparable, the self-named Three Musketeers, except for those times, as they'd segued into their junior and senior years of high school, when Zoe had begun spending more and more time with Seth Harper.

Pulling into a parking spot, Brianna sat in the car, watching as Kylee posed the couple in various ways while another woman set up reflector boards. They were apparently coming to the end of the shoot. After taking a few more photos next to the fountain bubbling away at one end of the green, Kylee exchanged a few words and hugs with the couple. Then, as she turned to walk away, Brianna got out of the car.

"Well, look who finally made it home," Kylee called out, emerald green skirt flowing around her ankles, revealing a pair of purple Chucks as she ran across the parking lot toward Brianna. The other woman, who'd finished packing up the equipment, followed at a more sedate pace. "I was beginning to think we'd lost you to Sin City forever."

Kylee threw her arms around Brianna and gave her an even more enthusiastic hug than she'd shared with the bride and groom.

"Wasn't going to happen."

Before her sudden change in her career, Brianna's destination track after Vegas had always been New York (her goal had been the Waldorf Astoria, currently under renovation), then London's Claridge's, before reaching her personal pinnacle: the Hôtel Plaza Athénée, which might not be Paris's flashiest hotel, but to Brianna's mind was the most luxurious, romantic and, with its glorious views of the Eiffel Tower, iconic.

Bygones.

"Do I dare hope you'll be here for our wedding?" Kylee asked. "Believe it or not, Seth's mother is going to be the officiant."

"Caroline Harper is a minister now?"

"She was ordained online about a year ago. She doesn't have an official church or anything, but has become very spiritual, in an earth mother New Agey way. More and more people have been turning to her for their weddings. And not just the retro hippy crowd, but remarrying widowers or divorcés, who want more celebration than signing papers at the courthouse, but also don't want to lock themselves into any established religious belief system."

"Trust you to have a unique wedding." Caroline Harper had always been a creative thinker and, like Brianna's own mother, was actively involved in community service. Performing weddings sounded like just another step along her life's path. She did wonder how Mr. Harper, who'd never seemed that conducive to change, had taken to his wife's apparent midlife transformation. "Now I'm even more looking forward to being part of your special day."

"So you're staying?"

"How could I not?"

"Oh, that's so great!" She pumped the hand not still holding the camera into the air. "I didn't want to dump any guilt on you, but I'll admit to being disappointed when you said you had that big deal convention to deal with."

Magic Marketplace, the world's largest fashion show, which attracted nearly a hundred thousand visitors, many of whom had booked Midas two years in advance, had been going to keep her in Las Vegas. Missing her BFF's upcoming wedding had been on the top of Brianna's list of life regrets. Now, thinking how events turned out, she should be grateful for Doctor Dick turning her life not upside down, but right side up.

"My priorities were screwed up," she admitted. Hyatt had denied her request for time off when she'd asked two months ago, but she'd also known that if she'd put her foot down and made certain her duties were well covered, he would have let her get away for at least the day of the wedding. But her damn pride, believing that only *she* could handle such a large event, had outranked what would be, so far, the most important day of her remaining best friend's life. Which went right along with her recent thoughts about not having any true friends. Because, in order to have a friend, you had to *be* one. Something she'd failed at. Miserably.

"Don't even worry about it. I totally understood." Kylee turned toward the woman who was, in appearance, her physical opposite. Where Kylee was tall, with wild masses of curly red hair that tumbled over her shoulders, her wife-to-be was petite with an asymmetrical black bob. "I'm sorry. I was so excited to see you, I got sidetracked. This is Mai, the grand love of my life. Mai, Brianna."

"I've heard a lot about you." The other woman's smile was warm. "Including that you're what keeps Las Vegas's most glamorous resort humming along."

"That's a major exaggeration. But it doesn't matter, because I no longer work there."

"No way!" Kylee's green eyes widened. "We talked just last week and you didn't give me so much as a hint you were changing jobs."

"It was sort of unexpected. And sudden."

"I guess so. So, what new gig did you jump up to this time? Social secretary at the White House?"

"Ha. Far from it. I'm opening a B and B."

"In Las Vegas?" Mai asked. Her tone remained neutral, but a slight lift of her brow hinted at skepticism. Which wasn't surprising since bed-and-breakfasts were rare in the city. Visitors tended to stay in the resort hotels, economy off-Strip motels or RV campgrounds as much as an hour outside the city. Although Airbnb had begun making inroads with budget travelers, hotels at Midas's level, where size always mattered, weren't the least bit concerned.

"As it turns out, I'm going to be doing it here." Brianna blew out a breath. This was the first time she'd said it out loud. And it sounded good. Good, but a little scary.

"Really? Wow!" Kylee's face lit up like a sudden sunbreak during a long winter of gray days. "And your timing's perfect because Herons Landing is for sale."

"I saw it on the website the other night. Other than paint colors on the exterior, it looks in pretty good shape compared to the last time I was in town."

"That paint was the previous owner's idea. While those

painted ladies may fit into San Francisco's street scene, the pink and purple look ridiculous with the wooded backdrop. And photographs can be deceiving," Kylee said. "Especially in these days when everyone knows how to Photoshop. The sales photo exterior shots only look good because Seth spent the entire last year fixing up the outside. Then the couple who'd hired him broke up and the place went into foreclosure."

Which explained why the price had seemed lower than Brianna would've expected. The real estate ad hadn't mentioned that little detail.

"The inside is definitely a work in progress," Kylee said.

"Which is a polite way of saying *wreck*," Mai murmured.

"True. But so was our new place not that long ago," Kylee reminded her. "Seth is a miracle worker. Even though his father is a bit of a challenge."

"He likes you," Mai said.

"That's because the caterers always let me keep the leftover wedding desserts. Which I take right over to the job. The man's got a serious sweet tooth," she confided to Brianna. "In his case, my mom was right on the money about the way to a man's heart being through his stomach. You can never go wrong with cookies. Or doughnuts. I'm not sure I could have convinced him to put coffering on the ceiling were it not for the fritters from Cops and Coffee."

Knowing how Ben Harper felt about her family, Brianna felt that even the entire contents of that towering glass case next to Cops and Coffee's take-out counter wouldn't be enough to win Seth's father over. Not that she was going to allow any negative behavior to dissuade her from hiring Harper Construction to create her dream.

"Anyway, Mai and I looked at Herons Landing while we were house hunting, but decided it was a lot more of a project than we wanted to deal with. And more rooms than we'd ever need. Even now that we're planning a family."

"You are? That's wonderful." Brianna shot a hard look at her only remaining friend. "Yet you accused *me* of holding back news? After, as you pointed out, we only talked last week." A conversation that had mostly been about the unexpected and ongoing trials with the Folk Victorian that Harper Construction was remodeling for them.

"I didn't want to risk jinxing things." Kylee ran a hand through her curls. "A few months ago I photographed the wedding of a woman who works with state and private organizations matching potential parents with children who need families. Which was when we decided to adopt.

"Meanwhile, our baby's birth mother isn't due for another month and we're hoping to move into the house beforehand so we don't have to bring her home to the apartment, then move again. It's not easy, but we're trying to stay patient."

"Which is proving a bit easier for me than her," Mai said with a laugh.

"What can I say?" Kylee shrugged. "We Scots have never been ones for red tape."

"I'd imagine there's quite a bit when it comes to adoption."

"Miles and miles of the damn stuff," Kylee agreed. "And it's a risk because the birth mother can always change her mind. However, despite some construction setbacks, like having to redo all the wiring in the place and getting rid of some asbestos, we're up for the challenge. The house is going to be perfect when Seth finishes.

"Speak of that handsome devil," she said as she saw a truck approaching. "There he is now." She stepped out into the street to wave him down.

Fortunately, the pickup had good brakes. He stopped on a dime, then pulled over next to the sidewalk. Brianna watched as the two exchanged a few words through the open driver's window. Then the door opened and the man she'd spent her entire adolescence fantasizing about climbed out looking like a cover model for *Hot Construction Guy Monthly*.

Over the years, partly in loyalty to her best friend and partly to keep her own hormones in check, she'd tried to convince herself that Seth Harper was just another guy. Okay, better-looking than most, but still, it wasn't as if he were movie-star handsome like Chris Evans. Or any of the other hot Chrises: Hemsworth, Pine or Pratt.

But she'd been wrong. As he strolled toward her across the street, she decided that just maybe he topped them all. He was tall, lean and lanky, which only emphasized the intriguing ridges visible beneath the black T-shirt he was wearing under a flannel shirt. Brianna didn't think it was possible to have a zero body fat ratio, but if it was, he was definitely pulling it off.

A black ball cap worn backward covered his hair, but his eyes were that same melted-chocolate brown she remembered, and above the hollows in his cheeks, his jaw bore a sexy scruff. Though, as he neared, she could detect lines fanning out from his eyes that hadn't been there two years ago.

"Hey, you." She hugged him, just as she had Kylee. But this hug was different. Even as Brianna reminded herself that he was her best friend's widower, despite all those years of telling herself that the man was off-limits, and not to even be fantasized about in her most secret moments, her breath caught in a way that could not be good.

"Hey, *you*." Was his voice deeper? Rougher? She wasn't sure, but it had definitely caused something inside her to jitter. He broke the brief hug off. "It's been a while."

"It has." They'd been standing side by side at the love of his life's funeral. She'd had no jittering that day. No unsteady breath. Just a deep, aching pain that went all the way to the bone.

"I've been meaning to get back for ages, but somehow days

flew by, then weeks, then months, then a year had passed, then two, and…"

She slammed her mouth shut. Of course he, of all people, would know how many days, weeks, months and years had passed. That wretched day had to have been etched forever in his mind. And in no way that had anything to do with her.

"Anyway, I've quit my job and come home for a lifestyle change."

"That's a surprise." His cocked brow echoed Mai's. "Zoe always talked about how much you loved your work in the fast lane."

"Well, you know how it is." Determined to appear casual, even as those butterflies in her stomach had turned into giant condors, she waved an airy hand. "Or possibly you don't, not because Honeymoon Harbor isn't exactly in the fast lane…"

Terrific. Now she was implying Seth Harper was some small-town rube. Could Mount Baker please just erupt and cover her in ash and lava now before she made things worse? "But you always knew exactly what you wanted to do."

Hadn't he built the tree house he and Zoe would hide out in with his own two hands from wood reclaimed from Harper Construction dumpsters? No. She was not going to think about what the two of them might have been doing in that house that Zoe had hung curtains in, because any thoughts of sex concerning this man were off-limits.

"I mean, you were the only person I've ever met who probably knew the difference between Italianate, Gothic Revival and Queen Anne styles of Victorians before the rest of us mastered long division."

She remembered, while they'd been running wild in Herons Landing, he'd stop and point out architectural details one of his ancestors had originally installed. Her brothers, intent on adventure, had never paused to listen. But she had.

Though, to be honest, back then she would've been more than happy to listen to him recite the tide tables.

Her thoughts were spinning even faster than she was talking. Even Kylee was looking at her strangely. She was saved from making a total fool of herself when a huge brown-and-black dog leaped out of the truck's window and came bounding toward them.

"Bandit!" Seth shouted. The dog's only response was to run faster, its tail wagging like a metronome. "Stay!"

Whether it was intending to obey, or it had finally reached its target, the dog came skidding to a halt in front of Brianna and, in way of greeting, thrust his huge nose into the crotch of her jeans.

"Hell." Seth grabbed its collar, and tugged. "I'm sorry. We're still working on manners."

"That's okay." She reached down and rubbed his broad head, scratching behind its ear. Her family had always had dogs, which, needless to say, hadn't been possible for her once she'd left home. Even if she had found a small couch potato breed, her long working hours wouldn't have been fair to any animal. "Aren't you a handsome boy?"

Moaning with canine ecstasy, he collapsed on the ground and rolled over for a tummy rub, exposing his male parts in all their proud glory.

"Don't get him started," Seth warned. He yanked off his cap and stuck it in his back pocket, revealing shaggy hair, streaked with the rich, golden brown of big-leaf maple leaves in fall. "Give him an inch and he'll take a mile."

"And probably deserves it." Crouching down, she obliged as eighty-plus pounds of dog wiggled on its back, huge paws waving in the air, a picture of pure canine bliss. "His name is Bandit?"

"Yeah. Because he's a thief. I adopted him partly to stop him from swiping all the workers' lunches. And not just food.

Shoes, socks, toothbrush, you name it, he'll take it. Last week he swallowed an entire dish towel, which involved a trip to the vet."

"Ouch."

"Bri's going to buy Herons Landing," Kylee said, jumping into the conversation.

The dark brow climbed again, practically disappearing beneath the strands of hair that had fallen over his forehead. "Seriously?"

"Seriously. And you sound skeptical." Now that they'd moved to talking about work, Brianna was back in her comfort zone, her mind returning to a more familiar organizing and planning mode. "Kylee said you restored the exterior. Which looks wonderful, by the way." She decided not to risk offending him by mentioning the exterior paint colors. "At least from the ad on the website."

"The rough edges on that ad were smoothed out by the real estate agent doing some Photoshop magic," he confirmed what she'd already been told. "Though that part's close to being done. The interior, however, is definitely still a work in progress."

"Which, I've learned over the course of our job, is contractor speak for 'It's going to take twice as long and three times the money,'" Kylee said.

"Especially when clients keep bringing up new ideas they want," Seth responded pointedly.

Bandit, realizing that he'd gotten as much tummy rubbing as he was going to get right now, was sitting in front of Brianna, his brown eyes giving her an adoring look she guessed often worked to his advantage.

"I can't deny that," Kylee said with a laugh.

"I keep telling her to step away from Houzz and Pinterest," Mai said. "But she's like an addict. Just one more picture. And the next thing you know, it's two in the morning and she's printed out a stack of photos and suggestions."

"I'm not that bad. And fortunately, Seth knows how to do everything."

"Far from everything. But having grown up on work sites, it's probably in my blood. I always knew I'd work to keep the town's old buildings from being turned into parking lots or strip malls." He turned to Brianna. "The same way you knew you wanted to work in hospitality. Whether it was finding a family the perfect Christmas tree, or creating a special hotel experience."

Brianna was surprised he'd listened to any of her grand plans when they'd all hung out together back in high school. Every atom in his body had always seemed to be honed in on Zoe.

She stood back up and shrugged with a feigned casualness she was a long way from feeling. "I did love my work. Especially in the beginning." Which she hadn't taken time to appreciate, being so focused on racing past each rung of the hospitality ladder. "But after a while, it became more a case of 'Be careful what you wish for.'"

"It happens." He didn't look all that surprised. On the contrary, his eyes, which she now noticed had deep shadows beneath them, turned sad. "So, what's your new plan?"

"She's turning it into a B and B," Kylee answered before Brianna could. "So why don't you take her over there and give her a professional opinion so she'll know what she's getting into when and if she ends up negotiating a price?"

"That'd probably be best for her contractor to discuss with her."

"I was hoping you'd take on the job," Brianna said, looking up at him in surprise. She'd never considered the possibility that anyone but Harper Construction would do the remodeling.

He put both his hands on his hips, his long, work-rough-ened fingers framing a part of his body that Brianna never allowed herself to even think about. Which was a lie. There'd been a time, during her freshman year of high school, when she'd first started having *those* feelings, that she'd definitely imagined what Seth Harper was hiding beneath those five metal buttons. He glanced over at her car with its back seat loaded with luggage and boxes. "Did you just arrive today?"

"On the four-o'clock ferry," she confirmed. "I'm staying with my folks for the time being until I find a rental in town. But I'm sure you have better things to do right now, so perhaps we could set up an appointment, since Kylee's idea for me to find out what I'm in for before I buy the house is a good one."

A silence hung between them. Everyone, including Bandit, whose gaze had begun going back and forth between them, seemed to be waiting for Seth's response.

"I don't have anything else to do," he said finally. A shadow had moved across those sad, dark eyes, like clouds drifting in from the coast before a storm. "If you don't need to get straight out to the farm, I'm up for showing you through the house." He looked down at her, studying her, his face unreadable. "Though I've got to warn you, it's a long way from being livable enough to open for guests anytime soon."

"It couldn't be any worse than back when we used to sneak in," she said.

"Got a point there." And then he almost smiled. At least that's what she thought that twitch at the corner of his lips might have meant to be. Though that could just be wishful thinking.

"I'll meet you there," she said.

"Works for me."

All three women watched as he walked back to his truck.

"I'm not into guys, but I've got to admit, that's one damn fine butt," Mai said on a long sigh.

"It's all those squats," Kylee said. When Brianna shot her friend a look, she lifted her hands and said, "Hey, he's working on our house. I'd have to be blind not to notice him picking up all that lumber and stuff."

"And those back muscles when he's pounding nails," Mai said on a sigh. "He's like a living work of art. You should shoot him," she told Kylee. "In the nude."

"I've thought about doing a calendar of Honeymoon Harbor Hotties to raise money for the food bank. Not entirely nude. Just suggestive enough for those of us with dirty minds." Kylee flashed a wicked grin. "He'd definitely fit right in."

"You could have a showing and auction of the photos at Mike Mannion's gallery," Mai said. "It would boost interest in the calendar. Especially if you had all the guys standing next to big, blown-up photos of their months. The place would be packed with women from all over the peninsula. Not counting our brother gays."

"She shoots. She scores. And the crowd goes wild," Kylee, who'd played center for the town's high school hoops team, said with a laugh.

"I'd buy it in a heartbeat," Brianna said. It would be the closest she'd gotten to a naked man in too long to remember. "And, as much as this has been fun, I'd better get going." Just the thought of a nude Builder McDreamy was raising her temperature.

"Good luck," Kylee said as Brianna opened the driver's door.

"Thanks. You know I've always loved that house."

"Oh, yeah. The house." Her friend's knowing look reminded Brianna of all those times when they'd talked about her secret crush on the third member of the Three Musketeers' boyfriend. "Good luck with that, too."

CHAPTER SEVEN

Driving over to Herons Landing, Seth passed two kids, about nine years old, racing their bikes down the quiet street lined with bright pink flowering plum trees and waved back at Otto and Alma Karlsson, who were sitting in rockers on their front porch. They'd celebrated their sixtieth anniversary in the town hall this past Valentine's Day. The party had originally been planned to take place in the friendship hall of the Swedish Seamen's Lutheran church, but when so many townspeople wanted to join in the celebration, it had been moved to the larger venue.

Turning left on Mountain View, the sight of Mellie and Jake Johnson pushing their two toddlers in a double stroller had him rubbing his chest. If he and Zoe had been successful in their baby-making plan, their child would be about the same age as the Johnson's twins. It also occurred to him that, in a space of less than three minutes, he'd witnessed a circle of life. From the babies and their parents, to the preteens, to the elderly Karlssons.

Although she might have arrived in Honeymoon Harbor from Astoria, Zoe's father's family, like Seth's own and the

Mannions, were early settlers. From time to time he'd be dragged into pioneer celebrations, which he'd always enjoyed growing up, but the last few times had only made him all too aware that Zoe wasn't there with him.

Putting that thought away in the mental lockbox, where he kept all things Zoe, he made another turn that took him past the high wrought iron gates of the cemetery, and along the water to the house in question.

The Queen Anne–era Victorian boasted three stories, four fireplaces, a turret and a curved porch with a view of both water and mountains. Back when it had been built by a timber baron in the late 1800s, at least two of the five acres it sat on had been gardens, which had long ago gone to weed.

He was standing on temporary gravel that had been planned to be a stone paver driveway, hands on his hips, looking up at the new slate roof that had cost an arm and leg but was historically accurate, when Brianna pulled up behind his truck.

The first thing he noticed when she climbed out of the snazzy red convertible, which wasn't all that practical for the rainy Pacific Northwest, was how long her legs were. Why hadn't he ever noticed that before? She was wearing a pair of cropped skinny jeans and a shirt blooming with hibiscus blossoms open over a white tank top. Her turquoise flats had little bows on the toes like the ones he remembered on Zoe's ballet slippers during those years her mother had made her take dance lessons. Hopefully, Zoe had complained, with a roll of her expressive dark eyes, to make her more girly so she'd give up any idea of being a soldier.

Which, duh, hadn't worked all that well since once Zoe Robinson got an idea in her head, it was impossible to shake it out. Still, those pale pink slippers with the lace-up ribbons and scuffed-up soles she was always having to clean were why those combat boots he'd last seen his wife wearing at her deployment ceremony at JBLM had always seemed so out of place.

Seeing his new best human friend again, Bandit loped over and jumped up, putting his paws on Brianna's shoulders. At the same time a cloud overhead started spitting rain, making her colorful Las Vegas–style outfit all the more impractical. Which, even as he yelled at his dog to get down, had Seth wondering if it would really be possible for a woman who'd harbored such glamorous, big-city dreams to come home again.

The sudden cloudburst had soaked her, revealing a lacy bra beneath the white tank clinging to her lean body. It had been nearly three years since he'd seen a woman's bra that wasn't on a commercial for the Victoria's Secret fashion show that'd pop up every year on ESPN. As an unbidden and entirely unwelcome feeling stirred, he snagged one of the emergency slickers he kept on hand for clients—usually Californians who didn't understand the concept of weather changing on a dime—from his truck's club cab back seat and held it out to her.

"Thanks." She shrugged into it, covering up that see-through tank. "I remembered to put the top up on the car when I crossed the border into Oregon, but forgot the cardinal rule of never being without a rain jacket." The sleeves fell nearly over her hands, which were tipped in coral lacquered nails that matched the flowers on her shirt. Each ring fingernail had a tiny white blossom with rhinestone centers painted on it, which was something he couldn't remember ever seeing in Honeymoon Harbor.

"You probably didn't need a slicker all that much in Vegas," he said.

"That would be true. I know people up here dream of retiring to the desert, and a lot do, if all those gray-, blue-and purple-haired elderly ladies who'd camp out at the slots were any indication, but I never got the appeal. Natives would say there were two seasons: hot and hotter. I always thought there were three: hot, pizza oven hot and hell." She lifted those colorful fingertips to her cheek. "And the lack of humidity, while good for hair, was horrible on the skin."

Her skin looked just fine to him. When he found himself wondering if her smooth cheek felt as silky as it looked, the resultant stab of guilt jerked his mind back to their reason for being here.

"The color leaves a lot to be desired," she said, looking up at what Seth personally considered an abomination, but the previous buyers had been adamant about wanting their very own painted lady.

"It's undoubtedly visible from space," he said.

"I would've gone with blue, to echo the water. Or perhaps yellow, to brighten the winter days. With crisp white trim."

"Both of which I suggested."

"Great minds." She flashed him a smile that was like a ray of sun shining from the quilted gray sky and momentarily warmed some cold, dark place inside him.

"You sure you don't want to come back another day? When it's drier?"

"The roof's new, right?" She glanced up at the randomly placed multicolored tiles in shades of blue and gray.

"It is. And not the fake stuff, but real slate formed by hand right here on the peninsula in Port Angeles. It'll last another hundred years."

"Then it won't leak on us."

"Not even during a downpour." Which this wasn't.

"So there's nothing stopping us from going in."

"It's a mess."

"I heard."

"And you're not exactly dressed for climbing over boards and nails." He looked down at the flats.

"Good point." She glanced over at the car. "Hold on a minute."

As he watched, she ran over to the convertible, Bandit right on her heels, popped the trunk, opened a suitcase and pulled out a pair of yellow Keds with perky white daisies printed on the canvas. She sat down on the edge of the trunk and changed. The Keds weren't proper boots, but if she was careful and he could keep her from climbing any leftover scaffolding, they'd work.

"Ready," she said. Since she hadn't pulled out any rain gear, he guessed she hadn't been exaggerating when she'd said that she didn't own any.

The snazzy car, along with the flowery blouse, which looked to be real silk and not the polyester Zoe had always bought at Target, suggested that she'd been well paid. But as two other owners in the last decade had proven, renovating a house like Herons Landing was neither easy nor inexpensive. And it also took time. He wondered if she ought to try staying in Honeymoon Harbor for a while before buying, just to be certain she found the town to be a good fit after all these years away.

"I've been homesick for a while," she said when he carefully brought the subject up. "The idea had been simmering beneath the surface for some time, but I was too busy and distracted by work to recognize it. The minute I saw it was for sale, I felt the tug to come home."

It was his turn to shrug. Hell, it was her problem, and her money. If it was what she really wanted to do, he'd make it happen. Not just because he was the best guy in Washington to pull the job off, but, other than himself, Brianna Mannion had been Zoe's best friend. He owed it to her.

"Some folks around here still claim it's haunted," he said, taking her arm as he led her up the steps to the front door.

"Some folks also claim Bigfoot's out there roaming around

in the woods," Brianna countered. "And if you believe the supermarket tabloids, actual sparkly vampires exist in Forks."

"True. But a couple who bought it three years ago believed the stories enough to hire a Ghostbuster."

She looked up at him. "You're kidding."

"Nope. Not to get rid of her, but to connect on some ethereal plane. They wanted a self-proclaimed paranormal investigator to make sure she didn't mind them living in her space."

"I guess she told them that she did mind? Since they didn't finish the project?"

"I've no idea since I didn't ask and they didn't tell."

"I never really believed in her," Brianna said. "Or, more, I never saw any proof. But I never disbelieved, either."

"Whichever, they were arrested for running a Ponzi scheme disguised as a hedge fund and the property was seized by the government." Leaving his bank account to take a huge hit when he'd been forced to pay for the materials and subcontractors out of his own pocket.

"Last summer it was bought at auction by a couple of doctors from the Bay Area who got tired of the San Francisco rat race and decided it would be fun to run a bed-and-breakfast. We'd barely started working on the interior when the docs realized what living in a construction zone would feel like. As their costs escalated, they got a divorce and bailed on the deal by declaring bankruptcy. We're far enough down the debtor's list, I doubt we'll ever see a dime."

"It sounds as if this place has turned into a money pit for you."

"Enough that Dad decided the house may not be haunted, but it's definitely cursed."

Having to listen to his father's nonstop bitching about Seth letting them get shafted, not once, but twice, had been the worst part of the deals. He'd have to remember to be outside when he told his old man about their new client. Because Ben Harper was flat-out going to hit the roof.

He wondered how much he should tell her about his parent's separation, then decided, what the hell. Since she'd undoubtedly hear about his family's domestic drama soon enough, he might as well let her know right off the bat.

"There is one thing that might cause a problem, so if you're going to be around the house during work hours—"

"That would be my plan."

"Then you need to know that my parents are currently separated."

"Oh." She tilted her head. "I'm sorry. That must be difficult for you. Being in the middle."

"It's not a walk in the park. But the reason I'm telling you up front is that it might concern you, too."

"Really? Why?"

"Because my mom's dating again."

"I guess that's a good thing? For her, anyway."

"It seems to be. But here's what could be a problem...the guy she's seeing is your uncle."

"Uncle Mike?"

"Yeah. I don't know how serious things have gotten between them, but I had dinner with them at Leaf—which is this new vegetarian place that's opened up since the last time you were here—"

"I saw the building. Near the park. Did you do the work?"

"Yeah. They hired a designer for the interior decorator stuff, but I drew up the plans and did the construction part of the job."

"You're awfully modest for a man who won an award for environmental historical renovation and remodeling."

"Sounds like you really checked out the town's website."

"As I said, I've been homesick. I saw your award. That's impressive."

He shrugged. "There's a lot happening in the historical environmental field right now," he said, shaking off the cloud that had returned to hang over them. "I enjoy attending seminars on the various views and options."

Not wanting her to think he was blowing his own horn, something his dad had taught him at an early age Harpers didn't do, he didn't tell her that he'd given a lot of those seminars himself. Just like they weren't that generous with compliments, Harper men weren't that good with accepting them. Another possible reason his mother seemed so attracted to Mike Mannion, who appeared to hand them out like penny candy.

Once again, Seth was forced to consider the idea that his parents' separation could well become permanent. Then, once again, he reminded himself that they were adults and their relationship, whatever the hell it was or wasn't these days, was none of his business.

"Anyway, getting back to Dad, he might not be all that cooperative."

"Believe me," she said on a laugh, "in the hospitality business you learn to deal with uncooperative people. Many of whom are males."

Her rich, warm laugh caused a tug of something he'd thought he'd never feel again. Something that was too close to desire for comfort. Which was why Seth immediately shut it down. Even if he were looking for any kind of relationship, which he wasn't, getting involved with his wife's best friend would just be too weird.

Which made Brianna Mannion definitely off-limits.

As he used his key to open the lockbox on the door, Seth reminded himself that he'd be wise to remember that.

CHAPTER EIGHT

He hadn't been exaggerating. However, from what he and Kylee had told her, Brianna had expected the cobwebs, mouse droppings and graffiti she remembered from those youthful days of breaking in. The graffiti was still there on the unfortunately ugly wallpapered foyer walls, but the only thing covering the floors was taped-down paper, sawdust and a few scattered nails. Scaffolding and sawhorses supporting long pieces of Sheetrock as tabletops took up much of the covered floors.

"The interior walls are all gone." That had been a spooky, but in a weird way, fun thing about the house. Going from parlor to parlor, never knowing what lurked around a corner. Pipes and wires between studs were all that remained.

Broad shoulders lifted and fell in what appeared to be a resigned shrug. "They thought open concept on the first floor would make for a communal experience."

"I can't argue with that. Especially when you're hosting a group that wants to spend time together. But they seem to have overdone the concept."

"Again, we're in full agreement."

"Could you put some walls back in?"

"Sure. We'll have to move some electrical and plumbing, and you'll probably need to change the HVAC, but it's doable. Were you thinking of going more back to the original layout?"

"A combination would be good." She'd decided that on the long drive home. "Some small parlor rooms for more intimate conversations, and even private meals. But I want a wide-open kitchen with plenty of room to serve breakfast."

Attacking her research the same way she had in her previous occupation, she'd bought two audiobooks about the business of establishing and running a B and B that she'd listened to along the drive, pulling off at exits every so often to write down notes in the three-ring binder she'd bought before leaving Las Vegas. She also had three more books on her Kindle waiting to be read.

She looked a long way up. "The mural is still there."

Rather than depicting the mythological figures popular at the time the house was built, these were scenes of the peninsula—from the cliffs and crashing waves, to the glaciers of Mount Olympus, standing tall over Hurricane Ridge, to the towering hemlock and Douglas firs, the fields of lavender farms, the strait leading to the Puget Sound cities of Seattle, Tacoma and Olympia, the dazzling blue bay that Honeymoon Harbor had been built on.

Scattered throughout the quadrants were the Native American original settlers, the ships, including Captain Vancouver's *Discovery*, fishermen and builders like Seth's family. Unsurprising, given that the house had been contracted by a timber baron, loggers claimed the center.

"I had to fight to keep that," he revealed. "The doctors wanted to paint over it and hang a massive chandelier they were bringing in from some old Italian chateau. Fortunately, the historical preservation folks stepped in to back me up since it turned out to have been painted by Whistler."

"*The* Whistler? As in James McNeill Whistler?"

"The very same. The original owner of this place had seen one he'd painted on the dining room in the home of some wealthy Liverpool shipowner and wanted something like it for this house. The fact that he was an American pulled a lot of weight with the historical committee."

"That makes it even more special. If I make a separate page for it on the website, it might even bring in historical art lovers wanting to stay here. Whistler's got to have a following, right?"

"Could be," Seth agreed. "The same way people go around the country searching out certain architects' work."

"Though, of course, that alone might not cause them to stay more than a single night. Fortunately, with the National Park and the proximity to the coast, and Victoria, BC, we've lots of other local things for visitors to do that will keep them here for at least a weekend, or longer. I'm going to make a list and put together packages on the site."

"You've thought this through if you've gotten to planning a website."

"It's a nineteen-hour drive and a two-hour ferry ride from Las Vegas to Honeymoon Harbor. That gave me a lot of time to think. And I can tell from the expression on your face that you think it's just a whim, but it's not. Maybe the idea sounds impulsive, but it's been percolating in the back of my mind for a long time. It just took an inciting incident to bring it to the surface."

Seth thought about asking what incident that might be, wondered if it had anything to do with a guy, then decided the less he knew about Brianna's personal life, the better.

"Except for updating all the wiring in the place to keep

the house from being a fire hazard, the second floor hasn't been touched," he said as they walked toward the back stairs.

Bandit usually took the opportunity to patrol the perimeter for renegade squirrels if no worker was around to mooch from, but today he seemed to have decided to tag along with the pretty new lady.

"The circular stairway in the front entry is a showcase, but if it were the only one, the owners—who I guess would now be you—would have to keep running into guests." Which he personally wouldn't enjoy. Then again, ever since his wife got blown up, no one would refer to him as Mr. Hospitality on his best day.

"Good point," she said.

"The third story attic's been turned into a penthouse with its own kitchen. The previous owners intended to live there."

She shuddered. "I remember bats."

"They're all gone. Though there is a bat house at the far end of the property, not far from the pond. Not only are they good for pollinating plants, one little brown guy can eat a thousand mosquitoes a night."

"That's a plus," she allowed.

"All the windows, including those in the attic dormers, have been reglazed," he assured her. "That wavy glass was a better insulator back then and, hell, it just looks better."

Brianna paused on the landing leading up to what was once an attic crowded with junk. And mice. And, yes, bats. She'd gotten one tangled up in her hair one night, he recalled. He'd managed to free her, but not before she'd practically blown out his eardrums with her screeching.

While Zoe had long dark curls, Brianna's hair was the color of caramel streaked with gold. As he got a whiff of its citrusy scent, he wondered if the streaks had been created by the blazing desert sun, or if she'd paid for them in some chi-chi salon. Not that he cared. It was just a random thought.

"I can tell why you deserved to win that award," she said, thankfully unaware of his thoughts. "You really care."

"Harpers built most of these old buildings," he said. "It only makes sense that I'd want them to stay true to the original vision."

"Yet with your credentials, you could work anywhere. You'd undoubtedly be in demand in lots of big cities where you could make more money."

"I have all the money I need. And I like it here just fine. Though I have done a couple jobs, for cost, in Portland and Seattle for preservationists wanting to save them from the wrecking ball."

She gave him another slanted-head look, as if working for free hadn't been a concept in her high-flying world. Which, he figured, it probably hadn't been.

"Let me show you the penthouse." As he followed her up the stairs, it would have been impossible not to notice that she had a very fine ass filling out the back of those skinny jeans.

Off-limits, he reminded himself firmly.

CHAPTER NINE

"Oh, wow." Brianna stopped in the doorway of what she'd remembered as a spooky, cluttered bat attic. "This is an amazing space." She walked in and turned around, arms outspread. "You could have the entire cast of *Swan Lake* dancing on these floors." Which were natural light maple coated to a soft sheen.

"Different strokes. I pictured the Trail Blazers running up and down the court."

"That's 'cause you're a guy." A fact that, as she felt herself drowning in two deep pools of hot fudge, she was all too aware of. She glanced a long way up. "I don't remember the ceiling being this high."

"It wasn't. We raised the roof another four feet, which brought it to twelve feet."

"I couldn't tell from the outside. But this makes it so bright and airy. Especially with the open beams and skylights you've added to the original dormer windows."

She walked over to the window and looked out over the water, where a successful haul had a pair of fishing boats moving slowly and heavily into port. A gleaming bridal-white and grass-green ferry chugged across the bay. In the distance, the wooded islands appeared like emeralds on a bed of sapphire silk.

He gave her a brief tour, showing her the small three-quarters bath with a large shower with two walls glass, and the other two subway tile with gray grout. There was also a long counter with double sinks. She would have liked a tub, but lounging in a tub probably wasn't something she'd have time for anyway.

The walls had been painted a soft grayish sage that blended with the various shades of green outside the windows. A kitchen area with maple cabinets and a gray quartz counter ran along one wall, and a large island divided the living space. The new gas fireplace featured a surround created by vertical strips of marble in grays and whites.

"It's interesting that they chose such calming colors when the exterior is so discordant," she mused.

"I figured they thought people would expect bright colors on a Queen Anne," Seth said. "Or maybe they'd always dreamed of owning a painted lady of their own back home in San Francisco."

"Whichever, paint can always be changed. Meanwhile, this space is lovely. You've almost made me forget the bats."

"All the vent openings are well screened," he assured her. "They can't get in."

"That's good to know." She crossed the room and looked out the windows facing the opposite side of the house, toward the snowcapped mountains, where blue and yellow wildflowers danced in the meadows. "The heron nests are still there."

The great blue heron was iconic to the Pacific Northwest, celebrated in art going back to the earliest Native Americans. The massive nests on this property had been built in towering Douglas firs over years of breeding seasons, with birds building new nests with sticks and twigs every year. Glancing out, she could count five, though she remembered as many as a dozen at one time.

"Lucky," he said. "Now you won't have to change the name."

She glanced over her shoulder and realized he was standing close behind her. Close enough for her to breathe in the brisk scent of his soap, like the towering fir trees blanketing the mountains, along with an undernote of workingman musk that was clouding her mind. "Lucky," she murmured, knowing that he was joking. Despite the town's long-ago name change, tradition was taken seriously in Honeymoon Harbor. Whoever owned the house, whatever it became, this would always be known as Herons Landing.

"As much as I love my parents, I'd feel like a teenager living there all the time it's going to take to remodel," she said, moving out of the danger zone before turning around to face him again. "I thought I'd rent in town for now, then eventually live in the carriage house for more privacy when I got up and running, but for now, this would be perfect."

"And noisy," he warned her. "Because you'd be living over a construction zone."

"Ah, but it'd be convenient, because I'd be on-site instead of having to drive in from the farm every day."

"You really do intend to be hands-on." The tone was neutral, but she sensed that he was wary about that idea. Given the previous buyers' choice of exterior paint, she understood his caution.

"I have some ideas," she admitted. "But you've been essentially living with the house, through two earlier owners, and from what you've told me so far, you and I are on the same page. Though you're way ahead of me because I never, in a million years, would've thought of this. Obviously you've drawn up plans."

"Sure."

"I'd like to see them."

"Absolutely. I also have the originals if you'd like to compare."

"The originals?" He might as well have told her he'd found the Holy Grail. "Seriously?"

"They were in some dusty old filing cabinets. Harper Construction built the most iconic buildings in town. Like the library, the city hall, the buildings where both your uncle and brother set up shop. We've always been proud of that."

"As you should be," she agreed without hesitation. "I just never expected them to still be around. What shape are they in?"

"A little yellowed. Brown around the edges. But they're still readable. And apparently Jacob Harper, Nathaniel's older brother who built the place in 1894, had a sense of history or immortality, or, if he was anything like Dad, worried about someone stealing them, because he signed every page."

"Oh, wow." Her heart began doing a happy samba at that news. "I don't suppose you'd be willing to let me buy the pages with the layouts of the room and exterior? To frame?"

"Sorry, they're not for sale."

"I understand." Which was true. Disappointing, but true. They might not be as famous as Captain Vancouver's ship logs, but they were a large part of Honeymoon Harbor's history. Why should he sell them off? Especially to a Mannion?

"Though I can give them to you. After I get them copied."

He'd been one of the nicest boys she'd known. Which was saying something, since she'd always found her brothers very special. It was also why, although there were times she'd admittedly been envious of Zoe, she'd never been jealous of her best friend for having Seth Harper fall in love with her. Apparently, despite the grief she could tell he was still experiencing, he hadn't changed. Now he was one of the nicest men she knew. Working with him, while not proving to be all that easy on her hormones, was going to be a pleasure.

"I'd love that. Thank you. But since they're a Harper family heirloom, I'd be thrilled just to have the copies." She could already imagine them on the wall. Not in frames, she decided. But shadow boxes to honor them with the importance they deserved.

"They're all yours."

An easy silence settled over them as they both looked around, imagining the house as it could be. "It's going to be wonderful," she breathed. "Since so many of the guests will be coming here for the outdoor activities, I want an easy, simple style they can feel comfortable in. Where they don't have to worry about knocking over a gilt-rimmed vase. But I also want to celebrate the curves and quality of the time."

"Dressing your Victorian dowager in flannel shirts, jeans, hiking boots, while keeping her good set of pearls."

He'd surprised her. Until she thought about it a second. This house might be her dream. But in a way, the entire town was both Seth's family history and daily reality as he brought Harper-constructed buildings back to life. He was the one who'd dedicated his life to blending the disparate eras.

"I wonder if people realize how lucky they are that you decided to stay here in Honeymoon Harbor," she said. She had no doubt he could make a great deal more in most older cities in the country.

He shrugged. "I never had any desire to go anywhere else.

"How about you drop by the office tomorrow?" he suggested. "About noon. We can go over the original blueprints and what I came up with, both before and after the lower floor walls came out, and you can give me your ideas."

"I'd love that. I'll bring lunch."

"You don't have to do that."

"Tonight's my first night home in two years," she said. "Which means Mom's going to make way too much fried chicken and potato salad." Although her mother might not have allowed processed food in her home while Brianna had been growing up, Sarah Mannion's fried chicken, which had won awards at the county and state fairs, was a family favorite for special occasions. "There'll be leftovers."

"I'd never turn down your mom's chicken," he said. "So, moving on, how would you like to see an idea I had for the second floor tower room? The previous owners turned it down, but I thought it wouldn't hurt to pitch it again."

"I'd love to hear any ideas you have." After checking out Harper Construction's website, she'd been blown away by their portfolio.

They left the large room and headed back down to the second floor, followed by Bandit, claws clicking on the wooden stairs. As he'd warned her, the second floor hadn't been touched except for all the open wall spaces where outdated electrical and plumbing had been replaced.

"We also added air-conditioning," he said. "Which didn't used to be needed here, but the past summers have had some hot spells, so it seemed prudent. There's a solar unit on the back side of the roof you can't see from the front that provides the power."

"Does solar really make that much of a difference here?" In Las Vegas, it made sense, but even here in the rain shadow so-called "banana belt" of Washington State, which received less rain than Seattle, winter days were still long and dark this far north.

"True," he said when she shared that thought. "But conversely, summers are sunny and clear and can stretch from a five a.m. sunrise to ten p.m. sunset. That produces a lot of free, clean energy, which doesn't all get used because the temperatures, which are admittedly rising, are still fairly mild. And here's the best part. When you produce more solar energy than you need, it gets sent back to the utility grid. Net energy metering rewards you for producing electricity for your neighbors by paying you for the extra solar power."

"Like spinning the meter backward?"

"Exactly." His smile wasn't as intimate as the ones she'd watched him bestowing on Zoe Robinson all during high school, but the warmest she'd seen since her arrival. Kylee might be right about food being the way to a man's heart, but just perhaps, talking construction and energy conservation was the way to Seth's.

But no… They were merely two old friends embarking on a joint project that would prove equally fulfilling and profitable. Reminding herself that she hadn't come back to Honeymoon Harbor to attempt to hook up with her best friend's widower, Brianna turned her mind back to their conversation.

"The credits show up on your bill, and the law requires that you be reimbursed for every kilowatt hour of electricity you produce. At minimum the power company has to pay you the same rate they charge you. So, the summer credits add up for you to use in the winter. Which, since we're doing a green renovation, with all the insulation and other stuff I don't want to bore you with until you're sure you really want to do this—"

"I'm sure." She'd thought it all through on the drive home and had convinced herself that she wasn't really acting on impulse. That returning home and buying Herons Landing was what she wanted to do with this next phase of her life. But, admittedly, there'd been those nagging little thoughts of, *Do you really want to throw away all you've worked for?*

Then, the moment she'd seen the heron nests, she'd been absolutely, positively certain.

"I'm not throwing anything away," she said.

He glanced over at her. His expression revealed she'd spoken out loud.

"I suspect a lot of people in the position I'd reached would probably think I'm crazy to do this," she admitted. Make that most, if not all. "I'd believed I was on the right track, but sometimes you can get so focused on moving forward, you miss whatever might be down a side road."

"That happens in hiking," he agreed. "I've been with people so busy looking at their Fitbits, counting their steps, or how long to their destination, they never pause to take in the view. But this isn't exactly a side road. Some might view it as more of a reversal."

"Or coming full circle."

He nodded. "Point taken. And it's not that I'd ever doubt you when you put your mind to something. To be perfectly honest, after two jobs falling through, I have a vested interest in this one reaching completion. If only to save myself from having to listen to Dad bitch at me for the next thirty or forty years."

A thought occurred to her. "Is working for a Mannion going to prove a problem for you?"

"As long as I've been involved in the business, Harper Construction only turned down one job. And that was from a Los Angeles architect who wanted to tear down a cottage house and build an ultra-modern concrete-and-glass box that would block the views of three houses behind him."

"Good for you. But did he get someone else to do it for him?"

"No. We were lucky in that case because although the boundary lines could admittedly be contested, part of the lot appeared to be in the historic district. When every historical preservation group in the Pacific Northwest threatened to help ours fight it, he decided it wasn't worth the trouble, gave up the idea and went back to California.

"And getting back to your question about us working for a Mannion, I did the pub for Quinn. As well as your uncle's gallery. And we built a new, larger barn out at your family's tree farm for various events your family's been holding there. Last summer your mom turned it into a summer theater for local writers and actors to put on plays."

"She wrote me about that." Having grown up attending

plays at the Theater in the Firs, which had always sold out early, Brianna had thought her parents' idea had been a brilliant addition to their revenue stream, along with strengthening brand loyalty since they definitely weren't the only Christmas tree farm in the state. But she hadn't made it home for a single performance.

Even as she reminded herself that she wasn't the only one of her siblings to leave the peninsula, Brianna felt a pinprick of guilt. "Mom's also a Harper." Brianna had heard stories of her parents' courtship, which often reminded her of *Romeo and Juliet*. Or the star-crossed Tony and Maria in *West Side Story*.

"Not the first case of our families marrying."

"True. My mom's great-great-aunt married your father's three-times-great-grandfather. Which makes my mom and your dad third or fourth cousins three or maybe four times removed. I never can remember how it goes, although Aunt Marian, who was into genealogy, once tried to explain her chart with dozens of connected boxes on it to me. I also have no idea what that makes us."

"Kissing cousins?"

Seth's out-of-the-blue question seemed to surprise him nearly as much as it did her. His shoulders and neck stiffened.

Meanwhile, an image of him pulling her into his arms, ducking his head, his beautiful, hot, hungry mouth claiming hers, flashed through Brianna's mind. Before the unwelcome fantasy could turn X-rated, the long and two short warp-and-woofs of the ferry leaving the dock shattered a hush as deep as the coastal rain forest that had fallen over the room. Saving them both.

"Well, anyway." She cleared her throat, and tried, with less success, to clear her mind. "Moving on from the logistics of our families' comingling—"

This time it was *her* very wrong word choice. She shut her mouth so fast and so hard she was surprised he couldn't hear the clang of her teeth. But the flare of heat in his eyes suggested he was thinking of more than the comingling of their families. When her rebellious mind conjured up another image of them lying together on a fluffy rug in front of the fireplace on a rainy winter night, every nerve ending in her body began to spark.

Dragging her hand through her hair, she took a deep breath. "Another thing that occurred to me during the long trip home was that all those years learning the hospitality business weren't wasted. When you only have an hour to find a doctor to come give a guest Botox—"

"You're kidding." He seemed as relieved as she was at any excuse to change the topic from kissing. And comingling.

"A provost for digital initiatives and dean of university libraries at a top Ivy League college was there to give a speech and had just learned that she was going to win a major award that night. She wanted to look her best."

"Makes sense to me."

Brianna knew that it didn't make a lick of sense to him. Which was okay, because there had been a time she would have found the request crazy, too.

"If there's one thing the past years have taught me, it's that no matter how well traveled a person is, there's always going to be times of stress, and different people have their own expectations of what will ease that stress. My job had been to make it happen."

As she could've done with Doctor Dick. If given the chance.

"I doubt any guest at Herons Landing will have a sudden need for face fillers," she said. "But unexpected things do come up."

She told him about a less than positive experience when a guest had gotten furious enough to pick up a lobby chair and throw it at her after she'd attempted to explain that she couldn't arrange for a live tiger to walk into their suite during dessert wearing a ten-carat engagement ring around his neck for his girlfriend.

"He was an heir to a fortune, and claimed that his about-to-be fiancée's spirit animal was a tiger. So he'd wanted to make his proposal one she'd never forget."

"She'd probably remember it a lot better if she weren't eaten," he suggested.

"That's pretty much what I told him." With a little distance, Brianna could laugh at the incident. "Those of us in hospitality share war stories, and I've come to realize there are very few problems I haven't faced."

Bouncing around the country had also had her realizing how regional guests' needs tended to be. Here in Washington she'd need to bone up on hiking trails and fishing location recommendations as opposed to knowing who to call to score tickets to some big sold-out show.

"So, the past years have been like getting your PhD in hospitality."

She laughed. "I like the way you think."

The tower room's bay windows offered a view of the waterfront, harbor and mist-draped islands that would allow her to charge more for it, but her takeaway from those audiobooks was that due to its size, it wasn't special enough to be a featured room.

"Here's my idea," he said. "Gut this space and the next two down the hall. Then open them up into one room that would give you both mountain and harbor views. Add grand, double hardcore entry doors, along with extra insulation to add more soundproofing, which I imagine would appeal to honeymooners. Since all the chimneys in the place are sound—I had them checked out early on—you could stick with wood. But if it were my decision, I'd change it out to gas that can be operated with a remote. Then turn the three separate rooms into one large honeymoon suite. You can separate an en suite bath with either pocket doors or even a sliding barn door."

She could envision it. So clearly. "I love the idea. Especially the barn door, which brings in a trendy feature with-out breaking the bank. And although a crackling wood fire is romantic, gas would be better for the environment."

"It'd also be better during red flag, no burn days," he said. "You wouldn't want to use a fireplace as a selling point, then have to tell guests they couldn't use it."

"Good point."

She turned from the view of a large, red-sailed ship that looked a lot like it might have been commanded by Captain Jack Sparrow, to look up at him. "Why did those other own-ers turn your idea down?"

"Because they'd read a bunch of books that said the entire point of an inn was to have as many rooms—and beds—as possible. They were focused on the number of heads in beds."

"That may be true for a highway off-ramp motel chain." During her college days, she'd worked nights at a couple of those herself, where room service didn't exist and the "con-tinental breakfast" consisted of a plastic-wrapped pastry of unknown age and coffee guests poured themselves into card-board cups from a huge stainless steel urn. "But the one thing bed-and-breakfasts, country inns and five-star hotels have in common is that they're offering an experience. Something special. And in a town that's literally named for a honeymoon, a honeymoon suite seems like a no-brainer."

"Thanks. That's what I thought, too."

"We'll need a statement bed." She slowly turned around in a circle, taking in the space, imagining the adjoining walls gone. "This big bay window bump out would be a perfect place for a nice skirted table and chairs for private breakfasts. And, of course, the room needs a Victorian fainting couch—"

"My mother has one of those. And I don't believe she's ever fainted a day in her life."

"I suspect fainting was more common when women were

all corseted up for hours a day. Body shapers are bad enough. I can't imagine being tied into whalebones."

He skimmed a look over her. If he'd been anyone else, she'd think he was checking her out. But this was Seth. Her best friend's husband. Well, widower. But still, any interest she might have thought she viewed in that dark gaze was undoubtedly born from whatever cooled ashes were lingering in her imagination from her youthful crush.

She was no longer a teenage virgin with a wistful, yearning heart. She was a grown woman who'd slept with not all that many men, but enough to know her youthful dreams of Seth Harper had been both overly romanticized and unrealistic.

"Also, there's another theory, but…" She felt the color, the bane of her fair skin, rise in her cheeks.

He tilted his head. "But?"

"That the couch was also used to keep women comfortable while they underwent a cure for female hysteria. Which, for a period of time, apparently was common. And often frequent."

"And the cure was?"

He'd already guessed it. She could tell from the slightest quirk of his mouth. "A pelvic massage." She'd gone this far. She might as well go full-out. "Often with specialized equipment."

"Well, then," he said, his tone remarkably matter-of-fact considering they were discussing vibrators, which was the only sex she'd had for far too long. "Sounds as if a fainting couch is a must for a honeymoon suite."

She slapped his arm, resisting the urge to feel up his brawny biceps. "You're terrible."

"You brought it up," he reminded her. "And now you sound like Zoe."

And, damn, there it was. The subject they'd both been avoiding. The dead wife in the room.

"I'm so sorry," she said. It was the same thing she'd said

two years ago. She knew it hadn't made a damn bit of difference then. And doubted it did now, either.

"Me, too," he said. Which was exactly the same thing he'd said. Thinking back, other than the required thank-yous to all the people offering condolences, she doubted he'd said more than a dozen words the entire day.

Brianna had dealt with this situation before. Often widows or widowers would return to special places they'd shared with their spouse. Many times one of those places would be a hotel. At The Royal Hawaiian, a woman who'd stayed there for her honeymoon sixty years earlier had returned with her husband's ashes for their anniversary. Every day for a week, she'd take off in the morning carrying that urn. Every evening she'd return to have dinner in her room with, in her mind, her husband. Many of the staff had thought it creepy. Brianna, on the other hand, could only hope that *she* could someday experience a love so long-lasting, faithful and true.

If she were going to be here only for a visit, she might not pick up this emotional conversational grenade. But because she was going to be staying, and because they'd be working together, but mostly because they'd been such close friends, she decided to face the situation now.

"How are you doing? Really?"

"Fine." His tone was flat. The single word sounding like something he'd say to anyone. Even a stranger on a plane, were the subject to somehow come up.

"I can't imagine experiencing such a terrible loss. But I do care. I loved Zoe, too."

"I have my work, which I enjoy. I eat six nights a week at the pub, where Quinn feeds me the best burgers ever. And I have dinner once a week with my in-laws."

"How about breaking with tradition and having dinner tonight with my family?" The invitation, while impulsive, sounded exactly right. It was obvious that he was still hurting, which wasn't unexpected considering how perfect a couple he and Zoe had been. What this Harper needed was to be surrounded by the exuberant Mannion clan. "I called Quinn from the ferry. He's bringing wings."

"None better than his maple whiskey bacon wing sauce," Seth agreed.

"You can't go wrong with bacon. But I prefer the sweet chili lime."

"He was making that back when we were kids. Burke used to bring them to team meetings."

"I always thought Quinn would grow up to be a chef," Brianna said. With two working parents, all the kids were expected to pull kitchen duty, but she and Quinn had been the two who'd enjoyed it. Quinn, especially, whenever it had to do with fire, which had made him the Mannion summer outdoor grill chef.

"He did all the cooking himself the first year at the pub. Before hiring Jarle."

"I know. Mom told me. And now he's brewing beer, which also makes sense because it goes along with his pub food. What I've never been able to figure out was how he stood all those years working in that stuffy law firm."

"Great minds. I wonder the same thing most nights I go in for my burger."

They were getting back on track. The tension that had stretched between them eased a bit.

"Life in a city's fast lane can be a draw when you grow up in a place like this," she said.

"For some," Seth agreed. "One of the major things Zoe and I had in common was that neither one of us ever wanted to live anywhere else."

"I know. And I'm belatedly realizing the same thing my brother must have. That sometimes you have to leave home to realize that it was where you belonged all along."

He glanced down at her Keds. And this time his smile reached his eyes. "Those don't exactly look like ruby slippers."

She grinned back at him and clicked her heels. "Ah, but appearances can be deceiving... So, speaking of home, do you want to come home with me? Did I mention my mom's blue-ribbon chicken?"

"I'd like to." He seemed to mean it. Then his smile faded. "But I have plans for tonight."

From the way he'd almost cheered up just talking about Quinn and his wings and dinner, Brianna almost asked if he couldn't change whatever the plans were. Then decided not to push. What if he had a date? Which didn't seem likely after how he'd talked about missing Zoe. But he wouldn't be the first guy to separate emotions from sex.

"Another time, maybe," she said mildly.

"I'd like that. Meanwhile, I'll see you at noon tomorrow at the office. And if there are any wings left over from your welcome-home dinner, I wouldn't turn them down."

"I'll make sure there are," she promised.

"And keep the jacket," he said. "Until you can go shopping. If you decide to stay after you sleep on the idea."

"I'm staying." He hadn't made it sound like a challenge, but Brianna took it as one. She realized that he wouldn't be the only person to question her reasons for returning home. But she was determined to prove any doubters wrong.

They made their way back to the main floor. The rain had stopped, and as he walked her to the car, Bandit bounding along beside her, Brianna watched the sun slowly sinking into the blue water, the golden ball tingeing the sky with shades of scarlet and orange, and decided that in spite of the potential problem with her lingering attraction to Seth Harper, she'd made exactly the right decision.

CHAPTER TEN

Although he'd never admit it, it hadn't taken long for Seth to find his weekly dinners with his in-laws more and more difficult. Just as there was no way he'd ever stop loving his wife, there were days when he'd be shooting nails into window trim, or laying hardwood floors, when he'd realize that his shattered heart might have begun stitching itself back together again. It would never be the same. There'd always be rough patches, like the ones scarring the old Boy Scout tent he used to take camping. But sometimes he'd have to stop and force himself to remember Zoe's face, which had begun to fade in his mind. Just a little.

But then he'd be back looking at the scrapbooks and photo albums and listening to her mother sharing all the stories of his wife growing up, going back to her birth three weeks early ("That girl was always in such a hurry!" his mother-in-law would say), and in his mind, he'd be back in that driveway, buffing the wax on her bright red Civic, watching the notification officers walking in slow motion toward him.

He parked in the driveway, walking past the trees that Helen Robinson had tied with yellow roses during Zoe's deployment, past the flagpole, where Dave had gone out on that horrible notification day and lowered the American flag to half-mast. A banner signaling that this was the home of a Gold Star family hung in the sidelight next to the blue door. Seth had never needed a banner to remind him that he'd lost his wife to war, but he hoped the symbol, like the folded flag they'd hung in a shadow box with her bronze star and purple heart over the fireplace, brought his in-laws some peace.

"I'm so glad you came tonight," Helen said as she brought the dinner to the table in the formal dining room, where a blue-and-white Greek flag hung on a wall painted bright red. Helen had once told him the color reminded her of the bougainvillea that climbed the walls of her childhood home back on the volcanic island of Santorini. She'd made pastitsio, Zoe's favorite.

"I'm glad to be here." It was Thursday night. Where else would he be?

And yeah, that was additional proof his life had fallen into a rut. If he didn't have the daily challenges of crumbling foundations, uncovering mold behind a bathroom shower, or discovering that an entire house still had knob and tube wiring that would have to be entirely replaced, putting the project overbudget—which would involve an unwelcome conversation with the homeowner—he'd be living his own version of that *Groundhog Day* movie. But without that happy ending.

"We have something to tell you," his father-in-law said as he passed Seth a basket of flatbread.

"Now, Dave," Helen demurred, placing a plate of what Seth had always considered a really good mac and cheese with meat in front of him. "I thought we'd agreed to wait until dessert." As she served her husband, she flashed Seth a forced smile. "It's *loukoumades*."

Another of Zoe's favorites. Seth figured if Cops and Coffee got hold of his mother-in-law's recipe for the fritters with cinnamon and thyme honey syrup with nuts, there'd be lines around the block waiting for the place to open.

"Sounds great," Seth said. As he always did.

"Might as well get it over with," the older man said. "Otherwise you'll be fidgeting all meal long, waiting for the right time to spill the beans."

They'd gotten Seth's attention. "Is something wrong?" He looked from one to the other, seeking any sign of illness. They were only in their midsixties, but logging and a three-pack-a-day cigarette habit had undoubtedly taken a toll on Zoe's father's health. "Are you both okay?"

"Oh, we're right as rain," Helen assured him quickly. Too quickly. As she shook out one of the cloth napkins she always got out for the weekly dinners, and placed it on her lap, Seth noticed her hands were shaking, just a little. "Aren't we, Dave?"

"I will be as soon as I can eat. So, are you going to tell him? Or should I just pull the damn trigger?"

Now Seth was beginning to get seriously worried. "Tell me what?"

"It's nothing bad," Helen assured him. "In fact, it's a positive thing." She took a deep breath. "We're moving."

"Okay." If people never moved, Seth would be out of work. Maybe they thought he'd be upset about them leaving the house where Zoe had grown up. Which wasn't that big a deal, even though he'd spent even more time here than he had at his own house all through high school.

"Out of state." Dave busied himself with slathering his flatbread with the olive tapenade sitting in the center of the table. Either he was hungry or didn't want to look his son-in-law in the face when he broke the news. Seth figured it was the latter.

"Oh."

"You know I have family in Arizona," Helen said.

"Tucson." Countless enthusiastic, talkative aunts, uncles and cousins Seth had met at the wedding.

Although Zoe had only spent a few weeks of her life visiting the desert, she'd talked about her mother's branch of the family often, filling him in on lives of people whose names he couldn't keep straight, and was always sending off stacks of birthday and Christmas cards. She had told him that she'd seen a certain beauty in the wide-open blue skies over a seemingly endless cactus-studded landscape, yet it hadn't taken her long to miss the lush greenery of the Pacific Northwest. Yet more irony at her having been deployed to sundrenched, dusty Afghanistan.

"My niece and her husband have taken over my brother's restaurant," Helen explained. "Which gives my brother and his wife more free time. Now that Dave's retired from logging, and I'm taking early retirement from cooking at the high school, we thought it would be nice to spend our retirement with family." Her cheeks flamed. "Not that we don't consider *you* family, because despite not being Greek, you are just like a son to us, but—"

"I get it," Seth assured her. If her niece and husband cooked anything like this, the Greek restaurant he'd never taken time to visit would undoubtedly continue to be a success.

"It's not like when my grandmother Stathopoulus took to her bed when I married Dave," Helen continued. "In her old-fashioned view, any girl who hadn't married a 'good Greek boy' and had her first child by twenty-three might as well be dead. We understand that the heart knows what the heart knows. And Zoe's heart knew, from that very beginning, when you were both so young, that it belonged to you."

"It was the same for me."

"I know. Which is another reason why you're like my own flesh and blood. But it's so hard to stay here." She pressed a plump hand over her heart as her eyes shone with tears. "In this town. And this house. I thought it would be easier. They *say* it gets easier with time. But whenever I drive past the middle school, I remember worrying that by switching schools midyear, she wouldn't have any friends."

"Which didn't happen." No one he'd ever met, or would ever meet, made friends as easily as his wife.

"That's what I assured her. But still she worried. And it's not just the school. If I go to a movie at the Olympic, I can see her doing pirouettes up on the stage, when the dance studio would hold the recitals there every year."

No one mentioned the arguments Zoe and her mother would have about those recitals. But she kept on taking those lessons, and dancing on that stage every spring, because not doing it would make her mother unhappy. And Zoe had never been one to make anyone unhappy. Until she went and died on him.

"We had to stop going to Friday night football games because she'd start bawling," Dave volunteered.

"Because of her cheerleading days," Seth said. And wasn't that one of the memories stuck in his head? Because nobody could jump as high or wave her pom-poms as enthusiastically as Zoe Richardson.

Some of the guys on his Sea Lions football team had envied his receiving skills, which, honestly, were more due to Burke Mannion's mad, crazy QB talent that could make any receiver look good. It was hard not to break the school's all-time receiving record when the passer put the ball on your numbers. But every single one of them, even Burke, who'd been a year ahead of him and would go on to be a superstar NFL quarterback, had been envious that Seth had been the one Zoe slow-danced with at the after-game dances in the gym.

"Whenever I walk by her room, I expect to hear her chatting away on the phone to you or Brianna, or Kylee," her mother said. "And many nights, on the way to bed, I imagine a light shining from beneath the door because she's staying up too late reading… She was so special," Helen said, sniffling. "Wasn't she?"

"She was one of a kind."

"Broke the mold when they made my baby girl," Dave said, sounding suspiciously choked up himself.

"Anyway." Helen blew out another breath and wiped her eyes and nose with a tissue she'd pulled from her apron pocket. "The counselor at the parents' grief group I go to helped me see that I'd gotten myself stuck in time. Like those dinosaurs in amber from *Jurassic Park*."

"Which is a fictional story," Dave pointed out.

"The story might be," she allowed with a flare of renewed spirit. "But that doesn't mean the problem isn't real." She reached over to touch Seth's hand again. Greeks, he'd discovered, were touchers. Harper men were not.

"I know it sounds selfish, Seth, dear, but I have to move on. I'll never forget my daughter—how could I?—but I can't stay in this place where everywhere I go and everything I do reminds me of how we lost her."

"I get it." Seth turned his hand and linked his fingers with hers. "I really do." Not only did he admire her ability to reclaim her life, he was tempted to ask her secret. "I think it's the absolutely right thing for you to do."

She managed a smile even as her dark eyes, so like her daughter's, glistened again. "Thank you for understanding. And, of course, you're always welcome to visit. You'd like the desert. Especially all that bright sun in the winter when you want to escape gray skies."

"Sounds like a plan." They both knew that wouldn't happen. That he was another of those painful memories she needed to move on from. Because with her daughter's widower still in her life, it would continue to be difficult to look back on their wedding and marriage without her heart breaking.

"Your mother volunteered to take over the gardening at the cemetery."

Growing up, having never had an up-close-and-personal encounter with death, Seth had never found the Harborview Cemetery a depressing place. It was pretty, with its tall trees and rolling lawns overlooking the water. Not that the residents could enjoy the view, but visitors could. He knew that, along with planting dahlias at Zoe's grave, Zoe's mother would also add seasonal bedding plants and go out every Sunday after church and "tidy things up." He knew because she told him, not because he ever went out there. He hadn't been to the cemetery since that day they'd handed him a folded flag that was a damn poor substitute for his wife.

"Mom's always liked gardening," he said mildly. "And she loved Zoe." Who, Caroline Harper would always say, was like a second daughter.

"Everyone loved Zoe," Helen said with another sniffle, this time dabbing her moist eyes with the corner of her napkin since she'd already shredded the tissue. Oh, yeah, this was turning out to be a fun evening.

"Okay. So, I told you he'd be okay with it," Dave told his wife. "Can we eat now?"

"Just one more thing."

Seth's father-in-law didn't quite roll his eyes, but he came close.

"We're hoping to put the house up for sale next month, because our Realtor says spring's a good time to sell. Since we'll be moving into a condo, we'll have less room. So, if you wouldn't mind coming by when you have a little time to choose what you'd like to keep…"

"Sure." The idea of dragging home even more than the stuff he'd spent the past two years of Thursdays looking through was less appealing than drilling an electric Phillips screwdriver through his eyeball. "Why don't you choose first?" he suggested. "Then give me a call when you're ready for me to collect the rest of her things."

"Great idea," Dave said, digging into his meal. "Now let's eat."

Ben Harper sat in what these days guys were calling a man cave, sipping Crown straight and watching the Mariners spank the Rockies at Seattle. It was potting soil night at the stadium. "Only in the Pacific Northwest," he muttered. Which might not be true, but it seemed everyone he knew went crazy this time of year, planting all sorts of stuff. While flowers were pretty much useless to his mind, at least the vegetables made sense, except those radical organic farm-to-table folks got on his last nerve.

He glanced out the window at the garden, which was, after a long winter, a mess. By now Caroline would've had him turn the soil for new plantings to go along with the azalea bushes and rhododendrons, which, luckily, seemed to care for themselves. At least they were beginning to bloom, no thanks to him.

Although it grated, he had to admit that he hadn't noticed all she did around here. Not only had she taken over all the company's bookkeeping, she'd drawn those illustrations that she'd framed to hang in the public areas of the office. When she built a website, she put them up there, too, and kept the social media pages going, which was a good thing since there was no way in hell he'd ever go chat with strangers on Facebook. But it had brought in business from all over the country, so, hey, he couldn't complain.

Except she wasn't here now to do that. He didn't know how to log on, but by clicking on the little square box on the website, he'd gone to the page this afternoon and noticed that there'd been no new postings for a month. But since they were doing okay, he didn't see any reason for writing anything, even if he could think of anything to say. And God knows, there was no way he wanted his down-in-the-dumps son posting. Hell, if that sandwich-stealing mutt, Bandit, could type, he'd probably be better than either one of them.

The truth, which he'd never admit to anyone, especially his boy, was that he missed his wife. And not just her cooking, and cleaning, and bookkeeping, and the flowers that had once filled the home he'd built for them when they'd married. But because she'd always been the bright and shining sun around which his entire life had revolved.

Since that very first day. She'd always called their meeting kismet.

Caroline talked that way, using words he'd have to look up. He'd called it luck. Because it was, flat-out, the damn luckiest day of his life, the second being when she'd agreed to marry him, followed by her telling him that he was going to be a father. Which had scared the piss out of him, but he'd never felt more pride than when he'd stopped at the diner the next morning and told the guys chowing down on their early Lumberjack Specials before work, and casually, as if it were just any other day, of his impending fatherhood to everyone in the place. Dinah, who'd run the diner forever, had insisted the special occasion called for a breakfast on the house. She'd also planted a big kiss on his cheek, which had caused more hooting than he would've cared for.

It had been summer when Caroline Lockwood had driven into Honeymoon Harbor with three girlfriends on a cross-country trip to explore various regional arts. He hadn't seen her arrival because he'd been working on building a set for a play put on by the Theater in the Firs group for the annual Harbor Days festival. The work didn't pay much, but while he might admittedly not be the most sociable guy on the planet, Ben realized that if he wanted locals to hire him, he needed to be part of the community. The work, compared to remodeling hundred-year-old houses, was easy, and he had to admit that the theater group, most of whom could have come from a different planet than the one he'd grown up on, were friendly. Although they often had to take up collections to pay for paint and other supplies, they never once missed paying him for the work.

So he hadn't seen Caroline and her girlfriends drive off the ferry in that pink Cadillac. Nor had he been there when she'd checked into the Lighthouse View Hotel. But he had been working the lighting the night the three woman had shown up to see a production of the story of the town's name change. Being a distant descendant of Nathaniel Harper, the one man who'd voted against the change, Ben wasn't enjoying the annual retelling of the story all that much. Especially since the director had talked John Mannion, who'd just returned home from two years in the Peace Corps—which was having everyone treat him like a damn hero, although all he'd been doing was building gardens and planting trees, not fighting the enemy like Ben had done as a Marine—into playing the Teddy Roosevelt role.

Sitting at the back of the action, Ben was able to watch Mannion and Sarah Harper huddled together in a cozy way that suggested they hadn't been talking about the weather. They'd been a couple for a while in high school. Then her parents had managed to break them up by sending her off to one of those fancy women's colleges back east. Not that they could afford it on Jerome Harper's fisherman's salary, but being supersmart, she'd managed to get scholarships and a work study program that took care of the costs.

John's return had definitely put a monkey wrench in her parents' plans.

He'd been thinking that Mannion was probably going to

get lucky that night when the sight of a pretty blonde in a pair of sprayed-on purple jeans, a blinding pink top and a multicolored flower jacket hit him like a sledgehammer. She was flirting with Mike Mannion, John's artist brother who'd painted some of the scenery. Like the Mannions didn't already have enough going for them? Not only was the family practically damn Honeymoon Harbor royalty, they had to get all the good-looking women, too?

He'd just decided the blonde and the artist would probably hook up for the night, when suddenly he got lucky. Although Caroline would later laughingly insist it was fate, a sudden downpour sent everyone running to wait the rain out in the building the theater company used to store equipment.

The outdoor bleacher seats had all been filled, and the building wasn't that big, so Ben found himself squeezed into the back with the blonde in those purple jeans whose voice had him imagining moonlight, magnolias and mint juleps. Which, he'd thought, probably meant he'd been spending too much time around the theater people, because guys like him never dreamed of women in picture hats sitting on wicker chairs on Southern verandas.

But on this rainy night, Ben sure as hell did think of that. And a lot more.

She'd been impressed when he'd told her he'd built the sets. And although he feared it might give Mannion more points, he told her that he hadn't painted those forest scenes. He'd just done the construction.

"Without you, they wouldn't have had anything to paint," she'd said. "So you're indispensable."

No one, in his entire life, had ever used that word to describe him. Ben had never been much of a talker, but bedazzled as he was, he could only mumble something incomprehensible.

"And you do the lighting, as well?" she asked, making him think she might have noticed him behind the bank of lights.

"It's not that hard." He tried to shrug the compliment off, but his chest swelled with pride. Although he'd only graduated high school, he'd studied damn hard to get those working right. "Until recently, you'd need different lights for different colors. Now they're automated."

"Yet you still need to know how to utilize color and varying levels of brightness to set the proper ambience," she said. "Where did you study?"

"I guess you could say I'm self-taught." Another shrug as he tried to untie his tongue. He could tell she was easy with conversation. Ben was not. "I restore old houses, so I've had to learn about electricity. When the theater company asked me a few years ago if I could do the lighting, I read up on it and realized I enjoy it." The same as he'd always enjoyed creating the proper lighting in the town's old Victorians.

And weren't those the most words he'd strung together in a dog's age?

"It shows. I can tell when someone loves their work. Your lighting deepens the emotional experience."

Ben had no answer to that, but it didn't matter, because she continued on, as if not expecting a response. "I'm a student at the South Carolina School of Art and Design," she said.

"Are you a theater major?" She was damn well pretty enough to be a movie star.

Her laugh was rich and warm, and made the back of his neck sweat. "Heavens, no. I'm already the black sheep in the family," she confessed, dimpling pretty in a way that reminded him of Vivien Leigh charming the Tarleton Twins. He wasn't much for that kind of movie—he was more a John Wayne guy himself—but his mother had made the family watch it once when it showed up as the Saturday night TV movie.

"Daddy's one of those 'respectable'—" she made air quotes

with fingers tipped the same bright pink as her blouse "—Southern lawyers. Mama comes from a long line of famous belles and if I ever considered acting, she'd undoubtedly swoon from the vapors. Bad enough I decided that I wanted a career, but I managed to win them over by choosing to major in interior design. I'm certain they both believe that once I get married and start having babies, I can dabble in designing pretty living rooms and nurseries for my friends."

"But you have other plans." He could hear the steel beneath her soft Carolina drawl.

She bobbed her blond head. Squared slender shoulders in that pretty flowered jacket. "I most certainly do. Oh, I'll probably get married someday," she allowed. "Because I do want to be a mother. But it would have to be to a man who considered me an equal. And not some decorative arm candy. I'll probably go to Atlanta. Or maybe even New York City. Then, once I get established, I'll start looking for a man who ticks all my boxes."

Despite his lack of social graces and not being a high and mighty Mannion, Ben had never had trouble getting women. He knew he was good-looking, but except for when he was shaving, wasn't one to spend any time looking in a mirror, because in his business you could probably look like Sasquatch and still get work if you knew what you were doing. Which he did.

But he'd never, ever, met a female who had him feeling so undermatched. Which was why, once the rain had stopped and everyone began leaving the barn, he was amazed when she'd put her hand on his arm.

"Are you doing anything later?" she asked, looking up at him with eyes as clear and blue as Lake Crescent, the jewel of the Olympics, where, years in the future, their son would get married.

"Later?" The warmth of her touch on his bare skin had tied his tongue up in knots again.

"After the play." Her stroking fingers were as light as thistledown, but still made his head start spinning like he was out of control on the Tilt-a-Whirl at the county fair. "I thought maybe you'd be hungry after working all day."

"Are you asking me out to dinner?"

"Well, since I had the feeling you weren't going to ask me, the answer to that question would be yes." Her smile brightened her big blue eyes. Ben could tell that she was teasing him. And the thing was, he didn't give a rat's ass. Just as long as she kept talking. "I realize that convention requires me to wait on you to make the first move. But I told you I'm the family's black sheep."

She swept a long, considering look over him. From his boots to the top of his head, then back again. As if he were a sofa she was considering buying for one of her girlfriends' living rooms.

"I like the cut of you, Ben Harper. And unless all my feminine instincts have gone on the blink, I believe that you're interested in me, too."

He gulped. Then managed to admit, "I am."

"Well, then. Why don't you pick me up at the Lighthouse View Hotel? About eight? Surely there's someplace on this peninsula where we can find a late supper."

"What about your friends?"

She laughed again. Damn, he could get hooked on that soft, musical sound. "They can find their own men."

She hadn't gone to bed with him that night. Although she might be a black sheep, she'd told him that she never slept with a gentleman their first night together. But she had let him kiss her at the door of the inn. A long, deep kiss that had tasted like honey and left him going home with aching balls.

It had been a small price to pay when the next night, on a

blanket on the bank of Mirror Lake, beneath a slice of crescent moon, she'd given him her virginity. Which had come as one helluva surprise because he would've figured that a fancy, worldly woman like Caroline Lockwood would've had her share of admirers.

Which she had, she'd assured him when he'd cautiously brought that up afterward as they lay on a blanket on the deck, bare arms and legs entwined, while shooting stars streaked across the midnight sky. But she'd been waiting for the right man. She'd kissed him again. Turned into him, breast to chest. "My forever man," she'd said, as she'd taken his hand and led it down to those silky blond curls between her legs.

They'd made love three times that night. Even though he'd been no virgin, he'd never done that before. But this sweet-talking Southern belle had Ben doing a lot of things he'd never done before. The most important of which had been to fall in love.

She'd been his forever woman. And, as far as he was concerned, she still was.

She'll come back, Ben reassured himself as he turned off the TV, poured himself another glass of Crown, tossed it back, feeling the burn go straight to the gut, then headed off to the king-size bed that these days seemed even larger. Colder. And a helluva lot lonelier.

It's just menopause craziness. She'll be back.

Because although he'd throw himself off Mount Olympus before admitting it, the simple truth was that Ben had no freaking clue how the hell he could survive without her.

CHAPTER ELEVEN

The Mannion Christmas tree farm was located about thirty-five minutes out of town on a road that twisted in sharp switchbacks. The evergreens lining the edge of the road created a green tunnel, and the road was striped with rays of stuttering sun that managed to slip through the bank of trees and clouds.

Every so often the trees would open up to a waving green meadow where white Sitka valerian bobbed like sailboats riding the harbor tides, and ferns were uncurling new frothy green fronds. Because it had been so long since Brianna had experienced the absolute, total silence that could be found here on the far northwest corner of the country, she didn't listen to any of her audiobooks. Nor did she try to search out a radio station. Instead, as she continued through the trees, around tree-fringed jetties and past tumbling creeks, the only sound was the hiss of the tires on the wet pavement and the *swish*, *swish* of the wipers clearing the splash of raindrops from the windshield.

She slowed for a herd of magnificent Roosevelt elk, some just calves, that had emerged from the screen of trees. As many places as she'd been, nothing could ever replace these sights and sounds of home, and while waiting for the elk, who were taking their own sweet time, to cross in front of her, Brianna felt like Dorothy waking up back home in Kansas from bright and glittery Oz.

She passed a farm, its acres of colorful flowers and freshly tilled dark brown earth dotted with young, spring-green plants surrounding the blue clapboard house that had given Blue House Farm its name. Just beyond the farm, she took a fork in the road, and past the old abandoned logging skid road, seemingly endless acres of conical blue-green fir, bright pine and spruce trees came into view. Rising up from the center of the trees was a bright red barn with Mannion's Family Christmas Trees, est. 1983 written on the side with white paint. Below that was Delivery or Cut & Carry.

Although it was still raining, she cracked open her window to breathe in the familiar pungent scent of fir and earth along with a faint tinge of salt riding in from the Strait of Juan de Fuca.

The road dead-ended at a pair of red gates leading to the farm. The fact that they were open suggested her parents were waiting for her. A fact proven out as soon she'd reached the end of the road leading to the white two-story farmhouse with ruffled fiery-red-and-yellow tulips blooming in front of the wide wraparound front porch.

The apple-red door opened and her mother, wearing jeans, sneakers and a black T-shirt stating, *I'm not Superwoman. But I am a high school principal. So...close enough*, came running out. Her smiling face was framed with a wild cloud of coppery curls brightened with strands of silver. Brianna, whose hair was as straight as Washington rain, had often envied her mother those curls. At the same time, Sarah Mannion had always said that Brianna was the lucky one to have that golden slide of hair that didn't frizz up like Little Orphan Annie's at the least provocation.

"You're finally here!" She gathered Brianna into her arms for a huge hug that she hadn't even realized she'd needed until now.

"I told you when I called that I ran into Kylee and Mai," she said.

"We're so excited about their wedding," Sarah said. "Jim Olson—you remember him, he was a few years behind you in school—is providing the flowers from Blue House Farm next door. He started out with organic vegetables, but recently added flowers for the wedding business." She waved toward the tulips. "These bulbs are from his farm."

"They're stunning."

"Aren't they? They're called Flaming Parrots. As soon as Kylee saw them, she decided she had to have them for her bouquet."

"They're perfect." As bright and colorful as the bride who'd be carrying them.

"That's the same thing I said... So, are you going to be able to come back home for the wedding?"

"I am. I also have something else I want to talk with you all about."

Brianna had held off telling anyone that she was returning home for good because she hadn't wanted to get her mother's hopes up. There'd always been a chance, she'd considered, that once she was on that ferry, she'd suffer doubts and perhaps even change her mind. Before her mother could ask what was up, Brianna turned to her father.

"Hi, Dad."

"Hi, daughter." The lines extending from John Mannion's blue eyes, which had provided the gene for her own, crinkled at the corners as he gave her a slow, easy smile. He'd always been the calm to her mother's seemingly unrelenting energy. "It's about time you found your way back home."

He gathered her into his arms, and although she knew it was silly, Brianna felt her eyes sheen. How many times had those strong arms held and comforted her? Too many times to count.

She'd always felt safe here. Which, she realized as the thought hit like a lightning bolt from a clear blue sky, was why she'd had to leave. Even when she'd come home from college during vacations, going on and on and on about her big plans, she'd understood that just as her parents had provided the anchor for her life, they'd also encouraged her to spread her wings. Which she had. And now, like the swallows returning every year, those same wings had flown her back to Honeymoon Harbor.

Two rescued Australian shepherd mixes, Mulder and Scully, came racing out of the house, circling around the group, herding their family like they were the cattle they'd been bred to gather. She'd always had dogs growing up, and now, as she crouched down to pet these, she wondered if getting a dog of her own would put off potential guests.

A moment later, Brianna decided she didn't care. The entire point of buying Herons Landing was to finally design a life she loved. To follow her heart and not her head. And if anyone was put off by sharing space with a dog, well, she could survive without their business.

Her mother glanced over at the car, with its back seat piled with suitcases and boxes. "Are you moving again?"

"Good guess." She also wondered what it said about the rootlessness of her life that all her possessions fit into the back seat and trunk of a car. She'd always been prepared to move at a moment's notice. Now, by buying the landmark Victorian house, she'd made a one-hundred-eighty-degree lifestyle change.

"John, start bringing Brianna's things in," her mother instructed her husband. "I'll send Quinn out to help."

"Just the two suitcases," Brianna said. "I can deal with the rest later." In the next day or so, when she moved into Herons Landing.

"So, where are you off to this time?" Sarah asked as she linked her arm through Brianna's and walked toward the house, the dogs close on their heels, noses nearly pressed against the back of her leg. If she attempted to break away, they were ready to circle and bring her back into the fold. "Chicago? Maybe your dream of New York? Even London?"

"Nope." She paused, waiting for a tinge of regret and felt none. At all. "And I'm not dodging the question, but I'd rather share the news with everyone at once," she said.

"You know I hate suspense," her mother said. "I bite my nails to the quick every election night."

"Yet Dad always wins." He'd been mayor of Honeymoon Harbor nearly all of Brianna's life. He always joked that he was stuck in the job because no one else would take it, but everyone knew that he loved the position.

The house she'd grown up in was both the same and different.

The rooms, which had once all been different colors, were now painted in neutrals that provided a perfect backdrop for paintings she recognized as her uncle Mike's work. The heavy bark-brown leather chesterfield couch with its thick rolled arms and high, deeply tufted back that had held up to five children had been replaced by a more modern but still comfortable-looking sloped-arm, pillow-backed sectional. It, too, was leather, but in a red shade lighter than rust but not as bright as a fire engine. Instead of the brown tweed rug that had easily handled puppies and rambunctious boys, the couch sat upon a lightly looped rug in shades of oatmeal, brown and taupe, the design reminding Brianna of Persian tiles. All the old heavy hand-me-down furniture her parents had inherited when they'd married had been updated to lighter pieces that made the rooms she passed through look larger.

"I love what you've done."

"Caroline Harper talked me into taking a design class at Clearwater CC," her mother revealed. "You know she studied at the South Carolina School of Art and Design."

"I remember hearing that."

"Well, she says that I have a natural talent I owe to it to myself to pursue. And I'll have to admit that I've always enjoyed puttering around the projects on the house. It's mostly online, with a weekly Saturday morning in the classroom. I'll be retiring after this school year, and since so many friends have asked me to help them with their decorating, I thought I'd try hanging out a shingle."

For as long as Brianna could remember her mother had taken classes at the local community college, covering a range of topics from archeology to art history. All while working as an English teacher at Honeymoon Harbor High School (taking extra summer courses at UW as she worked her way up to principal), running a lot of the farm business, planning the Christmas tree seasonal celebration and raising five children. Why would anyone have expected her to sit home and knit once she retired?

"I think that's a wonderful idea." Brianna followed her mother into the kitchen and watched as she took a platter of breaded chicken from the wide Sub-Zero refrigerator and turned on the six-burner gas range. When Brianna had been younger, there had been one refrigerator in the kitchen and two additional ones out in the garage in order to keep enough food on hand to feed all the growing Mannion boys. Despite her mother's protests, Burke had insisted on using a portion of his NFL signing bonus to remodel the kitchen.

"I've worked at some hotels that paid big bucks for design-

ers who didn't do half as good a job as you could have." Brianna was grateful her mother had never taken her up on an
offer to visit the Midas. Although a part of her had wanted
to show off how far she'd come, she'd also been concerned
that the amount of gilding might have put her into cardiac
arrest before she'd gotten across the lobby.

"Seth told me his parents are separated. Are you and Caroline going into business together?"

"Oh, no. She's hoping to travel. If she can talk Ben into
retiring. I was there the night they met and remember how
hard he fell for her. I hope they work things out."

"I hope so, too." Personally, now that she was home again,
Brianna would be happy to stay right here in Honeymoon
Harbor forever. On the other hand, except for a short trip to
Disneyland, she couldn't remember Seth's family ever going
anywhere, so she suspected Ben Harper wasn't all that big on
the traveling plan. "Can I help?"

"No, everything's done but the chicken. I wanted to wait
to begin cooking it until you arrived." She took out another
platter and a bottle of wine. "You can pour us both a glass."

"Sure." The wine, which she recognized as a very good
label, was from one of the Oregon wineries going to screw
tops. She twisted it open and poured it into the glasses she
retrieved from the open shelves. "Will Dad want one?"

"No. He'll be having one of Quinn's beers. The Jack Sparrow Rum Ale won a medal at a national craft brewery competition last month." She said it with the same pride she'd
always shown for her children's accomplishments. And her
students'. Although there had been times growing up when
it hadn't been easy having your mother as school principal,
Brianna couldn't think of anyone more suited to the job.

"I'll admit I was surprised when I heard about Quinn making such a drastic career change."

"He's happy as a clam." Oil sizzled as the chicken thighs

and drumsticks entered the pan. "Confidentially, although I never said anything, because your lives were your own business, I always suspected of all my children, you and he would be the ones of my chicks who'd return home. But I suppose, if I'd given a great deal of thought to it, I would have expected him to set up a small-town law practice."

"I guess he wasn't into property disputes, divorces and defending teenage mailbox bashers, which is pretty much what legal life exists of here."

"As ideal as it may seem from the outside, like any other community it has its problems. I see students who're obviously not getting enough to eat. And others who are taken from unstable homes due to neglect or abuse. And although it's less common than the larger cities, there's a fair amount of bullying."

"Which has always occurred," Brianna said, thinking back on Jolene Wells, a girl in her class who'd earned an undeserved reputation only because she'd grown up in a trailer outside of town with an alcoholic dad who'd been convicted of theft and a mother who was rumored to be a prostitute. Although Jolene hadn't been one of Brianna's closet friends, they were friendly, and once Gloria Wells, Jolene's beautician mom, had insisted on giving her a free cut and blow-dry after she'd invited Jolene to her fifteenth birthday party.

Being that the Mannions were unofficially Honeymoon Harbor's first family, that had shut down the gossip. For a time. She'd heard Jolene, who'd left town before high school graduation, was living in LA, doing makeup for movie stars. Which was yet more proof that you could probably never predict anyone's future.

"Well, at any rate, it's cool my brother's going back to the family's roots."

"You talking about me?" Brianna spun around at the sound of the deep voice, her face breaking into a huge smile as she viewed her older brother standing in the doorway, a suitcase under his arm.

"We were," she said.

"All complimentary," their mother assured him.

"That's good to hear." He shot Brianna a look. "Why don't you come up and see what Mom's done to your room?" he suggested in a mild tone that didn't fool her for a minute. While everyone might consider Quinn the easiest-going of the Mannion brothers, he was also the best at getting you to talk about things you'd rather not. Which undoubtedly had made him an excellent lawyer and probably served him well when he was working behind the bar of his brewpub.

"So," she said brightly as they headed up stairs lined with photos of first communions, school photos, graduations, sports, Christmas festivals and all the other family events that she'd never properly appreciated while they were happening. "Mom tells me your new beer is winning medals."

"No point in doing something if you don't do your best. Can I take from all that stuff you've got crammed into that shiny red car that you're not here for a short stay?"

"Aiden's supposed to be the interrogator in the family," she complained. Her brother, a former Marine, was, the last she'd heard, an undercover cop in Los Angeles. "Especially now that you've given up cross-examining people for a living."

"That doesn't mean I don't still enjoy it from time to time. And you're dodging the question."

"Okay." She blew out a breath. "I wanted to talk to you alone anyway. About my plans."

She stopped in the doorway. The honey pine furniture was still there, but the walls had gone from the pink-and-white-striped wallpaper that had been on the walls since her freshman year of high school to the blue-green color of beach glass. The crazy Leonardo DiCaprio, Luke Perry and NSYNC collage that had taken up an entire wall behind the bed had been replaced with an oversize scenic photo of the Sequim lavender farms overtop an eggshell–color shiplap. The bedding was no longer a riot of colorful flowers, but an inviting mix of white, ivory and cream.

"Oh, wow. I am so stealing this idea for one of my rooms," she said, more to herself than her brother. It was the perfect retreat, giving off a calming aura that would encourage guests to relax as soon as they walked in the door.

"Your rooms?" He put the suitcases down on the wide-planked wood floor.

"That's what I wanted to talk about. But first, I have a question. Was it hard moving back home?"

"Not at all." He arched a brow and gave her that same stern big-brother look he'd shot her back when she'd been fifteen and he'd caught her climbing up the apple tree to her bedroom window. She'd been coming home from a party she and Kylee sneaked out to at a sprawling waterfront house. The rich boy who lived there had put out the word that he was throwing a bash while his parents were away in Hawaii. Fortunately, they'd decided to leave before the police showed up after a noise complaint, so she'd gotten busted only by her brother. At eighteen, Quinn had pretty much been allowed to come and go as he wanted. "Is that what you're doing? Coming home?"

"Yep." Each time she said the plan out loud, it sounded more real. And after going through the house, both exciting and a bit daunting. Okay, more than a bit. A lot. "I'm buying Herons Landing. And turning it into a B and B."

"Huh." He rubbed his jaw as he considered that idea. "You may want to talk to Seth Harper about that."

"I already have. He showed me through the house before I came here."

"You don't waste any time."

"Seeing him wasn't planned. I spotted Kylee and Mai at the

park and stopped to talk with them, and he drove by. When Kylee spilled the beans, he agreed to give me a tour."

"Did he mention that two other owners gave up on the place?"

"Well, the first ones were arrested, so I'm not sure they gave up by choice," she said. "And it's possible the ghost scared off the other."

Quinn literally rolled his eyes. "Yeah. That's undoubtedly the reason."

"Skeptic." She conveniently ignored the fact that she didn't believe in the ghost, either. Though the supposedly widowed fisherman's wife could be an attractive marketing aspect. She'd have to give that some thought. "Anyway, as you already know, he's done amazing things to the exterior."

"You always did have a thing for that house. Did it live up to your memories?"

"It did. Except for a new paint job, it looks as if all the outside needs are some sod, trees and gardens."

"That's probably the easy part. From what I hear, the inside is a wreck."

"The first floor is a work in progress," Brianna admitted. "But it's not that bad. The second will be a challenge, but Seth had some wonderful ideas for that. I'm meeting with him tomorrow to go over the plans."

"Definitely moving fast," he murmured. "Like mother, like daughter."

She wasn't going to argue that. "Mom was a great role model. I love the idea that she's starting her own business."

"She's never let any moss grow beneath her feet, that's for sure. Having watched fun, loving, married friends turn into frazzled, overworked parents, I've no idea how she managed five kids of her own, as well as an entire school of teenagers, while helping run the farm and keep the house going. So, getting back to your formerly crumbling old house…"

"The third floor is amazing."

"I remember bats. Including one who tried to nest in your hair."

"It wasn't nesting." She didn't think. But that didn't stop the memory from giving her shivers again. "It accidently flew into me while trying to get out of the attic. But Seth assures me that the bats are gone—they now have their own house outside—and it's an amazing space for a penthouse. I'm going to move in as soon as I round up some basic furniture pieces."

"You're going to live there during the remodeling?"

"That's the plan."

"You know, I had Harper Construction do the pub and the brewery. And as much as I like living over the place now, I'm not sure I'd recommend you living there while the work's being done."

"Are you suggesting I'm not as tough as you?"

"No. I'm merely saying I'm a guy. So being surrounded by guys didn't bother me."

"I grew up surrounded by brothers, who happen to be guys," she reminded him. "I'm sure I'll manage just fine. Besides, it occurred to me that if I'm on-site, I may be able to save money by doing some sweat labor." Not that she needed the money. But she liked the idea of taking part in bringing the house back to its former glory.

"When was the last time you took down a wall?"

"Smart-ass. Probably the last time you did," she shot back, but with a smile in her tone. "That doesn't mean I can't paint. Maybe hammer some baseboard. Or work on the yard. We certainly got enough practice with that growing up." Including trimming the trees every spring so they'd grow in their traditional Christmas pyramid shapes.

"Aiden always accused Mom and Pop of having five kids for the free labor," he remembered with a smile.

"To which Dad told him to be grateful he hadn't grown

up on a potato farm." Her mother had grown potatoes in her kitchen garden, and digging the crop up every year would leave Brianna's fingernails dirt-stained for days. And those bags got heavy fast!

"And now that we've settled that, it's your turn to answer my question about whether or not you had any adjustments. Besides construction noise."

"Yeah, sure." His broad shoulders stretched the seams of his Mannion's Pub & Brewery T-shirt when he shrugged. "There were adjustments. Outside my own legal circles, I could be anonymous in the city. At the gym, going into a Starbucks, even when I asked a woman out, the only history she might have on me is what she could dig up on Google. Here, folks have known me all my life. And not only do they know my history, they probably know that I bought two glazed crullers at Cops and Coffee for breakfast this morning."

"I gained ten pounds from the aroma alone just walking in the door today. And admittedly, I hadn't given a lot of thought to the lack of privacy." Even though that had been precisely why she hadn't chosen to live on-site at the Midas.

"It's a fishbowl. A well-meaning one, but a fishbowl just the same." A grin creased his cheeks. Their brother Burke had inherited the same creases from their father, but he'd also lucked out with a pair of killer dimples. "After an unfortunate too-personal encounter with Mildred Marshall in the market, I learned to buy condoms online."

She laughed. "Given that she's at least seventy and been married four times, I suspect she's familiar with that particular item. But thanks for the heads-up."

"No problem. On the other hand—"

"Says the star of the high school debating club."

"As I was saying, while this town is a fishbowl, everyone will jump in to support their own. Like they've tried to do with Seth Harper. Who's pretty much become a hermit since losing Zoe."

"Understandable. They'd been a couple forever."

He looked up at the ceiling. Dragged his hand through his hair. "Okay, I'm uncomfortable with this, but family probably outweighs the guy code, so I'm going to warn you that he's in a dark place and it could be risky for you working with him."

"Surely you're not suggesting he's dangerous?"

"No. Not in any go-whacked-out-crazy-with-a-nail-gun way. But if you're thinking of trying to fix him—"

"That didn't even occur to me."

"Maybe not yet. But it will. Because that's what you do. You're like Mom. You fix things. It's probably the reason you were so good at your job. Same as my debating made me a good lawyer. But it's a rocky road that could end up bad. For you, and probably for him, too. Because he's a good guy who'd beat himself up for breaking your heart."

"How could he break my heart?"

"Because you were sweet on him for years."

"He never, not once, looked my way."

"Doesn't matter. The heart wants what the heart wants."

"Now you're quoting Emily Dickinson?"

"No. I think I'm quoting some country song. The thing is, you had a thing for him. Maybe you still do."

"I don't." Seth and Zoe had been the happiest couple Brianna had ever met. Their love, laughter and affection had always been absolutely genuine, and later, she'd often thought that they could have been naturals to play themselves in a Hallmark movie.

"Maybe it could come back, like the chickenpox, once you're together every day. Which brings me back to my point that he could hurt you. Even though he'd never mean to."

"Well." She blew out a breath. "Thanks for the advice,

counselor, but I'm an adult who's had my heart bruised from time to time. I know the pitfalls. And how to avoid them."

"Can't say I didn't try." He shrugged again. "It's your life."

"Exactly."

"So, putting that in the never-again-to-be-discussed category, the bottom line is that Honeymoon Harbor's glacial pace can be good for fresh starts. And for rebooting your life."

"Thank you. I bow to your wisdom." She could smell the chicken frying. Like the salt air and tang of fir trees, it, too, smelled like home. "We'd better go down before Mom sends Dad to look for us. She says you're doing some interesting things at the brewery."

"The Captain Jack Sparrow," he said. "Yeah, it took a few tries to get the alcohol bitterness from the rum barrel out of the beer, but we found that cutting the aging time, then blending it with the same blend that hadn't been in barrels, solved the problem. We've had a couple big breweries sniffing around to license it."

"Which you didn't do."

"I came home because I wanted out of the rat race," he pointed out. "No point in jumping back in with a new set of rats."

"I couldn't agree more," Brianna said, thinking of one doctor rat in particular. "It's going to work," she said. "I'll make it work."

He tousled her hair, the same way he had when she'd been seven and fallen off her bike while going too fast downhill from the lake and scraped her knee on a rock. The cut had taken seven stitches and she still had the faint scar. "I have not a single doubt."

"Thanks. And although we have a lot of time before it opens, I'd love to talk to you about adding brewery tours to my local attractions list. I noticed you weren't offering them—"

"Because it's a working brewery."

"True. But just give it a thought. We'd work around your schedule. And just think, after the tour, people would drop into the pub for a meal. It'd be a win-win for both of us."

He laughed. "That's quite a persuasive argument. Maybe *you* should've been the lawyer."

"Absolutely not." One of the things she'd loved about her job was trying to help people avoid conflict. The law seemed to thrive on it. "Besides, it sounds as if we're both exactly where we belong. Doing what we were meant to do."

"Just keep that in mind when the tile saw is still screeching in your sleep."

"Oh, ye of little faith." Weighing the idea of hammers and tile saws on one hand, and spending the rest of her working years putting up with rude, narcissistic guests like Doctor Dick on the other, the choice was a no-brainer. "You'll see. I'll make it work and it'll be wonderful."

"If it's what you really want to do—"

"It is."

"Then I've not a single doubt you'll pull it off."

She leaned up and kissed his creased cheek. "Thank you. Don't tell the others, but you've always been my favorite brother."

"Which is exactly what you tell the others."

Because it was true, Brianna laughed.

CHAPTER TWELVE

As usual for a Mannion family dinner, the long wooden table was laden with enough food for an army battalion. Over her mother's famous fried chicken, potato and pasta salads, along with dressed tossed greens from the garden, mac and cheese, grill-roasted corn on the cob and obligatory deviled eggs from Caroline Harper's Southern family recipe, Brianna was filled in on all the local gossip about who'd married whom, who'd had babies, who'd broken up, who'd started businesses and who'd closed them.

Her uncle Mike had shown up, thankfully without Seth's mother, which could have made the evening a bit strange.

Now, at a break in the conversation, Brianna took a sip of wine for liquid courage and prepared to break the news. Which, she hoped, since it meant she'd be returning home, surely everyone would take positively, so there wasn't any reason to be so nervous. Maybe because once she shared her plans out loud with everyone, she'd definitely crossed that burning bridge from her old life to new. "I have news."

"You've come back to marry that Harper boy," her grandfather Harper guessed.

"Jerome!" Harriet snapped at her husband.

"Dad!" her mother said at the same time.

Her father merely exchanged a look with Quinn and shrugged.

"No," Brianna said. "That never crossed my mind. Why would you think that?"

"Maybe because it was as plain as the nose on your face that you had a thing for him ever since you were knee high to a toadstool."

"You'll have to forgive your grandfather," her grandmother told her. "The filter between his head and his mouth isn't all it should be these days."

"I'm fine," he shot back. "I just believe in speaking my mind."

When the others exchanged looks, Brianna sensed something was going on. Something they were keeping from her. "What aren't you telling me?" she asked.

"It's nothing that serious," Sarah said, not sounding convinced herself.

"Which is what I keep telling you all," her grandfather said, folding his arms across his broad chest. He'd spiffed up for her welcome-home dinner in his dress overalls, she noticed. They were the original dark denim, showing little wear and sharp creases. "It was just a glitch," he said. "Everyone made a big fuss about it. Even had me flown to Harborview in Seattle."

"You were in the hospital? And no one thought to tell me?"

"It wasn't any big deal," he insisted as the others exchanged looks. "I didn't want to worry everyone. Hell, Quinn's the only one of you kids who knew, only because he was living here at the time."

Brianna shot her brother a look even sharper than that her grandmother had speared her grandfather with.

"Hey." He lifted his hands. "Gramps swore me to secrecy."

"It wasn't a little glitch," Brianna's grandmother said firmly. "It was a stroke."

"A stroke?" Her own head felt on the verge of exploding.

"A TIA," her mother broke in. "Transient ischemic attack."

"*Transient* being the key word," her grandfather pointed out. "As in *temporary.*"

"I know about TIAs," Brianna said. "A guest once had one during dinner at the hotel in Hawaii. I also know that it's impossible to tell whether it's a TIA or a major stroke because the symptoms are the same."

She'd personally driven the man's sixtysomething wife to Honolulu's Queen's Medical Center and stayed with her for hours. She'd learned that night that TIAs were often labeled "ministrokes" because although they didn't leave permanent damage, "warning stroke" was more appropriate given that they could indicate the likelihood of a coming major stroke. Which had her worried about her grandfather, but she knew not to push. Not now, during her homecoming dinner.

"The point I was trying to make, before everyone got on my case about a stupid little head thing, which may or may not have even been a TIA, since I'm not forgetful enough to know that those don't show lasting damage and I sure as heck don't remember having one—"

"Which proves our point," Brianna's mother pointed out.

"Getting back to what I was saying," the older man forged on, "I wouldn't mind another Harper joining this family."

"It's not that way, Gramps. Seth is only an old friend."

"You say that now," he allowed, gentling his tone, "but you're a pretty girl, Bri. And smart as a whip. A boy would be a blame fool not to snatch you up. Especially one who's been moping around as down in the dumps as a rooster in an empty chicken coop."

"Great simile, Gramps," Quinn murmured.

"It's the truth," Jerome Harper said. "I realize it's got to be hard, losing his wife, especially the way he did, but life moves on. I sure as hell missed my Bonnie when I lost her." The story of the tree limb falling on the house where he'd lived as a young man with his new bride was archived in the museum as one of the tragedies of a historic massive winter storm that had swept in from the Pacific, picking up power and ice as it roared over the Olympics.

"But if I'd let myself turn hermit like Seth Harper has, I never would've met your grandmother, who gave me a wonderful daughter, your mother, who in turn gave us you. When you get to be my age—" he said, using his accumulated years to bolster his argument, despite having always been more likely to dismiss them, "—you can look back and see that life's a chain, with every event and every person just another link." He winked at her. "And you, my beautiful, bright granddaughter, are one of the golden ones."

She smiled despite her continued concern, not to mention her discomfort with the renewed topic of any relationship with Seth Harper other than her contractor, and hopefully still friend.

"Now that you're back home again, maybe you and that boy are meant to be each other's next links."

Her mother suddenly stood up. "Who'd like pie? I picked the rhubarb fresh this morning."

Everyone at the table immediately agreed. "Can I help?" Brianna asked, looking for a means of escape.

"Thank you, darling, but I've got everything under control. This is your night, after all. John, why don't you clear?" The warning look Sarah shot her father before leaving the room slid off him like water off the back of a trumpeter swan. "And you, Dad. Please behave yourself."

"I remember when I was the one telling that girl what to do," Jerome harrumphed. "The pecking order gets all mixed around when you get old. I'm not real fond of that."

"Being old's better than the alternative," Brianna's grand-mother reminded him.

"Got a point there, honeybun." Proving that his short-term memory hadn't been affected, he returned to the topic. "So, you think you and Harper might be forever-after links?"

"I'm not planning to be anyone's link right now," Brianna said mildly.

"Life happens when you're making plans," he said, caus-ing her to wonder if this man's genes were where her broth-er's debating skills might have come from. He'd always been up for an argument, but this was one of the few very times when Brianna had found herself in the crosshairs. "Just ask your mom and dad."

According to family lore, her mother's parents had done everything to keep them apart. But in the end, love had won out.

"I came back home with plans I hope you'll all be excited about."

Over the pie, which was the perfect blend of tart and sweet with a golden, flaky crust, Brianna told everyone what she'd told her brother upstairs.

"That's great," her uncle Mike said. "If you need some art for the walls, say some scenery, and maybe some indus-try fishing, lumbering, like in the foyer mural, I'd be happy to pitch in."

"I'd want to pay." Thinking of what his work commanded, inside Brianna went pale, but her concierge calm-during-all-storms smile stayed put.

"In the first place, you couldn't afford me," he said on a laugh, echoing her thoughts. "In the second place, you're fam-ily. And it'll be cool to have my work hanging in a historical house we all grew up breaking into."

She laughed. "And here I thought we were the first kids to do that."

He winked. "Who did you think broke the windows in the first place?"

"Truly, that would be wonderful," she said, imagining his paintings hanging on the walls. They'd be perfect. "Of course I'll have your gallery business cards to hand out." Another idea occurred to her. "Would you maybe, just possibly, consider doing a monthly wine/painting class during the summer months? I could add it to the events calendar."

"I don't have to think about it. I've considered the idea before but haven't gotten around to doing anything about it. Sounds like fun, and anything that brings people into the gallery goes right back into the hands of local artists, which supports the town. Win-win."

"Thank you." Brianna felt the sheen burning in her eyes and wondered how she could have stayed away so long. She was so fortunate to have been born into such a supportive, loving family. Which had her thinking of Seth and his father's always difficult relationship and hoping that she wasn't going to make it worse.

While they all seemed enthusiastic, with even Quinn seeming to have gotten on board, she thought she viewed seeds of worry in her mother's hazel eyes.

As the men worked in the kitchen, Brianna sat with her mother and grandmother on the front porch, watching the stars wink in a midnight blue sky.

"I'd forgotten how many stars there are," she said, as one went streaking across the sky over the snowcapped mountains that gleamed in the slanting silver light of the moon.

"You don't see anything like this in the city, that's for sure," Sarah agreed. "I missed it when I was away at college."

"I thought I wanted bright lights," Brianna murmured, as much to herself as to her mother. "That's why I left."

"Is it?"

Her mother's quiet question surprised her. Since changing

her mind her final year of college, she'd probably bored everyone past tears with her talk of bright lights and big cities. How could her mother not remember that?

"Of course. Why did you think I left?"

"I doubt there's ever just one reason any of us do anything. In your case, I think it was to explore new territory, to test yourself to see if you were up to the challenges without the support of your family and friends." Her mother took a sip of her wine. "Small towns can be wonderfully safe places to grow up, but there comes a time when most of us need to test ourselves. Or, as your grandfather would say, test our mettle."

"That's it, exactly," Brianna said. And now that she'd proven herself, to herself, she was ready for the next chapter in her life.

"And you've succeeded, spectacularly." Sarah ran a tender hand over the top of Brianna's head. "But I also always thought another reason you took off to parts unknown had something to do with Seth and Zoe."

"What?"

"You changed your life plans shortly after their engagement."

"I guess." She thought back to the timeline. "But it wasn't because of that. It was simply triggered by what I'd learned in school opening up my mind."

"Which is what college is supposed to do. But did you ever consider that you didn't want to have to see them together every time you came home? To have to stand by, watching them build the life you'd once dreamed of?"

"I was a young girl when I had those dreams."

"As was I when I fell in love with your father."

"But he refused to let your relationship get serious for years. Because of the Mannion/Harper feud."

"People like to tell the story that way," her grandmother, who'd been quietly rocking, seeming to only half listen, jumped in. "But I wouldn't call it a feud. At least not in our branch of the family. Though I will admit that Jerome and I weren't real happy about our girl falling in love with your father."

"Because you worried he'd keep me here," Sarah said. "I'm not sure either of you ever understood what a big responsibility it was being the first Harper to go to college." She looked down into her wine, as if it were a window into the past. "The family had so much invested in my succeeding."

"We did and we didn't," Harriet said. "You did more than your part, mostly paying your own way and getting all those scholarships and work study at that fancy school back east and even on to Oxford, but your father and I wanted you to do better than we had. Which is what all parents want for their children."

"Your great-great-grandfather was a fisherman who risked his life much of the year in the Bering Sea." Her mother picked up the story Brianna knew by heart. "A sea that took his life and left his wife, Ida, a widow with a six-month-old boy his father had never seen, along with a toddler daughter and four-year-old son."

Ida Harper had lost her daughter at age eight to the Spanish flu, and the older son would be killed in the Japanese bombing of Alaska's Dutch Harbor. The youngest, Jacob, Brianna's great-grandfather, who'd also taken to the sea, had passed away in his sleep at the ripe old age of one hundred three.

But Jacob's son, Jerome, with constant pressure from his parents, had raised the family's lot a notch by owning not just one, but a fleet of three wooden fishing boats. While life had gotten considerably better for that branch of the Harpers, both Brianna's grandfather and grandmother had still wanted more for their only child.

Brianna had heard the story how, having lost three children to miscarriages, and another to stillbirth, Sarah had been

Harriet and Jerome's "miracle daughter." Thus the expectations to succeed that Brianna suspected her mother had carried on her shoulders most of her life.

Which might be why she'd never pressured any of her own children.

"Your grandfather didn't have anything against your father, personally," Harriet stressed. "I didn't have any problem with him being a Mannion, either. Which, like I said, is an overexaggerated disagreement that didn't start because of that vote on the town's name, like most people think, but like most foolishness concerning men, over a woman."

"Really?"

"That's what I was always told," Sarah said. "That Nathaniel Harper and Gabriel Mannion were both courting the same woman, Edna Mae Kline. Who chose the Mannion boy. And while I can attest to the fact that some of the Harpers have long memories, your grandparents believed that I was like you turned out to be, destined to live in big cities, doing important things."

"Well, we were wrong about that," Harriet allowed. "What you're doing here, in your hometown, is just as important as heading up some English department in a big Ivy League university."

Sarah smiled. "Thank you, Mother. I like to think so."

"Do you know the most important thing I did last week?" Brianna asked. Then answered her own rhetorical question. "Arranged, and attended, a mid-six-figure high-society wedding."

"Well, although I don't understand when or why weddings became such major productions, I suppose it was important to the bride," Harriet said.

"It was hard to tell since she wasn't talking. Being a dog. Though she did take a nip at the groom when he tried to mount the bridesmaid."

Her mother, who'd just taken a sip from her glass, spit out wine. It wasn't easy to rattle Sarah Mannion. Brianna felt a spark of pride that she'd come up with a first for her. "Well." She bit her lip, obviously trying to keep from laughing.

"It's okay. You can laugh," Brianna said. "It was a circus. Or a zoo. But my point is that I was merely catering to rich people who didn't have anything better to do than throw their money around to prove their importance."

"I'm sure some of them must have supported charities and done good things with their money," her mother said diplomatically.

"There was a family, the Johnsons, outside of Port Angeles, we bought our pork from when growing up," Harriet volunteered. "When I was just a girl, about ten, maybe eleven, they had themselves a big barn dance to celebrate breeding their prize hog with a blue-ribbon sow they'd had trucked in all the way from Iowa. Guess your dog wedding party doesn't sound all that different. The ham dinner they served all the guests ended up worthy of that shindig."

This was why she'd come home. Not the scenery, which was famous, nor the quaint, familiar town, nor the local history. But to be with her family, most of all these two women who could always look on the bright side and find good in anyone. Even, probably, Doctor Dick.

She leaned over and kissed first her grandmother's cheek, then her mother's. "I love you both."

"And I love you," her grandmother said.

Warmth flooding from Sarah's hazel eyes went straight into Brianna's heart. "I love you, too, darling. I know it's old-fashioned, especially coming from someone who's taught feminist literature and believed every word, but a part of me hopes that you'll settle in back here, be loved by a wonderful man and give me grandchildren to spoil."

"You never spoiled any of us." But, oh, how her mother

had loved each and every one of them, encouraging her four sons and daughter to seek their own destinies.

"It's different with grandchildren," Harriet said with the authority of age. "Dinah Foster—you remember her, she owns Dinah's Diner—once told me that the reason grandparents and grandchildren get along so well is that they have a common enemy."

Brianna laughed. And felt a tug she hadn't felt since Zoe had emailed her from Afghanistan, telling her all about her plans to start making babies with Seth as soon as she got home. She hadn't given all that much thought to children. In her profession—former profession, she corrected herself—it hadn't seemed practical. Plus, there was always the pesky little detail of needing a guy to make a baby and again, with her long hours and changing cities every few years, anytime a casual relationship looked as if it might turn serious, she'd break it off. Better to end early than face a divorce down the road.

"Sorry, Mom, but you're going to have to talk to one of your sons. Because I'm going to be too busy getting Herons Landing B and B going to take time out to even date. Let alone procreate."

"I'm not going to push. But—" she held up a hand to forestall any objection "—if you still have feelings for Seth, if I were you, I wouldn't wait too long to act on them."

"Seriously? My mother wants me to jump the widower of my best friend?"

"Well, I wouldn't put it that way. But your grandfather did have a point. It was obvious to everyone except probably Seth and Zoe, who only had eyes for each other, that you had a crush on Seth."

"Like I said, I was a girl." Yet, as her mother had pointed out, she had decided against returning to Shelter Bay about the time Zoe and Seth had gotten engaged. Could she have been avoiding watching the two people she loved most, outside her family, build their perfect picket fence, two-point-five children, married life together? "But Seth and I are just friends."

"Your father and I are proof that friends to lovers to life mates can be a real thing," her mother reminded her. "Just saying."

Then, having said her piece, Sarah switched gears. "Now, tell me all about your plans for the B and B. I do hope you'll let me help."

Grateful for the change in subject, Brianna polished off her wine. "Believe me, I'm counting on it."

CHAPTER THIRTEEN

Harper Construction was located in a stand-alone building at the end of Old Fort Road, right before the jetty that housed the lighthouse. Unlike many in the main part of town, the two-story building had been built with Western cedar siding milled on the site. Over the years it had expanded, but while the Harpers might be a bit difficult to deal with from time to time—at least if you were a Mannion—they were artisans, who'd built the additions to look as if they were part of the original structure.

The porch was wider than when Brianna had left town. And the siding, which had been a faded brown, had been restained a soft gray with toned-down blue trim. The door was a deeper burgundy red than her parent's bright one, and green landscape bushes had been added at the foundation. The Harper Construction sign hung on a black wrought iron frame topped with a pelican on a post.

An old-fashioned ship's bell rang as she opened the door. Which wasn't needed since the receptionist was seated behind a desk facing the front door.

"Well, if it isn't Brianna Mannion!" A pleasingly plump

elderly woman with a cloud of pink-cotton-candy-hued hair accented with purple streaks jumped up and ran over to practically smother Brianna in a huge bear hug. "I heard you were in town and was hoping to see you before you headed off again so soon like last time. Not that I'd blame you for leaving, since that was such a sad time and your mama said you were as busy as a beaver down there in Vegas."

"It's good to be home." Brianna's words were muffled by her face being buried in Ethel Young's pillowy bosom.

"Home's where the heart is, that's for sure." Ethel backed away, put her hands on Brianna's shoulders and gave her a long look, from the top of her head down to her feet and back up again. "You brought all that desert sunshine with you."

· "I need to go shopping." Brianna had decided that all her Las Vegas casual clothes, like today's red, orange and hot-pink paisley leggings and hot-pink tunic, were not going to work if she was planning to spend every day at Herons Landing while it was being remodeled.

"Well, you're just in luck. Doris and Dottie Anderson have the cutest dress shop. The Dancing Deer. They're identical twin sisters who originally had a shop in Coldwater Cove. But then they retired when they got an offer to sell the store to some Seattle software mogul who wanted to escape city life. To hear them tell it, after six weeks of watching daytime TV and puttering around in their gardens, they realized they'd made a big mistake.

"So, they moved down to Oregon, started over and were doing well, when a tidal wave took out their shop and the greedy owner refused to renew their lease. So, looking for a new place, and being originally from Washington, they decided to settle here. They're a hoot." She laughed. "You're going to love them. They're probably in their nineties now, and still going strong. We should all hope to live as long."

"That's a great story, except for the tidal wave," Brianna

said when Ethel, whom she guessed to be in her eighties herself, paused to take a breath. "I was going to order some things from the internet, but I'll start there."

"Oh, Doris and Dottie will fix you right up!" She ran a plump hand laden with jewelry over the front of her purple shirt, which featured a red hat with Red Hot Grandma spelled out in red rhinestones. "It's where I got this, for my Red Hat Club outings." She patted Brianna's arm. "But don't worry. They've got lots of clothes for a pretty young thing like you."

She paused for another breath, then said, "I guess you're here to see Seth."

"I am. We have an appointment." Brianna lifted the small insulated cooler she'd brought with her. "And lunch."

"Do you happen to have your mama's chicken in there?"

"Yep. And her potato salad, my brother's wings and rhubarb pie."

Ethel nodded her approval. "Best way to a man's heart is through his stomach," she repeated what Kylee had said. Before Brianna could clarify that their meeting was strictly business, she'd turned and walked across the room to a double door. "I'll just go fetch him."

She wasn't after Seth Harper's heart, Brianna assured herself. But that didn't stop her own from taking a little jump when he came out of the office. The heck with lunch. The man looked delicious enough to eat up with a spoon.

The good news was that Seth hadn't suffered any nightmares last night. The bad news was that was probably because he hadn't slept long enough to get into REM mode. His mind had gone round and round like a hamster on a wheel, spinning between the dread of taking all Zoe's stuff home from his in-laws to Bri being back in town.

One thing he never would've admitted to anyone, especially his wife, was that he'd started to notice Brianna

Mannion. All through their childhood, she'd just been that girl who'd palled around with her brothers and him. She'd also been gutsier than any girl he'd ever met. Hell, Seth had known guys too chicken to go into that ramshackle old house.

"I ain't 'fraid of no ghosts," she'd quoted the *Ghostbusters* movie that first time, before squaring her skinny shoulders and marching right into the door that had lost its padlock long before Seth had started exploring all the nooks and crannies.

While her brothers were acting like fools, leaping out of dark hallways and rooms trying to scare the shit out of each other, except for that little encounter with the bat she'd ignored the dust, the cobwebs, the signs of rats nesting in the gnawed-up upholstery. Instead, she'd talked to the house like it was a person, sympathizing with its neglect, assuring it that someday she'd come back and save it and it would be beautiful again. Although he hadn't realized it then, they'd bonded over Herons Landing. While her affection for the place seemed to be mostly emotional, he'd been drawn to the workmanship, pointing out things that no one else was willing to listen to him talk about.

Then one day she'd come to the school Christmas party wearing a fuzzy red sweater and a perky green-and-red-plaid pleated skirt that had showed off her surprisingly long legs and yeah, he'd noticed her in a different way. A way that didn't have anything to do with coffered ceilings, dado rails or plaster molding.

He'd spent the entire Christmas break thinking about what those suddenly budding breasts might look like beneath the stoplight-red sweater, at the same time feeling guilty because a guy wasn't supposed to think about a friend that way. Fortunately, his family didn't interact with hers, so he wasn't in danger of screwing things up by acting weird around her before he could figure out what he was thinking. And, more importantly, what he was feeling. Even if she turned out to be thinking the same stuff about him, there was one—no, make that *four*—problems looming on the horizon.

Her brothers.

Which not only meant he was outnumbered, but if he had a sister, and there was a boy even thinking about what he was thinking about Bri, he'd probably have no choice but to take the dirty-minded kid out into that icy bay and toss him overboard for fish bait.

But then they'd gone back to school after the Christmas break and suddenly a new girl from Astoria had shown up in class. Just looking at Zoe Harper was like gazing at the northern lights. He'd fallen right then and there and neither his heart nor his body had ever wavered.

Until last night. When, during that brief time he had managed to sleep, he'd had an X-rated dream about Brianna with a red spritz can of whipped cream and chocolate sauce, neither of which involved anything to do with an ice-cream sundae.

And now, after about a gallon of coffee and three glazed doughnuts, all he'd done was make himself as jittery as an alcoholic coming off a bender, and listening to Ethel's non-stop chatter on the other side of the door was about enough to have him slam his head into the wall.

And then he'd walked into the outer office, and the bane of his long, restless night was standing there, backlit by the sun, which seemed to be casting a halo around her blond head.

"Hey. Good to see you." Smooth, Harper. Real smooth.

She blinked. A small frown etched its way between her brows, as if wondering why he sounded surprised that she'd come to the office. "I brought lunch." She held up a cooler. "Because we were going to talk about Herons Landing?"

"Yeah. We were. Sorry, my mind was somewhere else." No way was he going to share what he'd been doing with that whipped cream.

"I know the feeling," she said, bending down to pat Bandit, who, having probably gotten a sniff of the contents of that cooler with his superpower canine sense of smell, had followed him into the reception room.

"Don't worry," she told the dog, who was literally prancing back on his hind legs into the office/client conference room. "I brought enough for everyone. Including you."

The dog dropped down to all fours, drooling on the wooden floor as he followed her over to the wall, where Seth had hung colored pencil drawings next to a matching photo of jobs Harper Construction had completed over the years. Which only had him noticing how those leggings clung like a second skin. And had him remembering how, in his dream, her legs had been wrapped around his waist while he'd taken her against the wall beneath the Whistler mural. "These are wonderful," she said.

"I only took the photos. Mom did the drawings."

"But you turned those drawings into reality. Creating homes and businesses, like Quinn's brewery and pub. That's so special. My work was ephemeral. A situation would arise, I'd take care of it, then move on to the next one. Guests would come and go, and it was just a constant stream of people and situations. But this—" she stopped in front of the library that had earned him the award "—is permanent. Your work is something people will enjoy for generations. Something your children and grandchildren will be proud of."

When he didn't respond to that comment, which he knew was well-meaning, she suddenly flushed. "Damn. I'm sorry. I wasn't thinking."

"Don't worry about it." He slammed the mental door to the nursery that was still sitting there, with the crib, rocker and orcas mobile. "I get your meaning and thanks." Because she looked so distressed, he walked to stand beside her and, he couldn't lie, did experience a sense of pride in the work he'd done. "There have been times over the years, when I've taken classes or attended seminars on historical reconstruction, that I've thought maybe I should have gone to architectural school."

"You'd have gone crazy stuck inside at a drawing board all day," she said.

"You know me well." Maybe too well. "Anyway, Mom's the artistic one in the family. She's always done these illustrations from the architect's renderings. But now that she's been taking classes from your uncle, she's apparently moved on to watercolors." He pointed to the painting of the forest she'd given him at the dinner at Leaf. Fortunately, his dad didn't come into the office often enough to have seen it yet.

"That's lovely." She paused. "Uncle Mike came to dinner last night."

"Did he bring a guest?" Seth asked with careful casualness.

"Your mother wasn't there," she assured him. "He did insist on providing some original paintings for the house."

"That would be cool. And make it even more of a personal experience for your guests."

"That was my thinking. I'm sorry if our families' situation is complicating your life."

"All three people involved are adults. They'll work things out." He hoped. "And speaking of work, I got out the original blueprints and the plans, so why don't we sit down and see what you think?"

"Great idea." She went over to the long conference table at the far end of the room and began taking plates, glasses, forks and knives from the cooler. "Though I'm apologizing in advance if I get distracted. It's been a very long time since I had a working lunch with a lighthouse view."

She laid out the blue-, yellow-and white-striped cloth napkins. "This is quite a step up from my usual sub from Mike's on the Bay," he said. Rather than being recycled brown paper, cloth napkins matched the yellow plates and deep cobalt blue glasses.

"Mom's taking a design class these days." She dished up the food, cutting up a chicken thigh and putting it on a plate, which she then set on the floor. Unsurprisingly, Bandit finished it off in a gulp and turned his big brown begging eyes on her. But having grown up with dogs herself, she managed to ignore him. For now. "She's designing a color palette for Herons Landing for her end-of-semester project."

"You're definitely keeping it in the family."

"Which is what I came home for."

"Lucky you for the paintings and the palette. Lucky me for the lunch."

Over Sarah Mannion's award-winning chicken and Quinn's wings, with sides as good as anything he'd ever had anywhere in Honeymoon Harbor, or even Seattle, topped off with a thick slab of rhubarb pie that could make the angels sing, they went over every square foot of the house. Unlike the last owners, Brianna was on board with every one of his ideas. More than on board. Her genuine excitement stirred cold, dead ashes of his own enthusiasm, which he hadn't felt for a very long time.

After the initial devastation of losing Zoe had worn off, he'd fallen into his pattern of work, dinner at Mannion's, some TV that he'd watch without paying all that much attention to, and what had come to pass as sleep, but was in no way restful. It wasn't that he didn't feel good about Kylee and Mai's house, because he did. If he hadn't been able to give them his very best work, he would've passed on the project. But satisfaction at the end of the day wasn't the same thing as pleasure. Or even, as he'd once occasionally felt, joy.

"As you can see from the original blueprints, the kitchen was really small and tucked away in the back of the house." He tapped on the space, which must have been difficult for a staff to move around in. "Like I said, the owners before you wanted a full open concept so we tore it out."

"I like opening up from the small individual rooms," Brianna said. "And one of the best things about a B and B is having a kitchen large enough to have guests in with you while you cook."

Although he'd been moving things around on the computer screen, she picked up a blown glass paperweight shaped like an orca and placed it on the blueprint. "What if we keep the kitchen here? Then," she continued, positioning his letter opener, "we can put a dining room over here, for guests who want a quieter space."

Her brow furrowed again as he took her suggestions and moved the templates to where she'd put them up on the screen. "I also want to maintain the cozy feel of guests being able to go downstairs in the night to get a snack, like they would in their own homes. Or, if they're going out hiking early in the morning, be able to heat up some oatmeal and coffee. The rooms will have coffee makers, a microwave and minifridge, but that's not enough."

"How about a butler's pantry?" He moved his mouse over to a space near the bottom of the stairs. "This used to be a ladies' sitting room. If you put in a fridge, a counter, microwave and one of those do-it-yourself coffee/espresso machines, along with either some cupboards or a small pantry, they could get the basics themselves whenever they wanted. And maybe a place to eat so they don't have to carry it back to their room." He moved in a template of a round table and chairs near the small kitchenette, then a love seat, coffee table and two armchairs on the other side of the small room.

"I love it." She crossed her hands over her heart. Which, dammit, drew his attention to those breasts he'd dreamed of having in his mouth last night. *What are you? Thirteen?* No. Just horny.

"I interned at a small hotel in Spokane during the semester between my junior and senior years," she said. "It didn't have a restaurant, but it did have a desk in the lobby with fresh-baked cookies for guests. And there was also another little room on each floor near the soft drink machines, where people could get those same cookies, and in the morning, a local baker would deliver fresh-baked muffins and pastries. It added a homey touch to something that could have, under other management, felt like just another chain motel."

"If you don't want to do all the muffins and pastries yourself, you can probably contract out to Ovenly. It's a new place where Fran's Bakery used to be. Mom and Caroline bought pastries for a brunch out at the farm to raise money for new runs at the animal shelter."

"I'll check that out, thanks." Rather than make a note on her phone, she wrote it in an old-fashioned paper day planner a lot like the one his mother used. But his mother had decorated hers with all sorts of colored ink and stickers that tended to make it look as if every month was filled with holidays.

"I'll also want to make breakfast available in the garden in the summer. And before you point it out, I do realize that the gardens are currently overgrown with weeds, trash trees and Scotch broom. But I have plans for that."

"Actual plans? Or just a vague plan to somehow restore them?"

"The latter," she admitted. "That's why landscapers were invented."

"That's why I asked. You might want to try Amanda Barrow. She's a landscape architect who still occasionally consults from San Francisco to Seattle, but moved to town and opened up a garden place not far from here. She can do it all—design, plants, hardscape, water features, whatever you want. Kylee and Mai are having her do their garden for the wedding."

"Sounds good." She took the card he handed her. "Wheel and Barrow?"

"With her name, what would you choose?"

"Good point. I think I like her already."

"I know you will. So, we're good? For now?"

"For now." Her smile reminded him of an auditorium of lighters flicking during a rock concert. Not that anyone used lighters anymore, but still. "Of course, I'll undoubtedly come up with changes down the road."

"Everyone always does." Though he doubted she could top Kylee. "The sooner you start looking at finishes and appliances, the sooner I can nail down a bid price."

"Super. I'm eager to get started so I'll shop today for things that aren't dependent on color while Mom works on the design palette. Can you give me a list of suppliers you've worked with who are dependable and won't jack up the price because I'm a woman?"

"Sure. And you'll get the contractor discount. But again, none of this is going to be cheap."

She shook her head and this time her smile was indulgent. "It's only because you've been left holding the bag twice before that I'm going to tell you that I have more money than I'll need."

"Either you hit the jackpot in Vegas or you've taken to robbing banks."

"No. I inherited a bundle."

He knew his surprise showed on his face when she laughed. "Not from my family." Who, while being comfortable, could in no way be considered wealthy. "There was this couple who I'd often work for during my vacations. Despite being rich enough to buy this entire town, they were lovely people and because of them, I was able to travel to places I'd never have seen otherwise. They weren't young when I met them, and although they quit wandering the globe, they continued to hire me to do special events like charity dinners, family reunions and a big party in the Caribbean when their grandson graduated from Georgetown Law. Sadly, the husband died recently. There was no way I was going to miss his funeral, because he'd become, in a way, sort of another grandfather. But I'd never expected that he was going to leave me anything."

"I'm not going to ask how much." But he wouldn't deny that he was curious.

She shrugged. "If anyone has the right to know, I suppose you do. And I trust you'll keep it confidential. Only my family knows."

"My lips are sealed." Which was a moot point, since he didn't talk to all that many people anyway.

"A bit shy of a million."

"Wow. The guy must've been megarich."

"Obviously I knew they had a great deal of money. But I didn't realize how many billions he had until I read his obituary," she admitted. "His wife assured me that my inheritance wasn't that much in the grand scheme of things, so I should accept it in the spirit in which it was given."

"Nice folks."

"They were." Her lips curved at what he assumed were fond memories. "And, truthfully, most of the people I worked with were lovely. It's the others who tend to stick in my mind."

"Tell me about it." It didn't help that his dad wouldn't let him forget.

"I donated some of it to a Las Vegas food bank, a refugee resettlement program and Doctors Without Borders. But in addition, I've also saved a lot of my salary because I wore an uniform at work and either lived in the hotels where I worked or received a housing allowance as part of my employment package. So you needn't worry about me going broke on you."

"Unless you decide to go with gold fixtures."

"Believe me, having just escaped a place called Midas, I've been surrounded by more gold than anyone should have to live with in a lifetime," Brianna said with a laugh that got the attention of Bandit, who'd given up his begging stare and settled back down on the rug. A whine that Seth had come to know well got him the leftovers on a plastic plate.

"Okay. So I'll put in for the permits. By now the county's used to me coming in with paperwork for that property, so it shouldn't take long. I'll start calling subs while you go shopping."

He opened a folder and took out a list of subcontractors and suppliers he kept on hand for clients. "You can get some stuff, like the paint, locally at other towns on the peninsula. For the bigger, more pricey items, you'll probably have to go over to Seattle."

"As much as I believe in supporting local businesses, I'd already figured that out."

"Since you're determined to go through with this, let me give you a key so you and your mom can walk through the place while we're waiting for the permits."

"Is that allowed? I haven't even been to the Realtor yet and have put my years of breaking and entering behind me."

"It is if the owner allows it."

She paused in the act of putting away the picnic dishes. "Are you saying *you're* the owner?"

"I bought it at a short sale, which made it affordable. The bank mostly just wanted to get rid of it and there weren't a lot of prospective buyers. Like none."

She frowned. "I can't take your house."

"You're not taking it. I have it up for sale. You're buying it."

"Don't you want to live there?"

"It's got eight bedrooms," he pointed out. "When it's done, it'll have ten bathrooms. What's a single guy like me going to do with all that? Besides, I have a house."

"So you bought it to flip it?" He could tell she was some-what disappointed by that.

"No. I bought it to keep anyone else from screwing it up." He paused, then decided what the hell. She wasn't like one of her brothers, who'd rag him for his sentimentality. "Besides, you weren't the only one who developed a strong emotional connection for it back when we were breaking into the place."

Her troubled eyes cleared. The smile returned like the sun coming out from behind a cloud. "This is going to work," she said.

"We'll make it work," Seth agreed.

Ignoring Ethel's knowing look, he walked Brianna to the outer door, watching as she headed to her car parked out in front. How had he forgotten those legs?

CHAPTER FOURTEEN

Because her mother was still in school doing her principal thing, Brianna decided to enjoy her first day off in years and stroll around the town, checking out both the familiar and the new.

Olympic Mountain Paints was still there, next to Dinah's Diner, which looked like a frozen photo from the 1950s. Around the corner was the Big Dipper, making Brianna wonder if kids still hung out there after movies at the art deco style Olympic theater. Though these days they'd probably be drinking frozen lattes instead of chocolate shakes.

What she remembered to be Fran's Bakery had been given a face-lift and, as Seth had told her, was now called Ovenly. From the display of elaborate pastries in the window, the new owner catered to a different clientele than Cops and Coffee. Since she'd need to know how much the house was going to cut into her savings before she could fully come up with a detailed business plan, she decided against going in to talk with the owner right now. But she did think that contracting out the pastries could be a good plan.

The Quilters Garden was new. Across the street, Rain Or

Shine Books—its hanging sign featuring a smiling sun peeking out from behind a gray umbrella—had moved into a store that had, when Brianna was younger, housed a camera shop. These windows were decorated for spring, with brightly covered romances depicting happy couples in meadows dotted with wildflowers and kissing beneath umbrellas and English gardens, along with tartan-kilt-clad men wielding swords, and kick-ass futuristic heroines wearing leather boots while wielding swords of their own as cityscapes smoldered behind them.

There were also children's books featuring flowers and bunnies, spring cozy mysteries and a display of cookbooks with spring meal themes arranged next to a coffee table photography book by, coincidentally, "local author" Mai, titled *A Pilgrimage with Tutu*. The cover showed an elderly Hawaiian woman placing a lei on an aged white tombstone.

While Brianna paused in front of the inviting store, thinking of all the to-be-read books already on her e-reader, but unable to pass a bookstore without going in, Kylee and Mai came out with bright white bags bearing the store's logo.

"There you are!" Kylee greeted her with her trademark hug that suggested she was a natural at calming stressed out brides and grooms, along with soothing any demanding mother of the bride that might threaten to cast a pall on the couple's special day. "I was just about to call you and see if you wanted to come have tea at the Mad Hatter with us."

"I just finished lunch," Brianna said.

"With Seth Harper. We know."

"Already? How?" It had been scarcely twenty minutes since she'd left Harper Construction. The Honeymoon Harbor grapevine had definitely gotten faster during her years away.

"We were at the Dancing Deer—which, by the way, is the coolest place to buy clothes on the peninsula—when Ethel called Dottie and Doris to tell her you'd shown up at the construction company with a cooler. So, you're already doing the picnic thing?"

"Good ploy," Mai said. "I snagged Kylee with a picnic in the French countryside the day after we met."

Kylee shook her head. "That was my idea."

"You *thought* it was your idea," Mai corrected her. "Which was my even more brilliant idea to have you think it. Since you like to be the one running everything."

Flame hair fanned out as Kylee shook her head. "I do not."

Mai just tilted her head, crossed her arms and waited.

"Okay," Kylee caved. "I may just be a bit of a control freak. But, excuse me, pot...kettle." She turned back to Brianna, who'd hoped that the subject had moved away from her. "We had cheese, amazing chocolate and wine. What food of seduction did you use on Seth?"

"There was no food of seduction. No picnic. We ate in his office. It was a working lunch. Mom made extra chicken and potato salad for my welcome-home dinner, so I brought some to eat while we went over plans for Herons Landing."

"Was there pie?" Mai asked.

"Rhubarb."

"Your mother makes the best pie ever. We were at the farm last week for a fund-raiser for the animal shelter, and her key lime nearly made me change plans from having cake to pie for our wedding supper," Kylee said. "But we've already ordered a dynamite cake from the place that took over Fran's Bakery."

"I saw that it had changed. Seth recommended the pastries."

"They're to die for. Fran retired to Palm Desert to spend her last years letting the California sun bake sixty-plus years of damp out of her bones, and she sold the place to this marvelous baker from New Orleans, Desiree Marchand. She changed the name to Ovenly, updated the design with help from your fabulously talented mom, and updated the menu, including adding a great selection of gluten-free pastries and cakes that taste like the real thing."

"Our cake is going to be gluten-free," Mai said. "And I swear you won't be able tell the difference. Better yet, she didn't even balk when we ordered a pair of Wonder Women for the topper."

"I can't wait to see it." Brianna laughed.

"We have photos of what it's going to look like." Kylee waved her phone. "Come to tea, even if you don't want to eat anything, and we'll show you. And plan what you're going to wear at the bachelorette party. Which, as maid of honor, you're technically in charge of, but don't worry, Mai and I will give you a list of our ideas and we can work it all out together."

After nearly missing her friend's wedding because of misguided priorities, there was no way Brianna was going to turn down a bachelorette party. Even though there were ones she'd arranged at hotels over the years that still gave her nightmares to remember.

"Tell me there won't be strippers."

"Not a one," Kylee assured her.

"We're remodeling a home and adopting a child," Mai said. "Strippers have no place in that agenda."

"And we're not going to get drunk and throw up all over the back seat of the limo, right?"

"Absolutely not. We're adulting," Mai said firmly. "So, we're just thinking of spending the weekend at this new spa resort on the coast."

"Where we can be massaged, buffed, polished and pampered in the style to which we're entitled," Kylee said. "It'll be a weekend of good food, good conversation and girlfriends. Along with a reasonable amount of adult beverages to get us tipsy enough to share secrets."

"I have trouble believing you have any secrets." Of the

three of them, Kylee had always been the most extroverted. "That's what you know. I didn't come out until I was in college."

"Zoe and I knew by the end of middle school."

"You did not."

"Did too," Brianna shot back, then laughed when she realized they sounded as if they were back in middle school.

"How did you know?"

"I guess I always knew, without knowing what I was knowing. But what nailed it for me, figuratively speaking, was when you never joined in to the Team Dawson versus Team Pacey *Dawson's Creek* debates. Even girls who mistakenly went with Dawson early on would swoon whenever Pacey would smile right into Joey's eyes."

"I may have already been leaning toward swimming in the girl pond," Mai said, "but even my heart melted when Pacey painted that wall for Joey."

Kylee let out a bright peal of laughter. "Okay. That was romantic," she admitted. "But when they took off on the boat, I was fantasizing sailing off into the sunset with her, not him."

"Katie Holmes is still hot," Mai agreed.

"Even I can't argue with that," Brianna said. "As for the party, it sounds as if you've already got it all figured out."

"We pretty much do," Mai admitted. "But we're open to ideas."

"A coast sleepover sounds great."

"Super. I hope you don't mind, but since I didn't think you were coming back home, we added a couple attendants who'll be joining us."

"Of course I wouldn't mind. Anyone I know?"

"Do you remember Chelsea Prescott?"

"Sure. She was a year behind us. She had a sister who died, right?" Brianna's memory was vague, given that Chelsea had always been one of those kids who stayed beneath the radar.

"She hung out in the library a lot." And had never shown up at any of the games or dances, or worked on homecoming floats, like the kids Brianna and Kylee had hung out with. "Her parents got divorced." That part stuck out because Kylee and Chelsea Prescott had both ended up being raised by single moms, which, despite Honeymoon Harbor not exactly being the Pacific Northwest's Mayberry, still hadn't been all that common.

"That's her. And all those hours in the library must have had an influence on her because she's now the head librarian."

"Mrs. Henderson retired?" The woman had been a fixture at the library for all Brianna's life.

"Well, she is in her seventies," Kylee said. "But, according to Chelsea, she still stops by at least once a week to make sure the place hasn't fallen apart without her guiding hand."

They shared a laugh. "I also asked Amanda Barrow."

"The landscape architect who's doing your yard?"

"That's her. Wheel and Barrow," Mai confirmed. "We've become friends. She's supertalented. And nice."

"And the only attendant who's married," Kylee said. "Her husband used to work for a tech company somewhere in Silicon Valley. But now he's gone freelance, developing games. They moved here because apparently he thought he could be more creative away from the pressures of the tech world of incubators, beehives and, in his words, 'sucking dick' for funding."

Brianna heard the odd edge to her tone. "You don't like him."

Her friend shrugged. "I don't really know him. He just seems sort of off."

"He's a techie," Mai said. "Those guys are all from a different planet."

"That's probably it," Kylee agreed. "You'll meet him at the wedding. I'll be interested in your take on him."

"Sure." There was more there that Kylee wasn't saying. But knowing she'd never been one to gossip, especially about her friends, Brianna didn't push. "I'd love a chance to pick her brain about the landscaping."

"She's brilliant. Wait until you see the wisteria arbor she's created in back where we'll say our vows."

"It sounds lovely."

"Doesn't it? We can work out all the details over tea," Kylee said. "So, do you have time to catch up?"

Being with Kylee again caused another familiar click of being home. And going to the Mad Hatter reminded her of when they used to hang out at the Big Dipper and made her all too aware of Zoe's absence. Which, in turn, had her wondering if it was this way for Seth. That he'd just be slipping into a good time and suddenly, out of the blue, the loss would hit. Of course it would. And how much worse would it be for him?

"Tea it is." It wasn't as if she had anything else to do at the moment, which was a strange feeling and gave her a sense of how her mother must view retirement. "I don't think I've been to the Mad Hatter since my sixteenth birthday."

"With Zoe and me," Kylee said. There was a brief moment of silence as her brilliant smile faded. "I really, really miss her." Her wide eyes glistened. "It's not right that she's not here for my wedding. I went to hers. We all pinky swore that whatever we were doing, wherever we were, we'd show up to take part in each other's weddings."

"I know. And it's not fair." Kylee's passionate words also had Brianna feeling even more guilty for having been about to blow off this wedding for work. "But she'll be with us in spirit." Which sounded lame, but she hoped the others would realize it was heartfelt. "Before tea, I want to run in and buy Mai's book so she can sign it."

"You don't have to do that," Mai said. "I'll give you a copy."

"You have a baby coming. You can't afford to give away books. Why don't you guys go on ahead, and I'll catch up."

"All right," Kylee said, spearing her with a stern, you'd-better-not-flake-out-on-us look. "Because I'm going to grill you about what you plan to do with Seth."

"What Seth and I plan to do with Herons Landing, you mean," Brianna clarified.

Kylee flashed her cover-girl grin and laughed. "That, too."

The place was looking good as Seth worked his way through the final punch list on Kylee and Mai's house. For some reason his dad hadn't shown up, so he didn't have to listen to him gripe about the state of the world, or try to dodge veiled questions about what his mom was doing, not that he'd tell if he knew. Which, thank God, he didn't.

Life was weird, he mused, as he took out a screwdriver and lined up all the screw slots on the wall switch plates to a perfect vertical because anything off-center made him itchy. Watching his mom with Mike Mannion had him realizing how both sets of parents had openly worried about his and Zoe's behavior. Especially that last summer after she'd graduated high school. He knew her parents had worried that he'd get her pregnant and from the safe sex lectures his mom had doubled down on, he knew the Robinsons weren't alone.

They needn't have bothered. Because Zoe had her (and therefore *his*) life all planned out. The military would fund her nursing degree, and she'd pay the government back with her service. Then, once she'd settled that debt, she and Seth would start their family while he restored houses for other families. Families she would take care of at Honeymoon Harbor General Hospital. Seth's masculinity hadn't been threatened that she was the one making all those plans because they'd sounded great to him.

Unfortunately, life had turned out to be a lot like restoring a hundred-year-old house. You could do all the damn planning, spreadsheets and blueprints you wanted, but something unexpected was bound to prove the old saying about God laughing while people planned.

Brianna had always been a planner, too. Although she'd talked only in generalities about her previous gig, he suspected that something unexpected had popped up to throw a monkey wrench into her life's plan. Why else would she suddenly come back to Honeymoon Harbor without letting either her parents or Quinn know until she arrived that she was returning to stay?

Not that it was any of his business. All he had to do was remember that she was, first and foremost, a client.

"Seth?" He was in the master bathroom, checking out the faucet flow, when he heard his mother call.

"Just a minute," he called back. "I'll be right out."

"Stay there," she said. "I'll find you." Since the cottage was small, it didn't take long. "Wow." Caroline Harper stood in the doorway and stared up at the crystal chandelier designed to look like water flowing down one of the waterfalls that were so prevalent in the Pacific Northwest.

"Mai wanted a spa look," he said. "Kylee wanted bling. This was the compromise." The gray-veined white granite, white cabinets and gray wood-look floor said "spa." As did the sea-glass-hued tile backsplash behind the double sinks that he'd also installed as an accent design in the shower's gray-grouted white subway tile.

The deep, freestanding soaker tub was admittedly a modernistic anachronism to the Victorian age, but it was one of the few things the two women had immediately agreed on. Kylee had found it romantic, whereas its clean, curved lines appealed to Mai's aesthetics. And while it did have an old-fashioned floor-standing tub filler, both women had been chosen a model without the period claw legs, which would have made cleaning the floor more difficult.

"I love it." She stepped inside. "I especially like that the shower door doesn't have a frame. It makes the two walls appear almost invisible."

"Kylee had to give up the second showerhead for that end glass wall. But she agreed Mai was right not to tile it in."

"Absolutely. It makes the room look so much bigger."

"Always a plus when you're dealing with a house where the historical committee makes you keep the same footprint."

"Well, it's perfect. I know the girls are going to be so happy here. And soon they'll be decorating that nursery across the hall." She cringed as her words sank in. "I'm sorry."

It was the second time this week Seth had heard that apology, making him realize that that he was getting as sick of people still tiptoeing around the subject of Zoe's death as he'd been with their earlier condolences.

"It's okay." Which was true. He didn't feel that familiar stab to his heart at the mention of the room two women from The Clean Team had been keeping dust-free since he'd first closed the door. "Really. So, what brings you here?"

"I thought I'd let you know that I dropped by the office with this month's accounts."

Which she could have emailed, but his dad had been old school, insisting on keeping the books in an old green-papered accounting ledger. The subterfuge was that his mother, who'd been handling the business end of Harper Construction, had moved over to Quicken years ago and only duplicated the numbers on paper to keep the peace.

"Thanks." Something in her voice had him eyeing her more carefully. There were shadows beneath her eyes that hadn't been there when they'd had dinner at Leaf and her bright enthusiasm seemed to have deflated. "Are you okay?"

"Of course. I'm just a little tired." She put her hand on her chest and coughed. "I think it's from spring allergies."

"Probably." With all the Scotch broom blooming wild all over town, the explanation made sense. Even Bandit had been sneezing.

"Or it could be hot flashes."

Jesus. "I think that falls under TMI, Mom."

"Unfortunately, it's part of female biology," she said. "And considering that same biology had me spending hours pushing you out of my body, you don't have any right to squirm with embarrassment."

Having no response to that, he decided to accept the hot flash explanation, which was preferable to the idea of those shadows having come from still-hot Mike Mannion keeping her up all night.

"I'm not sleeping with Michael," she said.

"Did I say anything?"

"No, but I'm your mother. You should know by now you can't hide anything from me. Along with eyes in the back of our heads, mothers can also read minds." As she'd just done his. "And you certainly wouldn't be the first person to wonder." She held up a hand when he opened his mouth to argue. "Oh, I've heard the rumors. But despite having moved out of the house and served your father with those separation papers, I'm still a married woman. I take those vows I made at the altar seriously. I'd never break them."

"Okay." And could this be any more uncomfortable?

"The same promise you made when you married Zoe in that lovely ceremony at Crescent Lake."

It had always been one of their favorite places. They'd always planned to return. And never had. *Yet more opportunities lost.*

"Why did you leave Dad?"

The question came out unfiltered. But it had been on his mind. A lot. "Sorry." He held up a hand. "Again, none of my business."

"We're your parents. If you were a child, we'd have to give you some reason. I was thinking this morning that we hadn't granted you that same consideration. Which is why, when Ethel told me you were over here, I decided to drop by and let you know that whatever happens, you'll always be our son and we love you."

"Now, that sounds exactly like what a mom would say to a six-year-old."

She laughed. Then wheezed. "Damn pollen," she muttered, echoing his earlier thought. "But I apologize for talking to you as if you were a boy, even if you'll always be my child. Long story short is that your father and I cut a bargain years ago, when I accepted his proposal. I'd make my life here in Washington if he promised that someday we'd take time to travel."

Just like the Robinsons. What the hell was it with his parents' generation? Had they all received some memo that after spending their lives creating suburbia it was now time to hit the road like a roaming band of boomer gypsies?

"Dad hates traveling." They'd taken a trip to Disneyland when he was eight. The plan had been to stay in Southern California for a week, visiting other amusement parks and going to the beach. By the third day, as Seth had been riding the small waves on the new boogie board his parents had bought him at a Huntington Beach surf shop, Ben had gotten antsy and begun to worry about work that wasn't getting done.

Declaring the vacation over, he'd called Seth out of the water, and they'd all piled into the car and gone back to their motel. They'd packed up and headed home to Washington in the dark. "He always says he doesn't want to sleep in some bed total strangers have slept in," Seth reminded her.

"I don't share that aversion, but I'm willing to accept it's a thing with him. Like me and spiders. So, the deal was that when he retired we'd buy a brand-new, never-been-slept-in-before motor home and drive around to all the national parks."

"Sounds like fun." Living at the edge of one of those parks, Seth thought that it sounded great. A bit of a cliché. But he wouldn't mind doing it himself someday. Him and Bandit. Like Steinbeck's *Travels with Charley*.

"Doesn't it? When we were younger, I was thinking more along the lines of adventures to Paris, Rome and Barcelona. But life changes, and exploring my own country has grown more and more appealing."

"What's stopping you?"

"Have you happened to see a motor home in the driveway?"

"No."

"He insists that he's still working."

"Only part-time." Great. Now he was throwing his dad under the bus. Could this situation get any more complicated? "And while he's great at his work, he's not the only guy in the Pacific Northwest who can do plaster."

"That's exactly what I told him! I've also reminded him that Brian Murphy, over in Gig Harbor, filled in for him after his appendectomy put him in the hospital ten years ago." Refusing to give in to the pain, his father had continued working after it had burst, finally causing him to pass out. Fortunately, he hadn't been on a ladder at the time. "And it would be one thing if he was moping around the house, having retirement depression, like I've read about. But all near-retirement seems to have done is give him more time for those damn poker games and fishing."

She folded her arms as a bit more color came into her

cheeks. "Do you have any idea how it feels to come in second fiddle to a salmon? Or those ridiculous-looking gooeyducks?"

Seth scrubbed a hand down his face. "Have you told him that?"

"Of course. Several times. You know your father. He only hears what he wants to hear."

Another statement he wasn't touching. "Brianna Mannion's back," he said in an attempt to change the topic.

"So I hear. That must be nice for you." The frustrated lines in her face eased. "There was a time, when you played together as children, I hoped she'd be my daughter-in-law. Until you fell head over heels for Zoe, who quickly grew to be the daughter I never had."

"She always knew that. There were times that she said it was like having two moms."

"That's nice, knowing she felt that way. Heaven knows, mothers-in-law don't exactly get the best press."

"Not all mothers-in-law are you."

Her laugh was quick and delighted and took some of the fatigue from her eyes. "If only your father had your silver tongue."

Not wanting to get into comparisons with his father, Seth opted against pointing out that no one, ever, had described him that way. In that respect, he took more after his dad than his mother. Although there'd been a time when his thoughts had been a helluva lot more positive. It wasn't as if he'd taken on his father's negativity. More that he'd just gone numb. When you didn't have anything to say, what was the point in trying to come up with any inane conversational filler?

"The reason I brought up Brianna is that she's planning to restore Herons Landing," he said.

"I heard that, as well. And it's partly why I'm here."

Okay. Having nothing to say to that, either, he waited, hoping she wasn't going to suggest that he might want to do something about there still being a chance that she could be Brianna's mother-in-law.

"I want—no, I *need*—you to do me a very big favor."

"Sure."

"When I say big, I mean seriously big. As in life-chang-ing." She took a deep breath. "I want you to fire your father."

"What?" At first he thought she must be kidding, but her expression was as serious as a heart attack. "You're not joking."

"It's not a joking matter. I'm fed up with living in limbo," she said. "I thought, erroneously, that my moving out and serving those papers on him would get his attention. But ap-parently I was wrong."

"It's gotten his attention." How the hell had he landed in the middle of all this damn marital drama? And more to the point, how did he get out? "He's convinced you're coming back."

"Stubborn old goat," she muttered. "Well, he may just dis-cover that he's wrong. My point, and I do have one, is that it's bound to take months to complete that old house."

"Several weeks," he said. "Maybe months, depending on how long it takes Brianna to pick out the finishes."

"She and her mother are in Seattle today, doing exactly that."

Something he didn't know.

"Well, then, if they find everything they need, we could be done in six weeks," he said. "Now that this place is fin-ished up, I can concentrate on Herons Landing. So, maybe eight weeks, allowing for inspection delays."

"That's six to eight more weeks of my life I'll never get back," she said. "I can't continue to live this way."

Opting not to mention that she hadn't exactly seemed to be suffering over dinner at Leaf, Seth swiped a hand through his hair and wished he could beam himself to anywhere but here. "Don't you have a woman friend to talk about this with?"

"Yes. She's currently in Seattle shopping for toilets and bathtubs with her daughter. But Sarah agrees with me. That I've been patient long enough and if I leave it the way it is, Ben will just keep playing cards, fishing, letting the dishes pile up and the house go to ruin, all the time having convinced himself that I'm merely having a menopausal female snit."

"The dishes aren't piling up and the house won't go to ruin because The Clean Team comes in every Friday."

"Your father has hired a maid?"

He wasn't surprised *she* was surprised. With the exception of a tackle box of fishing lures, Ben Harper never spent any money he didn't absolutely have to. He could, in fact, make Scrooge look like a spendthrift. Seth had always thought it was because he'd carried the heavy weight of not being the Harper that had allowed the family business to go under. But the truth was that business was booming, as it had even during the recession, when people were all fixing up their old homes rather than buying new. It had been his dad who'd focused the company on strictly remodel and restoration work because he'd figured out that people were always either modernizing a house they were living in, or updating one they'd just bought. New construction was riskier and more dependent on the fluctuating marketplace.

"Dad didn't hire them. I did."

Her mouth drew into an uncharacteristically firm line as she folded her arms across the front of today's flowing tunic. "And thus enabled him."

"Geez, Mom."

"I'm sorry. But he's a grown man and should be able to take care of himself."

Seth considered falling back on the "old dogs, new tricks" cliché, but kept that idea to himself because he couldn't disagree with her point. "Would you rather the health department condemn the place?"

"No. I'd rather he realizes that he needs me for more than cooking, cleaning and keeping the damn books."

She closed her eyes. Drew in a ragged breath as she put her hand to her heart as if to quiet it. Which was out of character because she'd always been the one to soothe everyone else. And not just in the family. Anytime anyone in the town needed something, she'd be there with her BFF, Sarah Mannion. The two of them had been best friends for longer than Seth had been born. They'd met that night at the Theater in the Firs, the same night she'd met his father. Their long friendship was undoubtedly another reason he and Bri had always been so close. Due to day care not being an industry business back then, like in larger cities, they'd both been dragged by their mothers to more civic events than he could count.

"I'm not going over to the house because I'll get pulled back in," she said, more to herself than to him, as if deciding out loud. "I never could resist the man when he turns on the charm."

There were many descriptions that Seth could imagine being applied to his father. Charming had never been one of them.

Her lips quirked in a half smile. "I know. You don't see it. That's because you're a male. But believe me, I had to fight my way through a crowd of local women, who were buzzing around him like honeybees around a lavender bush, to get to your father. He was considered quite a catch back in the day. And not just because he happened to own his own business," she said, once again demonstrating the ability to read the thought that had just popped into his mind.

"I was used to Southern men whose never-ending compliments were as smooth as butter. A strong, silent, Western alpha male was as rare to me as a unicorn. Though," she said as an afterthought, "I'd prefer you keep that information to yourself."

"Your secret's safe with me."

"Thank you… I'll text him."

"Good luck with that. He never turns on his phone."

She chewed on a nail, which brought his attention back to that wedding band. "Does he still play poker on Tuesday nights?"

"Yeah. But they moved the game to the Stewed Clam after they got tired of take-out pizza from Luca's."

"Ha! He always complained about my sandwich plates. Said they were too girly for poker."

The sandwiches in question were typically created from croissants and green or red pepper tortillas, given cutesy names like Highroller Ham, Texas Hold 'em Beef and Turkey Roulette Rollups. She'd also made platters of poppers, dips and deviled eggs because she'd insisted that in the South, no social occasion was complete without that special plate with the indentations for deviled eggs she'd inherited from her grandmother. It had not escaped Seth's notice that his father's poker buddies didn't seem to share his complaints. There'd never be anything but crumbs by the end of the night.

"You spoiled him."

She shrugged. "What can I say? It's in my blood and it's hard to escape my upbringing. But I'm tired of playing mealy-mouthed Melanie. It's time I embraced my inner Scarlett."

Oh, Lord. "This could get ugly, couldn't it?"

She tossed up her chin and looked as determined as when Hollywood's most famous Southern belle had held up those turnips in *Gone with the Wind* and sworn to never be hungry again. "That depends on your father." Then, softening, she reached up and framed his face between her palms, the way she had when he'd been six years old, and kissed his forehead.

"I'm so proud of you, darling. You've created the perfect home for Kylee and Mai to begin their new life."

"They'll create the home," Seth said. "I'm just fixing up their house."

"True," she agreed. "If only your father understood that concept, he'd realize that a motor home could be just as much of a home as the one he's stubbornly refusing to leave. Even better. Travel is stimulating."

It hadn't been for Zoe, but then, his wife hadn't traveled to Afghanistan on a tourism visa.

"I hope it works out for you," he said.

"Oh, it will." Her shadowed eyes flashed with a bit of her usual spirit. "One way or the other."

CHAPTER FIFTEEN

From the moment they'd left the farm, Brianna's mother had been snapping away with her camera, capturing the varying shades of green of the Douglas firs, western hemlock, Sitka spruce, the reddish brown bark of the western red cedar, along with the brighter hues of the leafy spring sword ferns. Fortunately, meadows, mountains and lowlands were in wild spring blooms, so the scarlets of rhododendrons and paintbrush, delicate whites of the trillium, blues of the starflower and reddish-pinks of the bleeding hearts also ended up in Sarah Mannion's extensive photo files.

The sky, even more unpredictable than usual this time of year, would change from gray to bright blue with all the combinations in between. The water, too, ranged in shades, and as they stood on the outer deck of the ferry chugging out of the harbor, her mother aimed her lens at the shades of white and gray in the driftwood lining the beach, and the varying colors of brown in the aged pilings.

"I love the bright orange of the pelicans' beaks during their breeding season," Sarah said as a pod flew by, as if in parade military formation. "You could use that as a pop of color somewhere. Or soften it to a coral. Oh, and how could I forget?" She turned, focused on Brianna's paper cup and snapped. "You can't not include the Northwest's most famous drink in its palette." The deep, almost black–brown was added to the palette.

Three days later, they were back on that same ferry. Brianna had often felt exhausted at the end of a long day's work. And she was admittedly tired to the bone today. Although she hated to admit it, she suspected she might be out of shape because her mother had definitely seemed to have far more energy as they'd gone from store to store, wholesaler to wholesaler. By the time she'd collapsed into bed last night, Brianna was surprised that her credit card hadn't burst into flames from having been run through so many readers.

The difference between today and other times she'd been worn out was that beneath the fatigue was a buzz of exhilaration. "It's all going to be so stunning," she said as the gleaming white boat with its iconic green stripe plowed through the water.

"It's a good thing you're doing," her mother said. "Not just for your own business, but for the town. That poor house has stood there like a destitute bag lady for too long. Now you're going to bring her back to life as a dowager. Not a stiff, formal dowager, but one suited for her place and time."

"That's pretty much what Seth said. He called it dressing my Victorian dowager in flannel shirts, jeans and hiking boots, while keeping her good set of pearls."

"He's a talented young man. Not only is his workmanship impeccable, he has an artist's eye. Which I suspect he inherited from his mother. Mike and I were talking and I mentioned how, if she hadn't married and settled down to work at Ben's construction company, she could well have had a successful career as an artist."

"It's not too late for that," Brianna pointed out. "Look at you."

Sarah laughed. "And isn't that exactly what your uncle said? I'm so excited for Caroline. She's possibly going to have an exhibition at the Honeymoon Harbor Days boat festival."

"I saw her illustrations in Seth's office. I was already planning to drop in to the exhibition, of course, but now I'm going to make sure I get there early so I don't miss out."

"Oh, I don't think you need to worry about that, darling. She'd be more than willing to paint whatever you'd like. You are, after all, almost family. And, although I realize it's a topic you're not comfortable with, I will admit that there were several times that she and I would be sitting over glasses of lemonade and shortbread cookies watching you and Seth playing in the sandbox or running through the sprinkler, and indulge ourselves in planning your wedding."

"Mom..."

"I know. But since you've never mentioned anyone you were dating—"

"Because there wasn't anyone to mention. My work took up nearly all my time and with the frequent moving, a relationship didn't seem practical."

"I understand your point, though I'm not certain practicality is the first thing a person should be looking for in a relationship."

"You won't get any argument from me," Brianna said. "I suppose the fact that I never felt inconvenienced proves that I've never met Mr. Right."

"Or the time wasn't right. Unless you plan to flip Herons Landing—"

"I don't. I dreamed of that house growing up. Did you know that Seth owns it?"

"I do. I also know that after having two failed starts, he was determined to sit on it until the right buyer came along. Obviously, he realized that you're the one he's been waiting for."

"To buy the house," Brianna clarified. There was too much

baggage between Seth and her to even think about anything but a contractor-client relationship. She'd do well to remember that.

"Of course," her mother said with a look of pure innocence.

"Well, I'm glad he did hold on to it because now that it's mine, I'm not going anywhere."

"Then, just take things a day at a time," Sarah advised. "You never know what the future's going to bring."

And weren't Doctor Dick, her out-of-the-blue inheritance and her house suddenly coming on the market proof of that? Still, as tempting as it might be to see if there were any embers left to be stirred from her old crush on Seth Harper, Brianna had way too many things on her plate to even think about.

Just keep telling yourself that, a dry voice somewhere in the dangerous zone of her head advised. *And maybe you'll even believe it.*

Since her mother had a PTA meeting to attend, they'd driven to the ferry dock in separate cars. Brianna hugged her goodbye, and thanked her for being the best mom ever. Then she decided that rather than go back to the farm, she'd show Seth her purchases. It wasn't that she was dying to see him again. Not even a little bit. He was her contractor, after all. He needed to know what she'd chosen in order to price out the job. And start planning the plumbing, framing, all that contractor stuff.

After dropping by the office, and suspecting her excuse didn't fly with the sharp-eyed Ethel for a minute, she tracked him down at Kylee and Mai's house, which was only the cutest Folk Victorian ever. The robin's-egg-blue siding set off with snowy white shutters and trim was perfect for brightening gray days. A welcoming front porch just made for sitting and watching your neighbors featured a cedar ceiling and white railing that echoed the picket fence surrounding the lot. Instead of a more formal, and to her mind, boring lawn, the front yard was a wild and free cottage garden. Patches of bright green Scotch moss edged a stone paver pathway.

She'd just gotten out of the car when the front door opened and Bandit shot out like a bullet. Bracing herself for impact, she reached out and slowed him down as he barreled toward her, a muddy green tennis ball in his mouth.

"Sorry," Seth said. "I think he's in love."

"It's mutual." She bent down and rubbed behind his velvety brown ear, which had the dog immediately swooning to the ground in dog ecstasy as he wiggled on his back next to an old rain barrel with pillowy flox spilling over the edges. "You're a good boy, aren't you!" She rubbed his belly, causing more grumbling moans.

"I heard you were in Seattle with your mom," he said, crossing through the spikes of delphinium, hollyhocks and scarlet foxglove that were starting to bud.

"I was. And I have so much to show you." Bandit, who'd gotten up, dropped the ball at her feet. She picked it up and threw it away from the garden.

"He'll chase that all day if you let him."

"Exercise is good, isn't it, handsome boy?" she said as he brought it back. She threw it again, this time harder. Farther, which caused it to roll beneath her car. Which appeared not to deter the dog as he began to shimmy beneath it.

"While he's busy fetching, will you give me a tour of this adorable house? It looks like a blue-frosted gingerbread house. But without the witch. You've created magic."

Seth rocked back on his heels and looked up at the house. "It was easy. Kylee and Mai were very specific."

"Oh." As soon as they'd entered, she paused in the doorway, looking up to where a high ceiling crossed with beams painted buttermilk white added the illusion of yet more space. "It's so much larger than I would've guessed."

"We ditched the dining room and blew out that wall into the kitchen," he said.

"Just like on HGTV."

"Yeah. Although I'll admit it drives me crazy when everyone on those shows blithely says 'blow out the wall,' as if contractors all have magic wands. Fortunately for Kylee and Mai's budget, it wasn't a load-bearing wall. The dining room and laundry became the third bedroom and three-quarters bath they wanted for guests, especially when Mai's family comes from Hawaii to visit."

That room, too, was done, although not yet furnished or decorated. "We didn't have a separate room for the laundry, but we put a stacked set in that closet with a set of open shelves." He opened the folding closet door, showing off the stainless steel washer and dryer. "I was worried they wouldn't go along with the idea, but Mai really likes it because it got her out of laundry duty."

"Because she can't reach up inside the dryer to get the clothes out without a ladder."

"Exactly." When Seth felt his lips doing that odd, tugging, smiling thing again, he realized that the muscles around his mouth seemed to have gotten out of shape from disuse. Who knew?

"They should put the bed against that wall," she decided. "That way they can look out at the mountains."

"That's exactly what they decided to do. It'll be delivered in the next few days."

While Bandit, seemingly bored with a tour of a building where he'd spent so many hours, went outside to patrol the perimeter in hopes of finding a rabbit or squirrel, they went back through the great room and kitchen to the other side of the house, where the other two bedrooms were located. She paused on the way, checking out the cabinets and beadboard on the small but efficient island and the ceiling.

"I want that in my kitchen," she said, looking up at the white board ceiling. "But in a different color. I'm still working on shades with Mom. There are so many hues on the peninsula to bring in. I'd never imagined. I found this amazing French oven that's hand-built with an enamel exterior. Since that's going to be the focal point of the room, everything else will have to work around it."

"Hand-built French," he murmured. "How much did that set you back?"

He prided himself on not blinking when she tossed off an amount that was probably equal to at least 10 percent of what her entire budget would turn out to be. "But it has five sealed burners, dual ovens, true European convection, a 15,500 BTU triple ring burner that can hold five pans at different heats at a time and two rotisseries."

"Plan on doing a lot of rotisseriing for breakfast?"

"Hey, you never know. Maybe down the road, I'll add dinner. Besides, did I mention how beautiful it is? And that it comes in the most scrumptious colors you've ever seen?"

"Jack down at the Olympic Mountain Paints spray-painted a fridge for me last month." It was a damn good thing she had deep pockets, because apparently the girl who'd grown up on a Christmas tree farm in the far northwest corner of the country had come back to town with champagne tastes.

"How handy of him," she said dryly. "But wait until you see it, Seth. It's so gorgeous. Herons Landing was once a spectacular house. It has a Whistler mural, for heaven's sake. This stove is like the best kitchen jewelry. She deserves it."

He wasn't surprised that she'd anthropomorphized the house. He'd done that before on occasion. Including a former sea captain's house that from the moment he'd first walked in the door, he'd always thought of being a manly place. Fortunately, the wife of the couple must have shared his vision, because she'd ended up with a home that an old whaling captain like the bearded guy in *The Ghost and Mrs. Muir*, which his mom had watched about a bazillion times, would've felt right at home in.

"You look great."

She'd been checking out the walk-in pantry when he'd heard himself saying the words. Turning, she appeared as surprised as he felt.

"Thanks." She ran her hands over the full short skirt. Like seemingly all her clothes, it looked like a garden in bloom and showed off those long, long legs even better than the jeans and leggings had. "It felt a little bright for the Pacific Northwest, but even though Seattle's more casual than some cities I've lived in, I didn't want to go serious shopping in jeans."

"This part of the country could use more brightness." And so could he. A video flashed through his mind of her standing in front of her colored jewel of a stove, bustling between all those burners, while he was outside searing meat on a grill the size of Alaska, and a passel of kids ran around an emerald lawn, chasing each other with water blasters. Just as she came outside, a bright red bowl of potato salad in her hands, she walked straight into a stream of water, which soaked the front of her dress, turning it almost transparent, revealing a lacy bra and, oh, hell, was that a thong?

No. Just freaking no. Don't even go there.

"Seth?" Her voice held a question, with a touch of concern.

"I was imagining the backyard." The fantasy, in vivid technicolor with surround sound, had seemed to last only a fleeting moment. But from the way she was looking at him, a vertical line between her worried eyes, he realized he'd zoned out. Something he hadn't done since those first weeks after Zoe's death. "Maybe you might want to add an outdoor kitchen. For entertaining."

He nearly groaned when she touched her index finger to her glossy lips and considered that suggestion. "We could have event nights for the guests," she said. "Like on the Fourth of July, since you can see the fireworks over the harbor from here. Or Labor Day. It'd be a short season, but it could be an extra draw. I know there's not a motel or hotel in town offering anything like that. Oh, and it stands to reason we'd get wedding parties staying here. Maybe we could offer the space for the rehearsal dinner. And I don't know why I didn't think of this before, but Kylee could offer photos of the patio dinner as part of the package. Or I could include a discount at the B and B with her wedding photo gig."

With every atom of his body focused on those lush, pink lips, her words were an incomprehensible buzz in his ears. "Sounds good to me," he said, figuring that was a safe enough response since, rerunning it through his suddenly sex-flooded mind, he didn't remember hearing a question.

"Doesn't it? I'm so glad you thought of it because it'll be easier to plan in an outdoor kitchen from the start, right?"

"Sure. Right. Definitely easier. And less expensive." His tongue, which had tied in knots, weighed a ton. Fortunately, judging from the light in her eyes, she was too busy imagining and planning to notice.

Seth was trying to think of something, anything to say, when he heard Bandit barking. Not the wild, crazed bark of a dog in hapless pursuit of a squirrel, but a sharp, all-too-familiar demand. One Seth knew he'd keep up until he got his canine way.

"Your dog's barking," she said as the earsplitting barks became louder and closer together.

"Yeah. He does that. I told you he was a stray."

"Who stole food."

"Yeah. Well, the thing is, he was pretty much feral. So, Cameron Montgomery, he's the new vet in town—"

"What happened to Doc Palmer?"

"He retired last year. Cam grew up in Port Angeles, but

was working down in Sacramento. He wanted to come back up here, so he bought Doc Palmer out. Anyway, he suggested putting Bandit on a schedule, to give his life a structure he'd probably never experienced before. Unfortunately, not only did it work, he's smarter than he looks because he latched onto the concept of daily repetition."

Given the rut Seth's own life had dug into, that hadn't proved a problem.

"I see. What are you supposed to be doing now?"

"Going to Mannion's for dinner."

"Quinn lets dogs in his pub?"

"Naw, he can't do that, though he does bend the code and allow them on the deck on nice days. But it doesn't matter, because we always do takeout."

"Oh." Again that slender finger to her lips, which caused another tug. This time not in the gut, but lower. "Would you like some company?"

"For dinner?"

"I didn't come by to see this house, as fabulous as it is," she said. "I wanted to talk to you about all the fixtures Mom and I found. I thought, since you're going to the pub anyway, that we could do it over dinner."

Unfortunately, *do it* were the words that got through the buzz in his head.

"After all, we both have to eat," she was saying when he regained his focus. "So, this will save time. And it's a gorgeous day. If we eat on the patio, Bandit can join us."

The dog's bark, which had changed from demanding to enthusiastic, suggested he might have actually understood her. Which made one of them.

Dinner on the patio overlooking the water. Wasn't that like a date? Which he hadn't done in so many years, he wasn't sure how dates worked. She'd spent a lot of time traveling the world and living a city life. Would she be expecting to hook up?

And your problem with that would be? the devil that had suddenly appeared on his shoulder asked.

The problem was that if he ever got to the point he was going to give up celibacy, it wasn't going to be relationship sex. And there was no way he could have booty call sex with Brianna Mannion, who'd not only been Zoe's best friend, but a lifelong friend of his. Even the idea of it was too messy and complicated to consider.

"But if you don't want to—"

"No." Damn, he'd hurt her. Although outwardly, she appeared as calm as a sea on a soft summer day, that little line had appeared between her blond brows again. "It sounds great and you're right, I need to know what you've chosen to start working on a cost analysis, and this is the most efficient way. Give me a second to lock up, and I'll meet you there."

The line smoothed, and her smile lit up those lake-blue eyes. "I'll snag a table."

She headed back toward her car, stopping to pat Bandit on his broad head, which set his tail to wildly wagging.

"It's just dinner," Seth reminded himself. "The same as every other night."

The same he might have with any other client. In fact, he'd broken his pub habit last week when Mai had insisted on making him a Hawaiian dinner and although he'd never in a million years thought he'd eat raw fish, the poke bowl of ahi tuna she mixed up with scallions, soy sauce, avocado, white rice and a bunch of other stuff had been one of the best meals he'd ever had. He'd even suggested she open up a food truck, which had made her laugh, and he'd enjoyed the evening.

So, the thing to do was to think of dinner with Brianna the same way. Simply a client dinner, and the one thing he was sure about was that Quinn wasn't going to be putting raw fish on his menu anytime soon. Like ever.

CHAPTER SIXTEEN

What had she done? The suggestion had come out of the blue, but as soon as she'd asked him to dinner, it had seemed the right thing to do. It was, after all, logical. She had to eat. He had to eat. They had business to discuss, so why not do it over dinner?

How about the fact that she'd eaten a huge salmon salad for lunch before leaving Seattle and, if she'd planned to eat anything at all for dinner, it would've been a bowl of cereal? But maybe everyone was right about her and Seth. Although there was no way she ever would have wanted Zoe to die, perhaps fate had given her a second chance. As loath as Brianna was to admit it, her feelings for him hadn't changed.

If anything, having had her share of hit-and-run relationships over the years, she could tell the difference between lust and something deeper. She wasn't yet prepared to use the L word. But neither was she going to shut off her emotions, as he'd obviously done.

Even if she did fall in love, only to have her feelings continue to be one-sided, the least she could do was try to help him past the pain that he'd admitted he'd become mired in.

"That's what friends do," she said as she drove past the storefronts that were looking fresher than when she'd been growing up. There'd been a time, when the logging industry had slowed, that Honeymoon Harbor had fallen into a slump. But thanks to all those who, like the original residents, had stayed, it was on the rebound. And that she was going to be part of it had her putting away her concern about any possible awkwardness with Seth over dinner. As she glanced up into her rearview mirror, she could see herself grinning like a loon.

Quinn was behind the bar, blender whirring as he whipped up a frozen strawberry margarita, when Brianna walked in.

"You're wearing a date thing," he greeted her after she'd woven her way through the tables, which were beginning to fill up.

"Shows what you know. It's a shopping thing. I just got back from Seattle. Mom and I were finding stuff for the house."

"So I heard. Sounds like you're determined to do this."

"Considering how much of a hit my credit card took with order deposits, that would be a yes." She picked up the menu from a stack at the end of the bar. "You have more than burgers."

"It's a pub. Not a burger joint."

"True." She glanced around. "I love what you've done with it."

He shrugged. "Seth did the construction, and Mom helped source the tables and decorative stuff, while I worked with a former client, who owns a national chain of steak houses, on the menu."

"So it wasn't an impulse."

"Not at all. I ran the numbers, and worked on the concept for over a year."

"Unlike me."

"I didn't say that."

"You were thinking it."

"No. And I wasn't being judgmental or negative. You're my little sister. Wanting to protect you comes with the job description."

She flashed him her brightest, most phony smile. One she'd perfected over the years to use with obnoxious guests. "I'm so flattered that you consider me a job."

He laughed. "Brat."

"Bossy big brother. Instead of insulting your customers, why don't you make yourself useful by mixing me up a margarita?"

"Top-shelf?"

"Sure. Why not." She was, after all, celebrating. And besides, she was going to insist she and Seth go Dutch and she could definitely afford it.

"You got it," he said, preparing it with real limes, not a mix, which didn't surprise her since he'd never settle for second best.

Feeling more upbeat than she had in a long time, she was skimming over the menu when her phone chimed. The screen read Harper Construction.

"Hi." Did she sound breathless? Yeah. She most definitely did. "Just a second. I dropped some stuff when I went digging for my phone in my purse." And didn't that lame lie cause her brother to cock a knowing brow? She rummaged around in her bag for a moment, hopefully making enough noise that he'd believe her. "I have a head start on you. Quinn's mixing me up a margarita as we speak."

"That's what I'm calling about." Seth paused, and she could sense the words she didn't want to hear coming at her, like the slow-motion bullet Keanu Reeves dodged in *The Matrix*. "Something's come up. I'm going to have to take a rain check."

"Oh. Okay." She was not going to ask what. "No problem.

I have things to catch up with anyway. Like working on this online program to come up with a logo and do website stuff."

"I'm sorry."

"Don't worry about it. It was just a spur-of-the-moment idea anyway. Not like a date or anything." This time Quinn rolled his eyes. Which, Brianna thought, was awfully juvenile for a man who'd once been featured on the cover of *Seattle Metropolitan* magazine as one of the top West Coast fast-track litigators. "I've got to go shopping tomorrow. For some clothes for Kelly and Mai's bachelorette party. My Vegas bikini just isn't going to cut it on the Pacific Coast."

She waited for him to laugh at the idea of anyone wearing a bikini on a coast that could require a parka this time of year. But there was only a deep, dark hole of silence.

"Anyway, I'm obviously keeping you from something. So, how about we meet tomorrow. Around two? Or I could just email you the fixtures and stuff Mom and I found. Including the stove."

"Sounds good." He sounded distracted. "Let's meet at the house."

"I'd like that. I want to measure for furniture anyway. I'm not going to get a lot, but I'm not wild about the idea of sleeping on the floor, either. Mom suggested Treasures."

"Zoe got stuff there," he said. "She called it going on an attic safari since the stock's always changing."

Okay. She'd gotten the message, loud and clear. It was definitely not a date when a guy made a point of bringing up his deceased wife right after you'd mentioned buying a bed.

"Mom said pretty much the same thing. I'll check it out before I meet Kylee and Mai for lunch, in case I find anything I might want to figure out how to use in the space."

"Okay." He'd gone beyond distracted to wanting to escape this conversation. Which made two of them. "I've got

an appointment in the morning and don't know how long
that'll take."

"Okay, then." She took a long swallow of the drink Quinn
had put down in front of her. "I'll see you tomorrow. Two
p.m. At the house. Bye." She escaped, just barely, having him
hang up on her, by pushing End Call first.

"Still on for dinner?" Quinn asked.

She glanced around, looking for someone, anything she
knew. She'd never liked eating alone in a restaurant. Eating
alone after being stood up would be even worse. Worse yet
would be running away like he'd broken her heart or something.

"Sure." She skimmed through the menu. "I'll have the
Dungeness crab and shrimp mac and cheese." She was tempted
to order another margarita, maybe one of those bathtub-size
ones she'd just seen one of the servers deliver to a table of
young women who reminded her of how she, Kylee and Zoe
had been when they'd been younger.

All three were laughing and working their way through a
platter of grilled clam chips, pretending not to notice the trio
of hot guys who'd just strutted in wearing tight navy blue
Honeymoon Harbor Fire Department T-shirts.

"Carb loading," he said. "You're either about to run a mar-
athon or in need of comfort food."

"You do know that you're not the only restaurant in town,"
she said. "I could go down the street and get a big bowl of
carbonara from Luca's."

He lifted his hands in surrender. "One crab and shrimp
mac and cheese coming up. You good on the drink?"

Wine would be better with the mac and cheese. But reminding herself that she had a long drive back to the farm,
she opted against additional alcohol, ordered soda water
with lemon, took the folder from her tote and began leafing
through it. As she sent Seth the photos from her phone, the

beautiful stand-alone slipper tub, sinks, cabinets and quartz countertops she and her mother had chosen with such care didn't give her nearly as much pleasure as they had just a few hours ago.

"Well, you sure as hell screwed the pooch on that one," Seth muttered as he stared down at his phone, wishing he could take the damn call back. But then what? Then he'd be out on Mannion's patio, breathing in the citrusy scent of her hair over the salt breeze, trying not to notice her legs. And all the other parts he had no business even looking at, let alone thinking about. He'd never kissed her. Except for that long-ago Christmas break back when he was twelve, he'd never even pondered the idea.

Correction. Except for that suspended moment at Herons Landing when kissing cousins were mentioned. He hadn't been the only one hit by a bolt of lust. He'd seen the lightning hit those big blue eyes. He didn't care what they called it, having a sunset waterfront dinner with her in that summery dress wasn't a business meal. It was a guy/woman thing. A first date. Which he hadn't had since his parents had driven Zoe and him to the Olympic Theater to see *The Princess Diaries*.

The movie about a geeky teenage girl who suddenly discovered she was heir to a European throne wouldn't have been his first choice. If he was going to be honest, and he was smart enough not to be, it would have been his last. But no way was he going to turn down a chance to spend two hours sitting in the dark beside her, getting a forbidden thrill that one time their hands had brushed while diving into the popcorn barrel at the same time.

So, rather than revert back to the almost-thirteen-year-old he'd once been, he'd chickened out, making up an excuse so lame Bandit wouldn't have bought it. And now he couldn't even get his burger, because what if 1) Brianna *had* stayed there for dinner, or 2) Quinn knew why she'd been there in the first place and that he'd stood her up? Neither scenario was appealing, and even worse was the thought that her brother might cut him off entirely for hurting his little sister's feelings.

Which was why he'd called into Luca's for a loaded pizza, which had caused Bandit to whine all the way home, letting him know that there was a piece of pepperoni with his name on it. A piece? He'd considered himself lucky when he got home without the mutt scarfing down the entire thing, box and all. And now here he was, drinking a Captain Jack's Ale while having a dinner date with his dog and trying not to think about Brianna Mannion. Or tomorrow morning, when he'd agreed to go over to Zoe's parents' house and go through her stuff.

And yeah. Wasn't that going to be a fun time?

CHAPTER SEVENTEEN

The Stewed Clam was located just across the town line and had always reminded Caroline of the darker side of Bedford Falls from *It's a Wonderful Life*, which it would have become if Clarence the angel hadn't been there to stop George Bailey from committing suicide.

The few times Caroline crossed the line was to get her hair done at Gloria Wells's salon. Gloria, who'd been doing her hair since she'd first come to town, had originally lived in a singlewide trailer. She was dirt poor, due to her husband getting in frequent trouble with the law, and rumors had floated around Honeymoon Harbor that Gloria was a prostitute. Which both Caroline and Sarah Mannion had never believed for a minute. The reason for men showing up at all times of the day and night was that Gloria was barely supporting herself, her daughter, Jolene, and her ne'er-do-well spouse by cutting hair cheaper than anyone else on the peninsula.

Caroline and Sarah hadn't gotten their hair done at Gloria's just because of the low price. Or because they'd wanted to show solidarity with another woman who hadn't been as fortunate as they'd been. But also because she was kind and as talented as any stylist Caroline had gone to when she'd been growing up in the South, where hair was a big deal, as anyone who watched SEC football would realize. Having become an environmentalist on her trip across the country years ago, she didn't even want to think about how much Aqua Net she and her girlfriends had sprayed into the environment.

Unfortunately, Gloria also possessed a lot of stubborn and a strong streak of pride, and except for the food stamps to feed her daughter, wouldn't take charity from anyone. Clothes were bought at the Goodwill in town, and although both women had offered her loans, or even to invest in her business, she'd turned them down flat, not trusting her husband not to mess things up and cause them to lose their money.

Jolene, who'd swept up the hair, had dropped out of school at sixteen, gone to cosmetology school, then bought an old clunker and taken off down I-5 to Los Angeles, where, after a series of fortunate circumstances Gloria was always proud of sharing, she'd gotten a job working in the movies. Which had allowed her to send her mother enough money for a manufactured home, where Gloria had set herself up an actual, licensed salon in one of the bedrooms. The business had taken off, and now, with a small business loan and undoubtedly another investment from her daughter, she'd recently hired Seth to remodel the old, abandoned lighthouse keeper's house into what would become a salon and day spa.

As furious as she was at her husband, Caroline smiled as she passed Gloria's current salon with its Thairapy sign in the front window and a tidy front porch where customers could wait their turn outside during nice weather. Even now a mother, a daughter and an elderly man were sitting on rocking chairs. The mother and man were talking, while the little girl's head was buried in a book that was undoubtedly taking her to faraway places that would seem so much more exciting than Honeymoon Harbor.

Another ten minutes past that bit of cheerfulness, she'd reached the bar, which, going back to the Bedford Falls/Pottersville analogy, reminded her of Martini's, after the cheerful bar in the movie had turned into a sleazy dive run by a nasty and insulting bartender. The Stewed Clam was one of those places that didn't even need a top shelf, because the clientele mainly came there to drink cheaply and get drunk quickly. Which explained the rule posted next to the door and above the bar that more than a single drink required a designated driver. It might be a dive, but the owner, a former alcoholic himself, was smart enough not to get slammed with accessory to any DWI accidents that might occur.

Compared to the darkness outside, the light, when she opened the door, caused several men to shout out a complaint and shield their eyes. She scanned the room, didn't see Ben at any of the tables and decided he must be in one of the back rooms.

Playing poker for money was illegal outside the casinos or licensed poker rooms, which the Stewed Clam wasn't, but the local law had always turned a blind eye to the poker games everyone knew went on in the back room, since the pots never got over twenty dollars, if that.

Heads swiveled, following her as she crossed a floor that was covered with peanut shells and probably hadn't been washed since the Clinton administration. The wood-paneled walls were darkened by decades of smoke from before Washington State added bars and restaurants to their Clean Indoor Air Act.

In no mood for chitchat, she abandoned her Southern manners and simply asked the bartender, "Ben Harper?"

No more verbal than she, he merely continued to dry a smudged glass and nodded his head toward a door at the end of the bar.

Wishing she could hear what Sarah would have to say

about all the fish and animal heads hanging on the paneled walls, she scanned the room that held five round tables and, wouldn't you know it, her husband would be at the far one? Unlike in the main part of the tavern, no one paid the least bit of attention as she walked over the ugliest brown-and-orange tweed carpeting she'd ever seen. To high rollers in Vegas, the stakes might be penny ante, but apparently here the game was serious business.

Ben had his back to her, but when his longtime friend Jake Logan saw her coming, he said something that had her husband turning around.

She held up a hand before he could say a word. "I didn't come here to talk. Since your phone isn't taking texts, I just wanted to give you this."

She handed him an envelope. You might be able to take the woman out of the South, but you couldn't entirely take the South out of the woman. Eschewing email for notes handwritten on embossed stationery with matching envelopes for social or important correspondence was one of those things Caroline Harper had never given up.

"I'd suggest you take it seriously," she added. Then, her business concluded, she turned to leave, hearing Ken Peters, a grizzled old retired fisherman, mutter to Ben, "I sure as hell wish you'd apologize for whatever you did. Because we do miss that woman's sandwiches."

That almost had Caroline smiling as she walked out of the room and out of the bar. Whether she walked out of her marriage was now up to her husband.

CHAPTER EIGHTEEN

Seth let himself into the Robinsons' house with the key Helen had given him the night of their dinner. She'd told him that Zoe's trunk was upstairs in the attic, waiting for him. As he climbed the stairs, he felt like a man making that last climb up to a gallows platform. He hadn't even opened the box the military had sent him. It crossed his mind that he could just take the entire chest and hide it away somewhere in the garage. How would his in-laws ever know if he never looked inside? It wasn't as if Zoe's parents were going to quiz him on the contents. At least, Dave wouldn't. But Helen? Just maybe.

Okay…probably. There might be more tears. He doubted she'd ever stop talking about the daughter she'd lost too soon and too cruelly. He had a feeling Helen's brother and sister-in-law were in for some very long road trips as they all took off traveling together.

Despite his mother-in-law's rosy scenario of the mother and daughter relationship, the truth was that it had always been tempestuous. During Zoe's youth, there'd been a lot of shouting and door slamming. As she'd grown into a woman, the slamming had mostly ceased, but there had been arguments over things both large and small. Despite Helen and Zoe's various tempests, Seth had never doubted for a moment that they loved each other. The Greeks, he'd determined, lived large, embracing life with enthusiasm. Zoe had been the same way. Despite being an all-American girl, she was proud of her heritage, taking on every challenge presented to her as if she were following instructions sent down from Mount Olympus from Zeus himself.

Most of what was in the trunk was stuff he'd expected. Like yearbooks from middle school, high school and college. Although she'd framed her college diploma, she'd left her high school one behind. He supposed in her mind, there was no point in keeping it since she'd already moved on. There was also a handwritten copy of her valedictory speech. She hadn't let him read it before she'd given it, but he could see how hard she'd worked on getting every word right by all the red-lined cross-outs.

There were the inevitable prom photos. He still remembered when she'd walked into the living room in a strapless, floor-length gown of some floaty material she told him, as she'd twirled, was chiffon. The daffodil color showed off her olive complexion, and she looked exactly like a princess even before she'd put on that tiara when she'd been queen of the prom. He'd looked like a geek in the royal-blue tux, yellow vest and yellow bow tie. Although she hadn't let him see the dress beforehand, she had told him the color and instructed him that he was supposed to match.

His dad, he remembered, told him he looked like a girly boy. His mom, on the other hand, had told him he looked handsome and got a little teary as she'd straightened his tie, which was one of those snap-on things because no way was he going to learn to tie a bow tie for just one night.

He found a collection of diaries and told himself that he shouldn't look through them, but unable to resist, he picked up the first one, and leafing through it, found the movie ticket stub to *My Big Fat Greek Wedding*. While romantic comedies definitely weren't his thing, he'd figured he could see *Terminator 3*, which was playing in the theater next door, with Burke Mannion while she was at cheerleader practice.

She'd talked nearly all the way through, pointing out over-the-top stereotypes. Later, over shakes—vanilla for him, chocolate for her—at the Big Dipper, she'd turned serious, explaining that, like the bride in the movie, although she was born in Oregon and was a red, white and blue American, she'd never be able to completely abandon her family and Greek heritage. Fortunately, loving her as he did, Seth had no problem with that idea and was more than willing to do his best to fit in.

He picked up another diary decorated with stickers of Greece and titled *My Best Ever Summer Adventure*. It was, he realized, the summer of her sixteenth birthday, when her mother had sent her away to camp in Greece. As she'd explained at the time, everyone in her family had gone to Ionian Village to learn about their faith and Hellenic culture. And to meet and interact with other people just like them.

To which he'd told her there wasn't anyone else like her. Which had made her laugh and kiss him and assure him that he always knew just the right thing to say.

"Don't read it," he told himself. "Journals should be private."

Yet if her mother hadn't thought it was okay, she wouldn't have left it in the box. Right?

He turned the pages, reading how she wished she hadn't argued so much with her mother about going to what, apparently, campers shortened to IV. Because she'd always remember it as one of the most amazing times of her life. And she couldn't wait to send her own children there when they got to be her age.

He rubbed his heart, which literally ached at that thought, imagining her all bright-eyed and animated, telling people about life back home, hopefully about him, and how, although he wasn't Greek, he was a great guy, and not to worry, their kids were going to grow up to know their centuries-old heritage.

From what he read, the camp, except for the religious classes and being coed, wasn't that different from the Scout camp he'd attended here on the peninsula at Camp Parsons. There were skits, singing, campfires. There was also swimming, though the Greek campers had done theirs in the impossibly blue Ionian Sea.

One of the photos pressed into the pages of Zoe laughing with a dark-haired boy caught his attention. The boy was wearing a pair of Hawaiian Jams, and she was in a blue one-piece swimsuit that showed off all her curves. They were lying on towels on the beach, and there was another girl with them, but there was just something about the moment that had him wondering why, when she'd come home and had been going on and on about the camp, she'd never mentioned any boys.

The brochures all state that Ionian Village is where kids from all over America learn about their faith, heritage and, just as importantly, themselves, she'd written, her loopy handwriting as large and open as she was. *But I know that Mama sent me here hoping I'd meet a boy that would make me forget about Seth. Like that's ever going to happen.*

Reading that had Seth exhaling a relieved breath. He didn't want to learn about some teenage flirtation. Or even worse, that she'd cheated on him during those weeks surrounded by hot Greek guys.

But Peter has me thinking, she wrote. *Not about having sex and stuff. He hasn't even tried to kiss me. But I think he just might if I gave him a hint I'd be interested. Which I haven't. In fact, he's probably getting sick and tired of hearing all about my boyfriend back in Honeymoon Harbor.*

Seth liked that she'd been thinking about him and even talking about him to this Peter guy. Until he read the next line.

If I were to be perfectly honest, I think I'm boring everyone with Seth stories as a defense mechanism. Because who'd have thought Mom and all my aunts and uncles who were pushing me to come here could be right. I have learned a lot about myself.

I'm always going to be passionate. I'm always going to embrace life to the fullest. And I'm always going to push boundaries, especially when it comes to what women can do. Because, let's face it, Greek culture will never be accused of embracing feminism. A lot of girls here worry that their Greek boyfriends might turn into their fathers. One girl's mother doesn't even sit down at the table to eat until her husband has finished his dinner. Can you imagine? In this day and age?

So, that's one thing I'll never have to worry about.

There's also such a big focus on family unity here. Since this is all about discovering ourselves, I'll admit, just to myself, that I'm jealous of all the stories of the big, connected families that get together for every occasion. Even if it's a Saturday backyard barbecue. My immediate family consists of just me, my mom and dad, and except for not fully appreciating the desert whenever we visited the family in Tucson, I'm remembering how exciting and how much fun it was to be part of such a special group.

Maybe, after we get married and I'm through with my military service, Seth and I could move to Arizona. It's not like he's got that good a relationship with his dad anyway. And there'd be houses for him to build and work on in Tucson, right? I always thought I belonged in the Pacific Northwest, because I was born in Astoria and have always loved the green of the Olympic peninsula, but now, being here, I'm realizing how similar Greek's dry Mediterranean climate is to Tucson's. Which may explain why my mother's family settled there.

So, maybe, if I wait until the time's right, and explain all my reasons for wanting to be among more of my own, he'd understand. The same way he always seems to understand me.

Except for the huge fights we had after he learned I'd signed up for high school ROTC, because he's worried I'll decide to go into the Army and get myself killed, he's always encouraged me in everything I wanted to do. Not that I gave him much choice. Because, as I've discovered, I'm more like my mom and my aunties than I ever could have suspected. I'm stubborn, a bit spoiled, and, to be perfectly honest, I like letting off steam with a knock-down, drag-out fight.

Peter and I had one the fifth day of camp. It was over a silly thing. About Greek men being the ones to cook the meat, while women are supposed to cook every-thing else. I told him, in no uncertain terms, that he was looking at one woman who had no intention of spend-ing time standing over a hot stove. That's why God had invented restaurants.

I, of course, also pointed out that his statement was not only hopelessly outdated, but misogynistic. Which, considering himself a very feminist guy (for having been raised in a traditional Greek-American family, mind you), had us shouting back and forth, right in each oth-er's faces, until a counselor came and told us to knock it off. Then we laughed and went back to studying about the saints. He, obviously, was named for St. Peter. I'd always known I'd been named after St. Zoe. Apparently it's required for all Greeks to be named after saints, but I'd never bothered to wonder how Zoe of Rome had achieved sainthood. When I read that she'd been devoted to St. Peter and had been praying at his tomb when she was arrested for her faith, I had to tell Peter. I mean, like how weird a coincidence is that?

Seth felt his concern spike again at the latest mention of a guy he was starting to view as a rival. Which was stupid. Because Zoe had married *him*.

Reading on, he learned that according to the book of saints, St. Zoe of Rome was hung over a fire and died of smoke inhalation, after which, her body was thrown into the Tiber River. Which, Zoe continued, *probably explains why Mom has never told me the story.*

The story of his wife's saintly namesake's death caused Seth's blood to turn to ice. His mother, even before she'd gone all New Agey, had believed in stuff like fate and destiny. But Seth, who prided himself on being a practical problem solver, never had. But still, the comparison between both Zoes' deaths weirded him out.

He turned a few pages, which were thankfully Peter-free, until he got to the last day's entry.

So, we're going home and I have a lot to think about. I love Seth, with all my heart, but I know that it hurts and confuses him when we fight. While with Peter, our passion about a subject builds up and if we don't agree, we'll explode. But then it's over and we continue on, because it was just an argument. Not the end of the world. It's the same way with Mom and me. I never even minded that much that she made me take all those years of ballet. Especially since Seth always looked at me like I was a princess whenever I wore one of my sparkly tutus.

Maybe my aunties are right. Maybe I should marry a Greek boy who'd understand me better. And who'd understand how our children might inherit my temperament. Like my camp BFF, Lori, said when I told her what I was thinking, being Greek is like having a powerful virus and once you get it, you never recover. And it'll affect everything you are and do.

But on the other hand—and isn't there always an other hand?—look at Mom and Dad. They stood up to her family, which couldn't have been easy, and she even moved to Oregon to be with him and that worked out. They're still in love after all these years.

To be honest, part of me wonders if perhaps Seth should marry Brianna, who, duh, anyone with eyes can tell has a thing for him from the way she looks at him when she doesn't think anyone's looking. She probably wouldn't cause him nearly as many headaches as I might, but the truth is that I'm too selfish to give him up.

I love Seth Harper. With my entire heart, mind and soul, and although he doesn't know it yet, when I get back home to Honeymoon Harbor, I'm going to love him with my body. Because, although our life together might not be easy, it'll never be boring. I love him. So, I'll make it work. We'll make it work. Together.

Seth blew out a long breath as he closed the journal. They *had* made it work. It hadn't always been easy, because, he'd discovered, love wasn't some magic potion or talisman that promised eternal bliss. They'd fought. Loudly, as she'd written they would, and more often than he would have liked. But their fights had been over as quickly as they'd flared, and he couldn't deny that make-up sex almost made up for the arguments.

It was Zoe's passion, her zest for life, that had turned his world upside down that long-ago day she'd walked into his classroom as if she already owned it. As if she'd been some long-awaited queen of Evergreen Middle School. It was also, he knew, what would have made her such a ferocious advocate for her patients. Like that little boy in Afghanistan.

There were two other things in the journal that had proven a surprise. That she'd been considering moving to Arizona. Had she changed her mind after they'd gotten married and started to settle down in Honeymoon Harbor? Or was she waiting for the right time to bring it up? Like maybe after they'd had their first child and she'd use all her persuasive skills to convince him that their son or daughter deserved to be among family? She was right about there being houses to build and fix up in Arizona. But his home had always been here, on the peninsula. He'd never, not once, considered moving.

And what about that part about Brianna? Had she had a thing for him? Enough that if Zoe hadn't shown up at school from Astoria, he and Bri might have become a couple? He'd never had any doubt that he and Zoe would've beaten the odds, stayed together and gotten married. As they had. But what if that success had partly been because of her determination to have things turn out the way she wanted them to?

Most of their high school friends' relationships had been lucky to last a couple weeks. Long-term wasn't something that guys, especially, thought about.

Looking back on those days, he remembered Zoe had always been talking about how their life together was going to be. And since it sounded just fine with him, except for that day she'd told him that she'd decided to sign up for UW ROTC and let the Army pay for her college, he'd gone right with all her plans. Right down to the color in that nursery he'd never walked into again since the day that had forever changed his life.

That idea led to another. Brianna had dated, but she'd never been part of a couple. Because, in her own way, she'd been as focused as Zoe. All she'd ever talked about back in high school was of someday buying Herons Landing, then turning it into a B and B. Not believing that would ever happen, everyone had humored her. But later, around the time he and Zoe had gotten engaged, her goal had changed to leaving the peninsula and seeking her fortune in glamorous places around the world. Zoe, he remembered, had been all for that plan, encouraging her as best friends do.

Could Zoe have been worried about the possibilities of him straying later on, when their marriage would get bogged down with work, babies and everyday routine life, if Brianna had returned home? Which he never would have done. Ever.

He put the journal in the discard pile. Hell. He never should have given in to impulse and read it. Because now that Zoe had put Bri's possible feelings in his head, he'd be wondering if she'd had a crush, if she might possibly be thinking back on those days. And how awkward could that make their working together?

"As if," Seth muttered, causing Bandit to glance up, hopefully for another piece of pepperoni to be tossed his way, "life could get any more frigging complicated."

CHAPTER NINETEEN

Brianna spent the night chasing sleep. She tried telling herself that it was because she was in a strange room. Which couldn't be the reason because, first of all, it was her old room. She'd spent her entire life in it from the moment her parents had brought her home from the hospital until she'd left for college. Maybe the bed was too hard. Or too soft. Or maybe it was the sound of the breeze in the trees. After all, it had been years since she'd heard that soft nighttime sighing. She'd become far more accustomed to the steady drone of traffic outside her bedroom window.

It couldn't be that Seth had broken their date. It wasn't even a real date. That would make her too pitiful for words. And would make working together impossible if she didn't get her act together and put the man out of her head. He had always been, and still appeared to be, in love with his wife. Maybe someday he might meet a stranger. A woman who worked for one of those charities he contributed his time to. Or a chef from a Seattle restaurant who'd decide to move to a small town that certainly could use a high-end restaurant.

The odds of him suddenly looking up and noticing her in

a romantic way for the first time in thirty-one years had to be about the same as being struck by a meteor while walking along the waterfront. It wasn't going to happen, so despite her well-meaning family and friends suggesting otherwise, she was simply going to put any romantic thoughts of Seth Harper out of her head and consider him solely as her friend and contractor. Period.

After stopping by Cops and Coffee for a double shot to add some much-needed caffeine into her bloodstream, she wandered down to the dress shop Ethel Young had told her about. A girl with blaze-red bangs and striped blue, magenta and fluorescent green hair pulled into a high ponytail was rolling down the blue-and-white-striped awning. Her clothing—black leggings printed with spider webs, a black T-shirt that proudly proclaimed I'm the Black Sheep of the Family, and lace-up over-the-knee boots wasn't all that encouraging.

"Don't worry," the girl said, her silver nose ring and multiple ear studs sparkling in the morning sun. "I just work here. I'm not the style director." Hazel eyes, emphasized with heavy cat-eye liner and kohl shadow, swept a look over Brianna's coral shirt and white clam diggers. "Dottie's going to love dressing you. I swear to the Goddess that woman's goal in life is to get every Northwesterner looking like a unicorn vomited out rainbows."

While that was neither an appealing nor complimentary image, given what Brianna was wearing, she decided to take it as an encouraging statement rather than criticism. "Ethel Young sent me here. And Kylee Cassidy recommended it, too."

"Ethel buys a lot of stuff here," she said. "Most people in town do. Kylee gets a lot of props for her photo shoots, too. My wedding dress was from here."

"You're married?" Since she was wearing rings on every finger, including her thumbs, and two toes, the one on the fourth finger of her left hand hadn't given that fact away.

"Yeah." She held out an arm sporting a tattoo of a guy who looked like a cross between a Hells Angel and Alice Cooper. "I'm Velvet. I chose the name because it means I'm excited by change, adventure and excitement. We're also visionaries and fight being restricted by convention, as my shirt obviously points out. But we're also optimistic, energetic, intelligent and make friends easily."

Her smile was as wide as a half moon. "Thorn is my life mate. People with his name are creative, drawn to the arts and often choose careers in the limelight. That's why he's a musician. He's a wonderful man, but a little reckless with his time and money, which is why I had to put him on a budget. I may be a rebel, but we have a child coming, so we have to work on our adulting skills."

"I've never had a child, but that seems like a necessary skill," Brianna said, thinking of Kylee and Mai.

"I used to babysit my brothers and sisters, so I'm really good with kids. I'm going to be a great mom, and although Thorn was an only child who was left with nannies all the time, I know that once he gets the knack of it, he'll be great. He's already recording the playlist for our baby's birth. He's very techy and can change the songs and rhythms to match how I'm supposed to be breathing."

She splayed fingers covered in silver-and-black-striped glitter over her stomach. "We're doing natural."

"That's great." Personally, if she ever did have a child, Brianna thought that she'd rather have drugs. Lots of them. And often.

"What's your name?" Velvet asked.

Since the sign in the window showed another five minutes before the store's opening, and she was enjoying a conversation that didn't demand much back from her, Brianna responded.

"Brianna's a beautiful name," Velvet said. "It's not Goth, but it is Celtic, which is way special. Did you know it means *strong*? It also has the same psychic numerology number as Velvet, so we must be a lot alike."

"I grew up Irish Catholic. I tend to follow rules."

"So you say. But I bet you have an inner, adventurous rebel you just haven't met yet. I have a BFF who's a Celtic kitchen witch. She makes herbs that'll cure anything. Even morning sickness, which, don't worry, I checked with my ob-gyn to make sure they were safe."

"That's definitely adulting."

"Thank you. I can't tell you how relieved my parents were. But of course, they just think I'm going through a phase, because I changed my name from Madison to Velvet when I was seventeen, after I went to a Midsummer's Night Renaissance Faire. I went with friends dressed up like a tavern wench, because that was the cheapest costume I could find, but then I discovered they were having a Goth event, and although all the princess, fairy and pirate costumes were cool, Goth spoke to me in some elemental way and it still fits four years later, so I can't imagine changing. Did you ever have anything like that? Where you just know in your heart that it's where you belong?"

"Yes. I have. In my case, it's a house."

"Oh, wow!" The cat-lined eyes widened. "You're the one who's going to restore Herons Landing."

Brianna laughed, not as surprised as she might have been. "Word gets around."

"It's all everyone was talking about the other day in Cops and Coffee." She glanced at Brianna's cup. "I see you've already discovered it. I love those guys, even if, in another life, they might have wanted to take me to the gallows for witchcraft. You taking on a project like that also reveals that whatever you say about being a rule follower, you've got an adventurous streak because, like everyone's saying, you'd have to be crazy to even try a project like that. Which, thinking about it, gives you and Seth Harper a lot in common. It was obvious he loved the house when he bought it to keep it from greedy developers."

Brianna was saved from responding to any of that flurry of topics when the door opened and an apple-shaped elderly woman wearing an orange-and-yellow hibiscus-printed top with a pair of tangerine cropped pants greeted her with an even wider smile than Velvet's.

"You'd be Brianna Mannion," she said. "Ethel told me to expect you."

Of course she did.

"I've been living in Las Vegas," Brianna said, though she suspected the shop owner already knew that. "And before that, Hawaii. I haven't owned anything appropriate for the Pacific Northwest for a very long time."

"Well, you've come to the right place. I see you've already met Velvet. She's been a godsend to Doris and me. Doris is my twin sister. After nearly nine decades, she still has a tendency to play the older sister card, despite having only beat me here by four minutes. At any rate, although we didn't want to give up working when we lost our lease on the Oregon coast, we also worried whether or not, at our age, we'd be able to handle all the orders and paperwork and such that running a business entails. But then Velvet showed up. She'd just graduated with a degree in marketing from WSU and was looking for work. So, here we are. Still kicking."

She waved her into the store that, from what Brianna could tell, was divided in half, one side offering neutral colors, the other as bright as the talkative woman herself. One look at Doris, and Brianna understood the division of the store. Although they might be twins, while Dottie looked ready to take off on a Caribbean cruise, Doris could have fit easily into San Francisco, or New York. She was wearing a black twinset over tan slacks, and in contrast to the dangling shell earrings her sister was wearing, a pair of discreet but very good pearls adorned her earlobes.

"Sister, look who it is!" Dottie said. "Sarah's girl, home from the desert!"

"Ethel told us you might be dropping in. It's lovely to meet you." Doris's voice was as reserved as her clothing, but still warm, as she held out her hand. "Your mother has wonderful taste. She was the one who helped us arrange the store, which works much more efficiently than the jumble we had in our previous two locations."

"It was Sarah's idea to create zones," Dottie explained. "But the best thing is how she suggested we hang separates together, to encourage customers to mix and match between the brights and neutrals." She waved her hand, tipped with turquoise nails, at the wall displays that did, indeed, offer enough possibilities to have shoppers considering items they might have overlooked or weren't sure about pairing together.

"I like that idea. I've gotten used to colors, but thought I'd have to switch entirely back to Pacific Northwest colors. Then Mom showed me the variety of natural shades I'd always taken for granted."

"Dottie worried about giving up colors, too," Doris said. "Because most people think browns and dark greens because of the forests. And gray from the rain and fog. But we've always had a mix that reflects our disparate tastes. Your mother showed us how to display them."

"And Velvet pointed out that we were missing the wedding market," Dottie popped in. "After all, this is Honeymoon Harbor, so taking advantage of that natural customer base only makes sense. She built us a website and had us reprise our old slogan we had back in our first store in Coldwater Cove."

"You bring the groom; we'll provide the dress," Velvet said. "They were afraid it'd sound old-fashioned, like snagging a guy was still a woman's main goal, but I convinced them it was old enough to be retro."

"So, if you're ever in the market for a wedding dress, you won't have to go to Seattle or Tacoma," Dottie said. "And if we don't have what you want, Velvet can get it for you from anywhere in two shakes of a lamb's tail."

"That's handy to know." Brianna had no idea how fast a lamb shook its tail, but since she didn't foresee herself buying a wedding dress anytime soon, it didn't matter.

"This is the one Kylee chose." Velvet had gone over to an alcove that showcased the gowns and brought back a black strapless midi dress with oversize, embroidered and beaded red, yellow and purple flowers.

"It's stunning." And perfect. Trust Kylee not to go with traditional white.

"Isn't it? We ordered it from Italy. She'd met a designer on a train while traveling there and apparently swore if she got married, she was getting her gown from her."

"Mai's wearing a western-style white strapless sheath gown, with a red kimono sash embroidered with gold butterflies that falls down her back, instead of a train." Dottie reached beneath a shelf and brought out a sketched design. "In Japan, apparently it's traditional for brides to wear white for the ceremony, then change into red for the reception. So, wanting to be modern, but also wanting to pay homage to all the women in her family who were married in the traditional style, she decided to embrace both looks in one dress. We're having this custom-made by a seamstress we work with."

"It's beautiful." Which was a wild understatement. "My mother told me they were carrying red and yellow tulips from Blue House Farm," Brianna remembered. "These will be perfect."

"Won't they? It's going to be a lovely wedding," Velvet said. "Thorn is playing."

"They booked a rock band?" Somehow Kylee had forgotten to mention that part when talking about her upcoming wedding.

"Oh, no." Velvet laughed. "He graduated from the famous Berklee school of music in Boston. He can play anything. In fact, he did a chamber music gig last weekend in Tacoma. He and Kylee have been working on the playlists for weeks. It's going to be a nice mix of a bit of everything."

"I'll be needing a dress."

"Of course. Kylee will want you to go with whatever you like," Dottie said.

"But we can show you what the other two girls chose," Doris suggested. "I think the style would suit you well."

She turned the pages to a dress with short capped sleeves, a tightly fitted bodice and a shirred skirt that flared out just above the knees.

"Chelsea chose purple because it works so well with her hair. Amanda went with yellow, which is a hard color to pull off, but with her coloring it works. I think red would be very flattering with your hair."

"Red always stands out," Brianna demurred. "I'd feel conspicuous, and although no one can outshine Kylee, it doesn't feel right on her special day."

"How about this?" Dottie jumped in, pulling out a swatch of material. "This deep blue will be amazing with your hair and eyes. I swear, when all you girls get together, it's going to look like a garden sprung up in their backyard."

"Which already has a pretty special garden." Brianna ran her hand over the piece of silk and decided that Dottie and Dorothy arriving in town must've seemed like a godsend to all the women in Honeymoon Harbor.

"Oh, so you've seen the house?" Doris asked.

"Yesterday. I love everything about it, including the landscaping. I've organized a lot of hotel weddings, but from what I've heard, this is going to top them all."

"Oh, it's going to be beautiful. Seth did such an amazing job on the house. It reminds me of something from a fairy tale," Doris said, revealing an inner romantic Brianna wouldn't have guessed was hiding inside her.

"Seth did an amazing job," Dottie echoed. "He's going to be a member of the wedding party."

"Oh?" Brianna did her best to hide her surprise, even as she wondered why he'd left out that salient fact.

"Well, it's only right, given how close they've all become. And it'll be good to see him have something to celebrate," Doris said. "It's been painful watching him grieve."

"I still miss my Harold." Dottie put a hand over her heart. "He passed last year when a brain aneurysm we didn't even realize he had burst. I wasn't there, but his pickleball partner told the EMTs that he was running to return a serve, then just collapsed. And that was it."

"I'm so sorry."

"So was I. Especially since I felt guilty for not having been there when it happened. Fortunately, I had Doris and Hayden, Harold's twin brother, to lean on. It was Doris's idea that we open this shop. She thought I needed a new challenge." Eyes that had moistened brightened. "And she was right. Then Velvet and Thorn joined our little family, and now it's going to be like we're having a grandchild."

"Since my parents are still in Spokane, and Thorn's snooty, uptight parents don't approve of our lifestyle, you're going to be the *main* grandparents," Velvet assured them, gathering them into a group hug that Brianna could tell invaded Doris's personal space a bit more than she would have liked, but the elderly woman was kind enough to join in.

"I love this dress," she said. "I don't usually wear jewel tones, but I think this will work."

"It'll be fabulous," Dottie assured her.

"And elegant," Doris said.

"You'll rock the garden," Velvet assured her.

Getting down to business, the sisters fluttered around the shop like sandpipers skittering along the waterline, gathering up clothing from display racks. Doris, unsurprisingly, chose taupe, black and cream, while Dottie dove into the bright hues and floral prints. While they had her down to her underwear, they also measured her for the dress that would be custom-made by a local seamstress.

Nearly an hour later, longer than Brianna had ever spent shopping, she was wearing a pair of cropped khaki pants, a T-shirt with a bright blue heron printed on the front and a pair of blue-and-fluorescent-green tweed sneakers.

"We just got that shirt in yesterday afternoon," Dottie told her as she cut off the tag.

"Which is prophetic," Velvet claimed. "It's absolutely a sign that you were meant to be living in Herons Landing."

Just as she'd never believed in the ghost, despite her Irish heritage, Brianna had never been much for prophecies and other woo-woo ideas. But as she left the shop with bags bearing the store's dancing deer logo filled with jeans, shirts and several of the Pacific Northwest's ubiquitous hoodies, all in various weights designed for layering, and a scarlet red slicker, she decided she liked that idea. A lot.

CHAPTER TWENTY

Seth arrived at Kylee and Mai's house before his father. Deciding his old man must've gone fishing—he'd been talking about wanting to get out on the rivers and it wasn't as if he was needed today—he walked through the rooms one last time, making sure everything was in order. Which it was. All it needed now was a final cleaning and polish, which was about to happen when the bright blue Highlander with The Clean Team written on it pulled up outside.

Megan Larson, who'd been a couple years behind him in school, jumped out, wearing a T-shirt with her business's logo on the front and a pair of crisply pressed jeans.

"So, you finished ahead of schedule," she said as she popped open the back of the Highlander and began pulling out a bucket, mop and various other tools. "Never thought that would happen."

"You doubted me?"

"Not you," she said. "But I've watched Kylee and Mai in action just choosing what movie to go to while standing in line. I figured you'd spend a third of your time in negotiations."

"They were great clients."

She laughed at that. "I'll bet you say that about everyone."

"Of course I do." He helped her get the rest of the stuff out of the SUV. A toddler's car seat was strapped down in the back seat. At the moment it was being used to hold a mesh bag of microrags.

Megan had dated Gabe for a few weeks, but since his goal had always been New York City, she'd ended up marrying a local guy shortly after high school. Jake Larson seemed to spend a lot of time at the casino while she'd attended Clearwater CC, taking business courses, because it was obvious that her husband, who was always into some crazy get-rich scheme he'd read about on the internet, was not going to be able to support a family on his own. Or at all.

She'd been three months pregnant when Jake had left town with the female partner in his latest venture, flipping houses after he'd cleaned out their savings account and maxed out their credit cards paying for seminars assuring him that he and his partner/lover would be the next HGTV stars. Leaving Megan with an empty bank account and creditors calling day and night until Quinn, who was still licensed to practice law in Washington, had written a cease-and-desist letter for what had been harassment. He'd also used some legal eagle stuff to extricate her from the expenses Jake had taken on after he'd run off, and he handled her divorce pro bono.

Megan had moved back in with her parents, and from what he'd seen, she was a lot happier than she'd been when married to the dickwad.

"I'm lucky that all my clients are good ones," she said. "The ones who aren't, I fire because they're not worth the effort, you know?"

"I definitely know that." Looking back on it, there'd been something sketchy about both couples who'd bailed on Herons Landing. But at the time he'd been so eager to get his hands on the house that he hadn't paid enough attention to those inner alarm bells. He glanced around as he took the mop and a bucket stuffed with cleaning supplies from her. "Are you on your own today?" She ran a tight ship of five employees, was always on time and left a finished project so clean you could probably perform surgery on any of the floors or counters.

"Betty's coming right after she gets back from taking her mom to the doctor for her annual exam. But, unlike some contractors on the peninsula, you leave a house so clean, I could've polished it up by myself."

They both turned as Brianna's convertible pulled into the driveway. She jumped out, dressed more like the native she was in a T-shirt, khakis and a pair of bright sneakers that suggested she'd paid a visit to the Dancing Deer.

"I thought we were meeting at your place," he said, trying not to notice how her breasts bounced beneath that gray shirt as she ran over to them.

"We are. I was just passing by and saw the truck, and…" She paused, narrowed her eyes. "Megan?"

"About time you made it home," Megan said. "I heard you'd come back and hired our local hunk with a tool belt to fix up that old haunted house."

"Geez," Seth complained.

"If you're going to have to deal with all the hassles of remodeling, it's a plus to have a good-looking hottie to watch hammering and other building guy stuff." She flashed Seth a smile. "And you don't have to look so embarrassed. You know you're hotter than Sven Olson, who's the only other contractor in town."

"I hope so. Sven's thirty years older." And was bald with a beer gut.

"Age doesn't necessarily matter," Megan said. "I'd do George Clooney in a heartbeat."

"He's married. And a father of twins," Seth pointed out.

"True. But since the chances of me ever having an opportunity with the guy are slim to none, if you don't mind, I'm going to overlook the wife and kids in order to maintain a good fantasy life."

If there was one thing Seth didn't want to talk about, it was any woman's fantasy life.

"So, you saw the truck, and…?" he asked Brianna, trying to steer the direction back to the original topic.

"I thought I'd stop and talk to whoever it belonged to. I don't mind changing beds and cleaning bathrooms, but I realized that if I want any kind of life that doesn't revolve totally around business, I'm going to need someone to do a deeper clean, probably once a week."

"Well, you're in luck. Because I'm your girl," Megan jumped in. "And you don't have to worry about it being such a big place, because I have five women working for me now, so there will be no problem handling it. You're going to be a B and B, right?"

"Right."

"In the middle of the day guests will be mostly out and about, which means we won't be disturbing them. I'll wait to give you an actual quote until I see how many rooms you and Tool Guy here end up with, but I think you'll find me reasonable."

"The Clean Team is the best on the peninsula," Seth said. "Probably the state."

"Make that the entire Pacific Coast, and you won't get any disagreement from me," Megan said with a bold, strong laugh. Then turned thoughtful. "Do you think you could use any help with the daily stuff? Like dusting, making those beds you were talking about, light housekeeping?"

"I might. Especially in the beginning because although I grew up cooking with Mom, I think I've got a pretty big learning curve ahead of me turning out a B and B worthy breakfast for a crowd."

"I sure as hell couldn't pull off it off," Megan said. "Then again, I figure that's what Cops and Coffee's for. Anyway, I know a girl who's attending the college and needs to make some extra money. She couldn't commit to what I needed because one of the reasons I keep everyone happy is that I've got all my employees and jobs tightly scheduled. But if you were willing to let her be flexible during the week, working around her classes, it could turn out to be a good deal for both of you."

"That sounds appealing," Brianna said, reaching into her pocket and pulling out one of the brand-new business cards she'd gotten on her trip to Seattle. "Let me give it some thought. Meanwhile, if you can fit in a project as big as Herons Landing, that would be great."

"I'll fit it in if I have to hire more people." Megan pocketed the card and handed Brianna one of her own. "Not only have I always loved that place, taking care of it would be a feather in my cap and undoubtedly draw in even more business."

"Super. What a lucky coincidence to run into you." She turned toward Seth. "I'll meet you over there in about ten, fifteen minutes?"

"Works for me," he agreed. "I'm pretty much finished up here." He took a spare key off his ring. "Just lock up when you're done," he told Megan. "And thanks a bunch."

"Thank you," she said. "I always love doing your homes. They're like polishing up a jewel box." She looked over at Brianna, then back at him. Then back at Brianna. "That poor house has been through so much. But now that you've come back home, all the problems were leading up to you two working together. I know you're going to do amazing things together."

As color drifted into Brianna's cheeks, Seth wondered if she could possibly be contemplating some of the amazing things he'd been dreaming about.

Which then had him wondering, what would happen if she had been?

He'd locked his emotions in a deep freeze for over two years. But now, as he watched her walk back to her convertible, Seth could feel the ice melting.

"I want Herons Landing to feel like a sanctuary," Brianna said as she and Seth entered her house. And didn't that just give her a thrill, thinking that, after all these years, it truly was *her* house? "People will be coming here to get away from their daily lives. So, they should feel any stress they're carrying just melt away the minute they walk in the door." She heard the familiar sound announcing the arrival of the ferry.

"Of course, I'm lucky to have a head start," she said. "I was excited and admittedly a bit apprehensive about taking this on, but coming over here on the ferry, looking at the water and mountains, just made anything seem possible."

"It can be like going back in time," Seth agreed. "Which can admittedly get a little frustrating when you're in a hurry."

"That hurrying part of life is what I want my guests to forget." She walked into where they'd planned the kitchen to be. "Mom says that our gray skies and evergreens bring out green and blue tones in colors. So she suggested balancing soft but warm whites and grays in the cabinetry and wall colors. Mixing cool and warms."

"Definitely make a difference from the deeper colors the original owners would have had."

"I love Victorian homes," Brianna said. "But I have to admit that all the oversize furniture, ornaments, heavy drapes, lace and dark colors would have been overly depressing." Her Girl Scout camp had toured one of the local Victorians back when she'd been in middle school, a few months before Zoe had arrived, and even then, although she'd come to understand many people found the interior style comforting and elegant, it had given her claustrophobia.

"I've been studying kitchens on Pinterest."

"Of course you have." There was something in his tone that had her glancing up from where she'd been imagining an island. Something not at all positive.

"There are a lot of good ideas there," she said.

"I know." He dragged a hand through his hair. "Zoe bombarded me with links to photos when I was fixing up our place while she was in Afghanistan."

Damn. Brianna had accepted that having feelings for her old crush could be a problem. But not if she kept her thoughts and emotions to herself. If she stayed professional, he'd never have a clue and they'd be able to work together as a team.

But already the simplest topic was turning out to be a conversational minefield. And wasn't that a horrible metaphor considering what had happened to the person who'd always been at the center of their triangle?

"We have to talk about it," she said.

"I thought we were." Seth jammed his hands into the front pockets of his jeans and glanced around. "Blending warm and cool tones to balance the greens and blues. Got it."

"Not the color palette. Though yes, it's going to be important. But we have to be okay about working together."

"We've already agreed on that."

"In principle. But you can't deny that the reality is already turning out to be more difficult." When he failed to respond to that comment, Brianna decided this was no time for polite evasion and beating around bushes. "How are you doing? Honestly?"

"I told you, we're crazy busy. I have volunteer work I enjoy and that keeps me out of trouble. I talk with your brother every night, and visit my in-laws every week, which isn't going to be happening anymore because they're leaving for Arizona."

"That's a surprise."

"Yeah. I wasn't expecting it, either. Helen's brother turned his restaurant over to one of his kids, so now he and his wife and Helen and Dave are going to be spending their retirement traveling."

"How do you feel about that?"

He shrugged. "It's their life. I just want them to be happy. And it's not like I can't find another way to spend those nights. The truth is, the last year I've turned down a lot more jobs than I've taken on."

"That's a list of what you *do*," she pointed out. "Not *how* you're doing."

He gave her another of those long looks. "Dumping personal stuff on you could get in the way between us. Maybe even screw up work."

"Or make it easier, because working as closely as we'll be is going to require honesty on both our parts. But that's not why I asked. I asked because Zoe was my friend. I loved her, too, Seth. And I care how you're doing because she loved you."

"Okay." He rubbed the back of his neck. Rolled his shoulders, then looked up at the ceiling she'd been picturing covered with a warm white beadboard, as if seeking answers. Which apparently didn't come, because he took a deep breath, blew it out and cursed.

"The truth is, I'm fucked up. Everyone keeps telling me it'll get better with time. But what the hell do they know? It's been two years, and sometimes, when I'm out washing my truck, or Zoe's car—"

"You kept her car?"

She saw his jaw clench. "Yeah." His hard look asked her if she had a problem with that.

"It's a cute car. I love the red. And I'm sorry for interrupting." And wasn't that an understatement? She was trying to help here. Not criticize his life choices. "What about when you're out washing it?"

"Not always, but sometimes I see the notification officers walking up. Just like that day."

"A flashback."

"Yeah. I guess. But it seems real. Like that *Groundhog Day* movie. Which, since you're asking for honesty, is pretty much what my life's become. But without the romantic ending."

"I can understand how routine could be helpful, but also keep you stuck in time. Maybe you should try therapy. Do you think seeing them could be a sign of PTSD?"

Another mistake from the flash of anger, and something else in his dark eyes. "I went to a therapy group and hated it because all anyone wanted to talk about was feelings. Because PTSD doesn't happen to guys who remodel houses. It happens to men and women who put themselves through hell so the rest of us can stay home eating burgers, drinking craft beer and living our lives without worrying about being blown to bits at any moment."

Oh, wow. There was more than pain and anger here.

"You're feeling guilty."

"Wouldn't you?"

She managed a faint smile at that. "I'm Catholic. Guilt is in my blood. Like a virus."

She watched as his shoulders relaxed. Ever so slightly. "Zoe wrote that in her journal. Not the guilt thing, but about being Greek. It was a journal I didn't know about. One she'd written while away at that Greek summer camp her parents sent her to."

"I remember that. She came home and said she'd had a great time." But she'd been unusually quiet for a couple weeks afterward, Brianna remembered now. "Did you find the journal after she, well…"

"Helen asked me to go through her stuff and see what I wanted to keep," he said, saving her from having to say that horribly fatal word.

"That couldn't have been easy." How about terrible?

"No shit, Sherlock." He shook his head. Took off his Harper Construction cap and swept his fingers through his hair. "Sorry."

"You don't have to apologize." This was about him. Not her. She might not be able to hammer a nail into a two-by-four. She might not be able to hang Sheetrock or tile a roof. And she definitely couldn't bring his wife and her friend back. But she'd always had a talent for soothing troubled waters. Which, hopefully, she *could* do for him.

"I should have been there. In the war," he said.

Deciding that using soft soap wasn't the way to get through this conversation, Brianna opted for bluntness. "And how would that have changed the outcome? When she'd have still gone into the Army?"

"She wouldn't have had to. I would've sent money home for her to go to school."

"She'd already determined to do it her way. And we both know that when Zoe got an idea into her head, there was no changing it."

"She said that in her journal. But it's a husband's job to protect his wife."

"Even if you *had* been in the Army, even if, by some miraculous chain of events, you'd been in that Kabul hospital, you couldn't have protected her from what happened. The only thing that might have changed is that your parents would've lost their only son and your mother would have a gold star hanging in *her* window."

He gave her a hard look. "You're tough."

"I guess I am." Even knowing her skills of persuasion, Brianna was a bit surprised to discover that she could be. She'd always been a soother, not a fighter. "About people I care about… You were telling me about how angry it makes you when people tell you it gets better with time."

"Yeah, I guess I was. Which, by the way, your brother doesn't do, so I appreciate that along with the burgers and beer. But FYI, they're flat out wrong because it's not getting any better. It's all I can do to drag myself through the day. If I hadn't had people counting on me to finish their jobs, I just might have said the hell with it all—"

Alarm shot through her. "Are you suggesting—"

"No." He shook his head. Closed his eyes for a moment. Brianna could almost envision the word cloud swirling above his head as he carefully sorted out his emotions, choosing ones to most safely frame his response.

"I'm not going to say there weren't weeks, even months, when it was tempting," he admitted. "In the beginning. But I knew Zoe would never forgive me." Brianna was not surprised that she'd be his first reason. Zoe Robinson had always been first place both in his mind and heart. And probably always would be, she reminded herself firmly.

"I could also see, even from the bottom of the pit I was in, that I'd break my mom's heart if I took the easy way out, and there's no way I'd ever do that."

"And now?"

"Now I don't think about it. Or talk about it, even with your brother, because, well…"

"He's a guy," she guessed, even as she knew Quinn, especially, would be an empathetic listener.

"Yeah. And since my mom's going through her own problems right now, there's no way I'm going to dump more family drama stuff on her. And then there's Kylee and Mai, who are counting on me to finish their house for their wedding. Which I just did."

"And yay for you for that. Especially since while you were

doing that, I bought a dress for the wedding. And, bringing out my inner tough girl, I'm telling you that it would tick me off if I couldn't wear it because you decided to commit suicide, which would result in the wedding being called off, which, in turn, could cause Kylee and Mai to lose their chances of adopting, which would then result in some child not being able to grow up in a loving family."

"Wow. Not only did you use the forbidden S word everyone has been tiptoeing around, you also played the guilt card."

She folded her arms. "No one plays the guilt card better than we Catholics do. We've had a lifetime of practice."

"Now you're being smug."

She opened her eyes wide. Splayed a hand across her chest. "Who? Me? Smug?"

"Yeah. Tough and smug, though if you're serious about staying—"

"I opened a construction account at the bank today, so I'd say I definitely am."

"Then you could be right about getting things between us out in the open."

"That's always better than keeping stuff inside," she said without hesitation. "And feel free to dump on me whenever you want without worrying about it getting in the way of working together. When I came up with the idea of coming home, I automatically pictured you doing the work. It never occurred to me to hire anyone else."

"Because Harper Construction is the best restoration contractor in the state." The spark of pride gave her hope that things weren't as dire as they sounded. "Though there is this guy, Lucas Chaffee, down on the Oregon Coast, who's good," he tacked on.

"Who's not as good as you."

That drew a faint smile, although his eyes remained so,

so sad. "We've never competed head-to-head in any kind of build-off, so I guess we'll never know. For sure."

"I've got the man I want." And always had, not that still being drawn to him was at all appropriate right now. Especially after what he'd just told her about how much pain he was still carrying. Grief, she thought, remembering the elderly lady with her husband's ashes, took its own time to overcome. "And I'm sorry I've been such a bad friend."

"How?"

"I always thought of Zoe as my best friend," Brianna said. "But you two were a pair for so many years that she would have wanted me to have been there more for you. I'd like to say I figured you had male friends to make up for your loss, but having four brothers, I should've realized that guys don't talk about personal stuff like women do. If you and I had kept in touch better, we could have had this conversation sooner."

Sooner and, if necessary, often. She'd long given up on the dream of Seth ever loving her. But she could have helped him.

"I probably wouldn't have been ready before," he admitted.

"And now?"

"I guess I am. But I do have one question."

"Okay."

"Did you ever have a thing for me?"

"What?" The question had hit like a bolt of lightning from the clear blue sky. At the same time, although she wasn't about to complicate things by admitting to that, lying would be hypocritical after insisting he be honest. So Brianna did the only thing she could think of while an icy fog rolled through her mind. She hedged.

"I doubt there was a girl in Honeymoon Harbor that didn't have a *thing* for you sometime growing up."

"Seriously?"

She laughed at his surprise. "Seriously. Partly because you

looked so hot in those shoulder pads and tight football pants. I guess you were too starry-eyed over Zoe to notice."

He blinked. Slowly. Once. Twice. A third time, reminding Brianna of the great horned owl her brother Aiden had once found with a broken wing. He'd risked his hand being mangled to wrap it in his sleeping bag, then taken it to the Northwest Raptor and Wildlife Sanctuary, where he and Brianna had visited every day until the owl healed and was sent back into the woods.

"You could've probably had any girl at Honeymoon Harbor High. But we all knew that you and Zoe were a perfect match." They'd moved through high school and even Zoe's college years as if they lived in their own bubble of happiness.

"No relationship is perfect," he countered. "But I loved her."

"There's not a person in Honeymoon Harbor who doesn't know that. And no one will judge you when you decide to move on with your life."

"It'd probably get a lot of people off my back," he said. "But I'm not in the market for a new relationship. You realize with all the time we'll be spending together, they might start talking about us as possibly being a couple."

"You must've worked with other women clients."

"Sure. But most of them have been married. Or older. You're single. And sexy."

Wasn't he full of surprises today? She glanced down at her shirt, khaki pants and sneakers. "You think?"

"Yeah. I do. But you don't have to worry, because I'm not sixteen. I can control my hormones."

She'd wanted to know how he was doing. To comfort him. How on earth had they gotten on hormones? "Um. That's good to know. I guess."

He lifted a brow. "You guess?"

She was not having this conversation. Not until she had

time to sort it through. Brianna was not an impulsive person. She was thoughtful. She planned. Even though her idea to buy Herons Landing seemed like a spur-of-the-moment thing, she'd fantasized about it most of her life. And look, she was spending hours fussing over color palettes, instead of, as her mother kept suggesting, going with her instincts.

Which right now were telling her to jump Seth Harper and find out exactly how sexy she was.

Wrong choice. Wasn't it?

"I think it's best we just get back to work," she said, suddenly realizing that as they'd been talking, they'd been inching forward until the toes of her new turquoise-and-lime-green shoes were nearly touching the toes of his scuffed work boots. He was not only in jumping range, all she'd have to do was go up on her toes, just the least little bit, and press her lips against his, and...

Do. Not. Go. There.

"Work," she reminded them both before things got dangerous. "So, I was reading about kitchens. And what colors stimulate appetites. Turns out they're red, yellow and orange."

"So, you're planning to open a McDonald's in Herons Landing?"

She laughed, relieved to see that he'd lightened up, and hoped that she might have had something to do with his change of mood. "No. And although my stove actually comes in red, orange or yellow, I opted for the Provence blue. Many more formal restaurants use that color because it's calming."

"It seems you'd want people eager to start out their vacation adventures, rather than hang around the house all day."

"I do. But not everyone's a morning person, so I want to ease them into their day." She reached into the case she'd put next to the blueprints on the plywood board balanced across two sawhorses. "I was considering sage green, but I'm so in

love with the color of the stove, I decided to go with a blu-
ish gray for the cabinets."

"That'll work with the water and fog," he said, looking
at her paint chip and the brochure for the range. "And I can
see how it'd be soothing. But during the winter it could get
a bit depressing."

"That's why I decided to do this white subway tile," she
said, pulling out a piece. "I was thinking of doing it in a her-
ringbone pattern, but that costs more because it uses more tile
and might look busy. So I went with this one with a wavy
edge for interest. It's popular now, which could risk it becoming trendy, but it should be okay because it also dates back
to New York subway tiles in the early 1900s, which makes
it a classic."

"You're going to do all the walls in tile?"

The doubt in his tone confirmed that Seth was more than
a builder. That he had a visionary eye. "No, that'd be too
hard and cold. I was thinking either a creamy white shiplap,
or painting one wall yellow."

"The shiplap, if you're going with the ceiling beadboard
like Kylee and Mai's, would be a lot of wood."

"You're right. Then it's yellow. But not obnoxious fast-food
yellow, but a soft, pale shade to brighten up gray days." She
pulled out another paint chip and held it up to the one for the
cabinets. "I was going to go with all white dishes, but now
that I've chosen this, I think I'll have you put in some open
shelves and I can use some blue-and-white plates."

She could tell she'd lost him with that when he merely said,
"Sounds great." Then studied the brochure she'd put on the
plywood. "That's one helluva big stove."

"Fifty-five inches," she agreed. "But we've room, so why
not use it? I thought we could have this space over here—"
she tapped on the blueprint "—for a marble slab for rolling

out dough. And a wooden countertop next to the sink for cutting fruits and vegetables."

"We can do that."

There was a lot of back and forth, but she didn't mind because he knew the construction end of it, and she knew, with help from her mom, how she wanted the kitchen to look and function. The oven was, admittedly, a luxury, as was the matching hood, but she'd fallen in love with it and knew that it would make her happy every time she walked into her kitchen. Once again, she compared the satisfaction she'd felt in her old job with the exciting expectations of this renovation. She wasn't so naive not to think there'd be unwelcome surprises and setbacks. She had, after all, watched all those HGTV makeover programs.

Besides, all those renovation challenges would be worth it. They'd also require her mind to stay fully engaged on the house, which in turn should keep her suddenly mutinous lady parts in check.

Or so Brianna told herself.

CHAPTER TWENTY-ONE

Two hours later, Seth had made enough pencil sketches that they'd decided they were pretty much finished.

"I love the idea of the second butler's pantry," she said. "I can do a lot of food prep there that'll keep the kitchen area looking tidier. And the walk-in pantry is, I swear, nearly the size of my Las Vegas apartment." That was, admittedly, an exaggeration. But not by much. Not that she'd minded since she'd spent so little time there.

"It's going to be great." He hooked his hands in his belt loops and looked around as if imagining the room completed. "Better than great. You get photos up on that website of yours and you'll be drawing folks from all over the country. And beyond. I can imagine some French couple going gaga over that stove."

"And you thought I was being extravagant."

"I never said that. It's your money. Your business. Your stove. Which *is* pretty damn special. If you don't mind, I'm going to want to put it in our online portfolio."

"I'd be proud."

"Great… Well."

A little silence fell between them. Now that they'd settled that work issue, whatever personal feelings that had zinged between them was back. In spades.

"I like that shirt," he said.

"Thanks." She lifted a hand to the V-neckline and was glad he couldn't feel how her pulse was jumping at the way he was looking at her. "Dottie and Doris gave me the name of the artist who silkscreened it. He's in Port Townsend. I emailed him and asked if he'd be willing to reproduce the same image, but with Herons Landing written above it, and Honeymoon Harbor below. I could sell them here, in a little gift shop area—"

"The guys at Cops and Coffee seem to do well with theirs."

"I can attest to that." She lifted the travel mug with the shop's logo she'd bought just this morning. "The twins at the Dancing Deer said they'd put them in their shop, too. Which got me thinking about how many local artists and artisans we have here."

"Enough that your uncle's got a list of people waiting for him to finish that second floor work space."

"Which means I should talk to him about freeing up some additional room on the street level. The gallery could offer more high-end items, while the other space could sell more souvenir-type things. I ran into your mom as I was leaving the Dancing Deer and she agreed the two spaces could complement each other, drawing customers back and forth."

"From what I saw, she wouldn't have any problem convincing Mike of anything."

"I'm sorry. I was so enthusiastic about the idea, I forgot how it'd be one more complication in your life."

"Their life," he reiterated. "Between you and me, I think right now Mike and Mom are just friends. I'm pretty sure she wants to stay married. She just wants some changes."

"She's got her work cut out for her. But then again, she's

like my mother. I can't imagine her not succeeding in whatever she puts her mind to."

"It's up to Dad," he said. "Speaking of whom, if we've done enough for today, I'd like to run by his place and check on him. He didn't show up at the cottage this morning and he's not answering his phone."

"Did you try texting?"

"He refuses to text."

"Oh… Well, he *is* sixty."

"My grandmother—his mother—texts several times a day from her assisted-living apartment to fill me in on all the gossip and intrigue that goes on in the rec and dining rooms. And she's eighty-nine. It's more a case of him not liking change.

"I've been thinking about you," he surprised her by saying as they walked out of the house. His back was to her as he locked up.

"About the job?"

"No." He turned around, pocketed the key and looked directly into her face. "About *you*. In a way that's not at all job-related. But personal."

"Oh." Her rebellious heart took a hopeful leap. "Like friends personal?" she asked as Bandit came loping up with that ratty ball again.

He shook his head. "More than that… Damn." He picked up the ball and threw it far enough to put a runner out at second base if they'd been standing in a batter's box. It landed in a bunch of scrub trees and bushes, buying them more time. "I've also dreamed about you."

"Me, too. About you." No point in adding that those dreams hadn't only been lately.

"Well." He blew out a breath. "We should probably talk about it."

Well, her plan for keeping the naughty lady parts, which had leaped up at the mention of dreams, in check certainly hadn't held up long. Brianna had spent nearly all day, every day of her life talking. It had been her job. One she'd done well. She'd dealt with people experiencing all ranges of emotions, and would probably go back to doing exactly the same once Herons Landing opened. But for now...

"Or we could just give it a test," she suggested.

His chocolate eyes darkened, which made the gold flecks seem brighter. "What are you thinking?"

"That sometimes reality doesn't live up to the dream. Or any fantasy. So maybe we should just see, to get the wondering over with." Throwing caution to the winds, she went up on the toes of her new shoes and lifted her lips to his.

It was just a soft, gentle press of lips. Beyond what friends might share, but certainly not anything even R-rated. Even so, she felt her heart nearly stop with the sheer perfection of the kiss she'd waited a lifetime for.

It didn't last long. There wasn't any tongue tangling or lip nicking. But the scrape of his afternoon beard had her tingling and wanting more. Much, much more.

But then he leaned back, looking down at her, his hands on her shoulders. To push her away? Or pull her closer.

"Again," he said.

"Yes," she said on a shuddering, relieved sigh.

His hands moved from her shoulders to cup her face, and this time, as she parted her lips, his tongue brushed against hers. He tasted of dark coffee and, yes, although he might not be ready to admit it yet, desire. His palms and fingertips, so rough, yet tender, were beyond what she imagined. She wanted to feel them everywhere. In all those places that were already heating up.

As she breathed in the aromas of pine-scented soap, of sweat, the salt she tasted when she broke contact just long enough to kiss his dark neck, Brianna wanted to feel him all over. She wanted to run her hands across those wide, strong shoulders that had carried so many burdens for so long. She wanted to rip open his shirt, like some daring heroine in one of those historical novels she devoured like crack, and trace those solid muscles she could feel beneath his shirt. She wanted to rip away his belt, unfasten the buttons on those faded, torn jeans and…then, no!…he'd pulled away again.

Seth had felt the heat change from a simmer to a flash as hot as the forest fires he'd once fought to earn extra money during the summer fire season. Hotter than your average bonfire, it was a flat-out conflagration capable of incinerating them both.

He'd known he was in trouble when he'd realized that somehow, without remembering moving, they'd been standing so close together. Told himself that he should have backed away when she'd first lifted her mouth to his. Though, to be honest, he'd passed that point when he'd read her intention in those wide blue eyes.

Late afternoon clouds had begun to gather over the still snowy mountaintops, chilling the air as it descended through the town and over the water, causing a cooling fog to rise. Yet inside Seth, heat flared, and as his tongue thrust through her open lips, he knew her shiver had nothing to do with the drop in temperature.

He'd felt as if he were standing on the summit of ice-clad Mount Olympus. One false step and he'd fall the nearly eight thousand feet, crashing over rocks down to Honeymoon Harbor's sea level. While he was busy concentrating on breathing, other, long-neglected body parts had kicked in and were demanding attention.

One more minute, he told himself as he wrapped his arms around her and pulled her tight against him, breast to thigh. Just one more minute of this pleasure he'd forgotten. The glory of a woman's taste, of her breasts pressed against his chest, of her thighs against his, of, hot damn, a raw, sexual hunger he'd buried deep inside him, which had suddenly roared to life.

He tangled his fingers in the silk of her hair, imagined it against his thighs and realized that they were on the verge of doing something they could end up regretting. Which was why, even as she wrapped one long leg around his, rubbing against him in a way that had them in danger of spontaneous combustion, even though it took every ounce of self-control he possessed, he took hold of her shoulders and eased them apart. Again.

"We need to think about this."

"My brain may be a bit fogged at the moment, but I thought we'd agreed that we both *had* been thinking about it."

"True. But now that we've conducted your test, I'm thinking that maybe we're moving too fast."

"We've known each other forever."

"As friends, like you said. I don't want to screw that up. Especially when we're working together. Also, I need to be straight with you. I haven't had sex with anyone for nearly three years."

"Not for the lack of opportunity, I suspect."

"No." He'd been surprised how being widowed had seemingly moved him to the top of some eligible males of Honeymoon Harbor list. When he'd mentioned that once, in a rare open moment to Quinn, Brianna's brother had pointed out that he'd already proven himself to be good husband material. Therefore, he could be considered a catch.

When he'd admitted that it wasn't just single women who'd made it clear that they wouldn't mind taking a tumble with him, Quinn had just shaken his head, given him an "Are you nuts?" look and asked him if he'd happened to look in a mirror lately. And, although Quinn couldn't figure it out, women seemed to go for guys in tool belts. Maybe, he'd mused, the low-slung leather belts reminded them of gunslingers in all those old Western movies.

Which was when they'd both decided that the Mars and Venus deal was totally true.

"I've had my opportunities," he admitted. "But you know this town. Word gets around. One of the reasons why, if you and I did try being a couple, it would be awkward after the breakup."

"Which implies number one—" she held up a finger "—that you're assuming we'd even become a couple, and—" another finger "—that if we did, you expect we'd break up."

"I'm not going to remarry." Seth might not be entirely clear what was happening between Brianna and him, but that was one thing he damn well knew for certain.

"Not ever?"

"No."

"Because Zoe was your soul mate?"

His reasons were more complicated than that. But this was neither the time nor place to get into it. If he were lucky, she'd decide he was a lost cause, fall for some other Honeymoon Harbor guy, like Dan Matthew, who made a good living as a sports fishing guide, or Cam Montgomery, Bandit's vet, and they could go back to being the kind of friends they were in the old days. Before that sunny spring afternoon his world had stopped turning.

"Yeah, that," he said. Zoe had always claimed they were soul mates, and he'd never had any reason to believe it wasn't true. They'd fit. Not perfectly, but what marriage was ever perfect? Besides, perfection could become boring. And, as he'd learned in the building business, while it might be a nice ideal, it was impossible to achieve.

"I didn't mean to hurt your feelings," he said as a frown came into her eyes and her lips, which he could still taste, turned down.

"You didn't," she assured him even as her eyes said otherwise. "Did you hear me saying I wanted to get married?"

"No." He folded his arms.

"Although that kiss was off the Richter scale, I agree we should think things through. I'm nothing like Zoe. In fact, you could probably consider me the anti-Zoe. I always thought one of the reasons she and I were friends was because we were so different. I'm not impulsive. I make lists."

"Nothing wrong with lists. I couldn't do my work without them."

"Me, neither. And I'm sure that Zoe must have kept lists of meds, and protocols, and treatment stuff for her patients. But although she had her life all planned, those plans always came from trusting her instincts. Not from writing up detailed pros and cons lists."

Seth wasn't surprised that she'd nailed Zoe. They had been nearly as close as sisters. "A helluva lot of good that did her," he muttered. Hadn't she written in her journal that though some Greek guy might make a better husband, she was going to follow her heart and marry him?

"That was a horrible thing, Seth. I hope you're not blaming her for going into the Army."

"Hell, no. Of course I'm not." Which didn't mean that he still didn't get pissed off from time to time. But blame? Never. Who he blamed was himself. For not protecting her. Somehow.

"I didn't think you would. But getting back on topic, the thing is, I make detailed life lists, too. Brad, he was my assistant at Midas in Vegas, always called me the empress of planners and spreadsheets. The only impulsive thing I've done in years, probably going back to when I used to break into this house with you and my brothers, was to quit my job, come back here and buy this house from you."

"I could suggest that was a good outcome for both of us.

But it doesn't exactly make my point about keeping our distance."

"True."

She tilted her head, and dammit, chewed on a fingernail, which was turquoise today and not only drew his attention to her mouth, but had him wondering if her toes had been colored the same. And if she liked them sucked. He'd never done that because Zoe was ticklish, but while he might be celibate, he wasn't dead. He'd watched Kristen Bell getting her toes sucked on *House of Lies*—which, in Seth's opinion, had been basically soft porn with enough corporate drama to make it acceptable to admit you watched—and she sure had seemed to enjoy it.

"You're right," she decided. "We shouldn't be impulsive."

Pondering her toes, and other lady parts, as well, had him thinking maybe he'd made a mistake. It also had him realizing that if she knew what he was thinking, she'd probably decide he was a sexist perv and they wouldn't have any problem in the first place.

"Take things slow. It's not like either of us is going anywhere," he pointed out. He'd already gotten the notice of Brianna's construction account from Danni Douglass down at the Timberlake Savings and Loan before she'd told him about it.

"So, at least for now, we'll just work on the house," she said. "And keep things safely in the friend zone."

"Works for me." As long as she didn't show up barefoot. Which was unlikely.

"Okay." She blew out a breath. "One more thing... Is it going to be a problem having me live here while you're working?"

"I suggested it," he reminded her. "And the only problem would be if you get tired of living in a construction zone."

"I can deal with that."

"Says the woman who's never lived with nail guns blasting all day."

She laughed, and the tension that had strung between them as tight as a wire band eased. "Oh, and speaking of lists and planners, I'm going to be gone the weekend after next," she said.

"For Kylee and Mai's wild weekend of debauchery at the coast before they settle down and become a boring married couple."

"There will be no debauchery. We went over the entire plan at the Mad Hatter the day before I went to Seattle. They're not even having some fake cop stripper show up with handcuffs."

Damn. He wished she hadn't mentioned handcuffs. Not that bondage had ever been his kink, but it did get a guy thinking of things that were better left in the pages of sexy romance novels or on movie screens.

"So," she said, dragging his mind away from the plastic zip ties in his toolbox, "if we're okay, for now, I'd like to run down to Treasures and see if I can find anything to furnish my new apartment."

Seth watched her walk away. Not just because he enjoyed the view, but because he enjoyed her. Being with her, talking with her, planning restoring Herons Landing to its original glory. But better, in his view. The Victorian era, which always made him think of David Copperfield fleeing his evil stepfather, little Nell dying and Ebenezer Scrooge, had some positive things going for it. But overembellishment of their homes was not one of them. Which, in a way, made it ironic that he earned a good living bringing Honeymoon Harbor's historical Victorians back to life.

Seth didn't know what, exactly, was going to happen between Bri and him. But wasn't that, in itself, a positive? She seemed determined to get him out of his rut. And, he couldn't lie, the predictability that had once felt so comfortable was getting flat-out boring. It was the first time he'd kissed anyone since Zoe's death. He'd thought it would feel terrible. And wrong. But if he were to be perfectly honest, it had felt good. Damn good. He waited for the guilt, but it didn't come, which was both unexpected and weird. But sort of welcome, too.

He waved as she tapped the horn and drove down the tree-lined road. Then turned his mind to another problem. His father's seeming disappearance.

CHAPTER TWENTY-TWO

Seth was admittedly concerned. After all, Pete Harper, one of his dad's poker playing buddies, was currently undergoing rehab therapy in the Seattle VA hospital after having suffered a stroke. His dad wasn't getting younger, and although he'd always keep his feelings locked down tight, surely having your wife of forty years walk out on you had to trigger some stress.

He called the home he'd grown up in yet again, only for it to go to voice mail. The recording was his mom's voice, which probably meant that his dad still expected her to come back home any day.

He tried his dad's cell, not expecting anything, which was why Seth was surprised when he answered on the first ring.

"Where are you?"

"Why?" There was a challenge in his dad's tone.

"Because you didn't show up at the house we were supposed to be buttoning up."

"It's all done. You don't need me to go through the last of a damn punch list. And there's no reason for me to go over the plans with the Mannion girl, since you'll both do whatever you want anyway."

"You don't want any input?"

"I'm just a laborer these days." He could hear the shrug and dismissal in his dad's voice. "I wouldn't have handed the business over to you if I didn't think you could keep it going."

"You're a skilled craftsman," Seth argued the labor point. "There's a difference."

"Whatever." Another shrug in the tone. "My point was you don't need me hanging around today. Also, the mill on Water Street is still waiting for a permit from the damn zoning board. Seems a guy should be able to take a day off."

Seth couldn't argue with that. Then he heard a familiar sound. "Are you on a ferry?"

"Why would you think that? We have ferries coming and going all the time."

Seth glanced out at the harbor. "Not at this moment." And not for another ten minutes since they'd gone to a spring hour schedule. Come summer, when tourism picked up, the ferries would shift to every thirty minutes.

"Fine, so I'm going to Seattle. Do you have a problem with that?"

"Of course not." But his dad had always claimed to hate the city. He found it too crowded and too noisy, and hated the traffic. "Are you visiting Pete?"

There was a pause. Just long enough to tell Seth that whatever his father had planned, that wasn't it. "Yeah. That's it. I'm visiting Pete at the VA." Another pause, during which Seth could practically hear the wheels turning in his dad's head. "I figured he'd like some of those cinnamon rolls from Cops and Coffee, since hospital food sucks. And if the MREs I had to eat were any indication, VA hospital food probably sucks even worse."

He'd put in enough truth, including that bit about his own service before Seth had been born. But Ben Harper had always been a rotten liar (which was why he so seldom won a hand at those poker games), and whatever he was up to, dropping in on his old poker buddy wasn't his first destination. Hoping he wasn't going to find out that there was more to his parents' troubles than his mother had told him, that maybe Ben Harper had a woman on the side, Seth decided just to let it go.

"You going to be back tomorrow?"

"Yeah, sure. You know what I think about sleeping in hotel beds."

Which confirmed what his mother had said about his refusal to travel in retirement. Maybe, Seth thought as he ended the call, telling his dad to have a good day and tell Pete hi for him, he'd gone to the city to buy a motor home.

With that positive possibility in his mind, Seth decided to take a run by the country courthouse and see if he could speed up the permit on the eighty-year-old sawmill. Although he wasn't rolling in dough, and had donated his military survivor benefits to the Iraq and Afghanistan Veterans of America, he'd put enough aside to not only pick up Herons Landing on a short sale, but also the mill, which, after a fire, had closed in the '70s.

He'd had a lot of competition from commercial developers who saw potential profit in the building sitting on the water that had once provided power for the saws and planers, but with some zoning changes, and federal and state grants, and given that he was a local, not some outsider sweeping in to make a quick buck selling overpriced condos, he'd won the property battle.

When repurposed into studio, one-and two-bedroom apartments, the former town eyesore would provide much-needed low-income housing for up to fifty families, depending on the configurations of the units. Working with Amanda Barrow, he planned to turn the land in front of the building into a green space, with a small, two-level parking garage where the sawdust burner—which had sparked the fire that had spread to the mill—had once stood next to the main building. While he hadn't been all that thrilled with the idea of the garage originally, he had understood local business owners' concerns that residential street parking could cost them customers.

So he'd brought Mike Mannion into the project to arrange with art students at the high school and community college to paint murals on the garage. Three of the drawings were left unpainted, then filled in by members of the local Down syndrome group, Down Right Perfect, started by Jim Olson of Blue House Farm a few years ago.

He might not be able to cure cancer, fight terrorism as Zoe had done in her own way or change all the world's problems, but at least he could make his little corner of the planet a bit better. Which was worth getting up in the morning.

The counselor's room was painted the color of what Ben figured Caroline would call something fancy, like *biscuit*, or *cookie crumb*, or *cappuccino*, but to him was just boring old beige. Which might be the point, he considered as a small table fountain bubbled over a bowl of small round rocks that didn't look like any he'd ever seen in nature.

He'd chosen a female counselor because he figured she'd give him some insight into what the hell Caroline was talking about. Sure, they'd discussed travel in their early days, but he couldn't believe that she seriously wanted to leave the comfort of the home he'd built them the first year of their marriage, added on to and updated, because that's what women seemed to always want to do. Not that Ben wasn't grateful, because all that updating and adding had made him a comfortable living.

And having slept on trailer beds on fishing trips, he suspected that once she slept on a cheap foam mattress, she'd miss the adjustable bed he'd laid out big bucks for just last fall. And then, there they'd be. Stuck with a damn overpriced motor home that would depreciate big-time as soon as they drove it off the lot.

So far Dr. Alicia Blake hadn't done much talking. Just asked a few questions, nodding, made some low humming sounds and kept making notes on that legal pad she held on her lap. She was younger than his wife and him. Maybe she wouldn't be able to even understand his situation. He should've gone with the old balding guy on the website. The one who looked like he'd lived long enough to have a wife go menopause crazy on him.

"How old are you?" he asked, breaking off his story of how his wife had taken up with Mannion.

"Thirty-eight," she said.

"I've got a son that's thirty-one."

"That would be Seth. Who's taken over Harper Construction."

He hadn't remembered telling her that, but once he'd started talking about that day of the play when he'd first met Caroline, and their marriage, and how they'd been partners rescuing the business his father had, truth be told, left pretty deep in debt, the words had just started flowing like a river over a busted dam.

"Yeah, that's him."

"And you asked my age because you think because I'm closer to your son's age than yours, I won't understand the problem that brought you here today."

"I didn't say that."

She just looked at him straight in the eye, letting him know she knew exactly what he'd been thinking, and gave him a slight smile.

A silence settled over the room.

"I may have been thinking along those lines," he admitted.

"It's understandable and you wouldn't be the first client

to think that." She nodded toward the beige wall. "Did you happen to notice those degrees?"

"Yeah." He'd also noticed that they were all from fancy private Ivy League schools like the one Sarah Harper had gone off to before returning home and marrying John Mannion. That had sure as hell caused a fuss at the time, and not just because of the centuries-old Harper/Mannion feud, but because her parents had had a lot higher aspirations for her than marrying a local boy and settling down on some Christmas tree farm in Honeymoon Harbor. At least he hadn't had that problem with Seth, who'd married himself a local girl. Well, not exactly local. But Astoria-born was close enough to Ben's mind.

"Yeah. Those are good schools," he allowed. "My son, Seth, gave a seminar at Columbia. On green historical restoration."

"That's very impressive. Not because of Columbia's reputation for innovative thought, but because historical restoration is very important work that more people need to be taking on. Our entire planet depends on them. You must be very proud."

"Yeah." He was. Although a lot of the time his son's ideas seemed like a lot of extra work for not much additional profit, and Ben admittedly didn't understand all the technology and terms, he was impressed that Seth had made a name for himself. Even before she'd put the idea of his boy helping to save the planet in his head.

"And no doubt you've told him that."

"Maybe not in so many words. But he knows I'm proud of him."

"The same way your wife's supposed to know that you love her."

"Yeah." Too late, Ben realized the trap. "You learn that

trick at those fancy schools?" He folded his arms. Then unfolded them, realizing he was giving away his discomfort.

"It's not a trick," she said calmly. Mildly. "What I learned
was how to help others see what they might not realize on
their own because they're too close to the situation. To use
a timber country analogy, my job is to see the entire forest,
while you and your wife might be stuck down in the trees."

"I hadn't thought of it that way." Hell, he'd just come here
hoping for a quick fix. Now he was beginning to think it
wasn't going to be so easy.

"I'm trained to help my clients help themselves. Which
you obviously want to do or you wouldn't be here today."

He decided that after having gone online and looked her
up, then picked up the phone and made the appointment,
then come all the way over here, he might as well tell the
truth. Because after reading the ultimatum in Caroline's letter, he realized that this young woman with the citified black
jacket and beige pants could see right into his head through
the lenses of those black sexy librarian glasses. Not that he
was thinking of her as sexy, because, Christ on a crutch, she
was young enough to be his daughter.

"I came here so you'd tell me what the hell Caroline's
thinking."

"I believe she's already told you that," Dr. Blake said. "I
suspect several times over the years. But, having read her letter expressing her feelings and needs, and from what you've
told me about her having always had a mind of her own, including having stood up to her parents when she married
you instead of that young man from her own social circle—"

"She would never have been happy with him." He'd met
the guy when she'd taken him home to the Atlanta mansion
she'd grown up in to introduce him to the family.

Her parents had thrown a welcome-home cocktail party
and invited all her old friends, including the boyfriend. Ash-

ley Somersett's handshake had been limp and his palm as smooth as a newborn baby's butt. Although he'd been in his early thirties, his pale blond hair was already receding. Decades later, Ben's own hair was still thick, with only a few streaks of gray, which Caroline had assured him added dignity, not age. "She would've eaten him for breakfast and spit out his little bird bones."

Dr. Blake surprised him by laughing at that. A rich, bold laugh that had him smiling back. "I like you, Ben Harper."

"I like you, too, Doc."

"That's a good start," she said, crossing her legs and sitting back in the black leather chair that reminded him of the vinyl one his parents had had in the living room when he'd been growing up. They were calling the style "midcentury" now. Which made him wonder how the hell he'd gotten so old when he hadn't been watching. "Now let's get down to work and figure out how you're going to save your marriage and win your wife back."

CHAPTER TWENTY-THREE

Brianna was on the way to Treasures to look for some furniture for her third-floor apartment when her phone buzzed.

"Hi," she greeted Kylee, who, despite plans for the bachelorette party all worked out over tea and scones at the Mad Hatter, had kept checking in several times a day about every little detail. And Brianna had thought *she* was a control freak.

"If you're calling about the party, don't worry. I've got the menu planned, the grocery list made, and you and Mai are going to be taste testers for the B and B recipes Mom promises I can pull off for a crowd without any problem. With any luck I won't poison anyone."

"That's one of the reasons I'm calling. The party's off."

"Oh, no." Brianna's heart sank. "Don't tell me you and Mai broke up? You're so perfect together."

"We are. And we haven't. Broken up, that is. We're going to be moms."

"I know." Brianna had bought three sets of onesies and a padded piano keyboard that tied to crib bars to allow a baby to kick against it and play music. "But that's still two weeks away. What does it have to do with the party?"

"It was *supposed* to be two weeks," Kylee said. "But apparently our child is going to turn out to be more like me than Mai. Because our birth mother just went into labor."

"Wow! That's so exciting!"

"And scary," Kylee said. "But the doctor assures us that thirty-eight weeks is a safe zone. But, of course, I'm already chewing my nails off."

"I'm on my way." Furniture shopping could wait. Friendship came first.

"Thank you. Mai's her usual Zen sea of calm, but I can tell that she's as nervous as I am. I am upset about one thing."

"What?"

"One of the reasons Seth was rushing on the house was to get us moved in in time for the wedding before we became parents. I'm not worried about the wedding. That's just a technicality. But I did want to bring our daughter home to the house she'll grow up in."

"And you didn't let me buy any baby furniture," Brianna heard Mai say in the background.

"I didn't want to jinx the adoption," Kylee said. "I'm Scottish. We're a superstitious people."

"Don't worry about that," Brianna said. "This is an easy problem to fix." Certainly easier than many she'd handled over the years. "You just stay calm so you won't upset the mother. Calm's got to be better for the baby, right?"

"Right." She heard Kylee blow out a long breath. Then another. A third. "Okay. I've found my center. Now I'm going to go back into the labor room. See you soon."

"Soon," Brianna agreed. As she turned around in the direction of the hospital, she hit the icon on the phone.

Seth answered on the first ring. "That was fast."

"Change of plans. I'm on the way to the hospital."

"Is your mom okay? Your dad?"

"Everyone's fine. Kylee and Mai's baby has decided to make

an early appearance. I'm going to offer moral support, but I need a favor."

"Just name it."

"You and Dad are the only two guys I know in town with trucks. I need everything moved out of Kylee and Mai's apartment into their new house."

"Sure, I can do that."

"You'll need me to get a key."

"I'm a contractor," he reminded her. "I know how to jimmy locks."

Of course he did. "While you guys are moving furniture, I'm going to ask Mom to find something to put the baby in." Kylee's own mother had tragically died in a car accident four years ago. "I figure being the principal she can leave school early and find a bassinet or something either at Treasures or in Port Townsend or Port Angeles."

For a moment, when he didn't respond, Brianna thought she'd lost the connection. "Don't bother," he said finally. "I'll take care of that."

He didn't need to say any more. Remembering Zoe's emails about the nursery they'd been planning, she guessed that Seth must have furnished the room as a surprise for her. The same way he'd kept her car clean and running. As she realized that he must have kept that room the way it had been two years ago, and what he was now planning to do, her eyes misted. Wiping the tears away so she could concentrate on arriving at the hospital without having an accident, she bit her lip. "Are you sure?"

Another pause, shorter than the earlier one. "Yeah. I am... Tell Kylee and Mai not to worry. I'll pull some of the crew off the old lighthouse keeper's house they're working on and we'll have them moved in by tonight."

After thanking him again, Brianna called the farm. Then, with her heart and thoughts torn between the about-to-be mothers and the special man she'd given her heart to years ago, Brianna turned down Quinault Road to Honeymoon Harbor General Hospital.

It was even harder than he had thought it would be when he'd made the offer to Brianna. Seth hadn't opened the nursery door since the day he'd been notified of Zoe's death. Hadn't wanted to because everything inside the room represented a shared dream that, as much as he knew it would never happen, he couldn't let go of.

On the other hand, two women who'd become friends enough to ask him to be in their wedding needed him to step up and open that damn door. After all, someday he was going to have to. He couldn't spend his life like Miss Havisham, who, after having been jilted at the altar, spent the rest of her life alone in her decaying mansion, never taking off her wedding dress and leaving the moldering wedding cake on the table.

He'd had to read Dickens's *Great Expectations* his senior year of AP English. Okay, two chapters into the book, he'd thrown in the towel and cheated by reading the CliffsNotes. But they were still detailed enough for him to find the story ridiculously over-the-top melodramatic. People got ditched. They divorced. And sometimes the one you loved with your entire heart, the one you'd planned to live the rest of your life with, the one in which all *your* great expectations lay, died.

Although he hadn't set all the clocks and his watch to the time those officers had arrived at his and Zoe's house, the way the old spinster had kept the clocks in the mansion set to the exact time she got the letter from the con man who'd defrauded and jilted her, by keeping this door closed for the past two years, he'd metaphorically behaved the same way.

He took a deep breath, and turned the handle.

Thanks to Megan's Clean Team, unlike the decaying old

mansion, there were no cobwebs, no mold, no rodents. The crib, which was designed to turn into a twin bed when their child got older, was a bright white, painted with an enamel guaranteed not to chip off when a teething baby gnawed on it. The bars were close together, per the new safety standards she'd found online, and the mattress was covered with a quilt his mother had made. Hot air balloons, in all the bright primary colors Zoe had insisted on, flew upward in each of the twelve squares of blue cloth sky. Riding in the baskets were baby elephants, bears, dinosaurs, dragons, ducks and more. Along each of the borders read, "Oh, the places you'll go."

A mobile he'd found online of Zoe's beloved orcas, in bright, whimsical colors, hung over the crib.

His father had surprised him by building not just a rocking chair, but a white dresser with each of four drawers painted in the colors of the quilt. Zoe's parents had provided the changing table along with the best safety car carrier on the market.

In the corner of the room was the bassinet that would be moved into their bedroom when they brought their newborn home. Made of see-into mesh, it had all the bells and whistles. It rocked, swiveled and had adjustable white noise sleep sounds, and the sides lowered, allowing the baby to sleep at the same level next to Mom and Dad, but not in the bed, which, Zoe had read, and their own doctor had agreed, was a lovely idea, but also increased the risk of suffocation and SIDS. Needless to say, it was the most expensive one made, but he'd been willing to pay anything to keep his child safe and his wife worry-free.

But he hadn't been able to keep his wife safe. And the child she might have been thinking about in those last seconds of her too-short life would never be conceived. Never born.

When the pain hit him like a sledgehammer in the gut, he dropped the toolbox he'd been carrying, doubled over, hands on his thighs, head spinning as he struggled to keep from passing out.

"You can do this, dammit," he muttered as vertigo had him swaying on his feet. "Not just for Kylee and Mai, but for yourself." He also knew gifting the new mothers with this nursery Zoe had put so much thought and love into was exactly what she'd want him to do.

So, picking up the toolbox, he pushed through the pain and guilt that he'd been carrying around for all this time and got down to business dismantling Kylee and Mai's crib.

CHAPTER TWENTY-FOUR

Caroline didn't know what to think. After handing Ben that ultimatum letter at the Stewed Clam, she'd been expecting a call. Or maybe he'd even show up at her door. She'd been trying to decide what his silence meant. Was he merely ignoring her, still counting on her returning home and things continuing just as they'd been? Which, although she hated to think it, wasn't going to work for her. Maybe he was giving himself time to seriously consider the words that had come straight from her heart.

Could he be deciding how much he was willing to change to keep the woman he'd sworn to love, honor and cherish that day amid the moss-draped oak trees in her parents' backyard? If a green space three times the size of Honeymoon Harbor's park could be called a yard.

An army of gardeners had mowed, trimmed and clipped, so the lawn looked like a huge putting green and the gardens could have held their own against the Biltmore Estate, which, when built during the Gilded Age, had been the largest private home in the nation. Her mother was a renowned Southern belle who, after providing the family with both an heir—Caroline's brother—and a daughter born to marry well into their class, had handed her offspring to nannies and turned all her attention to gardening. Her passion for creating floral perfection had her making a pilgrimage to North Carolina every year to confer with the Biltmore gardeners. Other plants had been grown from heritage seeds from Monticello and were said to have been avid gardener Thomas Jefferson's favorites.

In addition to the arbor covered with a pink climbing rose appropriately called New Dawn, beneath which she and Ben had exchanged their vows, thirty more varieties bloomed in a rose garden that had won the city's garden show award every year for as long as Caroline had been alive. At the far end of the lawn, a white tent had been erected for the reception for three hundred of her parents' closest friends. In the kitchen (which was larger than the house she'd moved into after her marriage) another army of chefs and servers had kept the reception running like clockwork.

Caroline had known that Ben hadn't expected such an ostentatious display of wealth. But she'd been proud at how he hadn't appeared the least bit intimidated. After all, why should he be? Not only was he the man she'd chosen to marry, he was a far better man than others she'd grown up with. Including her own father who, despite having a law degree from Vanderbilt, spent more hours a day at the country club than his office. He had, she'd accidentally discovered when she'd been a junior in high school, a fondness for women around the same age as the twenty-four-year-old bourbon he favored.

She'd sensed, during their early years of marriage, that every time they had an argument, her husband had expected her to go running home to her parents. To her previous life of wealth and privilege. What she suspected he'd never entirely understood or believed was that she'd always found her parents' life suffocating. Everyone behaved exactly the same way, expectations remained the same generation after generation, and certain things just weren't done. Like choosing a career as an artist, or complaining about your husband's wandering eye. Having watched her mother suffer her father's adultery in silence for so many years, Caroline had decided, that memorable day when she'd gone into the pool house looking for a book she thought she'd left there, and walked in on her father and a woman who was definitely not her mother having sex, that she was going to break the mold.

The day had sparked the flame that had her taking that trip across America. The trip where she'd met a man with strong hands, a brilliantly creative mind (although he hated it whenever she told him that) and, although he kept it well guarded, a heart as big as the vast Western landscape she'd fallen in love with.

She hadn't understood how such a smart, manly male like Ben Harper had remained single, but deciding that the women of Honeymoon Harbor must be blind, stupid or both, she'd taken less than a minute to stake her claim on him.

Life experience had changed him over the years, given him challenges that she'd watched him fight to overcome. It had only been the past two years that she wasn't certain if he could find his way back to the husband she'd loved. The partner she'd wanted to spend the rest of her days with.

Then, just when she'd feared he'd given up on them, this morning he'd surprised her.

"Ben left flowers in front of my door this morning," she told Mike as they stood in a meadow, painting the wildflowers dancing like ballerinas in the breeze. It had been his idea that she try her hand at plein air painting, which was all about leaving the four walls of the studio and capturing the landscape in its natural setting. He'd told her that the practice went back centuries, but had been turned into an art form by the French Impressionists.

"I think you'd find the spontaneity suits you," he'd said.

And he'd been right. She was immediately drawn to the freedom, but was quickly discovering that it was also more challenging than it looked due to the constantly changing light and weather conditions. But she'd never been one to turn down a challenge.

"Has he mentioned your letter?"

She'd told him about Ben, not because she was attracted to Mike Mannion, though there had been that brief flirtation the night of the play years ago, the night she'd met the man who'd become her husband, but because he'd become a friend she could talk with to get a man's take on her problem.

"No. But they were roses. A beautiful hybrid that blends from coral to orange. They've always been my favorite because they reminded me of the honeymoon in Hawaii we'd been planning to take. But shortly before the wedding, he discovered that his father had driven the company deeply in debt. So, instead of flying off to paradise, we came back here, buckled down and got to work."

"Like the steel magnolia you are," he suggested, as he painted in the shadows of clouds moving over the mountains. Clouds that made the painting an entirely different one than it would have been two minutes earlier. Plein air, she was discovering, was all about change. Just like marriage.

"Ben's always called me that," she murmured, watching as a butterfly flittered over a flower, and trying to quickly sketch it in. "I'd told him that the only things I missed about my old life down home were the rosebushes my mother dedicated her life to cultivating. So he bought me that bush, the first of many, for our first anniversary," she said. "The same week we managed to get Harper Construction back in the black. We planted the bush together, then sat out on the deck, drinking mai tais he'd made from a mix he picked up at the market, and drinking in the scent of the flowers."

And talking about how someday they'd get to Hawaii. She

wondered now if he was sending her a reminder of that promise. And that maybe it was his way of saying he wanted to talk.

Then why the hell didn't he come by her apartment? Or
at least call.

"I've always envied him," Mike surprised her by saying.
"For having won you."

"You make me sound like some sort of prize."

"Yeah." He cringed a bit at that. "It sounds sexist, but the
thing was, I fell for you when I was putting those last-min-
ute touches on that forest scene that had gotten dinged while
setting up. You came over and we talked about painting."

"I remember it well." He'd been handsome and she found
their shared interest in art appealing.

"Then that damn rainstorm happened, and you started talking
to Ben Harper, and I realized, watching the two of you together,
and the chemistry was so electric, that I didn't stand a chance."

"I'm sorry. I didn't know." If she had, would she have ended
up with this man? No, she decided. She enjoyed his company,
he was still handsome, and she loved her classes and their
conversations. But Ben Harper had, and undoubtedly would,
whatever happened in their marriage, always hold her heart.

"It was a disappointment." Then he treated her to a warm,
wry grin. "But, as you can see, I've survived."

"But you're still single."

"When I find a woman as perfect as you, I'll give up my
bachelor days without looking back. Ben's a lucky man. Hopefully, only because I want you to be happy, he'll pull his head
out of his ass."

Well. The clouds had rolled over the meadow, bringing
with them a light rain that created drops on the flower petals,
but if it kept up would have them quitting for the day. Which
was probably a good thing. Because between the roses outside
her apartment door, and Michael's surprise admission, Caroline's life had just become even more conflicted.

CHAPTER TWENTY-FIVE

Kylee was in the waiting room, pacing like a stereotypical expectant parent, when Brianna arrived in the maternity wing. "Thank God you're here," she said. "I've been wearing a path in the floor and need comfort."

"Where's Mai?" One advantage of a small town with slow population growth was that they were the only people in the waiting room.

"She's in with Madison, our birth mother, and her grandparents. Apparently there's a rule about only three visitors at a time."

Brianna had learned over tea that the birth mother was a seventeen-year-old girl who'd be attending her freshman year at Washington State University. Her grandparents, who'd taken over the job of parenting after Madison's parents had died in a small plane crash in the Cascades when the girl was ten, were elderly and not well enough to take on the care of a newborn. Without any aunts and uncles to take up the slack, and the boy and his parents having no interest in helping raise an unplanned and unwanted child, the small family of three had agreed that it would be better for everyone, including the baby the teenager was carrying, to choose adoption.

"I'm sorry about you having to put your wedding off," she said.

"It's not that big a deal," Kylee said with a shrug. "Well, it kind of is, because I wanted to be married before I became a mother, but it can wait. It was just going to be a few close friends and a bunch of Mai's relatives, who unfortunately are all having to change their plane tickets."

"So, your dad's not coming."

"No." Another shrug, but regret momentarily shadowed Kylee's eyes. "He still hasn't forgiven me for my 'lifestyle'—" she made air quotes "—since I came out."

"His loss."

"That's what Mai always says. She's good for me, Bri. And her family's been wonderful. Her mom's filled in for mine and her dad assured me that he'd love to be my dad, too. Her grandmother's even coming. Can you imagine? She's in her nineties, and not only is she willing to fly across an ocean to share in her granddaughter's wedding, she's more open-minded than my decades-younger father."

"Some people just have more open hearts," Brianna said. "Plus, having been in an internment camp while her young groom was off fighting in Europe undoubtedly taught her a lot about the dangers of hate and the importance of love."

"'And to live every moment with positivity,' is the way Mai's grandmother put it to me," Kylee said. "Mai told me that when she was standing at her husband's grave, instead of saying how wrong it was that he'd been killed so young, all she could concentrate on was her gratitude that his final resting place was so beautiful and peaceful, and that he was surrounded by five thousand other Americans."

Brianna remembered the day Kylee had called her from France, telling her that she'd fallen in love. Mai had taken her grandmother on a pilgrimage to the American Cemetery in Epinal, France, to the grave of her grandfather, who'd been killed in action after volunteering to join the famed Japanese American Go For Broke 442/100th. With one third of the Hawaiian population being Japanese, the government had decided that it would be devastating economically to put them all into camps.

Still, those considered of higher community standing, or who "posed a threat against America," had been interned behind barbed wire. Having attended school for a year in Japan, which was where he'd met Mai's grandmother, although he was an American citizen, he, she and his parents were among those imprisoned. He, like so many others of his peers on the island and mainland, had enlisted in the Army to prove that they and their families were loyal to their country.

As opposed to how they'd been treated at home, those who'd made the ultimate sacrifice had been "adopted" by the French civilians who took care of the graves and continued to bring flowers and flags on special occasions. Brianna had seen the photos taken by both Mai and Kylee, who'd serendipitously been there that day on a trip through Europe, documenting World War II American cemeteries.

"She never remarried?"

"No." Kylee shook her head. "She says no other man could ever live up to her beloved Masato."

"That's both wonderful and sad." It also had Brianna thinking of Seth and wondering if he'd end up a ninety-one-year-old widower, still emotionally tied to his one and only love.

Which was too depressing a thought to consider on such an exciting day. Shaking off the negativity, Brianna smiled as Mai came out of the room, her grin as wide as the moon. "She's dilated to three centimeters. We now officially have an active labor situation."

"Oh, God." Kylee collapsed on the hard sofa next to Brianna. "What if we made a mistake? What do we know about taking care of a child?"

"We'll learn," Mai soothed her. "After all, we survived to adulthood. As did Brianna, all her brothers and millions of other children. We're smart, we've studied up and we've got an entire library from birth to dealing with an empty nest. Take a deep breath and let's go downstairs and have something to eat. The doctor says we've still got a lot of hours ahead of us."

"I want to go see her," Kylee said. "Let her know we're supporting her."

"You've told her that. She knows it. Right now what she needs is to get some rest between contractions, and your energy, bouncing off the walls like it is right now, isn't going to help."

"You're undoubtedly right, dammit. I could use some cake."

"Protein," Mai corrected her. "Sugar overload is the last thing you need. And no coffee. Tea. Herbal."

Kylee stuck out her bottom lip. "You're no fun."

"You'll thank me later."

"Besides, I need you calm so you can give me some advice," Brianna said.

"About the house?"

"No. Seth." She decided if anything would get her friend's mind off the birthing, her news would. "I kissed him. And he kissed me back."

"I knew it!" Kylee headed toward the door just as another waiting family entered. This was not a conversation to have in front of others, although Brianna suspected by tomorrow, somehow the story might even be replacing Honeymoon Harbor's Harper/Mannion love triangle.

Five minutes later, huddled together at the table in the far corner of the cafeteria, digging into pieces of three-layer choc-

olate cake—which Kylee insisted she desperately needed because chocolate was a far better cure for anxiety than an egg
salad sandwich or Cobb salad that had probably been packed
into the plastic box hours ago—Brianna was being drilled
about that impulsive kiss.

"I shouldn't have brought the subject up. Today's about you
two," she said. "Not me."

"We need something to take our minds off what's happening," Mai surprised her by saying. "While Kylee's pacing
around like a wet cat in a thunderstorm, inside, I'm curled up
beneath this table in a fetal position. Since we can't do anything to hurry up labor, talking about your love life is the
next best thing. Maybe after chocolate," she admitted as she
stabbed the mile-high piece of cake with a plastic fork. The
hospital had obviously outsourced since the label on the plastic box it had come in read Ovenly.

"I don't have a love life." Brianna took a drink of the
mocha caramel latte. Which just might admittedly be sugar/
chocolate overload, but the moms-to-be weren't the only
ones with tangled nerves. She pointed her fork toward Mai.
"That's the point."

"Who initiated the kiss?" Kylee asked.

"I did."

"You go, girl."

"The first time. But it was totally an impulse."

"The word *first* implies a second time," Mai pointed out.

"That was him."

"Ha! I'll bet you're the first woman he's kissed since Zoe
went off to the Army. Not that other women haven't tried,"
Kylee said.

"He sort of brought that up. But not in any bragging way."
Brianna was quick to defend him, even feeling as if he'd
stabbed her in her heart with one of those screwdrivers he
carried around in his tool belt. Because friends stuck up for

friends, in good times and bad. "He said he hadn't had sex for three years."

"Then he's way overdue," Mai said. "Lucky you. I'd only gone eighteen months when I met Kylee." She nodded toward her fiancée, who was scraping at least two inches of frosting off the top of the cake. "The next day, during my grandmother's afternoon nap, I felt like Kilauea Volcano erupting."

"She was hot," Kylee seconded that description. "You'd better be stocking up on condoms. Any he has lying around are probably long past their sell date."

"We're not going to have sex," Brianna said. *Memo to unruly naughty bits: the original "behave yourself" plan is back on.*

"You kissed him. He kissed you back. Was it a hot kiss?"

"On a scale of one to ten, for me it was a twenty." But then again, she'd been fantasizing about it since the days when she'd practice kissing the back of her hand in front of her bedroom mirror, so perhaps she was exaggerating. No. She wasn't. At all. "But there was no inappropriate touching."

Kylee frowned. "None?"

Brianna took another drink. Chocolate courage could be just as good as alcohol, right? Maybe even better, because all she'd be left with was a caffeine sugar buzz. Not a head-splitting, stomach-churning hangover, like the one she woke up with the morning after Seth and Zoe's wedding.

"Well… I may have sort of wrapped my leg around his."

"And bumped privates," Kylee guessed.

Brianna felt the heat rise in her cheeks. "Maybe a bit more than bumped." She would have climbed inside him if she could have.

"That's a start," Mai decided.

"You've got his engine revved," Kylee agreed. "Now Seth just needs to step on the gas and go for the checkered flag."

"She's become addicted to NASCAR." Mai rolled her expressive dark eyes.

"I had to find something new to latch onto after you and Seth banned me from Pinterest."

"We didn't ban you. Exactly. We merely pointed out that if you kept making changes, we might finally be moving into the house in time for our daughter's backyard wedding."

When Kylee didn't attempt to argue that point, Brianna laughed, feeling a release of the tension that had wrapped its tight hands around her insides as she'd walked away from temptation.

"You two remind me of my parents," she said. "You're like my dad," she told Mai. "Calm, steady and seemingly always in balance."

"Not always," Kylee said with a wicked grin and suggestive wiggling of her bright brows.

"She gets that we have sex," Mai told her fiancée dryly. "And, although I admire both your parents, Brianna, being compared to your father is a serious compliment. Thank you."

"I wouldn't mind being compared to your mom," Kylee pouted. Just a bit, which again made Brianna laugh.

"You're so much alike, you could be her natural-born daughter."

"You're just saying that to make me feel better."

"No. It's true. You both have Wonder Woman energy that can be exhausting at times. She practically wore me out racing around from wholesalers to designers while we were in Seattle. But my point is that you and Mai are total opposites, which seems to make for a good relationship. Zoe and Seth were like that. While he and I are more alike."

"Opposite attraction works well for us," Mai allowed. "But that's because, beneath the surface, our core values and ideas are the same. Studies have shown that long-term compatibility is more likely to be with someone like yourself."

"And the way you and Seth rhapsodized about Herons Landing showed you thought a lot alike," Kylee said. "Plus,

I always suspected that despite all that big-city talk, you'd eventually end up back home. The same way I did."

"We might have thought alike. But Seth and Zoe were a couple from that first day they met."

"True. But you've always loved him, and as tragic as Zoe's death was, it's your time. You'd be a fool not to go for it."

"He said they were soul mates. That he's never going to marry again."

"He actually told you that? After kissing your socks off?"

"Yes." It was depressingly definitive. But no way had she wanted him to see that his declaration had sent an arrow straight into her unsteady, and distressingly still yearning, heart.

"But he didn't fight you off when you went in for that kiss."

"No, he definitely didn't." He'd enjoyed that kiss as much as she had. Been rocked by it. But maybe he'd felt guilty? As if he'd been cheating on his dead wife? While Brianna had never really believed Herons Landing was haunted, now she was forced to worry that Zoe's ghost might be hovering between them the entire time they were working together on the house.

"Kylee told me about your grandmother, Mai. What if he ends up like her?"

"Unlikely. Those were different times. Women, especially conservative Japanese women like my grandmother, didn't get divorced, so there weren't that many second marriages. And there's always the possibility that she discovered she liked living her own life."

"He's a guy." Kylee polished off the rest of her cake, wadded up the paper napkin and, like the former basketball player she was, made a three-point shot into the wastebasket several feet away. "Unless he decides to become a monk, he's going to have sex and you're the obvious candidate.

"Also, he's proven that he's husband material by having

married Zoe. So, my guess is that deep down, he's going to realize that he misses that intimate connection with another person. So if you're the one he's with when that happens, the scales will fall from his scrumptious brown eyes, and he'll see that the woman he wants has been there all along. Admittedly it might take some time, but I have not a single doubt that you'll change his mind. Because you deserve to be as happy as we are."

When she linked hands across the table with Mai, two engagement rings, similar but individual, caught the light.

Brianna was about to tell them how fortunate they were, when both their phones chimed texts in unison.

"Madison's awake and up to five centimeters," Mai read.

"Time to start walking again," Kylee said.

"You or her?" Brianna asked.

"Both," they said together.

"All the books say the old belief that women in labor should stay in bed is uncomfortable and prolongs labor," Mai explained. "So, we've been walking a lot with her. It seems to help."

"I still love the idea of adoption because we're providing a home for a child who needs it and helping a young woman make a better life for herself," Kylee said. "But I think, for the next one, I might like to be the birth mom."

Mai's expression was both indulgent and overbrimming with love. Brianna thought if any man ever looked at her like that, she'd marry him in a minute. "Let's just get through this one," she said as she stood up from the table. "Then, once we recover from sleep deprivation and survive her toddler stage, we'll talk about a little sister or brother for our daughter."

"You're so sensible." Kylee, who'd jumped up when the phones had dinged, leaned down and brushed a kiss against her fiancée's lips. "That's only one of the things I love about you."

There was no way Brianna could envy her friend for having

found her life mate. But as they left the cafeteria to go down the hall to the birthing center, she found herself wondering if Kylee and Mai were right about her fighting for what, or technically whom, she wanted. Or if just continuing to hope that someday Seth could love her the way she still loved him might just be a losing cause.

But you'll never know if you don't try. She heard all the voices—her mother's, grandparents', Kylee's and Mai's—tumbling around in her head.

She'd never been a quitter. She'd chosen a goal and stuck with it, and although, sure, maybe she'd moved on, it wasn't as if she'd given up, but simply returned to her earlier first goal. Who was to say she couldn't have both Herons Landing and Seth Harper?

Or, to put it another way, she thought as she tossed her paper plate and utensils into the recycling bin, have her cake and eat it, too.

CHAPTER TWENTY-SIX

While taking apart the nursery might have been one of the hardest things Seth had ever done, short of getting through Zoe's death and funeral, watching Kylee's and Mai's faces as they saw the nursery for the daughter they'd brought home three days after her birth was definitely worth the pain. Kylee carried the newborn around, showing her all the wonderful things, telling her that they were just for her, and going over to the bookshelf, she literally teared up when she saw *Goodnight Moon*, which apparently her mother had read every night to her. The happiness literally radiating from both women caused an unexpected tug in his own heart.

It should have been Zoe showing their child the quilt and the dresser their grandparents had made, but life hadn't turned out that way. All around him, people he'd grown up with, had gone to school with, were coupling up, settling down and reproducing. All except for Brianna, though even she was nesting in her own way, bringing Herons Landing back to life.

Meanwhile, his already limited social life had become a blightscape.

But he had done this. He'd made a connection with the

new mothers and would now be involved in their daughter's life. That was something, right? He hoped if Zoe was somewhere watching, she'd approve.

"You did good," Brianna, who was standing beside him in the doorway, murmured, as if sensing his need for validation. "It couldn't have been easy."

"I thought it would be hell," he admitted. "And you're right, it wasn't at all easy. But watching them now, seeing them so happy, I realize that it was exactly the right thing to do. Thanks for putting the idea in my head. I should've thought of it while the three of us were working on the layout of the cottage and made room for the nursery."

She reached out and took his hand, linking their fingers together. Not as lovers, he reassured himself. But as friends. The same way they had when they'd jumped off the pier together into the bay when he'd been eleven and one of them—he'd forgotten which—had gotten the insane idea to join the crazyass Polar Bear Club, which, for some reason he still hadn't figured out, thought it would be a good idea to celebrate the first day of the year by freezing their balls off.

At the time, having recently become aware of his own, as he'd hit the icy water, he'd worried that he might have shriveled them beyond recovery. And wouldn't that have killed off any of his chances for sex with anyone but Mr. Hand, which even at his age he'd figured out wasn't anywhere near as good as having sex with a girl.

"You're a good man, Seth Harper," she said.

"You're prejudiced."

"You bet I am." Her smile was quick and easy. As if he'd only imagined that earthshaking kiss. Maybe it hadn't affected her nearly as much as it had him.

After all, she probably had lots of guys after her. Guys in Brooks Brothers suits, or Armani, or whatever the hell overpriced designer was in fashion these days, slicked-back Wall

Street hairstyles and money to burn. It only made sense that while she might have come home to Honeymoon Harbor, she couldn't have been working all the time. She'd undoubtedly spent some of those years kissing more than a few of those one-percenters who stayed at five-star hotels.

"I have another favor to ask," she said.

"Okay." It was crazy. He wasn't going to allow himself to get romantically involved with her, because she might as well be wearing a shirt that read Here There Be Dragons, but except for a marriage proposal, this woman could ask him for anything, including a kidney, and he wouldn't hesitate to give it to her.

"I found some furniture for the apartment on Craigslist, but it's scattered over the peninsula, and, just one more time, I need some big strong men with serious vehicles to pick it up for me and bring it back to the house. My dad's taking care of Port Townsend, Sequim and Port Angeles. I was wondering if you could handle Port Ludlow and Port Gamble."

"No problem. Does this mean you're moving in?"

"You've got the third floor all ready and now that Kylee and Mai have brought little Clara home, I'd like to be closer to them since they asked me to be her godmother."

"There's a coincidence. Because I'm going to be the god-father."

"Huh. Kylee had failed to mention that. You don't think—"

"That they made that choice to push us together?" Seth shook his head. "I doubt it. They're both only children. Kylee lost her mom, her douche of a dad is out of the picture, and Mai's family's all back in Hawaii, which means that although they're close, they're not going to all be able to get together that often.

"Plus, you don't spend all that time with people building their home without getting to know them. And they were easy to get close to, so I figure they just needed a guy and since my mom's officiating at their wedding and whatever type of baptism they're coming up with at the same time, asking me was the logical, and maybe only, choice they had."

"You're underestimating yourself. Personally, I believe they chose you because you'll be an excellent male influence. But whatever the reason, it's nice that we'll be sort of sharing Clara."

"We probably would anyway without any official designation," he said. "The four of us are connected in a lot of ways. Not only through the house—"

"Especially your giving them a dream nursery."

Zoe's dream, he thought, then forced his mind to shut down those voices that some days badgered him from the moment his eyes opened until he finally fell asleep. And even during too many nights they were like foghorns, tolling forbiddingly in the darkness.

"I'm just glad they like it."

"How could they not?"

"Hopefully, they won't feel superstitious since she died before we could have a baby." If it creeped them out, he'd remove it right away and take it all to Goodwill. Because someone's baby should be able to enjoy it.

"Kylee was also best friends with Zoe," Brianna reminded him. "I suspect that it will make it even more special to her. Because she'll realize all the love that went into it. Love that Zoe would've felt for Clara."

"She would have adored her." He tried not to think that their child would have grown up with Clara.

"It's almost as if she's here with us," Brianna said quietly.

"Yeah." He watched Mai showing baby Clara the orcas mobile that he'd searched all over for, finally finding a woman in North Carolina on Etsy who was willing to make him one. He'd planned it as a surprise.

It was only as she went over to join the new mothers and baby that he realized that, little by little, Brianna Mannion was unbreaking his heart.

★ ★ ★

The bed was going to be perfect. It was a sleigh bed style, made of iron rather than wood. The gracefully curved bars, along with the pewter finish that she'd worried she should have gone to see in person first, were unscratched and gleaming, making it look lighter and more modern. It had chosen to be a bit more of a problem trying to get it up the curving stairs, even after Seth had dismantled it to fit it in the truck.

"Did you have to get a king-size?" he asked as he and his dad, who'd returned to town and had been making templates for the bits of missing plaster molding he was going to have to replace, struggled to get the mattress up to the third floor.

"It was the only bed I found that I liked," she said. "And admittedly, it's larger than I need—" she could lie in the center with her arms and legs stretched out like she was making snow angels and still not touch the corners "—but the room is large enough to handle it. And after I move into the carriage house, it'll be a bonus feature."

"There's always the possibility that you can add a second ghost to the house's lore after this damn mattress knocks me down the stairs, cracks my head open and crushes me," he muttered, maneuvering it around another corner.

"Quit acting like a girly man," Ben said. "I'm not going to drop it on you. I may not be as young as I used to be, but I'm still strong as an ox."

"And stubborn as one, too," Seth muttered beneath his breath.

"I heard that. Just in case you were counting on me getting deaf in my old age."

Listening to them as they'd cussed and grumbled their way, first with all the iron railings, then the box spring pieces, and now the mattress, which wasn't turning out to be all that bendable, Brianna could tell that despite their differences, there was true familial love there. She also suspected that, at least in Ben's case, bitching and complaining was his way of showing it.

Once they had everything laid out on the basketball-court-size floor, Seth went back down the stairs and returned with a seriously big red toolbox, and father and son got down to work putting the frame together.

With the only power to the house being a cord plugged into a temporary electrical post outside, there was no air-conditioning operating yet. And making things worse was that the day had dawned a bright one, hinting at the upcoming summer.

Although she'd opened the windows to allow the salt air in, the third floor room grew much warmer than the outdoors.

Or, it could simply have been her reaction to him grabbing hold of the back of his T-shirt, pulling it over his head and tossing it onto the floor. There was an old saying that Pacific Northwesterners didn't tan, they rusted. In this case, it was wrong. Because Seth Harper's chest was a deep and tawny gold, much like the color that bathed the deep Olympic forest at twilight. And if she'd found his chest intriguing when she'd first seen him get out of the truck at the park, viewing it in its full, naked glory nearly made her drool.

And then, wow, Kylee hadn't been kidding when talking about those squats. When he went to work, screwing the end piece into the side, her eyes were drawn straight to his butt. And fit, defined, amazing thighs.

Just looking at him caused such a sheer burst of lust that either a bolt of lightning had struck through one of the open windows or she'd just experienced a decades-early hot flash.

"I think I'm going to go down to the ice chest and get a bottle of water," she said. Preferably to pour over her head. "Would anyone else like one?"

"I wouldn't mind," said Ben, who was holding the side rail steady, while his son worked the bolt into the slot.

"That'd be great," Seth agreed. When he glanced up at her over his shoulder, the gold flash in his brown eyes revealed that he'd caught her watching the flex of his back muscles while he'd been screwing in that bolt. "It has gotten warm in here."

He ran the back of his arm over his sweaty forehead, giving her an even better view of a physique that hadn't been created in any gym, but by hard, physical work. And the creative hand of God on one of his more generous days.

"I'll be right back."

She was not running away, Brianna assured herself as she practically raced down the curving stairs to the small ice chest sitting in the back seat of her car. She was merely taking a time out. To cool down. And try to clear her mind of that too-tempting fantasy of rolling around her king-size mattress with Seth Harper.

CHAPTER TWENTY-SEVEN

The next two weeks passed in a blur. Along with moving into Herons Landing, which, as Seth had predicted, was turning out to be hectic, dirty and noisy, Brianna continued to shop for all the innumerable details like door handles, faucets and even ceiling fans for all the rooms. Especially her bedroom, which, despite a spike in outdoor temperatures, hadn't reached the heat level she'd experienced watching him put together her bed.

And speaking of beds, she was discovering that her nights were as restless as they'd been at the farm. Her dreams were becoming more vivid, which wasn't helped by spending eight hours a day with the man who starred in her X-rated scenarios. Last night he'd used his leather tool belt, *sans* the tools, to tie her wrists to the top rail of the sleigh bed. Which had her waking up damp, needy and unsettled, because she'd never, ever fantasized about playing sexually submissive.

"You know what I miss?" she asked Kylee and Mai as she sat on their sofa holding baby Clara, who was wearing a pink onesie that read, "I get my 'tude from both my moms." Pleased that they'd chosen to dress her in one that she'd bought, Brianna brushed a thumb over the baby's pink cheek and felt a physical pull as ancient as time.

"The hustle and bustle of Vegas?" asked Mai, who was folding a stack of pastel onesies from a wicker laundry basket while Kylee heated up a bottle of formula.

"No. Never. I didn't fit in the entire time I was there. At least Hawaii had a welcoming aloha vibe. Las Vegas was nonstop. I'm realizing that I never caught my breath until I moved here."

"There are times I miss Hawaii," Mai confessed. "But I've also fallen in love with the Pacific Northwest."

"With our careers, we figure we can switch back and forth when Clara gets a little older. Then, once she starts preschool, we'll settle down and save Hawaii for those winter vacations when we can't work that much and are in serious need of sunshine," Kylee said, shaking the bottle and testing the temperature of the milk with drops on the inside of her wrist.

"Sounds like a plan." Brianna picked up a little foot wearing a pink sock with a ruffle around the top. Was there anything cuter than a baby's foot? She didn't think so.

Perhaps it was because after years of traveling, she was finally settling down. Adulting. Perhaps it was because for the first time in her life, she was able to take stock of what she wanted to do and what she felt she needed to do to get ahead. It could be the slower pace of life that gave her time to take a walk along the waterfront or into the woods.

Last Saturday she'd even picked up a chicken wrap and iced tea to go at the diner and driven up to Hurricane Ridge to sit on a rock wall and watch a herd of deer graze in the meadow. How many times, she reminisced, had a group of friends gone into the park for sledding or snowboarding in the winter, or picnics on sunny summer days? There were also swimming outings to Lake Crescent, Lake Quinault or Mirror Lake just outside the park, when Brianna had envied

Zoe's lush curves in those bikinis she'd shown off so well. Two weeks before she and her best friends had headed off to UW, six of them had spent the night camping out at Mirror Lake. They'd cooked s'mores, sung around the campfire and watched the sparks fly into a midnight-dark sky studded with diamond-bright stars.

Zoe and Seth had brought along their own tent, of course, and Brianna had done her best not to feel a little prick of jealousy. The next morning she'd been the first to crawl out of her sleeping bag into a dense layer of fog. The air was chilled and scented with old growth fir and cedar trees that made it smell like Christmas in August.

Remembering that time, when the entire earth had seemed to stand still, and she listened to a seabird call from somewhere in the mists, she wondered how she could have ever left this place that had always held a part of her heart.

"You were telling us what you miss," Kylee said, handing her the bottle. The baby, gurgling deliciously, latched onto the nipple. As she drank, Clara's eyes closed in what appeared to be more bliss than sleep. She was nothing short of a tiny package of awesome.

"Sex," Brianna admitted. "I haven't had sex for over two years."

"You've gone two years without an orgasm?" Kylee asked, her eyes widening.

"I didn't say that. I just haven't had sex. You know, body to body, that kind. With a guy."

"But you were living in the land of high rollers. You took trips with them—"

"With their *families*. Wives and children. Sometimes even grandchildren."

"Don't tell me none of those guys ever hit on you," Mai said.

"A couple. But I never had anything to do with them

again and turned them over to someone else the next time they came to wherever I was working. I'd never have an affair with a married man."

"From what you've told me over the years, you don't have affairs, period," Kylee said. "You're more into hookups."

"Not hookups. Exactly."

"You're right. That sounds too skanky for a good girl like you. But you were definitely into hit-and-run relationships."

"I could take offense at being called a good girl," Brianna complained.

"It wasn't a judgment call. Just a fact."

"You should have at least had a fling with one of those male exotic dancers," Mai said. "I've seen *Magic Mike*. Those guys are superhung and know how to move. I'll bet one could find your G-spot without you having to pull out a map."

"Mai!" Kylee covered Clara's ears. "No dirty talk in front of our daughter."

"She doesn't know what I'm saying."

"Not now," Kylee said. "But who knows when words start clicking in? Do you want our child's first word to be *G-spot*?"

"Or how about *vagina*?" Brianna suggested, enjoying watching her one and only remaining BFF blush to the color of a boiled Dungeness crab.

"You two are terrible." Still, her lips curved and it was obvious she was struggling not to laugh. Then, like so often could happen, Kylee's mood turned on a dime, her expression serious. "Did you ever, back in the day, consider stealing Seth away from Zoe?"

"Of course not! They were my friends."

"But you were hot for him forever and might have gotten him. Especially that time they had the big blowup over her joining ROTC."

"Would you have done anything like that?"

"No. But I wasn't carrying a torch for the guy all my life."

"We were lucky," Mai said. "We knew right away, so we didn't have to go through all the does-she-or-doesn't-she-love-me suffering."

"I did love him. But it was only one-way and later, once I started working, my career came first."

"And look how well that turned out. Here you are. Out of work and celibate."

"I'm not out of work." When Brianna went to wave that thought away, Clara grabbed hold of a finger. The newborn's nails were like pink pearls with white crescent half-moons and made Brianna's heart melt a bit inside.

"This isn't a big city, but there are a lot of single hot guys here. Like Flynn Farraday down at the fire station."

"You should see him playing hoops on the station court," Mai said. "Not only did the guy play basketball for Annapolis, he's built… He should go on the calendar," she told Kylee.

"Definitely. I'm thinking July. Dripping wet, wearing his helmet and turnout pants."

"Hanging low on his hips," Mai said. "So that hot V thing, whatever it's called, shows."

"And Cam Montgomery," Kylee said. "Since he's a vet, I could pose him bare-shirted holding a puppy."

"Dogs and guys are definitely hot," Mai agreed.

"You two are not helping," Brianna complained, thinking of the other day when Seth was outside by the trunk and dumped some of the water from the orange cooler over his shirtless chest. And surely those soaked raggedy cutoffs he'd been wearing couldn't be OSHA-approved construction clothing?

"Yes, we are." Kylee reached for her daughter, who'd polished off the bottle and put her over her shoulder, patting her back. "We're reminding you that if you're sexless, it's only your own fault. Have you seen Luca at the Italian place? He's hot. And he cooks."

"There's only one guy I want," Brianna admitted.

"Then go for it," both women said together, just as Clara let out a loud belch that sounded like a drunk frat boy at a spring break kegger.

"Maybe I will," Brianna said once they'd all stopped laughing.

Later, driving back to Herons Landing, Brianna pulled over at the park and watched the children playing on the swings and sliding out of purple tubes on the red, blue and yellow play fort. The noise level undoubtedly rivaled that of a jet engine, and every so often, as the laughing shrieks of the girls threatened to shatter her eardrums, Brianna realized that she wanted more than sex, even as she knew how hot sex with Seth would be. What she wanted, she realized, was what Kylee and Mai had. What her parents had. She wanted a family of her own. And not just that—she wanted to create that family with Seth Nathaniel Harper.

It was the end of a long day, but things were going smoother than he'd expected and Seth was feeling good about the project. As much as he liked Kylee and Mai, he had to admit that even with the chemistry vibes zigzagging around between Brianna and him, it was a lot easier working with her than it had been with the brides-to-be on their just-finished cottage.

He and Bri still thought a great deal alike, which helped because it saved him a lot of explaining when needing to make a point about a decision. Her mother, he suspected, had also proven a plus because the colors she'd chosen combined the more expected monochromatic Pacific Northwest shades taken from the grays, blues and greens, and added unexpected bright dashes of salmon and golden yellow to counter the rainy season.

As he'd expected, given her previous occupation, Bri was also the most organized client he'd ever worked with. Her spreadsheet was linked with her phone, iPad and computer, along with a paper printout kept in a three-ring binder for backup. Because, she'd claimed, it might be considered old-fashioned, but she liked being able to see the pages written down. The same as he did with his schedule coordinating subs. But in his case, the schedule was on a large whiteboard on the wall of his office, where he could see it all at a glance.

Herons Landing was going to be a showpiece, he decided as he arrived back to the house after a trip to Port Angeles for the barn door that would be going in the bridal suite. They'd already changed the exterior paint color to a soft yellow, which made him feel better every time he arrived.

She hadn't been kidding when she said that she'd wanted to be hands-on. Over the past week and a half, she'd painted the walls of the bridal suite and another room across the hall while managing to stay out of the way of the crews. Her work was as professional as that of the crew who'd be painting the majority of the large house.

Everyone else had gone home, or to their favorite watering holes, leaving hers the only car in the driveway. He found her on the second floor, using the steamer his dad had taught her to use, going to work on decades of layers of wallpaper. His mother, who watched all those TV remodeling and flipping shows, had told him wallpaper was making a comeback. Which meant that the entire cycle of papering and eventual removal would begin again. Thus keeping future generations of Harpers in work.

It had first occurred to him a few weeks after Zoe had died that unless he had any secret half sibling somewhere, there wouldn't be any other generations of his branch of Harpers to carry on the company. He was, literally, the end of their line.

Putting that idea aside, he entered the room that was becoming uncomfortably warm and decided he'd made the right decision putting in the AC. The ceiling fans Brianna had chosen to add to all the rooms would be a help once they got installed closer to the end of the job.

She was standing on a ladder, her back to him, earbuds in place, long, smooth arms moving the steamer up and down against the bright peacock-feathered printed paper, warming the room up even more. But not as much as the sight of her hips, clad in a pair of red cutoff shorts, wiggling along with her belting out "Fight Song" at the top of her lungs.

Her strong, slightly off-key rendition had him thinking back on that night when they'd all gone camping at Mirror Lake and had sat around the fire ring, toasting marshmallows in the last days of summer before Zoe, Kylee and Brianna headed off to Seattle. Leaving him behind. That night alone with Zoe in the small tent he'd brought along had been bittersweet, but once the trio was gone, he'd been surprised at how much he'd missed each and every one of them.

Every time she reached up, her tank top rose, displaying a mouth-drying display of pale golden Vegas tan that hadn't entirely faded. Although it was a ridiculous response for a man of his age, that bared bit of back and the thin pink-and-white polka-dot bra straps riding on her shoulders was all it took to make him hard.

Not wanting to surprise her and cause her to fall off the ladder and break her neck, he mentally went through the multiplication tables the way his high school coach had taught the guys to do whenever they got boners watching the cheerleaders flashing their royal-blue panties while doing flips on the sidelines. When the song ended with her still believing, he called out to her. When she still didn't respond, he carefully reached out and tapped her bare shoulder, which had her twisting around so fast, she slipped down a step.

Dropping the bag of tacos, he grabbed hold of her hips to steady her.

She jerked the buds from her ears. "You nearly gave me a heart attack!"

"Sorry." Not sorry. Not when she was safe and his fingers were splayed on her very fine butt. She kept having him feeling stuff that he didn't want to feel. But Seth was discovering that want and need could be two very different things. "I called out to you. More than once. But you were busy belting out about taking your life back and didn't hear me."

"I thought I was all alone." She looked around, as if checking to see if any others of the crew had witnessed her less than professional performance.

"You were. But I got the barn door, so I thought I'd bring it by."

"Oh, yay!" She'd never been one to hold a grudge. Either large or small. Another plus in the hospitality business, he decided. The same as his job. He'd had clients yell obscenities to his face after he'd been forced to break bad news about unexpected costs not covered in the original estimate, only to have them turn around a few years later and hire him to either do more work on the original project or fix up a new place.

Because she wasn't complaining, and he was in no hurry to move them, he kept his hands where they were as she backed the rest of the way down the metal ladder.

Before heading to the door, she stopped at the brown paper bag. "Are those tacos I'm smelling?"

"Yeah." He scooped up the bag. Fortunately, nothing felt crushed. "I stopped at that food truck, Taco the Town, and picked up dinner. I bought extra in case you wanted some." Stopping at the truck, which he passed every day on the way to the pub, had been an impulse. One more step out of his comfort zone.

"Are you kidding? Who'd turn down a taco? What kind?"

"Carne asada made with skirt steak. Rubbed with spice,

marinated in lime juice and topped with pico de gallo and lime crema."

"Oh, yum. With guac?"

"Absolutely. And chips. Also, there's Dos Equis in the cooler."

"That sounds fabulous. I haven't had a taco in, well, like forever, and didn't even know I was craving one until I smelled it. But what are you going to tell my brother when you don't show up at his pub?" she teased.

He put his arm around her shoulder, easily, not like he was hitting on her or anything, just like two friends walking out the door. *Liar.* "I'll tell him I found a preferable Mannion sibling to dine with."

"Ah." She lifted her brows. "*Dine* sounds a bit fancy for a taco truck meal."

"It's not as much the meal as the company."

She'd found an old iron bench at Treasures for the front porch, intending to spray paint it and buy some cushions. They sat on it the way it was, the take-out containers on their laps, enjoying the cooling breeze coming off the bay, the brisk scent of salt and fir mingling with the aroma of spicy grilled meat, and the sight of the sailboats skimming over the jeweled blue water.

They talked easily, about the changes that had taken place in the town while she'd been away, and how her house was coming together so well because, as she echoed his thoughts, they'd made such a good team, just as they had when they built the volcano for chemistry week in fourth grade.

She told him about Clara, about how, despite having been born early, she seemed to be growing every day. He laughed about the burp, as she'd meant him to, and then, once they'd wadded up their taco wrappers and put them and the cardboard containers in the recycling bin, that now-familiar sexual tension, which they'd both been trying to avoid, hung between them, sparking like a downed electrical wire in a thunderstorm.

Which was when Brianna noticed the red splotch between her breasts from the pico de gallo that had dropped unnoticed out of her taco. "I'm a mess."

"Tacos are supposed to be messy." He was definitely noticing her breasts. And not in a way that suggested he was thinking of taco sauce. "That's part of the fun."

"It's not just that." Brianna pushed her bangs back from her forehead, which had been dripping salty sweat into her eyes while she'd been steaming the wallpaper. Oh, yeah, she totally looked like a woman a guy would want to do. Not. "I need a shower."

"Me, too." With a guy's lack of body self-consciousness, he lifted his arm and smelled his pit. That shouldn't be sexy, but damned if her lady parts didn't begin to purr. "I heard on the radio that the weather bureau is predicting the hottest summer in a decade. They may even have to start limiting what days people can water their lawns and gardens."

"I hope we can get all the landscaping in and well-rooted before that happens."

"Conserving water is always a good thing," Seth said.

"I'm all for saving the planet." There was another, longer, more significant pause as she looked up at him through her lashes in a flirtatious way that she'd always considered overkill when she saw other women doing it. But if she was going to break through that damn stone wall he'd built around himself, she figured she'd better pull out all the stops. "Perhaps we should consider practicing conservation together."

The invitation was unmistakable. She held her breath as she watched him process it. Then a grin Brianna had feared she'd never see again spread across his face. And there was a sexy gleam in his eyes that she'd never, ever thought would be directed at her.

Then, just in case the lash-upward-gazing thing had been a bit too subtle, and, although he might have thought she'd been talking about saving the planet—which, while admittedly important, wasn't at the top of her priority list at the moment—Brianna considered WWKD. *What would Kylee do?*

"I need to take a shower," she repeated. "And I want—no, I *need*—to take it with you."

CHAPTER TWENTY-EIGHT

Proving that they were, indeed, on the same wavelength, Seth didn't hesitate.

He lifted her off her feet, and took her mouth with his as she wrapped her legs around his waist. The kiss, which had begun soft and gentle, grew firmer, more serious. As his early evening beard scraped against her cheek and she breathed in the erotic workingman scents of sweat and musk, she knew that there'd be no turning back this time.

"There are too many stairs," she said as he carried her into the house. Three flights. All tightly curving. She might not be as heavy as that mattress he and his dad had lugged up to her room, but still...

"Oh, ye of little faith." She felt him grin against her lips as he kissed her again, causing every bone in her body to melt like butter left out in the sun. Brianna had no choice but to trust him since she wasn't certain that she'd even be able to stand on her own legs—which had gone as limp as overcooked spaghetti—let alone make it up to the third floor.

Chest to chest as they were, she could feel his heart pounding as hard as her own and hoped that she wasn't going to cause him to have a heart attack. She unwrapped her arms around his strong, dark neck just long enough to slip her hand between them and press her palm against the front of his shirt. No, the beat, while hard, was steady. There was none of that jumpy fibrillation feel she'd seen on *Grey's Anatomy* right before a patient flatlined.

Once they'd made it to the bathroom, apparently deciding they'd wasted enough time, after turning on the shower, he quickly stripped. Like many men, he seemed totally comfortable with being naked and stood there, muscled legs spread apart, as she drank in the sight of him, the breadth of his wide shoulders and strong arms, before staring at those washboard abs Kylee totally needed to immortalize in her calendar. Her gaze followed the happy trail of brown hair down his chest, then further south.

It wasn't the first time she'd seen him naked. Once, while he and her brothers had gone skinny dipping at Mirror Lake, she and Kylee had sneakily followed them, hiding in the trees rimming the lake, getting their first glimpse of the male anatomy. Brianna had taken definite interest in the part that her Ken doll certainly didn't possess. But they'd been boys at the time. While Seth was definitely now all male. Every beautiful inch of him.

When she realized she was staring, she pulled her sweat-stained tank over her head and tossed it aside, where it landed on the closed seat of the commode. Then, although her fingers had turned to ten thumbs, she managed to unhook the cotton polka-dot bra, which—wouldn't you just know it?—didn't match her underpants. Because how could she have known this morning when she got dressed that unless she was in an accident that would take her to the ER, anyone would see her underwear?

Not that it seemed to matter to Seth. This time his slow, easy smile revealed pleasure at what he was seeing. A pleasure that couldn't equal the feel of his calloused hands cupping her breasts, roughened thumbs skimming across her ultrasensitive nipples.

She froze, for just an instant, when his hands went to the button of her shorts.

"Do you normally shower with your clothes on?" His eyes, which had turned a deep smoky brown while savoring her breasts, turned teasing.

"No." Her hands covered his. "It's just, oh, hell, I didn't expect to be doing this."

"We can stop."

"No." *Oh, please, God, no!* "It's just that, well, you'd probably have to be a woman to understand, but my underwear doesn't match." And could the tile floor now open and swallow her up before she could humiliate herself any further?

"Well, damn." Was he laughing at her? Now? While they were finally about to have sex? "And doesn't that just throw a bucket of cold water on my libido?" Risking a glance down, she saw it certainly hadn't seemed to.

He touched a roughened fingertip against her lips. Dipped his sunstreaked head and kissed her again, running the tip of his tongue along the seam of her mouth. Then drew back and smiled down at her. "I want to see you, Bri. Touch you. All of you. Everywhere."

How could any woman resist a line like that? But she knew he really meant it, because unlike her bad-boy brothers, Burke and Aiden, Seth didn't resort to lines.

He took hold of her hands and held them away from her body. Then got busy on her shorts, pulling them down her legs. He kissed her thighs, behind her knees, her ankles, before working his way back up again.

"Oh, yeah," he said as he stood there, checking out her undies. Which, since she'd known she'd be getting hot and sweaty, were comfy cotton. The color was technically labeled *blush* rather than a nun's white. But it definitely wasn't what she'd fantasized about wearing the first time this man undressed her.

He took her hand, circling her fingers around his length. "I just may need myself some Viagra after seeing those panties." Impossibly, since atoms were exploding inside her as he began to move her hand up and down, Brianna laughed. Which she couldn't ever remember doing before while having sex.

Steam rose as he drew her into the shower. He poured some tropical-scented body soap into his palms, rubbed his hands together, then moved them over her body, following every curve and hollow. And then, if that wasn't havoc enough, as the water flowed over them, his mouth followed the trail. His tongue dipped into her navel and made her moan. His teeth nipping against the wet, hot flesh of her inner thigh had her reaching for him, but he'd already moved on.

Clouds of steam surrounded them, filling her lungs. Her mind. Brianna couldn't breathe. Couldn't think.

And then, just when she was sure she was going blind, his mouth found her. Her head fell back against the tile as she gave herself up to the explosive orgasm rocketing through her. To him.

And that was just the beginning. Over the next ten days, it was as if they were both making up for lost time. Brianna was not only experiencing the most mind-blowing sex of her life, she was having a full-blown, no-holds-barred affair. She knew the shape of Seth as her hands explored his body. The weight of him as he lay on top of her. Inside her.

She knew how he tasted, the glorious roughness of his hands as they traced over her curves and hollows, which he declared to be perfection. They'd come to know each other's bodies as well as they knew each other's mind. And it should have been wonderful. Glorious. But having never been one to allow herself to live solely in the moment, she could sense problems on the horizon as sure as the clouds on the horizon of the harbor signaled a storm blowing in from the Pacific.

Meanwhile, somehow, by never going out in public, and him moving his truck behind the house when the crew left at the end of the workday, then crawling out of the bed to return to his own home before sunrise, so far they'd managed to keep their affair their secret. As far as she could tell, no one had caught wind of the fact that Seth Harper and Brianna Mannion were having hot sex in every room of Herons Landing.

Oh, Kylee and Mai knew. But her secret was safe with them. And Dottie and Doris at the Dancing Deer undoubtedly suspected because she'd bought out nearly their entire lingerie section in the past week. She could've bought online, but 1) she was impatient, and 2) she'd wanted to feel the material herself. To run her fingers over the panties, bras and camisoles and imagine how the lace and silk might feel to Seth's roughened fingers.

To their credit and her undying gratitude, neither woman said a thing as they ran her credit card. But Brianna did notice a glisten of moisture in Dottie's eyes as she wrapped the lingerie in pink tissue paper, and wondered if the elderly woman was thinking of her Harold. And remembering when she'd worn bits of lace and satin for him.

Although Brianna wondered why Seth hadn't spent the past two Saturday nights with her, when no crew would be arriving on a Sunday morning, she'd given him enough personal space not to ask. The same way she'd stayed away from the topic of marriage. It might be cowardly, but she didn't want to risk him backing away again. Better to leave things as they were for now, she told herself. Friends with benefits was, after all, downright amazing.

Like Kylee said, it might take time. And, as much as she

was already picturing their children—a boy and a girl would be lovely, but she wasn't particular—she was willing to wait. After all, part of her journey back to Honeymoon Harbor had been about slowing down her life. They weren't in any hurry. Neither of them was going anywhere.

Though there were admittedly times when she'd wanted to escape the daylong screech of saws cutting tile and ripping wood and the hammering of nail guns Quinn had warned her about. But since she could see the progress happening before her eyes, she wasn't about to complain.

Two evenings ago, as they'd sat on the front porch, drinking wine and watching the sunset on the water, she'd indulged in a daydream where they'd be slow dancing at Kylee and Mai's rescheduled wedding, when having watched the couple exchange their vows, followed by his mother christening pink-cheeked baby Clara, who'd be dressed in the same white dress Kylee herself had worn for her baptism, Seth would realize, like she had that day in the hospital cafeteria, that he wanted to build a new life. To create a family. With her.

Caroline had just packed her cotton canvas tote with painting supplies for another morning in the park with Mike when there was a knock at her door.

"You're early," she said as she opened it. "I'm almost…" Her words dropped off as she saw who was standing there, flowers in hand. Not roses this time. But the tulips were the same tropical sunset coral color.

"Hello, Ben." She struggled for calm, even as her heart was racing. He wouldn't bring flowers if he weren't going to finally cave in, would he? "Those are lovely."

"I got them at the Blue House Farm booth at the market," he said.

"Let me put them in water." When she had to practically

pull them from his tightly fisted hand, she realized he was as nervous as she. And wasn't that a thought?

He followed her into the apartment, glancing at the tote and easel by the door. "Are you going somewhere?"

"I'd planned to go up to the park." The furnished apartment hadn't come with any vases, but it did have a white pitcher she filled with water. "I've been working on plein air, which is landscape painting in its natural setting. It's tricky, but I enjoy it." She arranged the tulips and set them in the middle of the small circular table.

"That's good. That you enjoy it. I guess Mannion's teaching you."

She lifted her chin at the edge she heard in his rough voice. "He is the only art teacher in town," she said. "Did you come here for a reason? Other than to bring me flowers again? Because as lovely as they are—"

"I came to ask if you wanted to go out."

"Out?"

"Like…you know…" He sort of waved a broad, work-roughened hand.

"Are you asking me out on a date?"

"Yeah. I am."

"Oh." Now she was the one having trouble coming up with what to say.

"There's this restaurant in Port Townsend. It's got both meat and vegetarian dishes." Caroline felt her heart melting as he looked down at the wooden floor he was scuffing his work boot on like a bashful six-year-old. "I thought maybe we could have dinner there tomorrow night."

It wasn't a full surrender. But it was encouraging. "I'd love that."

He lifted his head, allowing her to see the surprise and what appeared to be relief in his eyes. "Really?"

"Really. It's been a very long time since we've been on a date together."

Before he could say anything else, there was another knock at the door. Terrific. And wasn't Mike Mannion showing up just what this situation needed? Knowing she couldn't leave him outside, she drew in a calming breath, then walked across the room and opened the door again.

"Ready for a great day?" Mike greeted her, his smile fading as he glanced over her shoulder and saw Ben standing there, hands now jammed into his jeans pockets. "Harper."

"Mannion."

The younger, more romantic girl she'd once been would probably have found the idea of two handsome men vying for her attentions wildly romantic. The woman she'd grown to be did not.

"I can stay if you want to talk," she suggested to Ben.

"No." He shook the tension from his shoulders. "You go ahead and paint your landscape," he said. "How about I pick you up tomorrow at six? I took the chance of booking a table on the patio, so we can watch the sun set on the water."

Now *that* was romantic. And definitely encouraging. "I'll be ready."

He blew out a breath. "Great."

"And thank you again for the flowers."

Proving he was still a man of few words—she'd probably never change that—he merely nodded. Then, mission accomplished, left the apartment. And if his shoulder just happened to bump Mike's on the way out, well, that could've been an accident.

Probably not.

"So, we're still on for a lesson?" Mike asked.

Sarah felt her lips curving. A day painting in the meadow with a man whose company she enjoyed, and a sunset dinner with her husband tomorrow night. Life was definitely beginning to look up.

"Absolutely."

On this Sunday morning, as usual, Seth had driven Zoe's Civic up to Hurricane Ridge, was waved through the station gate by the ranger on duty, then spent the next hour watching a pair of ospreys with at least five-foot wingspans sitting, feeding their nestlings with fish they'd fly in from the strait. Usually his trips up here caused an ache in his chest. One that, even though it had lessened over the years, he'd learned to live with. Today, after about twenty minutes, he realized that he wasn't feeling it. He waited a bit. Thought about his wife. Waited some more as the giant birds dutifully continued their flights back and forth between water and nest.

It wasn't that he didn't still miss Zoe. She'd always be a part of him. It was more that somehow, over this spring, it didn't hurt to think of her. And most of the anger he'd felt about the unfairness of what had happened was gone. People had told him that time cured all wounds. He'd never believed that, and he knew there'd always be a scar in that place in his heart where Zoe had resided for so many years. But it was no longer a gaping wound. Not healed by time.

But by Brianna having come back home and into his life. He wasn't sure where they were going, but perhaps that wasn't just a bad thing. Maybe, he considered as he got back into the Civic and began the drive back down the road that wound like a tangled fishing line out of the park, like his mother kept telling him, there was a lot to be said about living in the moment. Especially when a lot of those moments were spent having hot, blow-your-mind sex. And, something he'd really missed, sleeping with a warm, soft woman in his arms afterward.

He was passing the ranger checkpoint when the woman

walked out and waved him down. He stopped and she came over to the open driver's side window.

"Nice day," she said.

"Can't argue that," Seth said.

And it was going to get better once he got over to Herons Landing and spent some lazy Sunday morning time rolling around that wide mattress with Brianna. One cool thing about Sundays was that she'd try out her B and B breakfast menus on him. Last week she'd had him taste test a citrus berry pizza made with a cream cheese base on top of fluffy dough with a berry topping and whipped cream, which he thought was pretty good, for like maybe a breakfast appetizer. He'd admitted that male guests would probably prefer her hash brown/cheddar cheese/bacon casserole topped with eggs fried in fresh butter from a local dairy farm.

"Got a question for you," the ranger said as his stomach growled at the memory of that meal.

"Okay." He was expecting her to ask about doing more remodeling on her '70s rancher when she surprised him. "You ever think about selling this car?"

"Not really."

"I was just wondering. Now that you and the Mannion girl are an item, I figured you wouldn't need an extra vehicle in that two-car garage of yours. Course, I guess if you end up moving into Herons Landing, you can build yourself a bigger garage." She scratched her head like she was thinking on something, while Seth was thinking how the hell she knew about him and Bri. "I'm not sure I'd be that thrilled about having a previous wife's car parked next to mine if I were her, but hey, we all look at things differently, right?"

"Right. But what makes you think that Brianna Mannion and I are a couple?"

"Oh, honey, don't be so naive. Everyone in town knows that you and that girl are seeing each other."

Seriously? "I don't get into town gossip, but you're the first person who's brought it up. And if it is true, which I'm not saying it is, how would anyone know?"

"Maybe because you haven't been eating dinner at Mannion's every night?"

"Sometimes a guy just likes to mix things up. I've gotten take-out tacos. And pizza. And lasagna."

"You've also bought enough groceries down at the market for two. Unless you're storing up for some disaster like those survivalist types."

Seth realized he was busted. "Everyone knows?"

"Just about. But don't worry. We're all keeping it off the Facebook page to give you both some privacy."

"Now there's a concept." One that had, as far as he'd seen, never before existed.

"You deserve to have yourself a romance after what all you've been through," she said, her eyes warm with sympathy. "Being widowed myself, though not at a tragically young age like you, I know how it feels as if you've lost a major part of yourself. And how small towns can be like living in a fishbowl. When I started going out with my Kenny, who became my girl's stepdaddy, I felt like we were lit up in a spotlight whenever we went anywhere. Gave me an idea how those celebrities must feel, always being followed around by tabloid photographers looking to make a quick buck."

"I'm not planning to get remarried," he felt obliged to point out before everyone in Honeymoon Harbor had Brianna and him engaged, married and filling Herons Landing with a passel of kids. He didn't mention that more random scenes of imagined children—who'd grow up loving Herons Landing the same as the two of them did—had occasionally flashed through his mind.

"Neither was I when I stopped by Kenny's garage to have

my winter tires put on. But life goes on and love can happen just when you're not looking for it."

"Well, I appreciate everyone giving us some space," he said.

"No worries. And getting back to my original point, if you ever do decide to sell this pretty little red car, I've got a granddaughter who just finished culinary training at Clearwater Community College and got herself a job in Olympia at some fancy seafood place on the Sound."

"Good for her."

"We're real proud of her. The thing is, she's going to be working nights and I'd feel a lot better if she didn't have to walk over to the bus depot, then walk home after the driver lets her off a couple blocks from her apartment. I've been thinking that this baby would be affordable for her to keep up and keep her safer. Plus, red's her favorite color. So if you change your mind about keeping it, I'd like first shot at buying it for her."

"You've got it," Seth promised. Not that he intended to sell the Civic, but he did agree that while the state capital might not have a lot of big-city crime, a young woman walking alone on the dark streets at night probably wasn't the best idea.

"Thanks." She tipped her fingers to her Smokey Bear ranger hat. "I'd appreciate that. Have yourself a nice rest of your day."

"Thanks, I intend to. You, too."

As he drove to Herons Landing, Seth debated whether or not to tell Brianna that they'd landed in the town's social topic bull's-eye, apparently reclaiming the spot taken up by his parents' separation and the birth of Kylee and Mai's adopted baby.

CHAPTER TWENTY-NINE

Seth was passing Cops and Coffee, wondering what Brianna was making for breakfast, hoping it would hold because just the thought of her bustling around in the kitchen had him fantasizing about taking her on that matte quartz kitchen counter with her wearing nothing but one of those cute retro '50s aprons she'd begun buying—and maybe a pair of high-heeled pumps like all those TV housewives used to wear—when his dad came out and waved him down.

He pulled over to the curb and got out of the truck.

"We need to talk," his dad, never much for talking, said without so much as a "good morning."

"Is it about you and mom?" He'd been in Cops and Coffee the other morning just in time to see his dad getting onto the ferry. It hadn't made sense because Pete had returned home from the VA hospital last week. Unless something else was going on. A possibility he'd been trying not to think about. "Because I don't want—"

"It is. And it isn't. It's mostly about you and that Mannion girl."

"What?" As far as he knew, except for his poker games,

his dad never went anywhere, hardly talked to a soul. How
the hell did he know? And what had Seth done to be forced
to have this conversation twice on a morning when he could
be tasting not just breakfast, but every inch of Brianna's tall,
lean body, which he'd come to know as well as his own? "I
don't want to be disrespectful here, Dad. But whatever our
relationship happens to be, it's our business." *And no one else's,*
he left out, but the message was clear.

"It is and it isn't," Ben Harper repeated. "I've got some
stuff to say and you need to listen to it. Before you fuck up
the best thing in your life."

Only because his father hadn't offered him a word of advice
since he'd shown up at his bedroom door with a box of condoms and given him "the talk," Seth decided he must think
whatever he had to say was damn important. Which meant
the least he could do was hear his old man out.

"Let me get some coffee and something to eat."

"I got a bag of bacon maple doughnuts. There's enough
for two."

"Because everything goes better with bacon," Seth said,
thinking about Brianna's hash brown/cheddar cheese/bacon
casserole.

"You got that right," Ben said. "I'll meet you at the pier."

Surprisingly, the pier wasn't as crowded as Seth would have
expected on a sunny Sunday morning. He figured all the
serious fishermen were out on the water, other folks might
have been in church and there was a good possibility Wheel
and Barrow was doing a dynamite business with everyone
getting excited about a new season of planting their flowers
and veggies.

His dad was sitting on a green bench toward the end of
the pier, not far from a father and kid who looked about six
or seven with their lines dangling into the water. Walking

down the wooden pier, listening to the waves lap against the pilings, reminded Seth of those days when they'd get up early in the morning to go crabbing off the pier.

Although his dad seemed to take his crabbing super seriously, like he did most everything, Seth hadn't cared whether or not they came home with a catch. It was having rare time together that didn't have anything to do with work that was special. Although he wasn't expecting an easy talk, thinking back on those rare times caused a bit of the peace he'd felt up on the ridge to settle back over him.

Seth sat on the far end of the bench, folded the plastic top back on his coffee and dug into the bag between them. Even as he felt his arteries clogging from the sugar, maple and bacon at the first bite, he decided a heart attack just might be worth it.

"So," he said, breaking the silence that lasted through his dad's entire eating of the Long John. "What's up?"

His dad adjusted his Harper Construction hat, brushed some crumbs off his Tom Selleck mustache and said, "I've got something to tell you, and then we're not going to talk about it again, okay?"

"Okay."

"It's about my trips to Seattle. I'm guessing you didn't think I was visiting Pete."

"That became clear after Pete came home and you were still taking those days off." Seth hadn't wanted to know about that because it brought up too many possibilities. Like was his dad seeing someone because he thought his wife was sleeping with Mike Mannion? Or had his mother left because he'd had a woman on the side all the time?

"I've been seeing this therapist."

"A therapist?" Having just taken a drink, Seth spit out his Portside dark roast. "Like one who works on your bum knee?" Which had come from too many years of going up and down ladders. "Or like a shrink?" Unlikely. It'd be easier to believe his father had been beamed up by a spaceship.

"She's a licensed therapist with a bunch of psychology degrees from fancy universities hanging on her wall."

Seth took another long drink of coffee, willing the triple shot to pump caffeine into his brain. "You've been taking the ferry to the mainland, then driving to Seattle, to see a shrink—" he raised his hand to take that word back when his father speared him with a look sharper than the fillet knife he'd used to clean steelhead "—*licensed therapist*."

"You got a problem with that?"

"No. It's just not what I was expecting."

"You thought I was seeing another gal."

"No. Yes. Well, okay, since you brought it up, it did cross my mind." Returning to his spaceship analogy, Seth wished that he could just call on Scotty to beam him up to anywhere and any other time but here. "Maybe."

"I'd never cheat on your mother. Ever."

"I believe you." Ben Harper was not without his faults, but Seth had never known him to lie. Which was why his lack of openness about his reasons for suddenly disappearing every few days had been troublesome. There had been one more possibility that Seth hadn't wanted to consider. That he was getting some sort of medical care he was keeping to himself. Like he had with his damn appendix. "I'm also glad that you have neither another woman on the side or cancer."

"Why the hell would you think I had cancer?" Ben dug into the bag again and pulled out a second Long John.

"No reason." There was no point in bringing up him almost dying once for having been a damn fool when his appendix had burst. "Why didn't you tell me? Does Mom know?"

"Not yet. And before you play Dear Abby and say I ought to tell her, I'm planning to. I just wanted to make sure I could also tell her that I'd gotten my head straight and would spend the rest of my life making up for past problems I'd caused her."

"Well." What did a guy say to that? Especially when it came from your own father, after you'd already told him that you didn't want to get mixed up in his marital drama? "That's good." He nodded and took a bite himself. "Real good," he said around a mouthful of doughnut.

"You know I was in the military before I met your mother."

"Sure." Though his dad had never talked about his military days, Seth had seen a photo of him on his boot camp graduation day looking ready to take on all the world's bad guys single-handed. "You were in the Navy."

"Though it pissed off my dad, I didn't want to stick around this town. So I bought into the message on those posters in the recruiting office window telling me that if I joined the Navy, I could see the world."

"Did you? See the world?" Another thing his dad had never mentioned.

"Some of it. But only after having a long talk with the recruiter my junior year of high school. I've heard a lot of them lie, but he was up front and told me that I wouldn't get to see much of the world from the deck of a ship or in a sub. Also, because I was captain of both the football and baseball teams, and had good grades in math and science, which probably came from years of working on houses with my dad growing up, he figured I might have a chance of making the SEALs. But having at least an associate's degree would give me a boost up. So I went to community college nights and Saturdays while working all day for my dad on houses. Then I joined up."

"You were a SEAL?"

"Yeah. Not right away—there's a helluva lot of hoops and training to get through, and they make it as hard as they can so they can be sure you can handle the job—but I made the grade. And I got to see some of the world, though not places most people ever want to go." He took a long gulp of coffee and looked out over the water, but Seth got the feeling his dad wasn't looking at snow-clad Mount Baker towering in the distance, but something else. Something else in his past he'd never mentioned. "I was in Lebanon."

Seth skimmed through a mental history book and did the math. "In Beirut?"

"Yeah."

"For the barracks bombing?" That had taken the lives of how many Marines?

"Yeah. It was the deadliest attack on Marines since Iwo Jima, the deadliest single-day death toll for the US military since the Tet Offensive and the deadliest terrorist attack before 9/11." Seth didn't remember reading all that, but he figured if he'd been there for the bombing, he'd never have forgotten it.

"Were you in the barracks?" How the hell could he have not at least heard *that* story?

"No. We were five hundred yards away, up in the hills above the city on a reconnaissance mission. We came under artillery fire on the way back and by the time we got to our bunker, it was nearly five in the morning. We could have taken our mess kits and gone down and had ourselves a hot breakfast. But we were pretty wiped by then, so the effort didn't seem worth it.

"Some of the other guys were going to wind down from the adrenaline rush and read—Robert B. Parker had a new book out—and others got out some *Playboy* and *Penthouse* magazines. But I hit the rack...

"I don't know how long I slept, but suddenly the entire place shook like it had been hit with one of those bunker buster bombs. There was a lot of confusion while we were all trying to figure out what the hell had happened, but then

Benson, one of my teammates who'd been out taking a piss, came running in shouting that they'd hit the barracks.

"It was hard to believe what we were seeing. Some days it still seems more like one of those end-of-the-world movies. While we'd been safe, sleeping or looking at porn, what turned out to be a truck bomb had damn near vaporized a four-story building.

"We went racing down the hill into this enormous cloud of ash and debris falling everywhere, and everyone who was mobile began digging out our dead and wounded from the rubble while snipers kept shooting at us. For days. A lot of guys got hit by bullets, others by cracking and spattering concrete.

"Meanwhile, down the road, another truck took out the French barracks. Many of those killed were paratroopers standing out on balconies, trying to figure out what had happened where we were."

"Jesus." Seth had seen old news videos during his American history class. But never in a million years had he imagined his dad in those scenes.

"It was the closest thing to hell I ever hope to get," Ben said. "It took days, and eventually the voices of guys still trapped quit calling out for help. That was the worst. But at the same time, it was so fucking overwhelming that we became frozen to it. We just kept working. All night and day."

"I don't think I could've done that," Seth admitted.

"Yeah, you could've, but I wouldn't have wanted you to," his dad said. "And I'm not telling you this to make you feel worse about your own grief over losing your wife in the same damn way. I wasn't happy about her going off to war, but hell, it wasn't any of my business. That gal was always going to do exactly what she wanted to."

"You're not going to get any argument from me about that." As Seth said the words he realized that along with the peace that had come over him, he was no longer as angry as he had been even a few weeks ago. Not at Zoe, and not at himself. Which didn't mean he didn't still wish he'd been able to stop her, but like his dad said, she was a woman who knew her own mind.

Just like Brianna. But in a different way.

"But you got over it?"

"You never get over a thing like that," Ben said. "You put it away, in a box, where you don't ever have to think about it." He looked at Seth. Long and hard. "I imagine you know a lot about that."

"Yeah. I do."

"The thing is that it doesn't work forever. The Trade Center bombings brought it all back to me. That was the first time I had to tell your mother about it. Not the entire story. Just that I'd been there."

"Mom hadn't known before then?"

"Like I said, it was in a box. We didn't meet until I got out, so there was no point in mentioning it... I don't know what I would've done without her... Yeah, I do," he said. "I just would've ended it after the PTSD came back."

And didn't Seth know the siren's call of doing exactly that? Maybe that was another thing he and his dad shared in their DNA. The inability to take the easy way out.

Ben blew out a long breath. "So I built myself another box, even stronger than the first, and made sure I stayed away from the TV during September every year. That was working. Kind of, anyway, although your mother might claim differently, because things were more strained from time to time, though we got through it. Until all this damn terrorist stuff started up again all over the news and it's like I'm right back there in Beirut... She wants me to quit my job."

Seth decided against saying he knew that.

"I promised her, when we got married, that someday we'd

travel. So she's got this idea about buying a motor home and driving across America, seeing all the national parks and stuff."

"Sounds like a good plan."

"Yeah. But it also means that we'd be stuck together in a damn metal box for twenty-four hours a day. And because I love her more than life itself, I just couldn't dump all these ugly dark memories and feelings I've locked up inside me on her."

"Has the therapist helped with that?" Seth asked hopefully. Now that he'd heard the story, he had a lot more invested in his parents' marriage succeeding. But not if it was going to cause them both pain.

"Yeah. She has, which is surprising, because she's, well, a woman. And young. Just a few years older than you."

"Maybe that's a good thing. PTSD has been around forever, but it hasn't been studied that much. She'd probably be more up on treatment," Seth suggested.

"I'm comfortable talking to her," Ben agreed. "I didn't think I would be."

Probably because he didn't experience any male competitive feelings, Seth suspected. And there was also the fact that being a man of a certain age, he'd be more likely to accept a woman as someone who could understand emotional problems he couldn't talk about with the guys.

"I'm glad for you."

"Yeah. She's helped a lot with what she calls coping techniques. I've been doing some deep breathing and visualization. But I drew the line at taking up yoga."

"Can't say I blame you there." Just the idea of his father doing a downward dog made Seth grin.

"So." Ben brushed his hands together to shake off the sugar. "The thing is, you've probably got a lot of stuff in your box, too."

"Maybe."

"You've also got yourself a good woman who's had a thing for you all her life."

"Geez. Does everyone know that?"

"Everyone but you, it seems. You were too young to be looking in that direction early on. Then once you met Zoe Robinson, you were blind to seeing any other girls. The past few weeks I've realized that a lot of guys are probably okay with living alone. But you and me, we're not them. I'm going to do my damnedest to get my wife back from Mike Mannion."

"She's not with Mike."

"Not yet, maybe. But if I lose her, he'd be the obvious choice to be her rebound guy. I'll take care of my relationship. I've been working on it bit by bit and it's getting easier. We're going out on a date tomorrow. To this wine bar bistro place in Port Townsend so she can eat her veggies, but it also serves steak, so I figured that'd be a good compromise."

"It is. And a good start."

"That's what my therapist says. She also taught me some conversational tricks that don't risk us getting into any argument over me quitting work or any future plans. We're supposed to just experience living in the moment together, she says." Deep color flushed up his neck. "She got me to do this conversational dinner-talking role-playing thing."

Despite the seriousness of the discussion, Seth struggled not to laugh at this news flash. "And how did that turn out?"

"Pretty damn well. She had your mother down pat. Meaning I guess she listened to everything I'd said about Caroline."

"I think that's what they're supposed to do. Listen."

"Yeah. It was a lot like when Tony'd talk with Dr. Melfi on *The Sopranos*. So, hopefully we'll make it through dinner okay."

"My money's on you."

"Yeah. Like we used to say in the SEALs, the only easy day

was yesterday and failure's not an option. Which you need to keep in mind and not let that Mannion girl get away," Ben warned. "She's a keeper, and if you lose her, you'll end up spending the rest of your life regretting screwing up a relationship you both deserve."

As weird as it was getting romantic advice from a man who'd probably, even a month ago, choked over the word *relationship*, Seth only wished things between him and Brianna were that simple.

CHAPTER THIRTY

Seth found Brianna in the kitchen as she was most Sunday mornings—unfortunately not naked beneath a blue-and-white-gingham apron with a ruffle around the bottom—but slicing white button mushrooms with a lethal-looking knife at a speed that would put his nail gun to shame.

"I hope you're up for another hash breakfast," she greeted him with a smile that soothed the still ragged edges from his conversation with his dad. At the same time, the way she'd put her hair up into that messy high bun revealed a long smooth neck he wanted to lick. And that was just for starters.

"Sounds good." Lifting her up on that counter and burying himself deep inside her sounded even better.

"It's a Pacific Northwest take on corned beef hash, with Dungeness crab in place of the corned beef. I picked the crab up fresh at Kira's Fish House this morning."

One of the aspects of her business she was highlighting on her website and brochures was how all the food served at Herons Landing was both locally inspired and locally sourced. In these days of more and more foodies finding their way to the peninsula, he figured that would prove a strong draw.

When she turned and bent over to get a box of eggs from the oversize fridge, a jolt of lust had him groaning, which caused her to glance back over her shoulder.

"Are you okay?"

"Yeah." From the concern in her blue eyes as they swept over him, he guessed she might be wondering why he'd been so late arriving this morning. "On my way here, Dad was coming out of Cops and Coffee. He waved me down and wanted to talk."

"Is everything all right?"

"Yeah. Mostly, I guess. You know he's been taking time off the job."

"Because he's cutting back to part-time, right, now that this place is coming along so well?" She began dicing the red potatoes for the hash. "I also figured he's probably finishing up the last of those plaster molds at his workshop."

"Both those are true." Seth weighed breaking a confidence, but it wasn't like his dad had instructed him to keep it under his hat. And Bri wasn't just anyone. She was the woman he was having sex with.

No. It was more than that. His dad was right about one thing. They were in a relationship. Where they were going, he still wasn't sure, but they'd shared the most intimate parts of themselves. He knew, if their situations were reversed, not that he could ever see John and Sarah Mannion having marriage problems, she'd share with him.

"But another reason is that he's been seeing a therapist in Seattle."

"Seriously?" It was a good thing she'd already put the eggs down on the counter, because as she spun back toward him, she probably would've dropped them.

"Really. Apparently he's been seeing her twice a week."

"Wow. I never in a million years would have imagined that."

"Join the club."

"He must truly love your mom to do something that must be incredibly difficult for him... Did you say *her*?"

"Yeah. It's a woman. A young woman, but he assures me she's got a lot of fancy degrees and licenses, and she seems to be getting through to him."

"Oh, Seth! That's so wonderful." Her face lit up like the morning sun. Those lips he'd been thinking about tasting since he came back from the pier curved in a dazzling smile that brightened her eyes, like the diamond lights that danced on the surface of Mirror Lake on a summer day.

"He's taking Mom on a date."

"Oh." She sighed. He thought he saw the glisten of a tear in one eye. "That's so sweet. Here in town?"

"No. Port Townsend. He figured they'd have more privacy that way."

"Good idea." Brianna nodded her approval. "The therapist must really have him working hard on this."

"Seems so." He decided she didn't need to know about the role playing. Seth sure as hell wouldn't want anyone knowing he was doing anything like that. "He's also working on some military stuff that he hasn't been able to shake."

"I'd forgotten he was in the military. That was before you were born, right?"

"Yeah. Get this... He was a SEAL."

She'd turned her knife skills to chopping some herbs. "I can see that."

"You can?"

"Absolutely," she confirmed. "If they're anything like in the movies I've seen or the romances I've read, they tend to be strong, silent types. And he'd never ring out." Which was a candidate's way of signaling that all the pain, misery, coldness and fatigue the training class was put through had become too much.

"You watched that documentary on BUD/S training?"

"I streamed it on Netflix. The books got me curious. He's one amazing man, your father."

"Don't tell him I told you this—"

"Cross my heart." Which she did with her fingers.

"He was a hero. During the Beirut barracks bombing."

"Oh. My. God." She took hold of the counter as if to steady herself, obviously stunned and envisioning the same videos that had flashed through his mind. He'd been too young to remember the stories growing up, but every few years, on the anniversary, one of the cable news programs or PBS would run a segment. "I can't imagine what that must've been like for him. So, that was before he met your mom?"

"Yeah."

"I know I'm repeating myself, but wow. That explains a lot. He'd have to have lingering PTSD. And all the other ter-rorist things that have happened since then must have trig-gered old feelings."

"Ever think of becoming a therapist?" he asked.

Her smile lacked its usual brightness. It was a little sad, and her expressive eyes revealed how deep her sympathy went. "I told you, my job was about more than getting show tickets or restaurant reservations. People were either celebrating some-thing important that I needed to ensure became a memory, or they were stressed out and needed calming, or they had personal problems they thought maybe they could escape by coming to a city that's a twenty-four-hour, seven-days-a-week carnival. Which, of course, didn't work. So there were times I had to deal with the aftermath of self-medication."

Her smile softened. "Then there were others who still had personal reasons for coming." She told him about the elderly lady who carried her husband's ashes back every year. Not having visited his wife's grave once, Seth felt guilty about that one. But then again, the Zoe he'd married was no more in the ground than the widow's husband had been in that urn.

"Well." She blew out a ragged breath. "This conversation has certainly turned depressing."

"I have an idea." He went around the counter and brushed away two tears that were trailing down her cheek. The other hand brushed along the outline of her lips that he'd gone too long—hours—without tasting. "When does that hash need to go into the oven?"

She covered his hand on her cheek with her own softer, smaller, smoother one. "It can wait." Then went up on her toes to meet his mouth.

"I have something to ask you," Brianna said after they'd dressed and were back downstairs in the kitchen.

"Okay. Did I mention this is the best yet?" he asked after plowing halfway through the crab hash she'd topped with a spicy sauce.

"You did. Thank you. And amazingly, I won that praise without including a single slice of bacon."

"I already had bacon today."

"You did?"

"Yeah. Dad got bacon maple Long Johns."

"A heart attack waiting to happen."

"Probably. But worth it. Though they were nothing like this. Your guests are going to lick their plates. And the fact that it has fresh Dungeness makes it even more of a treat for all those folks who aren't lucky enough to live on Pacific waters."

"Thank you." She got up from across the table, bent down and kissed him. "That's exactly what I was hoping you'd say. But what I was going to ask you has to do with the farm."

"Your parents' farm?"

"Yes." She seemed hesitant, which was unusual for her.

From the time she'd arrived in town, she'd seemed totally confident. "Next week is planting time."

"Which means the festival."

It wasn't that big a deal as festivals went, because it involved work, but a lot of townspeople came out to plant the trees and eat great food donated from local vendors like Luca's Kitchen, Mannion's, Dinah's Diner and Taco the Town. And this year, Cops and Coffee and Ovenly would be joining them. The cool thing for families was that the trees could be tagged with the names of the people who'd planted them. Then, seven or ten years later, they could come out and cut their own personal Christmas trees. Granted, not that many had the patience to do that, but Bri had told him that families celebrated the births of each of their children that way. Others bought living trees that they'd replant in their own yards.

"Yes. I was thinking that just maybe, you'd be willing to go with me."

"Even though everyone will see us together?"

"We've been working on the house for weeks," she pointed out as she sat back down in her own chair and put her napkin back on her lap in a way that revealed her surprising discomfort with the topic. Which left him thinking that in a way, by keeping their affair, or relationship, or whatever the hell it was a secret, he'd been behaving as if he was somehow ashamed of it. Or at least ignoring it the way his dad had with his mom. "It's not as if it would be that much of a surprise," she said. "Unless you felt moved to do something like kiss me."

"I always feel moved to kiss you."

It was his turn to get up from the table. From now on, he decided, they were going to sit next to each other. Or better yet, she could sit on his lap and he'd feed her. He bent and let his lips cling to hers for a long, delicious time that had him thinking he could probably warm up the rest of the hash later. After he'd had her again.

"And, FYI, everyone already knows about us," he said.

"They do not."

"According to Dad they do." And the park ranger, whom he decided wasn't relevant to this conversation. "There's no reason for us to try to keep it a secret anymore, Bri. It was probably an impossible idea in the first place."

"True," she agreed with a sigh. "But I've enjoyed having what I thought was our private time together. Time to get reacquainted, but in a new way."

A more intimate way, she didn't say. But he knew she was thinking it. And not just a sexual intimacy, but a personal one. She'd even told him about Doctor Dick, who'd been the inciting incident that had triggered her return home. Part of him had wanted to fly to Des Moines and punch the doctor in his smug, billionaire face. Another, stronger part thought he ought to thank the dick for his part in Brianna Mannion being back in his life.

"I always liked the tree planting," he said. Though back then he'd hung out more with her brothers, and they'd always seemed to end up more wet and muddy than everyone else due to pitching wet, packed balls of soil and mulch at each other. "And I can't think of any better way to spend the day than planting your family's trees with you. On one condition."

She narrowed her eyes, hearing the sexual tease in his roughened tone. "What's that?"

"That we wash the mud off each other in that shower upstairs."

Her smile was both promise and temptation as she reached up, caught his face in her hands and drew his mouth back to hers. "Deal."

After another round of steamy sex that Seth figured would've set up earthquake alarms all over the peninsula, they were lying in bed, all warm in each other's arms, when his phone rang.

"Hey, Dad," he said, feeling far more cheerful than he had in a very long time. It turned out that Quinn and Jarle had been right that frequent and hot sex had been just the ticket to lift that dark cloud from his head.

But not with anyone. It was Brianna who'd changed his life. And as he lay there in the wide bed, with the quilt, top sheet and all those froufrou pillows women seemed to like knocked onto the hand-scraped wooden floor, he admitted to himself something that had been teasing in the background of his mind, but he hadn't dared put into words.

Just like the ranger had with her Kenny somehow, when he hadn't been looking, he'd fallen in love with Brianna Mannion.

"What's up?" he said, dragging his mind back to his father.

"It's your mom."

"Oh?" He exchanged a smile with Bri, who'd left the bed and was fastening a skimpy lace bra the color of a midnight sky. As much as he was enjoying all the fancy lingerie she'd picked up at the Dancing Deer, he would have found her just as sexy in that plain cotton she'd been wearing their first time. "Need some more dating advice?"

"No. She's in the hospital."

"The hospital? Why? What happened?"

He was out of bed like a shot, searching around for his own scattered clothing. Briana fell to her knees and crawled beneath the bed to retrieve the boxer briefs she'd sent flying.

"She had a heart attack while painting some damn deer in a meadow."

"Fuck." He yanked on the briefs and began hopping foot to foot, pulling on his jeans. "I'll be right there." This time the look he exchanged with Brianna, who was already fully dressed, was grim. And, he suspected, as terrified as he felt. "Do you need me to pick you up?"

"No. I just reached the ER." With that Ben cut off the phone.

"She'll be all right," Brianna assured him after they'd found their shoes, raced out to his truck and went roaring down the long driveway that Amanda, who'd had bulldozers working for the past week in front, had begun lining with tall, shaggy fir trees.

"You don't know that," Seth said through clenched teeth as he turned onto the road leading down the bluff into town. It was only because he didn't want to kill any innocent people on the way that kept him from flooring the gas.

"And you don't know she won't be," she pointed out with a calm that he figured had worked well with angry people for whom she couldn't get tickets for some stupid, overpriced Las Vegas show.

"Don't fucking patronize me."

"I wasn't," she defended herself with a flair of heat that, even as terrified as he was, Seth realized came from her own fear.

It was all either of them were to say until they'd reached the hospital. "You go in," she said as they pulled up into the yellow zone in front of the ER. "I'll go park the truck to keep it from getting towed, then come find you."

He wanted to thank her. Not just for that, but for being there for him. For being *her*. But not wanting to take the time to find the words, he burst out of the truck and raced to the door.

CHAPTER THIRTY-ONE

He heard his father before he saw him, standing in front of a window labeled Reception. Like they were checking into some hotel or something. On the other side, a woman stood at a counter, shaking her head.

Oh, yeah. This was going well.

"Dad." He put a hand on his father's shoulder. "Calm down."

"Calm down? You expect me to calm down when my wife's back there and they won't even let me see her?"

"As I've explained, Mr. Harper," the woman said, color beginning to rise in her cheeks, "your wife has been admitted and is undergoing tests."

"I need to be with her."

"I understand. But what she needs is for the doctors and nurses treating her not to be distracted. And, to be perfectly frank, the only thing you could do back there is increase her stress, which I'm sure you wouldn't want to do."

"You don't know a damn thing about us," Ben said. "Maybe she's worried that I don't know. Maybe—" he swallowed, like he had a boulder in his throat "—maybe she's afraid that she'll die without me with her."

"Both those scenarios are quite possible." Seth heard a calm voice behind them and realized that Bri had parked the truck and found her way here. "And you're right to be concerned. If I were you, I'd be frightened. But truly, the best thing you can do right now, Ben, is let the people who know what they're doing take care of her."

She took Ben's hand, which was curled into a fist by his side, and gently unfolded his fingers, lacing them with hers. Amazingly, at least to Seth, his father didn't pull away. Instead, he clung so tightly that he could see Bri's knuckles going white.

"Hello," she said with a smooth, professional smile meant to soothe troubled waters. "I'm Brianna Mannion. A friend of the family."

"I know who you are," the woman said. "You're the mayor's daughter. You're fixing up that old haunted house."

"I am. And I realize that you have a great deal to do, but Mr. Harper and I are wondering if there's any way you could get a message to his wife, to let her know that he and her son are both here."

"I could do that," she agreed.

"Thank you." The smile turned from professional to warm and grateful. Watching her, Seth realized that her former job had required more than organizational skills and a caretaker personality. It had also required acting skills. "We'd appreciate that so much, Ms. Banning. Would you be related to Jack Banning?"

"He's my grandson."

"Isn't that one of the benefits of a small town? We're all family, in a way. Jack sat in front of me in Mr. Clinton's social studies class. He was an excellent student."

"He's a teacher at the college," the woman said as Seth's father begin to shift from foot to foot.

"Isn't that wonderful! He was always the smartest boy in the class... And I don't want to put you to too much bother—"

"That's her damn job," Ben muttered.

Brianna squeezed his hand but ignored his statement.

"Let Bri handle this, Dad," Seth said quietly. "Trust me. She's got it."

"As I was about to say," Brianna continued, "it would be so helpful if you could have someone find us a waiting room. Mrs. Harper has a great many friends and I know that you wouldn't want all the other people who are waiting in the main room to be disturbed by the crowd that will undoubtedly show up. Especially since they have their own worries and don't need the distraction."

"I can do that." She scribbled a note and gave it to a young man sitting at a black metal desk behind her. "Go tell Mrs. Harper that her family's here," she instructed. "And the mayor's daughter." She added that as if Brianna were some sort of Honeymoon Harbor royalty, which, Seth considered, in a way she was. "Then take them up to the small waiting room by the CCU."

She turned back to Brianna, totally ignoring Ben as if he'd turned invisible. "Since the cardiac care unit was named after your family, it's only right that you get yourselves a private waiting room." She paused, shooting Ben a steely warning look. "As long as there aren't any Mannion/Harper *problems*."

"There won't be," Seth's father said, his jaw clenched.

"Good." The woman picked up a stack of papers, hit them against the counter to line up the edges and put them in a folder. "If you'll have a seat, Brian will be back in a moment. But he's only a clerk," she said, wagging a finger at him. "So don't be trying to get any information from him, because he's neither medically trained nor allowed to talk to families about such things."

"We'll wait for the doctor," Seth assured her.

"Fine." She smiled at him. Then at Brianna. Once again his father had turned invisible. Which right now could only be a good thing.

Caroline had been worried about Ben. Even more concerned that he'd be getting the news from Michael, who'd called 911. But the nice young orderly had assured her that her husband and son had arrived at the hospital with Brianna. And that a private waiting room was being arranged. She worried a bit that Ben might feel as if the Mannions were throwing their name around, which is certainly what she'd do if it would have made any difference, but she also decided to leave that problem to Seth and Brianna. Who, from what Sarah had told her over the years, excelled in making the impossible possible. This situation, which she'd gotten herself into by being a damn fool and not realizing that her symptoms had not been from allergies but heart problems, could well require every ounce of professional skills Sarah and John's daughter possessed.

On the plus side, she was feeling much better. The IV and meds they'd given her when she'd first arrived were obviously doing their job. And the sense of panic that had had her in its grip during the ambulance ride down from the park had eased. Though she figured she'd have bruises from that bumpy ride. You'd think, she considered as an orderly wheeled her toward the X-ray department, where they were going to take films of her heart and give her an echocardiogram, and possibly yet more tests, that vehicles transporting seriously injured patients would have softer suspensions. She doubted that the old iron-wheeled wagons that used to go up and down those mountain roads could have been any rougher.

Her last thought, as the door to the room closed behind her, was that she was going to miss a date with her husband.

CHAPTER THIRTY-TWO

The waiting was interminable. Although Brianna had sat with that woman in Honolulu, and cared about her husband's outcome, she'd still been there as what she saw to be part of her job. This, on the other hand, was intensely personal. Her mother and father had arrived, as had Quinn. Sarah had called other friends, but asked them to put off coming to the hospital for now. Knowing how quickly word would get out, she'd also had Caroline's condition put on the town's Facebook page with a note that she wouldn't be allowed visitors, so, not wanting to get in the way of staff trying to help patients, she requested that people not come to the hospital at this time. And please, no flowers, because, as they all knew, Caroline Harper suffered from allergies, especially during spring pollen season.

So for now, those waiting were just the small group of Mannions and Harpers attempting to reassure each other that everything was going to be fine. And repeating the cliché of all clichés—that no news was good news.

Ben, unsurprisingly, couldn't sit still. Although his pacing was getting on her nerves, she understood. Taking in his complexion, which had turned from the angry red it had been when she and Seth had arrived to a sickly gray, she was grateful that medical care was close by. And wouldn't that be all Seth needed? Both his parents admitted to the hospital on the same day.

Finally the doctor arrived.

"Mr. Harper?" she addressed Ben.

"That's me. How's my wife?"

"She's doing quite well, actually. Especially considering that she's already had at least one heart attack."

"What? How could she have a heart attack and not know?"

"Women's symptoms often go unnoticed. They can be mistaken for cold, fatigue, flu, general malaise. Even, this time of year, allergies."

"She complained about that," Seth murmured, closing his eyes and shaking his head, giving Brianna the impression he was wishing he could turn back time.

"It well could have been allergies," the doctor reassured him. "This year's Scotch broom is the worst I've seen in years… At any rate, as a precautionary measure, we performed blood tests to measure the levels of cardiac enzymes that can indicate heart muscle damage. The results of your wife's test revealed that she did indeed have an attack today."

Ben's low, pained moan was easily heard in the silence of the small room.

"Not to get too technical, but troponins are proteins found inside heart cells that are released when damaged due to a lack of blood supply to the heart. Her levels also indicated an attack."

"Christ." The way Ben collapsed into a chair had Brianna worried he'd pass out.

"I'm not going to sugarcoat this," the doctor said briskly. "It's definitely serious, but not nearly as bad as it could be. The echocardiogram revealed enough damage that, since you'd signed permission for any necessary tests—"

"Hell, yes. Do whatever you need," Ben said.

"We did a coronary catheterization, which you may have heard referred to as an angiogram. Liquid dye was injected into the arteries of Mrs. Harper's heart through a long, thin catheter that was fed through an artery in her leg to her heart."

She paused when he slumped and dragged both hands down his face. "Are you all right?"

"Yeah." He took a deep breath. Blew it out.

"It's a very standard test," she assured him. "The reason we do it is the dye makes the arteries visible on X-ray, revealing areas of blockage. In your wife's case, it appears not to be a problem we need to worry about at the moment. She was fortunate to receive good care from the start. She'd taken a small aspirin last night, but EMTs gave her an additional one, which reduces blood clotting to allow the blood to flow through a narrowed artery. They also gave her nitroglycerin to dilate the vessels, and oxygen, and installed an IV so she'd be ready for us to give her clot busters as soon as she arrived. Time, as you may know, is of the essence."

"Both my parents died of heart attacks," Ben said. "Both on the same day. Mom in the morning, Dad at night."

"That, unfortunately, occurs," she said. "It's been recognized as sudden adult death syndrome, triggered by emotional stress. I'm sorry that you had to experience such a loss."

"I got through it." He brushed her sympathy off with his typical Harper male bravado. "All I want to know is when I can see my wife."

"We'll be moving her upstairs and settling her into a room," the doctor said. "She'll need to stay for three days, possibly more, until we're sure it's safe to release her. But she can't resume her normal work life for probably eight weeks."

"I'll take care of her." Ben shot a look at Seth. "I'm nearly retired now. She needs me more than you do."

"Absolutely," Seth agreed. "And don't worry about the work. We'll be fine."

"All right, then." The doctor glanced down at her watch. A code coming over the loudspeaker called her back to her duties. "We'll talk again over the next days. Meanwhile, if all goes as well as I expect, she should be able to go home in a few days. But you need to remember that she's still at risk. I'll want her to undergo a stress test as a follow-up to see how her heart and blood vessels respond to exertion. However," she said, more gently than she'd spoken since entering the room, "on a positive note, I'd say she's a lucky woman, Mr. Harper. And I suspect, from the bit she and I have talked, she's very special and you're a very fortunate man."

"You've got that right," Ben agreed with more heartfelt emotion than Brianna had ever heard from him.

Caroline had to be all right, she thought. Because all of the Harpers, who were in new phases of their lives, needed her to be.

Ben had just finished taking a much-needed piss, which he hadn't allowed himself to do because he'd refused to leave the waiting room for a second for fear of missing his wife's doctor, when of all the damn people in this town, Mike Mannion strolled down the hall.

"My wife isn't allowed visitors," he growled as his hands, scarred from a lifetime of saving Honeymoon Harbor houses, fisted.

"I understand. I've already talked with the charge nurse."

Of course he had. For some reason Ben hadn't been able to understand, every female in Shelter Bay seemed to go into estrogen overload whenever the artist was around.

"She told me that she was holding her own."

"She's a tough girl," Ben said, softening a bit as that night they'd met flashed back through his mind. "One of those steel magnolias. She's going to be fine."

"Of course she will," Mannion said in an agreeable way that made Ben want to punch him in that pretty black Irish face. "But I came here to talk with you."

"What about?"

"Why don't we take it to the coffee shop?" the other man suggested. "Or outside."

If they went outside, he'd risk slugging the guy. Which Caroline would probably never forgive him for. He shrugged, even as his gut clenched. Ben didn't want to hear anything Mike Mannion had to tell him. Especially anything to do with his wife.

"I guess I could use some coffee," he said. His nerves were already jangling with worry and all the toxic sludge they called coffee from the hallway vending machine, but he figured the cafeteria was better than discussing their situation somewhere private.

After dropping back into the waiting room, letting everyone know that he was just getting some coffee and needed some time alone, Ben was sitting at a corner table, hunkered over a cardboard cup of joe he didn't want, waiting for whatever Mannion had come here to hit him with.

"I'll get straight to the point," Mike Mannion said. "I love Caroline. I've loved her since that first night of the play, when she came over to talk to me about the set."

"She left with me."

Mannion nodded. Eyed Ben over the rim of the brown-and-white cup. "She did, to my everlasting regret. To tell the truth, I didn't think you two would last the summer. You're very disparate personalities. Different."

Ben's fingers tightened on the cup enough to send coffee splashing over the top onto the table. Both men ignored it.

"I know what the hell *disparate* means. Just because I work with my hands doesn't mean I don't have a brain. Or a dictionary." He'd like to see artsy-fartsy Mannion do a damn day's work with his hands creating something that people, families, could build a life in. He painted pretty pictures that went on walls the Harpers had once built and now restored.

Another nod. "I didn't mean to sound condescending."

"Like you didn't mean to take up with another man's wife?" Ben challenged. His teeth clenched so tight he imagined he could hear them cracking.

"I haven't taken up with her. She's merely a student. And a friend. She appreciated the roses, by the way. Nice touch."

Ben wanted to hate this rival. But gave him credit for offering some kernel of hope. He wasn't sure that if he'd been in the other man's shoes, he would've been that generous.

"But here's the thing," Mannion continued, his own jaw stiffening. "I know she's given you an ultimatum. I suspect this incident could well tilt things. Whether toward or away from me, I've no idea. But I imagine when you think you might die, you take stock of your life."

"Makes sense to me," Ben agreed.

"So if you can't pull this off and give her what she wants, what she *needs*, I'm giving you fair warning that I can. And I will. And you'll be the one out in the cold, remembering a night when the most amazing woman you'd ever met in your life drove into town, showed up at a small-town Theater in the Firs, then left you to spend the rest of your days thinking about what might have been."

His piece said, Mannion picked up his cup and tossed it, untouched, into the recycling bin on the way out of the coffee shop.

Brianna wasn't that surprised when Seth's visit with his mother was short. Although she hadn't kept track, she doubted it lasted more than three minutes. It must have been horrible for him, having lost his wife, then almost his mother, both without any warning.

"It's not your fault," she said as they drove back to Herons Landing.

"She was coughing."

"So is half the town. It's spring in the Pacific Northwest. My car got covered with tree pollen while I was having lunch up on the ridge. I've probably been going through a box of Kleenex a day." That might have been an exaggeration, but not by much. "It's one of the prices we pay for living in such a stunning part of the country."

"And she looked tired."

"Her marriage is rocky right now. Which, thinking about it, also means she could lose her income if she and your dad can't find a way to continue to work together. It only makes sense that she wouldn't be sleeping well. When I first arrived, you had enough bags beneath your eyes that if you decided to fly anywhere, they'd probably charge you extra luggage fees."

"Did you talk this way to those rich guests? Or am I the only one who's lucky enough to get the tough love lecture?"

Ouch. "I'm sorry. I just didn't want you to blame yourself. These things happen."

"Yeah. I'm very well aware of that."

He didn't say anything else on the way back to the house, but she could feel him silently berating himself, possibly going all the way back to those arguments Zoe used to tell her they were having about ROTC. Because best friends tell each other everything, she knew how hard he'd tried to talk her out of going into the military. Now, she feared, his mind was filled with if only's.

He wasn't a negative person like his father, but one thing they did share was that, even on a good day, Seth wasn't that talkative. So she decided there was no way to discuss this, at least not now, that would soothe his pain.

And this was one of the few cases when she doubted that food would work, either.

Which only left one thing.

CHAPTER THIRTY-THREE

As soon as they entered the house, Bandit greeted them as though they'd been gone a year instead of a few hours. Brianna gave him a huge bone and his ball, which would hopefully keep him busy, and put him outside.

Then, without a word, she laced her fingers together with Seth's and led him toward the back stairs.

"I'm not sure I'm up to this," he said. "Not right now."

"You don't have to do a thing," she said. "We both need something to hold on to right now. So, I'll hold on to you, while you hold on to me."

Except for that first time, when she'd embraced her inner Kylee and initiated the shower, Seth had always made the first move. Not that she'd minded. Because all his moves were excellent.

But this time she undressed him slowly, lifting his shirt over his head, then pressing soft, gentle kisses down his chest. As always, she felt that shock of awareness and sexual need when her lips brushed over his abdomen, but she forced herself to control it.

"Sit down," she said, pushing him onto the bed.

Although the color was impractical, she'd gone with a romantic, all-white bed in shades of cream, ivory and a soft snowy shade. For now, she'd draped a light taupe throw over the handmade quilt she'd bought at Quilters Garden, but come winter, she was looking forward to the fluffy white faux-fur throw her mother had put a photo of on the room's design board.

She knelt on the floor, unlacing, then removing, the black and white Converse All Star high-tops he was wearing today instead of his usual work boots.

She pressed another kiss against his bare ankle, pleased when he'd responded with a shudder. She'd discovered that surprising erogenous zone the second time they'd made love, and was even more pleased that he'd hadn't even known he had it.

And wasn't that the wonder of making love? Sharing and discovering new and special things about each other? It was hard to hide who you were when you were naked, open and, yes, vulnerable.

After kicking off her Keds, she climbed up on the bed, straddling his hips as she got busy on those five damn buttons that he insisted on wearing. Why couldn't he wear jeans with a zipper? Then again, being forced to slow down was probably a good thing today. As she pressed a series of kisses along his shoulders, she could feel the rock-hard tightness start to relax.

After unfastening each metal button, she pressed her lips against the placket of his navy boxer briefs.

"Bri…" He dragged his hands through her hair, but did not pull her head away. Oh, she was getting to him. As she had in years and years of forbidden dreams. But the reality was so much better.

"Soon," she promised, as he arched his hips off the bed. She was pretty sure that he wasn't thinking about either his wife or his mother right now, which was precisely what she'd intended. "I'll need you to scoot over so I can get these jeans off."

"If I last that long."

"This is for you," she reminded him. "Just do whatever comes naturally. Whenever."

"I want to be inside you when I come," he said, shifting so his head was now on the pillow. Although he was tall, the king bed allowed him to stretch all the way out with room to spare.

"Lift up."

When he arched his back and lifted his hips, it was all she could do not to just stop and take him in her mouth now. But this wasn't about her. She wasn't the one aching. Well, except in parts of her that would just have to wait.

She yanked the faded denim over his hips and down his legs, then stripped him of his briefs. Then leaned back on her heels and just drank in the sight of him so hard, so aroused. For her. The idea was thrilling. As she stripped herself, watching that wonderful dark smoke fill his eyes, she felt strong and invincible. Like Wonder Woman. And she wasn't even wearing magic bracelets.

"You're wearing too many clothes," he complained.

"Once again we're in perfect agreement." It wasn't the easiest thing to undress while kneeling on a mattress but she managed it with, she thought, a reasonable amount of sexiness. From the flame that flared in those smoky eyes, he'd definitely enjoyed her little impromptu striptease with her bra.

He finally lost his cool, giving in to the powerful needs within by ripping away the pretty little thong. "Sorry," he muttered against her bare hip as she felt and heard the ribbon tie rip.

"I'm not." She was about to straddle him again and regain the slow, dreaming and soothing pace. Then decided that there were many ways to soothe. If fast and hot was what he wanted, what he needed, Brianna was going to give it to him.

He rolled her over onto her back, put his hands on her inner thighs to spread her legs, then paused.

"You didn't take the quilt off. We're going to mess it up."

She almost laughed, but loved him for even thinking of it at a time like this. How many men would actually listen to all her wavering over the impracticality of white beds, and the care of cleaning, but they were so romantic...

"That's what washing machines are for."

They'd discussed condoms the first time and since they'd both been tested during routine physicals and hadn't had sex with anyone for such a long time, with her being on the pill, they'd decided not to bother. Although she'd always been a strong advocate for safe sex, she couldn't deny that bare hot flesh to flesh, which she'd only ever had with him, was sublime.

Reaching up, she wrapped her arms around his neck and lifted her hips in invitation.

He took her with a power he'd never revealed. With a force that she definitely hadn't expected. The storm sweeping over them was violent, but not dangerous. Trusting him as she did, it only fed an equally strong recklessness in her.

They rolled over the large mattress, hands grasping, teeth nipping and sucking, hips pumping fast and furious. He gripped her hips, lifting her up to feast on her, his tongue and teeth creating a hard, fast climax that lanced through her.

Then, grabbing her wrists in one hand, holding them over her head, he thrust into her, plunging hard and deep, taking her. Claiming her even as he relinquished demons who'd been tormenting him for far too long. But he wasn't finished. Even as she fell back to earth from her second stunning orgasm, he was hard again, pumping in and out as her legs wrapped around his hips. Looking straight into those flaming dark eyes Brianna surrendered to the fury. And to him.

What the hell had he done? After emptying himself in her again, leaving them both lying in a dampness that risked staining the precious antique quilt she'd been so excited about finding, drenched in sweat, Seth suffered a shame he'd never, ever felt. A feeling even worse than the survivor's guilt that had stalked him since Zoe's death.

He rolled off her, onto his back, and covered his eyes with his arm. "I'm sorry."

"Sorry?" Her voice was shaky.

"I used you."

The sex had been absolutely consensual. In fact, if he wanted to give himself a break, which he didn't, Brianna had initiated it. But in his heart, Seth knew that he'd used her. To overcome the guilt he was feeling about his mother, but most of all to burn away the pain and even deeper guilt that had been tearing at his insides since the day those officers had informed him that because of him staying safe at home in Honeymoon Harbor, his young, vital, beautiful wife had been blown to pieces.

Without a word—what could he possibly say?—he got off the bed, went into the bathroom and cleaned up. Then took one of the pretty white towels (which had to be the most impractical color on the planet—who thought that stuff up, anyway?), dampened it and brought it back to her.

His heart wanted to wash her. Tenderly. With the care and love she deserved. Shame had him unable to look at her as he simply handed her the cloth and began collecting his clothes.

"I think it was mutual," she said quietly. "And you're not going to hear me complaining."

"Because you don't complain." He yanked the briefs over his treacherous penis. It wasn't the first time it had taken on a mind of its own (hello, high school), but it had never, ever behaved violently. "Hell, crazy women needing emergency Botox, tigers with diamond engagement rings, Doctor Dick wanting you to pay back fifty thousand dollars he was stupid enough to throw away—you're unrelentingly nice to everyone. It's who you are. And it's why I can't do this."

"Do what?"

"I can't be with you." He still refused to meet her eyes as he turned his jeans right side out and pulled them up his legs. By the time he was ten years old, spending lazy summer mornings fly-fishing with his brothers, he'd been able to tie a full dress feather-winged salmon fly, which was still considered one of the most difficult to tie by fishermen his dad's age. Yet right now those same hands were shaking so badly he could barely fasten the damn buttons. Why the fucking hell didn't he just buy jeans with zippers? "Not in the way you want. In the way you deserve."

"I love you," she said quietly. But evenly.

He'd known that. Probably from the beginning. Even before people started telling him that she'd had that thing for him. He'd known it and had taken advantage of her feelings for his own selfish damn pleasure. Because being loved had him feeling human again. Making love had made him feel alive.

"And I'm falling in love with you." Hell, he was all the way there, but wouldn't admitting that make things even worse? He pulled the shirt over his head. It smelled like the hospital. Illness and antiseptic and urine and other things he didn't even want to think about. How did anyone work in a place like that? How had Zoe survived such misery every damn day?

"So, what's the problem?" She'd gotten off the bed and was standing there, all flush and pretty and naked, looking at him, her expression confused.

"It's not you. It's me." Oh, Christ, Jesus, had he actually said that?

"Okay." But it wasn't okay. "So, you're dumping me because you love me?"

"No. Okay. Maybe."

"Is it because you're feeling guilty because of Zoe? Like you're cheating on her?"

"No. Seriously. It's not that. I worried I would, in the beginning, a little. But I didn't. That's not it."

"I don't understand."

"I thought I could handle it. And, call me a coward, which I guess I am, but I can't risk losing another woman I love."

"The reason you're breaking up with me is because you're afraid of losing me?"

"Yeah." He dragged both hands down his face. "I've been through that pain once. And the ironic thing is, you're the one who made it better. Who brought me back from hell. Or at least the purgatory I was stuck in.

"But Mom's heart attack, watching Dad seem to shrink three sizes and look like he was about to flatline, too, reminded me that people die. Every damn day. Hell, right this very second, there are probably millions of people all over the world dying. And maybe some of the survivors who loved them are strong enough to put their hearts on the line again, but I'm not one of them."

"I don't really have any intention of dying anytime soon," she said.

Her tone was mild, but he could hear the tremor of strain behind her words as she grabbed the sheet from the floor and wrapped it around herself. Not that it was going to provide any real protection against the pain he was inflicting.

"But we just never know, do we?" He shook his head. "It's like life's just one big crapshoot. Just when we think we have things under control, shit happens."

Not only had he used her, both emotionally and physically, but now, watching the color drain from her face and the pain in her damp eyes, he knew that he was also breaking her heart. "Look. I'd better go before I make all this even worse."

She folded her arms, holding herself tight, as if to keep from shattering apart. "I doubt that's possible." She closed her eyes, drew in a breath, then, with the backs of her hands, wiped at the tears that were falling down her cheeks. "Dammit, I never cry," she said.

And didn't he know that feeling? So why did he feel on the verge of bawling like Kylee and Mai's baby now?

She lifted her head. Jutted out her chin in a way that was far more familiar. She'd probably looked like that when Doctor Dick had accused her casino's games of being rigged. "You're right," she said on a stronger voice. Going into the closet, she pulled out a duffel bag, some jeans, shirts and two pairs of sneakers (one Gore-Tex for wet days), then went over to the dresser and dumped her underwear drawer, along with the clothes from the closet, into the bag.

"This isn't going to work because you refuse to let it. And yes, I know you warned me up front, and yes, I've settled for a friends-with-benefits deal these past weeks, so I guess I shouldn't be surprised. Or have expected more. So go ahead and go home, or back to wherever the hell it is you go every Sunday, and I'll move to the farm while you finish work on the house."

"I can do that," Seth said, even as sharp claws ripped away at his guts.

"Good." She took her toothbrush and makeup bag from the bathroom and threw them into the duffel bag. "You know my plans for the rest of the rooms. Just send word through Quinn when it's done. Then I'll move back in."

He had to ask. "What about the carriage house?"

Her laugh, which surprised him, held no humor. "I've no

idea. I'm not really up to thinking about it today. I may contact that guy you told me about down the coast in Oregon."

"Lucas Chaffee. I'll have Ethel send you his card. Just in case."

"Fine." She shook her head as she zipped up the bag. "And aren't we being so very civilized?"

Funny, for once they weren't on the same wavelength. Because nothing about this felt the least bit civilized.

One advantage of her former occupation was that she'd learned to move quick and travel light. Brianna grabbed her purse from where she'd left it on the downstairs counter, and walked out the door. For the last time until Seth got her dream house done.

"Wouldn't you just know it?" Bandit was standing there with his ratty old tennis ball in his mouth.

"You're such a sweet boy," she said as she patted his huge head, starting his tail thumping on the wooden slats of the porch floor. Oh, how she was going to miss this goofy, adorable, loving rescue dog.

He dropped the ball at her feet, his request obvious. She picked it up and threw it as far as she could. She might not have played official sports like Kylee, but years of playing baseball in the baseball diamond they'd made in one of the farm's fallow fields had given her a strong throwing arm.

As he took off after it, she jumped into her car and drove away down the tree-lined drive that was going to be such a stunning welcome entry for guests once Amanda Barrow finished with it.

She'd sworn she wasn't going to look back, but couldn't resist glancing up into her rearview mirror. When she saw Bandit, ball in his mouth, chasing after her, Brianna allowed herself to sob.

CHAPTER THIRTY-FOUR

This welcome home was nothing like the earlier one. Instead of joy, her mother's face was etched with sorrow and concern. And not just for her daughter, but her best friend.

"Are you sure you want to be here?" Sarah asked.

"I need to be here. He practically threw me out of my own house. After he'd told me he loved me."

"Of course he does. Otherwise he wouldn't be so afraid of losing you," her mother said.

Brianna jammed her hands into the pockets of her jeans. "It's stupid."

"It's human."

"Like I told you, I never thought I'd get over Bonnie," her grandfather reminded her. "But then I met Harriet, who rescued me. Not only from my grief, but the bottle. I never talk about it, but I drank some back then. A lot, if you want to know the truth. I was in a dark place. But this woman—" he took hold of Harriet's age-spotted hand and lifted it to his lips as if she were a young woman he was courting "—she brought the sunshine back into my life."

"Your grandfather was a tough nut to crack," Harriet said.

"But he's been worth all the tears I shed until we made it to a good place."

"The best place," Jerome said. "Or would be if you'd take the same advice everyone wants to give that Harper boy and quit worrying that I'm going to keel over on you at any minute."

Her grandmother shook her head. "I hate it when he's right."

The laughter that statement encouraged lightened the mood.

"I'm making four-cheese mac and cheese. With some slipper lobster Quinn is picking up at Kira's Sea House for me."

"The ultimate comfort food," Brianna said. Her mother usually saved that decadent dish for New Year's brunch.

"That's the idea. Why don't you go settle into your room, then come down. We'll have wine or tea while your grandmother and I cook and the men go out to get an early start on the planting before the crowd arrives."

And didn't that cause a little stab in her heart, given that she and Seth should have been out there together planting with them? But she'd always enjoyed time in the kitchen with her mother and grandmother and it beat locking herself away in her room and feeling sorry for herself.

"That sounds great. But I'd better stick with tea." The last thing she needed was to get drunk. Which actually didn't sound like such a bad idea. But then she'd have to pay for it afterward, and although she still loved him, dammit, Brianna refused to give Seth Harper that much power over her life.

She'd just unpacked the duffel bag and moved her things into her old dresser when Quinn knocked on her open door.

"Come on in." The family was rallying around her. Which felt good and sad at the same time because, having prided herself on her independence, she'd never really needed to lean on them before.

He wrapped his arms around her in a hug, letting her rest her head on his shoulder for a long, soothing time. "FYI," he said against her hair, "Harper's been banned from Mannion's."

Brianna leaned back and looked up at him. "You've already talked to him?" So much for Honeymoon Harbor's glacial pace.

"Yeah. He thought I ought to hear from him that he'd dumped you. So I told him exactly what he could do with that announcement, punched him in his pretty face and threw him out before I came here."

"You hit him?" She grabbed his left hand, viewing the red skin on his knuckles that would be an ugly purple-blue bruise in a few days.

"You're my little sister. He made you cry and broke your heart. What the hell would you expect me to do? He's just lucky I didn't turn Jarle loose on him. He's had a crush on you since you arrived in town."

"Really?"

"Yeah. But don't worry about hurting his feelings if he asks you out and you turn him down. Jarle tends to fall in love with every good-looking single woman who comes into the pub. I think it's the Viking in him. So far he hasn't carried any off, and doesn't harass them, just admires from afar, so I figure putting all that emotion into his cooking helps improve business."

This time her laugh felt lighter. As did her heart.

Just a bit.

CHAPTER THIRTY-FIVE

"You do realize you're acting like a damn fool," Ben Harper told Seth three days later as they drove to the hospital to bring Caroline home. "Go out and grovel. Hell, get on your knees if you need to. Crawl naked down Water Street. Do whatever it takes to get her back."

"Is that Dr. Blake speaking?" Seth asked.

"No. She'd probably nix the naked public crawling because it'd land you in the clink. But she would tell you that you're the one at fault here."

"Don't you think I already know that?"

"You losing your wife was a tragic thing, I'm not going to deny that," his father said. "But fate, destiny, God, whatever, has given you a second chance for happiness. It's your responsibility to grab it with both hands and not let go. Then spend the rest of your life making up for your stupidity."

"That's a positive view of my possible future," Seth said dryly.

"Okay, here's this... Do you love her?"

"Hell, yes."

"Then do something about it. Mike Mannion told me that

if I didn't get my woman back, he was going after her. That lit a fire beneath my tail, let me tell you. Your mother is the best thing that's ever happened to me. You come in a close second, but I wouldn't have you if she hadn't been willing to marry me instead of that rich Southern lawyer or Mannion."

"She and Mannion had a thing?"

"He tried. But I won. Then I almost blew it. But I'm going to make it up to her. Starting today. And after we get her home, you ought to get your ass out to the Mannion farm and do the same thing."

That out of the way, he pulled up into the loading zone, cut the engine and said, "Let's go get your mom."

Caroline couldn't wait to get home. Oh, the hospital staff had been lovely, the view of the Olympics stellar and the food had been surprisingly good. Especially the couple bites of cake, which wasn't on her approved dietary list, but which Ben had sneaked up from the cafeteria when she'd complained about missing chocolate. She'd been moved to tears when he'd told her about going to the therapist, which had scared him enough that he was about to go running out into the hall to call for a nurse.

"It's okay," she said, pulling a tissue from the box on the rolling table next to the bed. "They're happy tears."

"How does your heart feel?"

"Fine. And why don't you stop asking me that? I have a better sense of the signs now and promise not to ignore them."

"Okay." He sighed. "I don't know what I'd do without you, Caro."

"You won't have to," she assured him. They still had years together. After all, everyone was saying the sixties were the new forties.

He'd stunned her by telling her about his therapy sessions. If there was anything more amazing—and undoubtedly difficult—he could have done to prove his love, Caroline couldn't think of it. Dr. Blake might have opened his eyes to many things, but he'd always be a man's man unable to fully understand the female mind. And, quite honestly, she wouldn't want him any other way. She'd merely wanted to feel appreciated. Which he'd definitely done, refusing to go home that first night when the nurses told him visiting hours were over. Eventually they'd caved in and brought him a cot to sleep on. And except for those trips to the cafeteria, and outside to call and update all her friends on her condition, he hadn't left her side.

She'd just finished dressing when the door opened.

"You're looking great," Seth said, giving her a careful hug that had Caroline wondering how long it would be before people would quit treating her as if she were made of crystal and easily broken.

"Thank you. I'm feeling great," she said.

Her son, on the other hand, looked nearly as bad as he had when his wife had died. Ben had filled her in on that breakup drama, which she had no doubt would eventually work out, but it was painful to see the man who'd always, deep down, be her baby boy so miserable. She'd also heard, from a nurse who'd been at the pub, about the altercation that had given him that ugly bruise. Although she didn't approve of violence, Caroline couldn't really fault Quinn.

She turned toward her husband. "I'm also ready to go home."

"The paperwork's been all taken care of," Ben said. "So, let's blow this popsicle stand."

Caroline wasn't all that happy about the hospital's insistence on patients being rolled out in a wheelchair, but apparently rules were rules.

The double doors opened, and there, beneath the canopy, was the most beautiful thing she'd ever seen.

"Ben Harper, you didn't!" The motor home was all shiny and new, painted in shades of smoke and gray and white with sweeping swoops that made it look as if it was all ready to drive them away on an adventure. A huge red plastic bow had been stuck on the hood.

"I know it's going to be a while before we can take off and start seeing all those parks and other places, because the doc's going to want you to stick around a couple months for those stress tests and such, but I thought maybe tonight, since we missed our date, you might want to try it out with dinner in the driveway. Luca made veggie lasagna and antipasto."

"That sounds lovely." Tears pricked at the back of her lids. Not wanting to scare the poor man to death, Caroline resolutely blinked them away. "Both the food and the company. And this is the most beautiful motor home I've ever seen."

"It's not real fancy, like those big buses people drive those days."

"They look like they'd be so much trouble getting in and out of places, and then we'd need a car to tow, and there'd be more to clean," she said. She'd never had one of those behemoths in mind. "This isn't so small that we'd feel cramped in a sardine can. It's absolutely perfect. I can't wait to go somewhere in it."

"I thought, while we're waiting for you to get the okay to take off, we could do day trips around here," he said. "Maybe spend some nights. The doctor said that'd be okay."

"I'd love that."

"Then there's something else I was thinking maybe you'd like."

He reached into the Gore-Tex jacket he'd put on for the spring rain and pulled out an envelope. Opening it, she gasped as she looked at the gleaming white ship floating on a cerulean blue sea.

"There are two tickets for a cruise to Hawaii," he said. "For that honeymoon I promised you. It's late, but—"

"It's better," she said. "Even without the money problems back then, we would have been too young to truly appreciate it. Now it's going to be perfect."

The aide had folded back the footrests, allowing her to stand up, twine her arms around his neck, and not caring who might be watching or if she embarrassed her son, she kissed this man who'd won her heart from the moment she'd seen him.

"Take me home, Ben Harper." It was what she'd said to him the night he'd proposed.

"I'd be right happy to, Miz Caroline," he said back to her. All these years later, the man still had the worst fake Southern drawl Caroline Longworth Harper had ever heard. Which was only one of the things she loved about him.

CHAPTER THIRTY-SIX

Five days after moving back into her parents' house, Brianna was already going stir-crazy. She kept busy learning breakfast recipes from her mother and grandmother, and helping organize the planting party, which had been put off again due to more spring rain, but she missed her house. She also missed Kylee, Mai and Clara. Especially baby Clara, who even as she made her yearn for a child of her own, also lifted her spirits and made her smile.

"I think I'll go into town," she told her mother.

"To the house?" Sarah asked carefully.

"No. I'm not ready to see Seth. But I miss the baby."

"Speaking of whom," her grandmother, who'd been rolling out cookie dough for the party, said, "I made her something." She left the room and came back with a pair of white crocheted newborn socks with pink toes and heels, with a row of pink at the top.

"Oh, these are darling! Kylee and Mai are going to love them." She embraced Harriet. "Thank you."

"It's good to have a baby in the family again," her grandmother said. As if just by Brianna's designation as godmother,

Clara had become a Mannion. Having Seth as her godfather would make her yet another link between the Mannions and Harpers. "Not that I'm pushing you to procreate. Just saying."

"I wouldn't hold your breath waiting for me," Brianna said. Except for yesterday's discovery of asbestos in a second floor bath that had been remodeled sometime in the sixties, she hadn't heard a word from Seth. And even the extra cost for the hazmat removal team had been relayed through Quinn.

As she drove past Blue House Farm and continued toward town, Brianna decided that she'd spent enough time hoping and crying over Seth Harper. The sex, admittedly, was off any scale. But although he'd beat himself up for "using" her, she'd felt claimed. Even owned, but not in a dangerous guy possessive way. What could well be their last time together had been raw alpha male, totally honest and, she couldn't lie, thrilling.

Still. Judging from his silence, it was time for her to move on and find someone else. Like the song said, if she couldn't be with the one she loved, she might as well love the one she was with.

She'd seen Flynn Farraday out washing a fire truck in the station parking lot a couple weeks ago. He'd been shirtless, and from the way he was ripped, looked capable of carrying an entire family, including the dog, out of a burning house on those wide, manly shoulders. But the only way she could think of to casually meet him would be to set the kitchen on fire while practicing flambéing the bananas Foster recipe she'd found on YouTube. Which would probably end up with Seth doing the repair work. So, scratch the hot fireman.

Maybe she'd drop into Luca's and pick up dinner for the family one of these days. While there, she could casually ask if he'd teach her how to make his light and airy Italian strata breakfast recipe. Then, maybe, while rolling out phyllo sheets on the restaurant's marble pastry counter together, their eyes would meet, bells would chime and little cartoon lovebirds would begin circling their heads. Her imagination wandered to the two of them nuzzling over a plate of spaghetti, like *Lady and the Tramp* in one of the most romantic movie scenes ever, while their personal couple's soundtrack played "Bella Notte."

"It could happen, right?" she asked herself as she stopped to let a herd of Roosevelt elk cross the road. They could be a perfect couple. Luca was sexy, with that romantic Italian accent and those hooded bedroom eyes. Plus, as a bonus, he cooked. And she ate. "Perfect fit."

The elk had finally moved on, and deciding that she was definitely putting Luca into her husband candidates folder, Brianna continued, just in time for a dawdling elk calf to sprint across the road to catch up with his family.

Acting on impulse, she yanked the wheel and swerved. Right off the road toward the trees.

After watching the budding young chef and her grandmother leave his house in their newly purchased Rallye Red Civic, Seth drove to the Harborview Cemetery, parked in front of the iron gates and sat there for a long, silent time, his hands draped over the top of the steering wheel.

The sky overhead was dark and gloomy, forecasting rain, as he climbed out of the truck and made his way past the earlier stone gravestones, many of the names long ago worn away by wind and water, to the newer section. He vaguely remembered some discussion about whether Zoe would be buried among the Robinsons or in the smaller veterans section. It had been her father, he seemed to recall, who'd decided she deserved to be with the vets. Where earlier generations of Robinsons already lay.

He was surprised that he found his way to Zoe's grave so easily, since everything about that time after the notification was so fuzzy. Apparently his heart had mapped what his mind had forgotten. Her family had ordered the stone, with her name—Zoe Robinson Harper—and below a line reading simply Loving Daughter. Beloved Wife. American Hero. Which didn't begin to describe all she'd been, but all those words were true. As he knelt on the damp green grass and ran his fingers over the letters, Seth was vastly grateful that cemetery guidelines established in later years had kept Helen from going all-out grief crazy with weeping angels standing eternal guard. A third line simply listed birth and death dates, revealing a life cut tragically short.

Someone, either Helen or Sarah, had placed some bright red and yellow tulips in the cup by the marker. He knew they were parrot tulips from Jim Olson's farm, because Kylee had shown him a picture on her phone of the same ones that she was going to use in her wedding bouquet. He might not remember much about the funeral, but he did remember Zoe and her mother's argument about his wife's wedding bouquet. Helen had insisted that peonies were more appropriate than the daisies Zoe had wanted because their cheery yellow faces made her happy. In the end she'd won, of course. Which was why he'd bought the daisies this morning at Blue House Farm's booth at the farmers market.

"I miss you," he said. He plucked at the flower petals, trying to find the words. "I thought I'd die in those days after the officers came to the house. I *wanted* to die. But I didn't, though all my feelings, any sense of love, just withered up inside, like they'd died. Because there was no one I wanted to share them with. And then Bri came back, which maybe you already know.

"If you do, then you'll know that she brought me back to life. And it's not that I love you less, Zoe." He put the daisies into the cup with the tulips. "You'll always be the first girl, then the first woman I ever loved. But I love Bri now. And I want to spend whatever time we're lucky enough to have on this earth together."

He leaned back on his heels, thinking of how the three of them had always been so intertwined. "Because she was your best friend, and you loved her, too, I'm hoping you're okay with that." He touched his fingers to his lips. Then to the stone.

As he stood up, he felt a little bit of air, like the wafting of invisible feathers against his cheek. It was only a breeze from the water, he assured himself. Or maybe it was more. Maybe it was Zoe, setting him free.

Whichever, as he walked away, Seth put away the pain and focused on his hope.

He was on his way, headed out of town, when he passed a tow truck going in the opposite direction. It was bright green, with Easton's Garage and Towing printed on the doors. On the flatbed was an all-too-familiar car, its front end smashed.

Seth's blood chilled. He instantly pulled a U-turn, easily caught up with the truck and laid his hand on the horn. When the driver looked up, he waved. Then, noticing Seth's hand motion toward the side of the road, pulled over. Both men got out of their vehicles at the same time.

"Hey, Mannion," Kenny Easton said. "Thanks for selling that sweet little car. It made my wife feel a lot better not to have her granddaughter walking at night in the city."

"What the hell happened?" Seth was in no mood for pleasantries. He gestured toward the truck. "To Brianna Mannion?"

"Oh." Kenny took off his Easton's Garage and Towing trucker hat and ran his hand over his bald head. "Seems she swerved to avoid hitting an elk."

"And hit a tree?" Everyone knew hitting an immovable

tree could mean death. Then again, so could hitting a long-legged elk. Either way was a crapshoot.

"No, she slid right through those and ended up in a deep creek wash."

"How is she?"

"I'm not sure. The ambulance had taken her to the hospital before I got there. But from what I was told by the cop on the scene, she was alive and talking."

The breath whooshed out of Seth. "Thanks." He ran back to the car and, ignoring all posted speed limits, went racing back to the hospital. Which had become his least favorite place in Honeymoon Harbor.

The same woman who'd been at the reception desk when his mother had been brought in looked up from her computer when he raced through the sliding glass doors. Her expression was anything but welcoming, which had him thinking she'd be a huge failure in the hospitality business.

"Brianna Mannion. She was brought in a little while ago."

"She was. But you can't see her."

Remembering how Brianna had finessed the situation after his dad had gone charging in like a bull in a china shop, Seth struggled for calm and opted for a middle ground.

"She's my fiancée." He hoped. "She'd want to see me."

"Heard you two had broken up," the woman returned. "So I'm not real sure about that. But it doesn't matter because she's not here any longer."

Seth didn't think his blood could go any colder. But it instantly froze to glacier ice. And he'd have sworn his heart had stopped beating. *Do. Not. Pass. Out.*

"She spent the entire time complaining that she was fine, but Flynn Farraday—you probably know him, he's the fire department EMT—decided that the impact was hard enough she needed to be checked for neck injuries. Like whiplash.

So he brought her in, they X-rayed her and then her parents came and got her and took her home."

His head cleared, his heart resumed beating, and though his blood was still chilled, a bit of the ice had melted.

"Thanks." He leaned over the counter and kissed her on the cheek. Which surprised both of them.

"You're welcome," she said, pressing her fingers to her cheek, which had colored slightly. He'd just reached the door when she called out to him. "You'd better be prepared to grovel," she said, unknowingly echoing his Dad's words. "That poor girl's had a rough week."

In large part thanks to him. If he hadn't broken her heart, she wouldn't have been out there at the farm in the first place, so she wouldn't have nearly run into that damn elk and possibly come within inches of dying. Unintended consequences. Life was fucking full of them.

Which, Seth knew both Zoe and Brianna would say, was no reason to stop living. And loving.

He was totally prepared to grovel. To get down on a knee. Hell, crawl naked down Water Street if that's what it took to get Brianna Mannion back.

It began to rain as he drove out to the Mannion farm. A deep, drenching spring rain that was good for the mountain snowpack and was what kept the Pacific Northwest so emerald green, but it had also turned the ground to muck. Which, Seth decided as he passed the blue house that had given Jim Olson's farm its name, could be a good thing, because if it got too muddy, they might have to delay the planting, which would prevent the entire town from witnessing him groveling. Not that it would've stopped him.

The gate was open to the farm, probably from having expected a crowd for the planting party, although it could be that the Mannions just got tired of having to get in and out of the car in Pacific Northwest weather to open and close it.

He'd been hoping that Brianna would open the door. Or her mother. Unfortunately, he got her dad, who, although always being known as an easygoing guy, didn't look all that welcoming.

"It's about time you showed up," he said.

"Hello, Mr. Mannion," Seth said. "I just had some things to work out."

"And now you have? Worked them out?"

"He better have," Quinn's deep, all-too-familiar voice said from behind John Mannion. Terrific. That was all he needed.

"I have." Seth refused to rub his bruised jaw. "I was actually on my way here when I ran into Kenny Easton, who told me about the accident. The woman at the hospital told me she was okay."

"Physically," Quinn said. "You going to make her cry again?"

"No. I'm going to do my best to convince her that I love her and I'll never hurt her again."

"Oh, you will," John Mannion said. "Even if you don't mean to. Marriage isn't always a smooth road, as you undoubtedly know."

"Bri thinks the best of everyone," Quinn said, folding his arms. As threatening as the gesture might be, it wasn't as bad as clenched fists. For a former attorney, Quinn had one hell of a left cross. "And she's always had a damn thing for you."

He didn't make it sound like a positive. "I'm going to prove to her that I'm worth her."

"I doubt any father ever believes any man's good enough for his daughter," John said mildly. "But my wife's always insisted that you were going to be my son-in-law, so if you can talk Bri into forgiving you for acting like a jackass, you've got my blessing."

"Thank you, Sir."

"You're welcome. Although we tried to get her to lie down after the accident, she insisted on helping her mother and grandmother get the barn ready for the planting party. You'll find her out there."

With her dad's blessing, he had one—make that two, since Quinn hadn't punched him again—obstacles down. One final, important one to go.

He found her standing on the stage he'd built at the far end of the barn, up on a ladder again, using a staple gun to put a THANK YOU FOR YOUR SUPPORT banner up on the wall. It wasn't the money the family saved by having volunteers come out and plant. That probably wouldn't cover the cost of the spread they put out for the planters. It was to show appreciation for the sense of community that had kept their family business thriving all these years.

With her back turned toward him, and her grandmother busy stacking red plastic cups, Sarah was the first to see him.

"Brianna, dear," she said. "You have company."

Brianna stiffened. Then looked back over her shoulder. And didn't say a damn word.

"Hello, Brianna," Seth said into the icy stillness. The temperature in the barn felt as if it had dropped at least thirty degrees.

"Hello, Seth." Her tone didn't offer a hint of welcome. But neither was it as angry as the last time they'd been together.

"Mother," Sarah said mildly. "Let's go in and make sure we have enough utensils."

"We already counted them this morning," Harriet said.

"Then let's count them again."

"Dang it all," the older woman muttered. "I always miss the good stuff." She looked up at Brianna, who was still standing on the ladder. "You make him work for it, sweetheart. A woman's gotta let her man know from the beginning that he's going to have to do his share in a marriage. We women shouldn't have to do all the heavy lifting."

Brianna's lips quirked. "Thank you for the advice, Gram," she said. Her tone was far warmer than the one she'd used on him.

"She's right," Seth said as the two women walked back toward the house, leaving them alone. "Fortunately, I'm good at heavy lifting."

"Lumber, tile and stuff," Brianna agreed with a shrug. "I can always hire men to do that."

She wasn't going to make it easy on him. And why should she? Her father was right. He'd been a jackass. Which was a lot kinder than some of the names Quinn had called him.

Outside the rain was pounding on the red tin roof he'd put on the restored building.

Inside, a silence as thick and dense as morning fog rolling in from the harbor filled the barn.

"I heard about the accident. Are you sure you should be up on a ladder?"

"I'm fine," she said, backing down the ladder in question. "And you have any right to question what I should be doing, why?"

"I was wrong."

"About what?"

Nope. Not easy.

"About all of it. Except the loving part. Because I do love you, Brianna Mannion. I want to marry you. And have children with you, if you're willing."

"What brought about this change of mind? And if it's because of my stupid accident—"

"It's not. I was on the way here when I found out about that. That woman at reception told me you were okay. She also told me to be prepared to grovel."

"Groveling might be a nice touch. An explanation would be better."

"It's like I told you. I was afraid of loving anyone after Zoe. Because loving and losing hurt too much." And wasn't that an understatement? "But then I fell in love with you."

"You said you were falling," she corrected him.

"I lied."

She arched a brow. And waited.

"I was going to tell you. I was waiting for the right moment. But then Mom had her heart attack, I watched Dad nearly die, and thought about *his* father dying of a broken heart the same day his wife had died, and well, I freaked out. You were right. I was a coward. But I loved you so much that I couldn't bear to lose you."

"That's pretty much what you said after we made love. What I'm waiting for is the change of mind part."

"I've missed you. Every minute of every day and night. I've ached to have you in my life. And yeah, it took time for me to wrap my mind around the idea that things happen that we don't have any control over. But that I'd rather grab every day of the rest of our lives together, even knowing that I could lose you—"

"Or vice versa," she said.

"Yeah. And you're braver than me."

Her expression softened. "No. I loved Zoe, but in a different way. I understood what you were trying to say. Mostly. Because no one can fully grasp a pain like you experienced. Which was why I wasn't sure your feelings would ever change... Mai's grandfather died in France, fighting in the war. Her grandmother was still a young woman. And never remarried. I thought you might end up like her."

"I went out to the cemetery," he said. "For the first time since the funeral. I told Zoe I loved her. And that part of me always will."

"I wouldn't want to be with a man who could feel otherwise."

"I also told her that I love you now."

There was a long pause as she took that in. This time instead of stopping, Seth's heart was hammering against his chest.

"I want children," she said.

That was a plus. She hadn't given him a flat-out *no*. Seth forged on. "Okay. Good. Me, too. And I want to live in the carriage house, and if that grows too small, I'll put on additions. Maybe a second story—"

Her brow furrowed. "How many children are you talking about?"

"However many or as few as you want. And I want to grow old together, watching our grandkids building sandcastles on the beach and enjoying the sunsets together."

"A lifetime of sunsets," she murmured.

"Once again we think alike. And we'll always hold on to each other, getting through whatever storms come together."

"Not just the weather ones."

"No," he agreed as she walked toward him. "*All* storms. The way your parents have done. The way mine have done. Because one thing our families have in common is that neither Mannions nor Harpers ever give up."

She smiled at that. Both with her lips and her remarkable lake-blue eyes. "No. We don't."

"I'm so sorry."

"I know. Like I said, I knew even as I left that I wasn't the only one hurting. But you had to find your answers on your own. So, is this a proposal?"

Oh, hell. He really was a jackass. "Yes. Absolutely it is." And although he never would've guessed he'd be taking relationship advice from his dad, Seth dropped to a knee on the wide-planked floor. "I love you. And I want to marry you."

"How handy, since I've wanted to marry you ever since you shared your Ding Dong with me."

"What Ding Dong?"

She laughed and waved his question away. "I'll tell you later. Maybe on our honeymoon."

"Thomas Wolfe was wrong," Brianna said as, after a long, heartfelt kiss, she and Seth walked through the rain, which had softened to a mist, back to the house.

"About what?" Seth dropped a light kiss atop her head, wondering what he'd ever done to deserve two such amazing women in one life.

She smiled up at him, their love, their bright future, shining in her eyes. "You really can go home again."

★ ★ ★ ★ ★

ACKNOWLEDGMENTS

While writing can be a solitary existence, publishing a book truly does take a village. I've been fortunate to have received a great deal of help and want to give thanks and a huge shout-out to my fabulous publishing team:

Dianne Moggy, who first reached out from our shared past. I'm so happy I followed that winding yellow brick road back to HQN Books.

Craig Swinwood, who welcomed me home with such enthusiasm.

Susan Swinwood, editor extraordinaire, who sees the forest when I'm down writing in the trees. Working together is a joy.

Sean Kapitain, for portraying my beloved Pacific Northwest so beautifully on Herons Landing's cover.

And everyone else working so hard behind the scenes at HQN to bring Seth and Brianna's story to readers.

Last, but certainly never least, heartfelt gratitude to my wonderful agents Denise Marcil and Anne Marie O'Farrell, for their steadfast encouragement, wise advice and work on my behalf. Who knew that first day that we could end up having such fun?